The Fall of Ossard

Book One

The Ossard Trilogy

By Colin Taber

COLIN TABER

Thought Stream Creative Services
P O Box 562 Mount Lawley
Western Australia 6929

www.fallofossard.com

First Published 2009

Cover art: Shaun Tan
Copyright © 1994

Edited by Cheryl Bettridge AE

ISBN: 1440475040
EAN-13: 9781440475047

Set in Goudy Old Style 11/18/36

The Fall of Ossard

-

Contents

COLIN TABER

THE FALL OF OSSARD

Dedicated to Dom Glenn
1968-2009

With thanks to;
Mum & Dad, Andre, Andrew & Heather, Andrew C, Andrew F, Basil
& Jim, Brad & Iris, Brad H, Donna, Elizabeth, Gary, James, Jaycen &
Peter, Jen, Jo, Lauren, Matt, Melissa & Brendan, Mike, Millicent &
Simon, Nick & Karen, Samantha, Sara, Stefen, & Paul & Suzanne.

COLIN TABER

The Truths of the World

Three races of man separated by the ages;
The high, the *Lae Velsanans*;
the numerous common-men of the *middling* nations;
and the lowly *Saldaens*.

Three branches of magic, each with a league to control them;
Mind, governed by the women of the forbidden *Sisterhood*;
Soul, wielded by the priesthoods of the faiths;
and Heart, regulated by the *Cabal of Mages*.

Three realms of existence;
Ours of soil;
the *Celestial* of souls, gods, and magic;
and the *Elemental*.

Three stages of godhood;
Avatars, seeds within mortal shells;
the *New-Born*, awakened gods upon our world;
and the *Elevated*, those matured and raptured to the next.

And all in a world forged by the goddess, Life,
in partnership with her husband, Death.
Yet now they are estranged and waging divine war,
a war that promises doom for us all.

Maps

Northern Dormetia

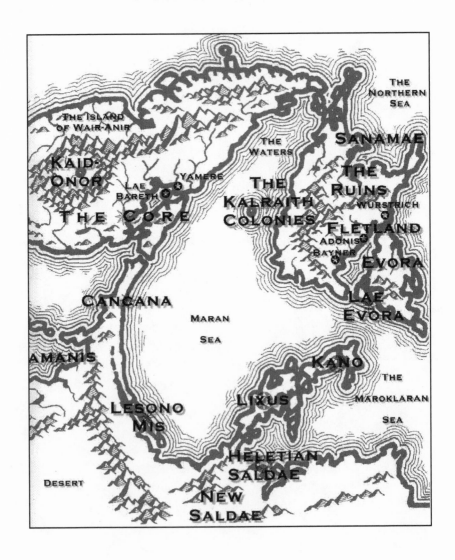

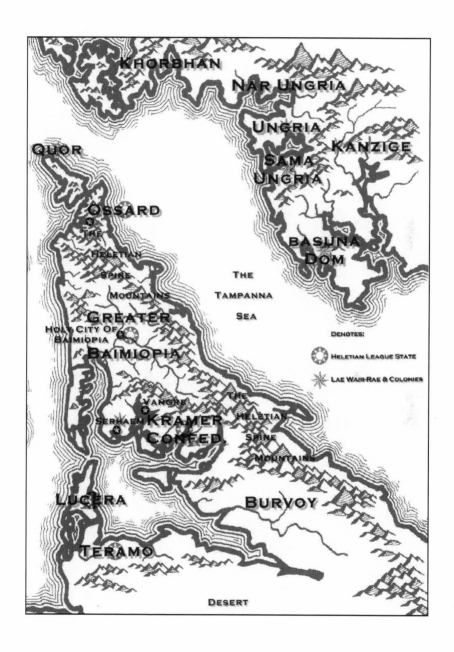

Ossard & The Northcountry

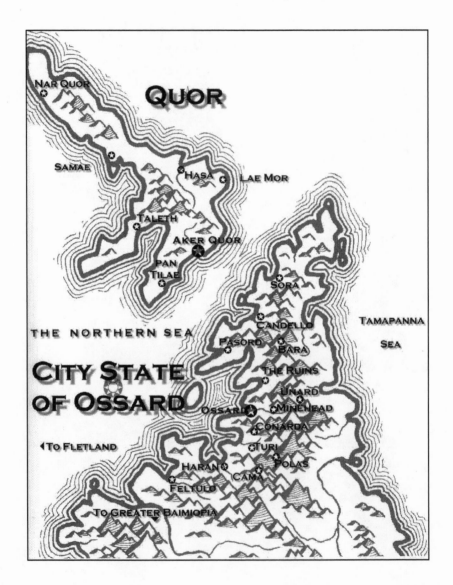

The City-State of Ossard

COLIN TABER

Prelude

-

The Witches of Ossard

COLIN TABER

Prelude

-

The Witches of Ossard

The fiery brand seemed weak, its flame all but lost under the glare of the summer sun, yet the black robed man who wielded it stepped forward with all the chill and menace of the deepest winter squall.

Vilma watched the young Inquisitor cross the cobblestones to the base of the long, stake-studded, and oil-soaked pyre. She wasn't alone. Four-dozen others also stood naked and bound as if some macabre forest had sprouted from the heart of Market Square.

Standing as straight as her bonds allowed, she tried to show her defiance despite her racing heart.

This wouldn't be quick, and by the gods, it would hurt!

-

Inquisitor Anton met her wide blue eyes, waiting for her to break – they always did. As a member of the Church of Baimiopia's *Expeditia Puritanica*, he'd already cleansed scores of souls across the Heletian League, yet here he'd truly excelled: His superiors had warned that the harvest in Ossard always came heavy and rich.

Thanks be to Krienta!

It was the Northerners' penchant for blood mixing, the intermarrying of pious Heletians with foreign Flets, that created such fertile ground for heresy. Ossard stood ripe for a good burning, and fortunately he had the faith to kindle it.

He could smell a witch at a dozen paces, tasting their vileness just as his keen nose could catch the dirty blood of a fertile woman. Anton was good at what he did, very good indeed.

The Flet bitch continued to stare at him. He smirked, letting her sample his smug disdain. Most of her fellows begged for mercy or persisted with cries of innocence, yet it was the few who maintained their silence that he focussed on. They were where the true danger lay.

He turned his back on her to bring his attention to the crowd being forced into the heart of Market Square. They needed witnesses, as many as they could get, to learn the lesson that the Inquisition dutifully taught: That none shall stray from St Baimio's righteous path, for that was the only way to Krienta.

Thousands of hesitant townsfolk came forward, forced by a reluctant city watch, they in turn driven by the *Sankto Glavos* - the Inquisition's holy knights. With barely a murmur, the two peoples of Ossard closed on the pyres, both the dark featured and olive skinned Heletians, and the blonde and fair Flets. Usually, their differences kept them apart, but today it was the true outsider - the Inquisition - that brought them together.

Vilma looked from her executioner's back to her poor daughter where two monks held her at the front of the crowd. Inger, only newly a woman, struggled against their hands as she tried to turn her tear-filled eyes away. They stopped her, forcing her to look on.

The Sankto Glavos stood solid in their fine armour with shields and breastplates bedecked in black, navy and gold. The townsfolk before them cowered, the Heletians shedding tears to feed seeds of resentment with their sorrowful water, while their Flet brethren's anger roused, fuelled by this latest act in an unfair history two centuries old.

Vilma whispered thanks to the gods that her daughter held no magic, but they'd also deprived her of the spirit she'd need to survive. She had to do something to give Inger a chance, something that might also spare her future children - for in their bloodline the ways of magic could skip a generation, but never two in a row.

She tried to keep her composure for Inger, to offer some kind of calm. It was hard, so very hard when she stood naked and bound to a stake rising from a pyre while so many different emotions rushed through her.

Her anger at her fate boiled, and that her daughter and her people should be made to watch the barbarity of it all only stoked that rage.

It also angered them; she could feel it. Her ability to delve into the *celestial*, the realm of magic and spirits, showed her the emotions entangling the souls around her. She would die today, but before her charred corpse fell crumbling and loosened from its burning bonds, the Inquisition would suffer the fury of the mob. Some already planned for it, both Flet and Heletian. By sunset the city would stand united, coming alive in riots led by the guilds and merchant houses. More would die. But dawn would see Ossard free of the Inquisition and their damned *Black Fleet*.

In a strong voice, Inquisitor Anton called, "Witches and warlocks will burn while cultists will drown. Yes, faithful people, the Church of Baimiopia will keep Ossard safe by picking the unfit hidden amongst you. Behold, the cleansing of the foul!" Then he dropped the burning brand, letting it fall through the silence and onto the edge of the oiled pyre.

The flames blossomed, rolling up to lick at Vilma's toes while their searing breath raced higher to singe her blonde hair and scorch her fair skin. She struggled against her bonds, but it was pointless. The shock of the pain didn't allow her to do anything more than jerk and buck. She needed to focus, to blind herself to the agony and avoid the madness it would bring.

She had to focus...

Flames raged to either side of her and all about the stakes rising from amongst the piles of oiled wood. Men and women screamed and writhed against their bindings while the crowd cried out in horror.

Vilma fought against the pain, pushing it down, back, and into her heart. There she worked to harness it, to use it for power. This would be her only chance.

And all the while the flames grew stronger.

Blisters rose along her reddened and swelling legs, and lower her feet blackened and charred. The scent of her own burning flesh haunted her nose, yet she found sanctuary despite the stink and searing blast.

She stared out into the crowd, her gaze locking on to her daughter.

Inger looked back, her head held tight by the monks. Tears ran freely from her wide and innocent eyes, rolling down her cheeks to her chin, from where they fell free to land on the cobbles.

What Vilma would have given to sup of them!

She whispered, a sound that couldn't hope to break above the hiss and snap of the roaring flames, yet she knew Inger would hear. Delving into the secret arts, she harnessed her boiling blood as it leaked from doomed veins to spend its power. This would be her last casting.

Yes, she was a witch, but what of it? She'd never burnt anyone at the stake or committed any other crime. She wasn't the monster!

She whispered to Inger, first soothing words and cooing.

Her daughter stilled her struggles, so much so that the monks holding her began to loosen their grip.

Vilma then gave her a message, whispering it over and over, "Remember your children, keep them safe."

The monks relaxed as Inger calmed. Now, her only sign of anguish came from the tears streaming down her pale cheeks. The monks stepped back, leaving her to her misery.

And all the while the fire raged.

Vilma's hair fell about her in burning strands with most of it breaking free, singed and ashen, as it was dragged up and into the afternoon sky. She couldn't feel her legs any more, but it was no relief, the worst of the pain had risen up her body, fully upon her blistering belly and breasts, and her arms tied behind her.

She had to end this and quickly. She'd also try to take the others being fed to the fire with her, but before she could, she had to give Inger hope.

Vilma saw a young man in the crowd, glimpsing him through the rising wall of flames. She knew of him. He was the only son of a well to do Flet family – and also come of age.

He looked upon the burnings in horror, yet had the strength to watch. She sensed his soul more deeply.

He was true...

She whispered to him, sending something that made him push forward to the front of the crowd.

Before him stood a lone Flet girl, the young lady's beautiful face wet with grief. Struck by the look of loss in her eyes, all he wanted to do was offer her comfort. He stepped past some monks and took her into his embrace.

Inger surrendered to him.

Her mother whispered, "Love her and care for her," sending the message directly to his soul as she reached into the celestial and bound them together.

Inquisitor Anton scowled. He could sense a casting, the cold tingle of its passing hanging in the air despite all the heat being thrown off by the flames.

It was the defiant bitch!

It ran weak and without danger, but still stood as sorcery. Guessing its target, he span on his heel to search the crowd.

There she stood, the witch's daughter, wrapped in the arms of a young man – *another Flet!*

Anton could taste her mother's bewitchment; the binding of souls and making of love. She'd crafted their marriage here. No doubt they would breed and more witchery would crawl from the filthy pit between the girl's legs.

No matter, he could check on their get during his next visit.

And then a dark smile broke his stern lips.

But for now...

For now rose the hungry fire and he would burn her mother, and if he found no satisfaction in that, he could always throw her daughter on the pyre as well. His gaze drifted as he thought, coming to a stop where it found a half empty barrel of oil.

He'd finish her casting now!

Anton strode across and tipped the barrel on an angle so he could wheel it along on its rim. He began moving it, it rumbling as it rolled over the cobblestones, bringing it closer to the witch and her coming end.

Vilma watched her daughter, the young man holding her tight. The couple were lost in each other as they mouthed her message of binding and love.

A smile split her blistered lips. The Inquisition had set many magical blocks about the pyre to stop any offensive sorcery, but because of her casting's harmless nature she'd been able to bypass them. It seemed that it had never occurred to the heartless bastards that someone might cast a love spell while being burnt alive.

Finally, it was time to end her own suffering...

Inquisitor Anton growled, "Put this in you!" And he kicked over the barrel, setting free its dark juice to spray onto the bonfire's edge.

The monks cheered.

The crowd cried out in horror.

And the fire around Vilma erupted into a ball of fury that lifted up to wash over her.

Her work done, she freed her perception and fell away from her mortal form to escape the pain, screams, and roar of her own boiling blood rushing through doomed veins. It was like backing away from two open furnace doors, her eyes, and into a dark cellar. With each moment the heat grew weaker and her view of *that* world diminished as she fell into the cool and soothing blue-tinged darkness of the next – the celestial.

She sensed for the others around her, seeking those also being fed to the flames. She grabbed at their desperate souls, mercifully dragging them and their attention away from their failing bodies, and into the cool of the afterlife.

Vilma would let them rest soon, but not before she used them to stir the emotions of those left behind. They needed to feed the crowd's anger – just as oil had been used to feed the fire. What she was doing would spare them the agony they'd felt, but also block their mortal forms from dying. The results would not be pretty.

Back in Market Square, the spiritless bodies convulsed and ruptured in a gory display. At the same time the crowd's anger also bucked to grow wild and ugly.

Anton shifted uncomfortably. He'd sensed the passing of souls, yet their blackened bodies still jiggled, moaned, and burst amidst the flames. It was as if they'd become zombies, the flesh alive, but the bodies without spiritual owners. Worse still, he could sense the shift in the crowd's mood; from one of horror to a deepening outrage.

In the celestial, her spirit smiled.

Tonight, it wouldn't be the witches and innocents of Ossard being slaughtered. Not any more. Tonight, it would be the false moralists of the Church of Baimiopia's hated Inquisition. And as for the Inquisitor who'd personally lit the pyre, the vile man taking power from the pain he inflicted - she'd get her own revenge.

COLIN TABER

By My Own Hand

-

A Belated Introduction

I am Juvela Van Leuwin, daughter of Inger Van Leuwin, and granddaughter of a woman burnt at the stake for being a witch. It seems that misfortune and tragedy are as common to my blood as its colour - and I assure you, it *is* red.

By my own hand I write this record using the skills that *they* forbade us to learn. For *them*, the ruling order of Ossard, such things as reading and writing were reserved for the mercantile-noblemen, most especially if they were of Heletian birth. In that, you see, is my failing, for I am both not a man, nor Heletian.

The Inquisition may have been expelled from the city after the riots, but the Church of Baimiopia and its prejudices were not.

My Flet parents taught me, their beloved only daughter, what they thought adequate. They showed me the basics of letters and numbers, but no more, worried if I learnt too much I'd be caught out. Needless to say, I've since improved my talents.Today, with the skills *they* forbade me to have, I sit down to tell the tale of how *their* mighty city, the city-state of Ossard, fell.

It all started about six years before my coming of age. The first signs were subtle, hidden amidst unrelated events and missed by most. It was eyes further afield that had spied the beginnings of the corruption. Those same eyes, Lae Velsanan eyes, imparted a warning that would save me. For that, despite their terrible part in the coming catastrophe, I will forever be grateful.

We begin in the late summer of the year 509 *Encarnigo Krienta* (seventeen years after *the Burnings*). I had just entered my teens...

COLIN TABER

Part I

Ossard, City of Merchant Princes

COLIN TABER

1

A Growing Shadow

My mother loved children. She cried if one suffered hurt and fell into despair at the news of an innocent's death. It didn't matter if they were strangers and news of their fate arrived as gossip, or if they stood as family or friends. Sometimes the grief came as a long and unwinding spiral of cold and numb mourning, others carried the explosive rawness of heart-wrenching cries and wails. There were always tears.

I hated it!

Every year that mourning built through Ossard's icy winter and thawing spring, only to mature into a deepening madness that rose with summer's heat.

Summer...

Those balmy days brought the fever; Maro Fever. It spread from the docks and through the slums to take the weakest into its burning embrace. It loved the young, for winter had already found the old to claim.

During the summer, instead of my mother hearing of a child killed in some misfortune several times a season she'd hear of fever deaths every other day. We tried to keep such news from her, it trapping her at home, yet the sounds of passing funeral processions marked by the slow beat of mourning drums could not be kept at bay.

Poor Inger, so sensitive and emotional, so busy feeling other peoples' pain – it almost drove her mad. Then one summer the real problems began...

Child-theft is a coward's crime; that's what my mother said.

At first I didn't even understand it. I mean, how could you? Why would someone want to steal someone else's child? But then it happened, marking the beginning of Ossard's fall from grace.

A little boy was the first to be taken. An infant girl went missing half a season later, stolen straight from her crib. More followed, and they were all Flets. I didn't know any of the victims, but I couldn't miss their families' grief.

The outrages went on, haunting the alleys of Newbank - the squalid Flet quarter of the city. The Heletian authorities ignored it as they did all the problems that plagued our district. In the end, any attempt at handling it fell to our guild, the Flet Guild, who unofficially governed everything on our side of the river. Still, as skilful as they were at dealing with our other problems, this was one that they couldn't overcome.

So the kidnappings continued, as did the misery they delivered.

Running our household kept Mother busy, it being one of the most prosperous in Newbank, and even of note in the larger and wealthier Heletian side of Ossard. She tried to keep an eye on me, as did Father, but that along with the family business, an inherited importing concern, just took too much of their time. One of our two maids could have watched over me, but they couldn't hope to defend me. If I was to be safe, it needed to be at the hands of someone suited to the task.

Father found someone, a man of battle that came recommended as honest and able. Still, on the day he started, none of us were sure.

Like any young adolescent I came with some attitude. At Sef's introduction, I displayed as much rebelliousness as I could muster.

"A bodyguard?" I asked.

"Just for now," said my father.

Mother nodded, her movements anxious.

I said, "It's because of the kidnappings, isn't it?"

Father nodded.

Mother said, "No, not at all, and it's just for a short while."

I turned to face him - *my* bodyguard.

He stood tall and solid, in his late twenties, with blonde hair and blue eyes spaced between the occasional scar. He tried to smile to win me over. It sat strangely on such a big man, one made bigger by an armour of leathers, and a scabbarded sword at his side. He looked like he'd just come from the bloody battlefields of Fletland, our people's war-torn homeland across the sea, so much so that I checked his boots for mud – to my disappointment they were clean.

He shifted, moving his imposing bulk awkwardly on our polished floorboards and setting them to softly groan. He just didn't belong in our *civilised* household, or for that matter any home.

I smiled; having him around would drive my mother mad. "Well, I guess it could be fun having my own bodyguard."

Sef's smile broadened.

Mother sighed in relief.

Father grinned. "How about we give it a try by letting him take you to the markets?"

I was making it *too* easy for them, so I let my enthusiasm fade. "I guess..."

Sef's smile faltered, making me feel bad. It was my parents I wanted to toy with, not him. He obviously didn't have a lot of experience with children.

I found a grin. "I guess. He looks like he could handle anything."

Their faces lit up.

Then I went on, "And he's got a great sword." I turned to him. "Can I hold it?"

He looked to my parents.

My mother paled while my father shook his head.

That's when I delivered the punch line, "Killed anyone with it?

Mother nearly fainted.

He squatted, coming eye to eye with me. "Only those who deserved it."

I looked into his eyes, cold pools that had seen a lot of worse things than a spoilt girl of thirteen.

Well, if I needed a bodyguard, I guess he could do the job. He was bigger than Father, and easily worth two maids and my mother in a fight.

Father filled the silence. "The markets then?"

Sef's smile dropped, now all business. "The markets."

I took a step back, my bravado dead.

All four of us took the family coach, Sef up front with the driver while my parents sat inside with me. My parents spoke of nothing in particular, just mundane household matters, both nervous as we headed out from home and away.

We arrived under overcast skies at the edge of Market Square. Crowds and stalls filled its wide expanse, all the way to its bordering sides marked by Ossard's grandest buildings; the guildhalls; Cathedral; and *Malnobla*, the residence of the lord of the city-state.

Sef helped my mother from the coach and then reached up for me. He tried to be careful, but his strong hands held too firm, seeing me twist against them. In response he tightened his grip.

I gasped, "You're hurting me!"

Father frowned. "Come now, Juvela, be good."

Mother stood to his side, worried but silent.

Then we set out.

Sef walked a pace beside me, or a step or two behind. He watched the crowd for trouble, and my parents for directions, but more than anything he watched *me*.

Mother looked at some cloth, and then some fruit, before we headed towards the livestock stalls. Amongst them we found a boar running around an otherwise empty pen. Alone and in a strange place, the brutish animal had become frenzied, to the amusement of a small crowd.

The owner was trying to calm it, but the tusked beast lunged at his handling attempts. We watched for a while as the owner called in two men to help. Armed with long poles, they began forcing it into a corner. Soon they'd have it. With the chase over we moved on, my mother not wanting to watch its likely death.

I led Sef and my parents down a narrow path that cut between two banks of pens, some empty, while most hosted goats, pigs, or sheep.

My mother complained, "Juvela, the animals' filth is everywhere!"

"But there are lambs ahead?"

Father looked to his women and sighed, then noticed my shoes already caked in muck. "Juvela, go and have a look, but take Sef. We'll walk around and meet you on the other side."

Sef offered an awkward smile.

My mother paled. "Can we leave her alone?"

Father put a hand to her back as he began to steer her away. "She's not alone, she's with Sef."

I skipped down the path. I could see a dozen lambs in the last pen.

Sef followed, but also kept his distance.

The lambs huddled in straw near the fence, it made from a tight weave of oleander canes. I went to them, squatting down as I slipped a hand through the lattice to offer the nearest my fingers.

Sef walked past, coming to a stop only paces away.

The owner of the lambs, a fat Heletian, approached him to see if he represented a possible sale. They talked while I patted the closest animal, marvelling at its innocent face.

That's when I sensed something behind me, it cold and sudden.

I looked down by my side to see a pair of black boots. A man stood there with his back to Sef, but Sef also had his back to him.

The man wore a dark cloak to protect against the coming rain that the sky promised, yet it also harboured something else - something akin to the chill that lurked in Sef's eyes. Earlier, I'd been a little spooked by Sef, but right now this stranger had me terrified.

He said, "It seems you've made some friends."

I just stared up at him.

"There are other friends you can make..."

Sef's voice came firm and hard, along with the ring of his sword as he unsheathed it. "She has enough friends, sir, such as me."

He'd escaped the lamb owner, moved around, and begun to push between us. I got up and stepped back behind him, putting a hand to his beefy hip.

Screams sounded from the other end of the pens. The three of us ignored them, caught up in our own intrigue.

Sef and the man locked eyes. At the same time, I swear, the very air chilled.

I looked down at the stranger's feet, his boots dulled by a sudden frost as strands of mist rose to drift about.

That wasn't right...

Sword in hand, Sef squared his shoulders and announced, "You'll need to do better than that!"

The stranger showed some surprise.

I didn't understand what they were doing, and had no time to think as I was distracted by a second set of screams. They were followed by a loud and bestial cry.

I turned to discover that the baled up boar was now charging towards us. Pink froth ran from its snout while blood streamed down its side; behind it, the beast's owner lay tripped up amidst the pen's ruined fence.

I cried out, "Sef!"

Following the narrow lane, the boar drew closer.

Sef hissed at the stranger, his sword held between them, "Get gone!"

The stranger chuckled. "So much to worry about!"

Sef said, "I can manage."

"But so little time!"

The boar neared. We only had moments.

I looked for a way through the fence, but the gaps in the lattice were too small, and the canes too thick. The lambs on the other side scattered. "Sef!"

The boar was upon us.

He swung his sword up from between him and the stranger, half-turned, and then brought it down from over his shoulder and out to his side. The move left me under his arm, and between him and his steel.

The beast reached us as the blade's tip flashed down.

The sword caught the boar on its great wet snout, with the charging animal's momentum driving its head onto the razor-sharp blade. Sef held it stiffly, forcing its tip into a gap between muck-covered cobbles where he strained to wedge it.

The boar opened its own skull and then collapsed into the path's mess. After a moment of spasmodic kicking, a wet squeal, and the spray of blood, it finally succumbed to a quick death.

Not wasting the chance, the stranger lunged around Sef's side and grabbed for me.

I screamed.

Sef brought his knee up to hit the stranger under the jaw, and at the same time lifted his sword and brought the hilt down on top of the man's head. He then turned and stepped back to pin me protectively between his back and the fence.

The stranger slumped to the ground.

Sef's blade hung in the air in front of me, half its length red. He asked, "Juvela, are you alright?"

I whispered, "There's blood on your sword!"

"Juvela, your parents are coming. Tell me you're alright!"

I took a deep breath. "Yes!"

He stepped away from the fence, freeing me, and then squatted down to be eye to eye. "It's alright, it's the boar's." He smiled.

Still giddy with fright, I threw my arms around his neck to hug him.

He patted my back with his free hand. "Your parents are nearly here. Please be brave, I really need this job."

I nodded.

Sef stood as we noticed that the cloaked man had gone.

I said, "He's gotten away!"

Sef frowned. There wasn't a trace of him.

My parents arrived.

Father cried out, "Well done!"

Mother dropped down to her knees in front of me. "Are you alright?" She was trembling and close to tears.

"Yes," I said, "I like Sef, he's great!"

Father laughed and nodded, while Mother sobbed with relief.

That night they discussed the terms of Sef's employment over a roast boar dinner.

Sef became my closest friend, and, for me at least, part of the family. He had great patience. Not only did he watch over me, but he also talked and played, telling me stories of his adventures in Fletland.

Few families in Newbank could afford such a luxury, but it did keep me safe. Meanwhile, around us, the abductions not only continued, but worsened.

My burly swordsman never again had to raise a blade to defend me – well, not back then. In my early years I thought it was because I was unique, you know, like most children.

I was special!

The adults around me reinforced the notion by the way they watched me grow. I thought they were looking for *something*, some telltale sign of my hidden glory beginning to bloom. There wasn't any. Later, I realised that they were just watching my all too ordinary progress into womanhood.

With its arrival the adults began treating me differently, like some kind of precious jewel. Only Sef didn't. Secretly we joked that the biggest threat to me came from my overprotective mother and her countless rules.

My father, an observant and warm-hearted man, asked me to be patient with her overbearing ways. He explained that my grandmother's dying wish was for my mother to take good care of her yet-to-be-born children. He said it plainly, telling me for the first time that Grandma Vilma had died in the riots that saw the Inquisition forced from Ossard, during the dark days known as *The Burnings*.

That moment had been a turning point for the city.

The expulsion of the Black Fleet marked the beginning of a new age of prosperity for Ossard, even for its marginalised Flets. Gradually the era faded, growing corrupt and wrong. That was when the child stealing had begun.

They never found the bodies, not even their clothes. Rumours abounded to blame everything and everyone. Occasionally, unfortunates would be set upon by accusing mobs, yet the kidnappings continued. It seemed that nothing could stop them.

The only thing the missing children *did* leave behind were their heartbroken parents, parents who carried unseen but deep wounds. Such hurts don't heal, instead they're re-opened by memories as if cut afresh every day. Left untreated they only spoil.

A city is the sum of its souls – when some begin to turn, all stand endangered.

It begged my maturing mind to ask what kind of city could allow such a thing? Perhaps a city too distracted by its own success.

Who cared if Flet children were being stolen from the slums? Not the Heletians ruling Ossard. In the city of *Merchant Princes*, anyone with the power to help was too busy doing business. In truth, it would take the theft of one of their own before they'd even notice the problem.

In many ways the city was as lost as its stolen children. And as the years passed and I began journeying through my teens, I felt lost too.

As my seventeenth birthday neared, my days revolved around little else than my mother grooming me for marriage. I didn't know to whom. Nothing had been arranged, but whatever the future brought, a pairing would have more to do with influence and wealth than love. I didn't care much for the notion.

The rude realisation that I'd soon have my own household and eventually children left me cold. I wasn't ready for it. I could only hope for a kind man with a good heart, with whom my feelings might change and grow.

In truth, I think my real fear was of becoming like my mother.

Meanwhile, the abductions continued, three or four a season and always of children under twelve. It was a tragedy, but it meant that I was well and truly safe, and that meant that Sef was no longer required.

We all seemed to come to that realisation at the same time, both Sef and I, and my parents. It left me numb.

Surprisingly, Mother insisted on keeping him on. We were too used to having him around and wealthy enough to afford it.

As it turned out, he was as relieved as me that he was being retained – if now on broader duties. I can still picture him standing in our sitting room, anxious, as my father gave him the news. It left him with a huge grin and trying to blink back tears. Seeing the big man so vulnerable made me giggle. He went a deep red at the sound, but then burst out laughing. Even my parents had joined in.

I was so happy. We all were.

If we hadn't offered the work, I think he would've returned to Fletland, but I knew he didn't want to go. He was afraid of that place, haunted by memories of bloody battles he'd fought, and adventures that hadn't always ended well.

Soon enough, he gave me another chance to giggle at him. This time it wasn't because of held back tears, but my approaching coming-of-age. He began to get awkward around me, just like my father. It was very endearing.

Mother spent her days teaching me the skills of a lady; etiquette; how to manage a household; and how to master various crafts.

It was a bore.

In the afternoons, she'd send me to my loft bedroom with stitching to complete or some other *enthralling* task.

I'd often end up sitting at my window lost in the caress of the summer breeze. Once there, it'd not take long before I'd let my thoughts escape the monotony of my work to seek the freedom of lazy dreams.

Being from amongst the wealthiest of Flet families, I was destined to marry a Heletian to help Father's business bridge Ossard's cultural divide. The thought frightened me. Unlike the blue-eyed and blonde Flets, the Heletians with their dark hair and eyes matched to olive skin seemed so different and stubbornly traditional.

My mother sensed my apprehension, so she started adding a lotus-based concoction to my meals. It was reputed to induce thoughts of motherhood, love, and even lust. I didn't notice any change, well, not at first...

Finally, and much to my mother's relief, I began to look at the idea of a husband, my husband, with a fresh and hot-blooded heart. He became the focus of my dreams, shameful things, as my mother strengthened the dosage so that the fantasies crossed increasingly into the waking day from the sleeping night.

It threatened to become an obsession.

I could see him, handsome and wealthy, but at the same time gentle and loving – a Heletian merchant prince.

He would be my hero, standing alongside me through the travails of life, living for me as I did for him. Together, as best friends, partners, and lovers – nothing less than a true couple. We would be inseparable...

Soon enough, bored with my mother's lessons, the daydreams became an escape. More and more, when I wasn't lost in a lotus inspired haze or taking lessons, I sought them out at my bedroom's loft window, most especially at the end of the day.

In contrast, in the waking morning, when the grip of the lotus ran at its weakest ebb, my head often grew heavy with pain. At such times I felt trapped by a destiny promising comfort, but no excitement, where I could see a lingering lifetime only to be mercifully ended by the hand of Death.

Such bleak moods only fed my hunger for lotus.

I dreamt of a sacred union, of two souls joined by all things honourable in a partnership heralded by angels. It would be so beautiful that even the gods would weep. In time, with the passing of many happy seasons, children and prosperity would strengthen our most important gift to each other – our love...

I knew it was just a fantasy, but I couldn't get enough of it.

I was being enslaved.

To my surprise, a respite surfaced in the strangest place; my sleep.

It began a little over a week out from my coming-of-age. At first it was just an image, like a glimpse of a distant land. It wasn't until after its first few visits that I realised how much I needed it – something to counter my growing dependence on the lotus.

Every night this new dream came stronger and longer. It pushed aside stubborn scenes of handsome husbands, breathless kisses, and naked, sweat-covered shame. It ran like a vision, as if I flew free with the birds, seeing me glide high above a green and beautiful land.

Without the passion and lust of the lotus dreams it might sound like a bore, but it stirred something deep within. It gave a sense of life, hope, and liberation: It was of freedom.

Within its sleeping caress, I dove down into steep mountain valleys and soared up by rugged, snow-dusted peaks. Eventually, that landscape gave way to a rock-lined sound where the sea spilled in. Behind that coast rolled green hills that grew in height and grandeur, and not much farther back, a shadowed canyon cradled in their midst.

A *sanctuary*.

The canyon was warm, lush with life, and full of water's song. Little streams trickled down tier after tier of the canyon's moss-covered sides, falling lazily to its mist-shrouded and fern-forested bottom.

But the lotus always fought to reassert itself...

> And out from that mist-veiled fern forest stepped my naked husband, his olive skin glistening, while the curve of his muscles caught the overhead sun. With a cock of his eye and a strong hand, he beckoned me, demanding that I come and make love to him...

Even my sanctuary could be violated.

My mother kept increasing the dosage, determined that I fall for the first man presented to me. She knew I could be rebellious and feared my initial reluctance. She wanted me nice and agreeable.

Amidst all this my headaches continued. At first I thought it was the lotus causing them, yet in the end I realised that the stronger doses actually worked to quell their pain.

After our courting, when finally he came to propose,
the question would be asked with flowers – red roses.
I'd always said; the first man bold enough to give me
such a gift of scandalously coloured blooms would be welcome to
my hand, for surely anyone so daring would have already won
my heart!

Such daydreams were best had sitting at my bedroom window
oblivious to the household and the crowded streets below. It was on
one such afternoon that I found myself settled in and looking out at
the maze of moss-covered rooftops, the whole vista still damp from a
long morning of showers.

The soft green ridges reminded me of the rolling hills of my dream
sanctuary as the afternoon sun peeked between clouds to highlight
them with passing shafts of gold. Beyond that living mosaic climbed
the sides of the steep valley we lived in; the Cassaro, Ossard's cradle,
and whose exhausted silver mines had given the city life.

The ancient range made the surrounding *Northcountry* difficult to
farm. All about us, its granite pushed through the thin soil to loom
rugged and stark.

The Northcountry was a treeless place.

The pine forests that had once veiled so many of its hills and
mountain slopes had succumbed to a blight over a century past, and its
few survivors long since been felled. The city's symbol, its famed rose-
tree, was also gone. Thickets of it had once lined the gullies and
riverbanks along the valley-floor, but the same blight had also stolen it
away.

Such a history saw the present slopes and valley-floor given over to
pasture and crops, or where too boggy or steep, abandoned to herbal
brush and a hardy oleander. The latter had spread without invitation
many years ago, growing its long branches full of thin and poisonous
leaves. The shrub's one blessing came in its bright pink blooms, while
pretty, they were also deadly. It was certainly no rose-tree.

But all that lay to the sides of my view and the inland depths
behind, in the distance spread something else; the Northern Sea.

The port crowded the far side of the city. There, the sea's deep
blue drew a dark line between the mossed roofline of Ossard and the

cloud-streaked sky above. In one place, partially hidden by a set of church towers, it glittered golden as it reflected the late afternoon sun.

A soft breeze tugged at my blonde hair, soothing in its caress. The sun also worked to seduce me as it set my pale skin aglow with its warm and sweet kiss. And all of it combined to make me sleepy.

I'd come here to daydream and endure a headache that had struck me earlier in the day. Its lancing pain had faded, but a muffled buzzing in my ears warned that it hadn't finished with me yet. The aches had haunted me for weeks now, at first soft and barely noticed in the morning, but recently they'd worsened to grow rough and breathtaking. My mother had been concerned at the news, overly so, but she'd always been prone to fretting.

I closed my eyes to let the sun comfort me.

A *mistake*.

With the distraction of my vision gone, I became aware of just how wrong things felt.

The buzz in my head gained clarity as it cleared into a chorus of whispered voices. I couldn't make sense of them, there were too many.

Was I imagining them?

While I couldn't understand them, the longer I listened the more certain I became. Soft and busy, like the hum of a distant crowd, it came from nowhere, yet everywhere.

What was happening to me?

And then, as if that question was the key to unlocking a door, images flashed through my mind in glaring white and blinding blue, all against a void of the deepest black. They were of flames, leaping sparks and billowing smoke, and at the heart of it loomed a forest of stakes with people bound to them. Those poor souls struggled against their bonds and screamed, but the inferno feasted on them nonetheless. In a stark moment of horror, I realised that the elementals fuelling it planned on doing so for eternity.

I was watching a witch burning, something from the past that the poor souls had been unable to escape even in death. It was of Ossard's riots, or more correctly, of the incident that had triggered them; The Burnings.

The vision left me shaken, but also *different*.

The tang of blood came to my tongue – *my own!*

Why was I bleeding?

The voices declared, "Magic!"

What?

They chorused again, "The coming of magic!"

No, not for me!

And my breath caught as I shivered.

I didn't want it, not to be burdened by the Witches' Kiss!

And then my headache subsided, the pressure binding it suddenly released.

My mind cleared only for it to succumb to a new sensation, it eerie, like a flow of iced water cascading *into* my core. Its brutal chill came as such a shock that I cried out as my eyes sprang open.

And the vista before me held such clarity it was as if every other time I'd looked out of my window it had only been for a glance.

Now I could see *everything.*

Everything!

Across the city, wherever I looked, I could see people walking, talking, working, loving, and so much more. It was as if I stood out there with every one of them. I discovered, to a degree, I could even sample their feelings and thoughts.

I turned in wonder from the city to watch the chores of a lone fishing boat crew far out in the sound. I took all of it in effortlessly and in beguiling detail, as three men cleared their nets while seven seagulls circled above them.

I could see everything!

That's when I noticed the sparks.

They rained down past my window to flare with an intensity that hurt to watch. It left me in no doubt, I wasn't supposed to see them, no one was; they were *black.*

Only one kind of spark could hold such a hue. I knew that from Sef's tales; they were of the celestial.

Magic!

The sparks stretched off in a narrow trail as they headed across the street towards Newbank's slums. I leaned forward in my chair, mesmerised. About me, the air grew cool and expectant.

It *was* magic, but not of me.

Someone else was casting.

The wind sounded, it heavy with the whipping of cloth. A moment later, a tall and ragged form with arms outstretched glided past. The robed caster followed the extending trail of sparks, their brilliance fading with his passage.

I supposed him to be a forbidden cultist or perhaps an outlawed mage.

The dark figure coasted on until he began descending towards a faraway alley lined with rundown tenements. Several balconies jutted out from those grimy three level buildings, all but one of them empty.

A boy with only a few years behind him and a crop of messy red hair stood there looking up. Surprisingly, the child could see him, but even at his tender age he sensed something was wrong.

I watched with growing fear.

The alleyway grew dark with the cultist's arrival, the light sapped away by some damning spell. The figure wore a hood, but I could tell by the strong jaw and a solid frame that it was a man, probably Heletian.

He landed.

This was no persecuted cabalist, a scholar of magic, instead it was a man who'd sold his soul to the diabolical, seeking favour in return.

Without a word, he offered his hand.

I held my breath.

The child looked up to the cultist, and then reached out to take it.

My vision, so strangely clear, marked the boy in the spoiled colours of death. I knew his fate, as though I'd be there when his blood was drained.

Under the weight of that feeling, the paralysing fear that had taken me finally released its grip. I stood and screamed, "Get away from him!"

The cultist's head snapped about, even though he was surely too distant to hear. His eyes sparkled coldly. He wasn't afraid, not of a Flet girl standing at a window too many streets away.

As if entranced, the child took his hand.

The cultist grinned.

It set me to tears.

The cultist and boy began to drift up, the two hand-in-hand. They followed a rising path of flaring sparks that trailed off towards the heart of the city.

I heard a scream and looked back to the balcony. The boy's mother, oblivious to her son above, looked to the street below.

With a thick voice, I yelled, "He's above you! He's taking him!" but she couldn't hear me. I was just too far away.

She rushed for the stairs.

My excellent vision faded, returning to the mundane. Sobbing, I dropped my tear soaked face into my hands.

Caught in my own grief, I didn't hear the hurried footfalls on the stairs leading to my room. The door burst open behind me. My mother charged in, Sef, of course, was right behind her. They'd heard my yelling.

She ran to me looking for any sign of what was wrong. Finally, as only a mother can, she took me into her arms.

Grateful, I took my hands away from my face.

Her supportive sounds died as her eyes filled with horror.

Behind her, Sef took a step back in surprise.

What was wrong?

She reached for my cheeks with hesitant hands. "Oh Juvela!" With trembling fingers she wiped at my tears – they came away bloodied. She whispered, "Just like your grandmother!"

And that is how it began.

2

The Mint Ladies

I tried to forget the dark happenings of the previous week by losing myself in the preparations for my coming-of-age.

It didn't work.

Nothing relieved the sense of guilt that haunted me. I just kept seeing that poor boy's innocent but deathly face.

I'd witnessed one of the child thefts, and the true nature of the crime; its link to magic was as much a problem as the abduction itself. Simply, I'd seen something I should've been blind to. To report it would incriminate myself.

The Inquisition might be forbidden to enter Ossard, but the Church could easily arrange my arrest and send me to them. I had to be careful. Such an arrest and consequent journey to the Holy City of Baimiopia wouldn't end well, particularly for a young woman, and even more so for a lonely Flet.

Mother demanded that I say nothing – *and damn the stolen boy!*

As a reward for my grudging agreement, she finally offered to explain something else; my bloody tears were a sign of my own awakening. She then made me vow never to speak of it again.

It was a vow I couldn't keep.

Two days later, I asked her about what she'd said regarding my grandmother. She snapped at me and reminded me of my vow. Her anger came fiery and quick, but it wasn't built of fury, instead it was founded on terror.

I am not and never have been stupid, even for a girl forced to suffer an education of little more than grooming, appropriate conversation, and how to smile without showing too much red lip or teeth. I suspected that my long-dead grandmother had also held an affinity for the forbidden arts, but confirming that wasn't going to be easy. Certainly, it was something that would take time, and that meant it would have to wait until after my traditional outing for my coming-of-age.

Ossard crowded at the Cassaro River's mouth, the river's waters passing through the city after snaking along the valley that stretched out to the east. Its chill flow ran for days through the rugged Northcountry, marked on its way by rapids, waterfalls, and a wild and icy source up amongst the interior's snow-capped peaks.

Those mountains rose up not just inland, but all about the Northcountry. They were dotted with exhausted silver mines – the same mines that had long ago fuelled the city's growth. Today, they hosted the miners' graves, along with gangs of bandits, and a thick spread of impoverished farming hamlets.

Once the Northcountry had built Ossard, now it fed it.

And just as the land had once brought riches to the city, now the sea likewise delivered. Its deep grey waters, Ossard's lifeline, brought food, trade, and on occasion even refugees.

The Flets, my people...

My family and I are descendants of refugees, from the thousands upon thousands who fled a war waged against our people by the Lae Velsanans two centuries before. Those dark days, *Def Turtung*, The Killing, lay behind our people, but far from forgotten.

We Flets are proud survivors of such catastrophe. In truth, if such calamities were omitted from our history little else would remain.

Today, the Flets of Ossard met passing Lae Velsanans with animosity and distrust, but preferably not at all. In such a climate, violence between our two peoples wasn't unknown.

Myself, I'd never seen any blood spilt in the feud, but for that matter I'd never even seen a Lae Velsanan in the flesh. I'd been told that they looked like us, but stood taller, leaner, and, it was grudgingly admitted, finer. I found it hard to picture such beings as Flet-hating beasts.

Since arriving in Ossard, our family's bloodline had mixed on occasion with our more numerous Heletian hosts, but our roots remained obvious – as they did for one third of the city. My family, with its blonde and blue-eyed Flet heritage, had never been able to climb above the rank of a relatively successful mercantile family, even with a good portion of luck. As I grew older, I realised that my birth had marked the end of that good fortune.

THE FALL OF OSSARD

My mother had suffered a terrible labour delivering me, something that had threatened her life, savaged her health, and brought bloody ruin to her womb. My parents needed sons, not a solitary daughter. Even before I'd taken my first breath I'd failed them.

Despite the disappointment of having only one child, and a daughter at that, our household was still full of love.

Our family stood as one of the most successful within the Flet community, we had not only wealth, but also respect – being generous benefactors to the Flet Guild. Due to our family's well-known civic nature, we even shared some goodwill from the Heletians, but in the end, to them at least, we were *still* Flets.

Growing up in a place where one's people are victimised can be a cruel experience, but also builds character. As my coming of age approached, and with the lotus warming me to the idea, I became determined to catch a man's eye that would help my parents. Simply, I had to marry a Heletian, specifically the son of a powerful family or a wealthy widower.

In Ossard, coming of age happened on a young man or woman's seventeenth birthday – a year late compared to most Heletian League states. As with so many things, Ossard was slightly out of step with the rest of the League, partly due to its Flets, but also because of its isolation. Regardless, when the day came I was ready.

At seventeen I stood slightly above average height with long arms and legs, all of it topped by blue eyes and wavy blonde hair. It was often said I had been blessed with the attractive looks of my mother.

Politeness is double-edged.

It's true that my skin lay smooth and unblemished, but it's also true that my face hung only neat and plain on an unremarkable frame. At the time I hoped it would grow into something worthy of the compliments. It never did.

It was the day of my first outing, an Ossard tradition at a young lady's coming of age. In essence, I would be dressed up, reminded of my manners, and then put on show with a chaperone. An outing's *new* lady was referred to as a *Mint Lady*, meaning *fresh*.

Wearing a new dress gifted to me by my proud parents, I was to be escorted out by a young group led by a distant cousin. On that sunny afternoon, my father and beaming mother saw our two open-topped coaches off at the door with Sef.

45

My father had arranged for us to go to a fine establishment that overlooked the sea north of the main port. The venue, Rosa Sorrenta's, was the place for the young of the Heletian upper ranks to be seen. In all, it was an outing someone such as myself should aspire to, but never too seriously expect to achieve. That I was going at all was a gift in itself.

We were all dressed in finery; in the lead coach my cousin and his new wife, and another relation with his betrothed. Also accompanying us were two family friends, both Flet Mint Ladies in their own rights. We three mints sat in the final coach.

I was so dosed up on lotus - courtesy of my anxious mother - that I kept forgetting my companions' names. Lost in that haze, I just knew that my objective was to find a husband, and looking at the competition, I felt that I wouldn't be hindered despite being so plain. Forgive my unkind honesty, but one sat as burdened as a heifer, while the other had the face of a horse - an old horse fed on lemons. We spoke little, those nameless girls and I, but we all knew the truth of the day. Following the coach of our chaperones, the three of us sat studying each other and exchanging the most cordial of pleasantries, Horseface, Heifer, and me - *Plainface*.

The three of us wore similar dresses in the fashion of the time. They were all substantial, well covering, of rich fabric, and showed off a little of the curve of the hip and bosom - a taste if you like. White lace showed through in places as a symbol of our purity, but lay amidst the strong colour of the main body of each dress; mine a deep blue, Heifer's an emerald green, and Horseface's a brave violet that verged on burgundy. No one wore red; that would have sent out a whole new round of messages, none that our families were ready to associate with.

The main streets of Ossard were cobbled, seeing our meandering ride towards the northern district in the late summer sun as one of lazy pleasure. Before long we were earning glances from men alongside the road, all flattering and good-natured. Our duties of maintaining fixed, polite, but disinterested smiles in response to their looks and whistles became a challenge in itself. The longer it lasted, the more we gave in to quiet giggles as the iciness between us melted.

During our progress through Ossard's streets another challenge brought itself to my attention; my undergarments were too tight. Some of the lacings felt as though they were cutting into me, a thing made worse by the constant rocking of the coach. I began rehearsing the conversation in my mind, the one that saw my mother scolding me for bleeding inside my dress. My reply would be that she shouldn't have laced me up quite so strictly just to hide one of my more popular attributes with the gents, my breasts.

The streets flew by, the buildings changing in nature from the stout stone buildings of the market quarter, all signed and well kept, to the less affluent districts that would never be as successful as those on the high ground and main streets. Here the buildings were predominantly wood, some little more than daub-and-cane.

Horseface spoke, dragging me from my whimsy, "There was another kidnapping last night."

I paled.

Heifer asked, "Where?"

Horseface indicated a passing alley. "This district, another boy stolen from his bed."

Looking down the shadowed lane, a place lined with litter, occasional stalls, and a steady flow of residents, it seemed so unlikely. I asked, "Another Flet?"

"Of course," she said with exasperation.

My father had said that the crowded slums, the most poorly governed districts of the city, were simply the logical place for such diabolical crimes. They were also home to the bulk of the Flet population, not just in Newbank, but also to a lesser degree in the low-lying districts on the Cassaro's other side. It was just a matter of circumstance. Regardless, we all knew it would take the theft of a Heletian child before the city's authorities took action.

In a fading voice, Heifer said, "My nephew disappeared a week ago."

Had he been the redheaded boy?

Horseface and I didn't know what to say. Her words left me numb, but nonetheless I found myself reaching across to pat her knee. "The Guild's looking to help, my father's talked to Heinz Kurgar, its head."

Heifer nodded as she fought to hold onto her composure.

Horseface thankfully changed the subject, putting on a mischievous grin, "Look, we're in the port!"

She was right, and we were all glad of it.

We passed along the edge of the district, one side of the road spreading as a seemingly endless row of warehouses, while the other lay thick with taverns, hostels, and brothels. We were supposed to be ignorant of the latter so we tried not to stare, but still took our time to look them over.

The amount of attention we gained from the stevedores, sailors, and other big men who worked the port thrilled us. From the small crowds outside taverns, to men walking the streets. None of them were shy or polite, and few of them settled for just a smile or a wink. They were free with suggestions, both in voice and action, and bold enough to see us blush while they cheered.

In front of a bar, to the roar of a crowd, one burly but drunk Flet stevedore pulled down his britches to let his proud manhood out.

I should have been mortified, instead I could barely contain myself.

I'd had far too much lotus!

We left that seedy place, heading up a rise to the northern district of the city. The quarter was built upon a small hillock that rose from the valley-side to loom over the port, it holding the homes of Ossard's elite. I looked upon the ornate facades of the exclusive homes we began to pass, many with manicured gardens, walls, and even guards. With few exceptions, the district held an exclusively Heletian population.

Fate would allow a few maidens of Flet-blood to be married to the district's eligible sons, but less than a handful every year. My plain looks could jeopardise my greatest hope. For a moment I considered my travelling companions; if I doubted my chances, what hope could they have?

For all of us, I slipped into nervous misery.

We passed by Ossard's *second* cathedral, Saint Baimio's, its two spires dominating the skyline of the quarter, and from the hilltop the city below. As with all the spiritual places within Ossard, it lay as part of the Church of Baimiopia, the only legal faith in the lands of the Heletian League. The stone building, vaulting and carved, stood exclusively for the wealthy locals, stopping them from having to mix with the commoners in Ossard's first cathedral and lesser churches.

While the city stood united in faith, it knelt divided in prayer.

Our coaches finally turned for the cliffs at the west end of the district. My heart fluttered, the sight of gulls and the scent of the sea telling me that we were nearly there.

In moments, I'd be helped out of the coach and into the glory of Rosa Sorrenta's.

THE FALL OF OSSARD

I prayed, a silent thing offered up to Schoperde, the Flet god of love and life. "May today find me a caring and wealthy husband, one who can uplift my family and me." Our people maintained no public temples to her or our other gods, but we kept our secret beliefs alive. The Heletians' faith didn't ring true to us, although we did feign piety.

The coaches rounded a bend and came into a street of brightly painted buildings, many fronted by window boxes full of well-cared-for blooms. There were wine bars, high-class taverns, theatres, and finally, up ahead, Rosa Sorrenta's. Upon sighting it a tingle of excitement started in my belly and grew.

Our coaches slowed to a stop, waiting for one parked ahead at Rosa Sorrenta's doors. I tried not to stare, but its dismounting passengers were young gentlemen, Heletians at that, and all tall, dark, and handsome.

I noticed the blue, red, and black crest of the Liberigo family, the rulers of Ossard, on the opened coach door. The Lord's youngest son then stepped out from the coach to the street. His appearance left me stunned and anxious.

Pedro Liberigo was tall and solid with an olive complexion of near perfect skin, well-tailored clothes hugged him tightly, showing off a good frame covered in muscles' meat. He turned to look at our waiting coaches, his sculpted face thoughtful and finished with dark hair and deep brown eyes. He exuded confidence, just like the man of my lotus-fuelled dreams. For a moment his mouth moved with the beginnings of a welcoming smile.

He then looked away to break the spell.

Horseface and Heifer gasped, one of them whispering, "He looked at us, did you see!"

Such hopeful words...

Then, as we watched, he glanced back and gazed directly at me.

My fellow mints let out another round of gasps.

In a heartbeat the moment was over. He and his friends had gone inside and their coach was leaving. It left me breathless, but also meant we were free to go forward: It was our turn to join the parade.

Rosa Sorrenta's stood three floors high with its exterior covered in a subtle pink render, something akin to that of sun-bleached oleander blooms. Planters full of flowering geraniums nestled beneath window frames finished in gold leaf, it all giving a taste of the reputed beauty within.

For my own part, I wanted to see the glory that had given the establishment its name, its rose garden – the cliff-side courtyard was said to be amongst Ossard's delights. But now, most of all, I wanted to catch another glimpse of Pedro Liberigo.

Had he really been looking at me?

Two doormen came forward to help us down from our coach. They wore cobalt blue uniforms, white leggings with matching caps, and reached up with white-gloved hands to steady our descent upon a set of portable steps. Once down, I looked about as I waited to be joined by Heifer and Horseface, and when reunited, we all shared a moment of innocent joy.

My cousin met us, leading the rest of our party.

Once everyone stood ready, he nodded to the doormen. Impassively, and in perfect unison, they swung open the gold leafed double doors.

The doors opened into a wide hall to reveal a beautifully chequered pink and white marble floor, from which the walls rose covered in burgundy suede, and highlighted in gold. Alongside both sidewalls climbed staircases leading to private dining rooms.

A uniformed host awaited us. Without speaking, our host dipped his eyes and gave a welcoming bow, then rose and turned to lead us through the hall and towards the open doors of a dim lounge. The room spread full of comfortable seats, all of them accompanied by small side tables lit by lamps capped with amber-tinted glass. We passed through the room towards another set of double doors manned by two more doormen.

The lounge was a social place, a space for fine liquor and smoking, and a place at the moment half full. Looking around, I was astounded by the faces I saw. I'd never met any of these people first hand, but I knew of more than half of them. Predominantly, they were of the establishment, and all here to socialise and do business. As we passed, conversations stopped and heads turned; the passage of Ossard's latest mints *always* demanded attention.

We left the lounge through double doors that opened onto a hall servicing half a dozen different rooms, and at its end we entered a long and light space; the Sunroom.

The radiance and beauty of the Sunroom can only be described as otherworldly. All the woodwork had been painted white, with an absolutely decadent amount of glass fitted into one wall and part of the roof. A floor of white marble spread before us sporting clusters of chairs, all wooden and whitewashed, with matching cushions. An assortment of lush potted plants, huge and outrageous, worked to break up the brilliant space. Groups of patrons sat back enjoying the room's light and ambience.

Midway along its glass wall stood another set of double doors, these also panelled in glass. Doormen opened the doors without a word, allowing our passage, and in a moment we went from the splendour of the Sunroom to the blooming glory of the Rose Garden.

The Rose Garden spread as a courtyard that ran the width of the building, making it perhaps sixty paces long and forty deep. At one end stood the glass and wood of the Sunroom, but facing it was a waist-high stonewall, also whitewashed in keeping. The cliff fell away beyond that, plunging to the sound a hundred paces below. The view was spectacular, and only challenged by the magnificence of the collection of blooms that lay within its walls. It was superb.

The area had been carefully planted to mature with an assortment of flowers. Jasmine climbed the tall, whitewashed sidewalls, and in some places the glass of the Sunroom. The rest of the plantings were made up of thick clusters of manicured roses, all perfectly pruned and magnificent in colour. Beneath them spread the soil of their beds, lying dark and moist, to peek from under a frosting of spent petals. The beds lay strung about to create between them large spaces amidst the paving for tables and chairs. All in all, with a variety of vibrant colours and luscious perfumes, the Rose Garden was a wonder.

All of it, its layout, colours, plantings, and the way it mixed with the sky's blue saw me sigh, yet it lacked something...

Alas, where was Pedro Liberigo!

Our uniformed host led us towards the cliff wall, to a table being prepared by more blue-coated staff. In a moment we were seated, the ladies first, each with our chairs politely pushed in behind us amidst words of welcome.

The other patrons ranged as a mix of Ossard's wealthy, but weighted with youth. The majority were male and Heletian, though there was also a smattering of Flets and women.

Many of the young men turned our way, some even getting to their feet and walking to the cliff wall to take in the view – a contrivance to enable them a closer look at the city's latest mints. At this my thoughts of competing with Horseface and Heifer came back to haunt me: They ignored the other girls, I was the sole focus of attention.

Me, simple miss Plainface!

My cousin ordered drinks, something cool to soothe the bite of the sun. They arrived in beautiful glasses, iced, coloured with fruits, and all of it mixed with watered-down rum.

Not long after, the gifted drinks began to arrive.

The majority came to me. The first took me by surprise, the second saw me abuzz with proud pleasure, while those that followed set me to wonder if I'd drown in such generosities. Nonetheless, as the uniformed servers whispered in my ear whom each was from, I offered a coached smile of thanks, while everything was monitored by my chaperoning cousin.

My mother had warned me to watch what was served, and never to take more than a sip from each. In particular, it was not unknown for men to send drink after drink to Mint Ladies in an effort to win their befuddled favour.

The afternoon passed, and the staff began to move through the garden and light coloured lamps. It was then, after losing count of the drinks I'd accepted, that I began to feel quite flush and full and knew with certainty that I needed to get to a privy.

I left our table accompanied by my cousin's wife, she leading the way. In trying to follow her I found myself delayed by a group of well-watered merchants, they weren't quick to pass or part as they took their time admiring the evening's favourite mint. I blushed at their leers as I rushed after Isabella.

The privy lay just off a small ladies' lounge. After tending myself, it was in the lounge that Isabella and I freshened up, spoke of the afternoon, and giggled as we compared our dresses. It was then, as she referred to one of my fellow mints as *Horseface*, that I nearly died of laughter. Still, the next moment saw me breathless because of my undergarments tight laces.

Isabella saw my discomfort. "Whatever's wrong?"

"My lacings are too tight, it's rubbing me raw."

Before I knew it, she'd whisked me away to a side room to open the back of my dress.

"The knot's tighter than a Burvois merchant's purse!" she cried.

I realised then that her drinks hadn't been watered down.

She managed to open my dress and began fiddling about with my undergarment's laces, all the while straining and cursing. The pressure being put on my chest and sides left me breathless. Worried, I gasped, "Just leave it, my mother can see to it later."

"Nearly there..."

"Really, it's not that bad."

"Almost..."

In the next moment, as she strained, our voices were silenced by the angry growl of ripping fabric.

I cried out.

She whispered, "Oh my!"

"What's happened?"

"It's the stitching on your unders', the laces have come off!"

"Oh!"

"I'll just leave them and do up your dress. No one will ever know."

I held still as she fastened it. "Please, don't do it too tight, at least let my dress survive the evening!" Already I knew the rest of the night would be a problem, without being restrained my breasts would be bouncing about like two drunken sailors in a brawl.

Isabella finished and appeared in front of me, laughing as she offered a glass flask that appeared from somewhere amidst the folds of her dress. "Take a sip, it'll help you forget about it."

I sulked, "Perhaps I should go home..."

"Go home? This night will mark out the rest of your life, and look at your competition; Horseface and Hog-hips!"

I laughed as I reached for it, and then took a long swig.

Isabella smiled as she grabbed it back.

My dress felt fuller now that my breasts weren't so restrained. I asked, "Do I look proper?"

A seedy smile came across her face. "You look *very* pretty."

We left, heading back to the Rose Garden.

Again Isabella and I became separated amidst the noise and crush of the crowd. I knew where to find her, so I wasn't concerned - besides I was preoccupied with trying not to stumble.

The drinks were taking their toll, and in that they weren't alone: My mother's lotus mixed with everything to make me feel quite hot and restless. My mind wandered from thoughts of husbands to lustful dreams, and even back to the big stevedore who'd exposed himself on the port road.

I was losing control.

The room buzzed with music, conversation, and laughter. Ahead, I caught a glimpse of Isabella as she reached the Sunroom. I'd catch up with her soon.

It was then that I heard a man speak from behind, his tone soft but commanding, "My lady?"

I stopped and turned.

Pedro Liberigo stood there with a bouquet of red roses. "May I present you with these?"

I thought I'd faint!

He reached out to give me the blooms, the stems wrapped in a length of white silk. "I'd be most honoured if you'd also accept a gifted drink?"

I felt vulnerable without my chaperone. What was I suppose to do? Taking the roses would be polite, but they were the most scandalous red. Was it wrong to take them? As for the drink, without my host I couldn't possibly accept.

He saw my hesitation and offered, "Would you like me to escort you back to your table? When you're seated, I'll again make my offer in front of your friends?"

To me, with my mind now swimming under the sting of Isabella's spirits, and my body burning with my mother's lotus, that seemed like a noble idea. I nodded, not even noticing in my befuddlement that his gaze rested solely on my breasts.

He offered me his arm, and as I took it the crowd parted so the most eligible bachelor in all of Ossard could escort a Flet Mint Lady, a plain face at that, back to her table.

Strings of coloured lamps lit the Rose Garden, now bathed in sunset's final glow. My cousin stood at our table searching the crowd for me while Isabella shrugged and sat down beside him. His eyes finally came to rest on me, and then my escort, seeing them fill with surprise. When we reached the table, it was an expression shared by all.

Pedro bowed before the table. "I must compliment the ladies for their beauty, and the gentlemen for escorting out such fine company."

My cousin replied in kind, "Thank you for your generous words, and returning *my* charge to our table."

Then, Pedro, as if he hadn't stunned me enough, worked to do it all again. "I'd be honoured to have such fine company dine with me tonight in the Pearl Room, if you'd care to join me?"

My cousin couldn't refuse the offer. It would be a great honour, and sate the curiosity of everybody; the Pearl Room wasn't open to the public.

"Thank you for the invitation, one we *all* are most happy to accept."

Pedro smiled. "Then allow me to provide some pre-dinner drinks." He looked over his shoulder to a uniformed waiter. With a quick nod and a whisper the attendant disappeared, only to return moments later carrying a silver tray loaded with an assortment of refreshments. Pedro reached for two, handing one on to me. I accepted it and wondered if I'd just been sold, but such was this man's charm that I didn't care.

He said, "My apologies for being so forward, but I saw you this afternoon and knew we had to meet."

A seat appeared for him beside me. He helped me into my own, and then took his before turning and taking my hands. "So, tell me young lady, what ever is your name?"

My heart raced while my tongue sat heavy, and I could only hope that my makeup hid my blushing cheeks. For a long moment I remained quiet, not even acknowledging his simple question.

Isabella, who'd been watching, broke in to save me from my paralysis, "The young lady is Juvela, Juvela Van Leuwin."

He raised his eyebrows in recognition of the family name.

I smiled, and he went on to speak of rare beauty, fate, and destiny. Like any young girl I believed every one of his honeyed words.

I was swept away.

We moved to the Pearl Room, a fine upstairs suite. The whole room glowed, its white marble walls and floor reflecting the flames of scores of candles, dozens of them alone lighting a chandelier hanging from the vaulted roof. Everything in the room was made or tinted in the colours of cloud-white, crystal, pearl, or silver. The effect was heavenly.

The meal that arrived was as rich and sumptuous, amongst its countless courses, truffle soup, honeyed lamb, and Evoran jellies, with all of it punctuated by yet more drinks.

The evening was graced by easy conversation amongst our selves and a dozen of Pedro's friends. Every member of our party seemed to be catered for, that is, everyone but me: Our host claimed my sole attention.

We seemed to be getting lost in each other, only momentarily distracted by the arrival of new courses, refreshed drinks, or our fellow guests. Finally, he asked my cousin, "May I have permission to escort Juvela for a stroll in the roof garden?"

My cousin quickly sobered, something spotted by Isabella. "I'll play chaperone," she offered, "I need to get some air." As she rose she placed a hand on her husband's shoulder to keep him in his seat.

Pedro pulled back my chair so I could rise, my vision spinning as I got to my feet. I tried to stifle a giggle as I walked as gracefully as I could manage, heading for the door where Isabella waited.

We left the room and passed down a corridor, moving towards a narrow staircase at its end. Isabella saw me on my way before dropping back, a moment later I heard her voice hiss in whisper. I turned to see Pedro nod to her as she took something from his hand. She then went back down the corridor, past the Pearl Room, and to a staircase that descended to the ground floor.

Pedro turned to me. "Don't worry, Isabella won't be long."

I laughed and continued to the stairs. What did I care? I finally got to be alone with the man of my lotus-fuelled dreams! I wasn't afraid, far from it! My thoughts ran drunk with wine and heady with lotus.

I just wanted him to kiss me!

I started to climb the stairs and slipped. Pedro's strong arms caught me, pulling me against his chest to keep me safe.

He smiled and held me close. "Come now Juvela, we can't stand like this forever. What will people say?"

With his arms around me, I really didn't care.

I let him steady me, and then he passed by to lead me by the hand.

Was he planning on taking advantage of me?

Such a fine host couldn't be doubted – even though I stood besotted by his charms and drunk on his liquor.

Above, the full moon glowed fat and bright, its blue, green, and tan face marked by swirls of white.

Everything was so perfect...

We walked amongst raised beds of herbs, roses, and hedges, all of it lit by occasional lamps. I stumbled several times as we walked along those dim paths, but every time he was there to catch me.

Soon we found ourselves entwined together, and staring into each other's eyes. He whispered, "You're such a rose."

"I'm so glad we've met, that you sought me out."

"How could I not?"

"Oh Pedro..."

And then he bent down to kiss me.

I should have slapped him.

His presence was intoxicating, his smell, touch, and warmth setting me afire. When his hands began straying, I didn't just give in, I welcomed them.

If I hadn't realised it earlier in the day, I did right now: This was what I wanted, and I wanted it very badly indeed!

He led me to a secluded corner of the gardens, a place lost to shadow and surrounded by tall hedges, all of it centred on a beautiful lounge. Once there, he untied my dress and helped himself to my breasts while I undid his britches to find the joy within. Finally, mostly naked, and as if the spell had to climax, I reclined as he climbed atop, eased my legs apart, and then slid inside me.

I had never been with a man before, and I swear it was like being born anew and dying all at the same time. It started with pain, but soon became a very morish pleasure, and one that put even my most shameful dreams well and truly in their place.

Amidst our passion, unbelievably, the voices that had haunted my mind chose that moment to return. I began to rock my head about, as if trying to cast them out. That's when I noticed the men watching; they were standing amongst the hedges.

I would have screamed, but one of Pedro's hands had come up to stroke my cheek seeing him inadvertently cover my mouth. I tried to meet his gaze, but he was looking the other way, and with his bulk astride me I was pinned and unable to move about. So, while I tried to get his attention, he just kept working me.

Deeper and deeper...

The robed men stepped out of the darkness to close around us in their long blacks, their features lost to hood and shadow. With them came a chill that stirred a fear in me that was nothing but primal.

We had to get out of here!

The voices in my head grew louder, no longer whispering mumbled words, but joining together in a rising wail.

I tried to scream to get my lover's attention, but his hand, once a tool of gentle pleasure, now pressed down so heavily that I barely raised a sound. Confused, I bucked, thrusting my hips up into his as I tried to throw him off.

He just rode out my efforts.

Harder and harder...

And then one of the robed men stepped forward.

Pedro turned his head in their direction, but instead of showing surprise, he nodded in greeting. My lover, with sweat from our efforts running down his brow, growled, "Hurry!"

He knew them!

The leader nodded and started a chant, the tongue of it foreign, but its rhythm making it ring out like a prayer. The others were quick to join in.

Panic finally overtook the alcohol and lotus in me, yet I lay helpless under Pedro's weight.

What could *I* do?

What were *they* going to do?

Were they all going to jump on top of me once Pedro had finished?

It was then that I realised I knew their leader. I was staring into the same cold eyes that had arrogantly watched me as he stole the redheaded boy away. As if in answer to the thought, he snapped his fingers, and the same child appeared, pushed forward to stand mindless before us.

The voices sounding in my head climbed higher, their choral wail growing more intense.

They were terrified!

I struggled again, trying to force Pedro off. His weight made it impossible, and my bucking only seemed to give him more pleasure.

I had to do something!

I bit down on his hand, but he barely flinched. Blood came into my mouth, but he just kept working me.

Faster and faster...

The leader stood there with the child in front of him.

The chanting built in crescendo and then finally peaked.

Casually, as if filleting a fish, the leader opened the child's throat with a blade and a quick flick of his wrist.

Pedro gave a throaty growl, pushing down so hard into me that I yelped. And with that deep movement my own body responded, trembling as it found its own release.

Then it was done, both he and I, and the red haired boy.

All of us finished.

I lay there with Pedro slumped on top of me, both of us wearing nothing more than sweat; his of exertion, mine of terror.

The boy still stood, held by two of the robed men. They were draining the life from his body, directing the red flow from his wound into a bowl of silver.

The robed leader wet a brush in the bowl, and then began painting something on Pedro's back.

I shivered.

The leader finished his marking, and then looked to me. He leaned down, his breath on my cheek, and uttered something in the tongue of the chant before kissing me.

Slowly, Pedro removed his bloodied hand from my mouth.

I tried to scream, but no sound came.

All of them laughed at my horrified surprise, even Pedro.

Their leader said, "You will remember this, all of it, but you will never be able to speak of it." And then he grinned.

He stepped back into the shadows, as did those with him. In a moment, only Pedro and I remained.

The alcohol had long ago relinquished its grip on me, replaced with horror and shame. Pedro knew, but refused to let me become a prude. He pulled out of me as he rolled off, and with his closest hand squeezed one of my breasts. "Perhaps I'll see you again, Juvela, you are too special to let go." Then he got up, turned around, and fetched our clothes from where they lay on the paving.

Under the silver-blue moonlight, I could see that the cultist had marked a four-sided diamond on his back. Painted in blood, it now trailed long dribbling lines from the base of his neck running all the way to his butt. He looked to me and smiled, but it wasn't of shared joy, instead it was of selfish power.

We seemed to be alone, leaving me to wonder if I was safe. I also worried about the time; Isabella had been gone for far too long.

I wanted to run.

I wanted to go home.

I wanted Sef.

Pedro dressed himself and then helped me. He pulled me up and off the lounge, forcing me into my dress with well-practiced hands. I wondered with disgust; how many other women had he been with?

Then we stood facing each other.

I scowled at him.

Would he or his robed associates ever want to see me again? I hoped not.

This would be the end of it.

He regarded me. "Your dress looks as it should, but let me fix your hair. He fussed over me, his touch lingering, and then he wiped away tears I didn't remember shedding.

As if nothing had happened, he asked, "How am I, orderly enough?"

Shocked and numb, I whispered, "Yes." He actually looked magnificent, truly alive and vital, as if he'd been blessed.

He took my reluctant hand and led me along the path.

I felt stunned and confused. My guilty flesh still carried his memory, worse still a part of me revelled in it.

I'd unwittingly been part of a ritual that saw my previous silence on the redheaded boy's kidnapping mature into the guilt of being present at his murder. I'd also shamed my family.

Voices rose from the stairs, we turned to meet them. I let go of Pedro's hand.

It was the rest of our party.

I would try and tell them, I had to.

Pedro stepped forward to greet them.

Horseface and Heifer looked tired and bored, but I couldn't hold their gaze.

My cousin carried the bouquet of roses. The sight of them hurt me; my perfect dream dead.

I tried to speak, to say that a boy had been killed, that forbidden magic had been worked, but my mouth would simply not move. Despite my efforts, neither my voice nor jaw would follow my command.

Pedro watched me. A sparkle in his eye told me that he knew of my plight. I could see his relief.

Isabella appeared out of the darkness behind us.

Had she been there all along?

Her face gave away nothing.

My cousin said, "It's a good night for a rooftop stroll, but unfortunately the evening must come to an end." He looked to Pedro and continued, "I must thank you for your invitation to dinner."

Pedro bowed and looked to me. "It was a pleasure, and a pleasure I'd very much like to have again."

I shivered.

3

The Coming of Shame

I went through the next few days as if in a trance.

My mother worried, I think she thought I was drifting off, somehow becoming lost to the magic. Struggling with my own guilt, I couldn't bring myself to tell her the truth. I convinced myself that I wouldn't have been able to in any case because of the binding their leader had put upon me.

Slowly, I pulled myself out of the haze, helped by my mother reducing the amount of lotus she added to my meals. In the end, I reminded myself, it hadn't been me drawing the blade across the boy's throat. I was just a witness. If anything, I was also a victim – if perhaps a luckier one.

And so I went on, trying to soothe my troubles away. It didn't work, not at first, but soon I found some solace and my malaise began to fade.

Pedro didn't call on me, and for that I was glad. I even began to think I could put the whole thing behind me and settle for a simpler man.

Until I discovered I was pregnant.

Before long I wasn't the only one who knew. My mother realised and told Father. The maids overheard, and through them the news of my shame spread.

Pedro's next visit started without the charm of our first meeting.

I was sitting in our household's courtyard, a place I'd tried to find peace in by greening like Rosa Sorrenta's famed garden. My efforts had shown some success, but early autumn in Ossard was no time for new roses to take.

I heard the bell ring, and listened as one of our maids attended to it. I expected it to be a messenger – since word of my pregnancy had got out, my parents' friends had stopped calling, all too embarrassed by my condition.

Soft voices hummed, followed by quiet as the maid hurried away to seek my mother.

My parents weren't speaking to me. They hadn't since I'd confirmed my pregnancy, something feared by my mother since she'd seen the state of my torn undergarments. Worst of all, she'd also forbidden Sef to talk to me.

The little I did want to say in my defence couldn't be said; the cultist's casting blocked every one of my attempts to talk of it. It left my mother and father, and even Sef to think the worst of me.

I heard the click of the front door's latch; our caller had either left or let himself in. The curiosity as to which saw me turn around. At the same time, a gentle whisper of warning swirled about me.

I looked up to see Pedro step through an opened door that led into the courtyard. Once on the cobbles, he just stood there and gazed at me. After a pause he swallowed and said, "Juvela, how are you?"

"I'm well," I said in a shaking voice as I got to my feet.

He came forward, retrieving something from his belt. He stopped before me and then moved to offer it; a small leather pouch. As our hands met, he looked to me and said, "This is medicine from Evora, it will end your *malady*."

Speechless, I didn't accept it.

His eyes widened. "You must take it. Have your maid mix it into a broth..."

"May I help you?" My mother's voice cut off his words.

We both turned to see her stepping into the courtyard, the maid behind her in the shadows. Sef also stood in the house, watching, but his hand rested on the hilt of his sword while his face flushed red. I'd never seen him so tense.

Pedro turned and bowed, closing his fist over the pouch. "Lady Van Leuwin, I am Pedro Liberigo."

She stared at him. "I know who you are." And it was obvious that she did. "Have you come to belatedly ask for her hand?"

Pedro stood stunned and for once his charming tongue lay still.

I paled at the suggestion.

My mother stepped forward. "Well, have you?"

To his credit, he stood his ground. "No, I've not come to ask for her hand. I've come to speak with her regarding topics of mutual interest."

I spoke up, my tone weak, "He's come to give me a brew to kill *our* child."

Pedro winced.

My mother's eyes gleamed, as if given permission to slake her thirst for his blood. She growled, "What kind of man are you? No Fletman would hear of such a thing. You Heletians have no honour!"

He nearly choked, his own face turning red. Finally, fired by his wounded pride, he spat back, "Maybe so, but Heletian men can't have any less honour than Flet women – she is looser than a tavern wench!"

My fists bunched and my lips trembled. "You liar! You have dishonoured me and my family, and stolen something precious and dear!" and then the rest of my words died, my jaw locking as my rage saw me try and tell of the ritual, his corruption, and the murder. Frustrated, I could only curse.

Pedro grinned, realising that his master's sorcery had silenced me. He turned back to my mother, but as men do, he lost his courage in the face of a woman so enraged. In that moment she had all the power – something I was famished for.

She walked up to him and pointed an accusing finger. "You will do the right thing, and there is only one right thing to do."

He stared incredulously. "What, marry her? A plain Flet maiden from a common family?"

My mother answered in a voice cold enough to silence the heavens, "Your family is hearing of this right now, as is the mercantile, stevedoring, seafarers', and Fletlander guilds. Our shame is becoming your shame, and there will be only one way to soothe it: You will marry her!"

Both Pedro and I were stunned by the news. The shame of it all, the whole city would know by dusk!

He glared at her, only to be distracted like all of us by the sound of urgent knocking from the front door.

My mother called to the maid, "See to it!"

We heard the door open, followed quickly by the stomp of booted feet. In moments the courtyard began to fill with men at arms in the livery of the Liberigo's, a dozen of them, and amongst them Lord Liberigo himself. The men at arms arrayed themselves to either side of their lord, a tall, broad, but lean man, without his youngest son's looks. Lord Liberigo stood stern and hard. This was a man who did business, and did it quickly.

Sef moved to stand beside my mother.

"Lady Van Leuwin, it is unfortunate that we should meet under such circumstances, but I came as soon as I received your message."

My mother answered, "My apologies for the harsh language within it, my Lord, but we share a problem that needs a just solution."

Pedro had paled at the sight of his father. He began in a quaking voice, "It's not..."

His father hissed, "Shut up, Pedro!"

The front door slammed again, followed by the sound of hurried feet. My father appeared, his satisfaction plain to see as he took in the sight of the Liberigos. My mother nodded, indicating that all was well despite the presence of the armed men in livery.

Put at ease, my father's gaze landed on Pedro. He strode straight up to him, his eyes boring into him as his anger built. "Shameless bastard!" Then he raised his hand and slapped him.

The solid blow reddened Pedro's cheek and saw him struggle to keep his footing. He looked to his father, waiting for him to intervene. He didn't.

Lord Liberigo clapped his hands together and growled, "You deserved that, Pedro, and you deserve so much more!" Then he turned to my parents and said, "You have done well in forcing my hand. You have succeeded in shaming my family, and your own, by making Pedro's part in your daughter's condition public – but I don't blame you. I can see you are merely trying to make the best of a bad situation. I imagine you want compensation?"

My father's fury settled, but he still stood angered. "You can't buy us off, not in this!"

Lord Liberigo shook his head and chuckled. "I'm not going to, in any case it's too late for that. Instead, I'll give you what you want. Pedro is a no-good playboy and has shamed my family with his exploits for years. It's time he settled down. *I* offer him in marriage."

I nearly died.

Pedro cursed, "Father, she's a Flet, and her family of no consequence!"

My father turned on the young man, slapping him so hard that he was knocked off of his feet.

Pedro looked to his father, his lips quivering and bloodied.

Lord Liberigo answered, "Pedro, you have much to learn. Yes, Juvela is a Flet, but so is much of Ossard. You need help, and I know of a good monastery that can see to it while your betrothed runs through her maternal peace."

If Pedro could have paled more he would have, he stood whiter than olive skin should go. I knew his fear; would the holy men of the church discover his shameful secret, his involvement with heresy?

I hoped so!

With his shoulders slumped, he whimpered, "I won't do it!"

Lord Liberigo hissed, "You will!" Then he turned towards my parents. "The union of our families has benefits for all. I lose responsibility for a troublesome son, your daughter salvages some dignity, and you receive the benefits of a close association with the most powerful family in Ossard. Will you be a part of this?"

Inger looked to Josef, he in turn turned to me. I knew what Father was thinking; what better solution? He asked, "Juvela, will you abide by this?"

Pedro turned to me, his pale face regaining some colour. This was his way out. He knew I didn't want to marry him, not after what I'd seen.

My parents expected me to say yes, it was my duty, but how could I?

Pedro couldn't help himself, a triumphant grin took to his face.

He would win!

Gently, like a chorus of angels, I heard the whispering voices rise again in my mind. This time they sang out, peaceful and welcoming, and lacking their previous confusion, they were led by one, strong and determined, it stirring to comfort me.

Could I become a lady of magic, a witch? And if I did, would I be strong enough to control whatever it was that Pedro stood mired in? Could I be safe?

He expected me to refuse, and to do it out of hand. The longer I stood there in silence the less smug he looked. Sensing my considerations, he began to panic. "This is insane!"

In that moment I tasted power over him - *and I liked it!*

He gasped, "This is madness!"

I considered what an opportunity it was for my parents.

He continued, "She's looser than a tavern wench..."

Could I do it?

And then his own words doomed him, "...and just a plain-faced Flet!"

I growled, "I'll do it, and if the monastery can't break him, I will!"

And the blood drained from his face.

THE FALL OF OSSARD

4

A New Life

We married in a simple ceremony held in St Baimio's Cathedral the very next day. My new husband spent the time in between confined to the Liberigo residence, and after our exchange of vows he was sent on to a monastery amidst the mountains of the interior.

His father said it would be best for all of us, especially me, if Pedro's selfishness was broken in such a place. He assured me that his son would return a new man.

In truth, I feared what might come of it. Would the monks catch the scent of ritual magic? A commoner would be burnt alive for such heresy, but the son of the Lord of Ossard?

Could I be fated to be a widow before I became a mother?

There had been a time, albeit for only half an evening, when I'd been infatuated with him and hostage to all his charms. It seemed an age ago. Since then I'd changed, becoming something other than the childish girl who believed in lotus-fuelled dreams. Now I stood determined to control my future. Never again would I submit to him, but to ensure that I needed to awaken and master my own power.

Throughout the term of my pregnancy, I sought more knowledge of the arcane. My mother was horrified at my interest. She begged me to abandon my search for answers. When I asked why, she'd just whisper the name of the Inquisition. At such moments I saw something in her eyes, something terrible.

I asked, "Grandmother?"

Tears came, running fast to flood down her cheeks. "Oh Juvela, they came for her. They took her away and burnt her at the stake!"

I was stunned.

67

The little they'd previously said about her death had led me to believe she'd died in the chaos of the riots, not in the mass burning that had triggered them.

And all the while a new life grew within me.

I prayed for goodly souls for my new family, for all three of us, but not to the Heletians' Krienta.

I followed Schoperde, the god of life. She'd given life to all of us, and the world about us; that included her divine children, Krienta and so many others. She was one of the two original powers of the universe, and partnered to the other, her husband, Death. Together they'd made all that followed.

Schoperde's faith arrived in Ossard with the Flet refugees. While my people found themselves grudgingly accepted in the city-state, their gods were not. Officially they converted to the Church of Baimiopia, but their beliefs survived in secret.

At the time, after having fled the bloody events of Def Turtung, enduring a harrowing sea-crossing, to only then be faced with the zealous Inquisition, the exhausted refugees of two hundred years ago had found the decision easy to make. Still, deep down, we Flets longed to practise our faiths openly.

Ironically, my faith stood as forbidden as whatever dark religion stained Pedro's soul. His spirituality was about death and power, while mine was about love and life. They couldn't have been more different, but not in the eyes of the Church.

The thought always brought a bitter smile: Pedro and I had more in common than we realised.

I never received any report on Pedro's progress. It left me wondering if his heresy had been discovered and fiery redemption granted, yet no word came.

My feelings for him were confused. At the same moment I felt repulsion and hope, anger and anguish, but certainly no love. To make this work I needed to be strong, but also to soothe my bitterness. We had to coexist and build a life tolerable for each other and our coming babe. Together.

Regardless of that understanding, even lukewarm feelings for my new husband struggled to find vigour.

In the meantime, the marriage had restored some of my dignity, was profiting Father's business, and had legitimised my coming child. I told myself that that was enough, but in the dark of night, I wondered if the best outcome was for Pedro simply never to return.

The passing months became seasons, and so my belly swelled. I thought of Pedro often, him carrying his own burden as he no doubt suffered through demanding religious training and trials. Sometimes I worried that he'd return charged with the zeal of a missionary.

He didn't.

Even ice holds more fire than what came back.

He arrived a few days before the birth, at a time when I was plump and rosy. He stood with slumped shoulders, ragged hair, sunken eyes, and pale sagging skin that let his bones show through. He'd lost a lot of weight, but a good deal more spirit. It was as though Death had taken him for a lover, and when done, spurned him.

His father was appalled.

Pedro would say little in general and even less to me. He was empty and broken. The playboy was dead.

I'd wed a phantom.

The birth came when expected, was thankfully easy, and almost beautiful in its own way. I think that deep down I'd feared that I'd bear some kind of cult-spawned devil, instead I delivered a little girl, an angel with a thick crop of red hair.

I wondered about that, thinking of the Flet boy who'd died at her conception. Any worries about her true nature faded after they gave her to me to hold. She was amazing, both cute and so very helpless. I knew then that nothing diabolical could hide in such a fragile shell. She was beautiful.

Pedro had been aloof prior to the birth, but the change was stark.

The maid and midwife wiped her over and checked her. They cleaned me, and then brought up the covers, while giving me a damp towel to refresh myself with. They were quick at it, getting us ready to receive my husband, parents, and in-laws. The midwife took the babe, wrapped her in fresh linen, and then sent the maid to fetch them.

I looked to the open doorway, apprehensive. How would he react to his daughter, to the very thing that had imprisoned him? I tensed, trying to lean forward and get the midwife's attention; perhaps she should just let him see our babe, but not hold her.

He stepped through the doorway, shoulders slumped, eyes downcast, ready to receive the ultimate reminder of his shame. Not a trace of interest or care marked his sallow face, he just wanted this over, not just the day, or the matter of his daughter's birth, but I think his entire existence.

He stumbled forward, pushed by two sets of grandparents trying but failing to hold themselves in reserve. Three more steps brought him to the midwife.

I opened my mouth to warn her, yet my voice faltered.

She offered him our babe.

I tensed, reaching out a hand.

He finally looked up.

Her eyes remained closed, but her mouth occasionally opened. She didn't make a sound.

His eyes widened as he took in the sight of her, but he didn't move to take her.

The midwife held her out to him afresh.

He raised his hands, his shoulders squaring.

The midwife asked, "My Lord and Lady, what will you call her?"

We hadn't even spoken of it.

My father looked over Pedro's shoulder. "She's beautiful."

The baby then yawned, leaning a little back as she opened her mouth. Her arms appeared, rising out of the linen wrap.

My mother giggled. "She's gorgeous!"

And Pedro smiled.

Lord and Lady Liberigo crowded past my father to also look upon their grandchild. My father-in-law said, "Beautiful indeed, and red hair – that's not quite a Heletian trait!"

His wife laughed.

I found my voice, "Perhaps she needs a good Heletian name?"

Pedro looked to me. "Yes?"

I smiled, trying to offer something of a peace between us. "How about Maria?"

His mother smiled. "A good name, your late grandmother's name."

My mother added, "And the middle name of *your* grandmother, Juvela."

Pedro straightened his back, raised his head, and grinned as he drew his daughter to his chest. "She *is* beautiful." He chuckled and then looked to me. "*Our* little Maria."

I nodded as both sets of grandparents gave a cheer.

He said, "It's a good name for such a beautiful little girl." And with each word his voice grew stronger, finding some of its old depth.

He stood there stroking her, marvelling at what had been made. I saw love in his eyes. My own heart softened at the sight.

He had changed.

In time Pedro and I built a better relationship.

I think he came to respect me; my strength and determination, but there was certainly no love. Maria had bonded us together. Sometimes I wondered if he loved her more than I did – and that would have been a marvel!

In her first season of life, she lost her red hair to have it replaced with something closer to Pedro's dark locks, and that better matched her olive skin. From me she carried a Flet's blue eyes and a petite nose. A child of two cultures, a bridge, she bound us together.

My parents forgot their shame, and their household thrived with its close association to Lord Liberigo as did the family business. In so many ways I'd achieved everything I should have. All that was missing was love and its peace.

I came to trust Pedro with Maria, anyone watching them could see the love there. He and I were another matter. Sometimes we sat and talked a little, managing to be company for each other, but more often we didn't. I could never forget his part in the boy's murder and the way he'd treated me, but I realised that I could live with it.

As the years passed, he began to talk about his experiences at the monastery, something he shared with me bit by bit. I pitied him when he told me of the season he'd spent enduring confinement in a cramped cell, it damp, dark, and cold, and with the barest of rations.

That imprisonment had ended when he finally accepted and confessed his sins.

When he talked of these things he looked to me for understanding. Never did he mention the cults, and I still couldn't get the words out of my ensorcelled mouth to ask, but I knew he stood ashamed. I think that's why he wanted to tell me of his bleak time in the monastery. He wanted to show me that he'd not only been punished, but that he'd accepted that he deserved to be.

He truly was a different man.

To see him remorseful gave me hope; maybe I could share my life with my husband and perhaps even come to enjoy it. But such remorse came couched with what had delivered it, the dogma of the Church.

We lived in a grand old house in Newbank not far from my parents. Pedro began working for my father, acting as a liaison between his own father's contacts and my father's business.

My own time was lost in setting up our household and tending Maria. I often visited my mother. We saw less and less of Pedro's family as they realised how much of a shadow he'd become; a man with no spirit.

All the while the kidnappings continued to not only plague the city, but worsen, yet my own magic lay stubbornly idle.

Four years after our marriage day, I took Maria to see an Evoran herbalist down near the docks. She suffered from a regular chill, something that came on seasonally, and that I'd come to think might be brought on by the flowering shrubs that covered the surrounding valleyside.

I took our coach and driver, Kurt, and Maria's bodyguard, Sef, who'd joined our own household. Ossard's children were still being stolen, the problem now so bad that it even plagued the Heletian districts.

The thefts occurred in groups twice each season. In each group five children would be stolen, all on the same day between sunrise and sunset. Lord Liberigo had tripled street patrols *and* called up the militia, yet the diabolical crimes persisted.

On the day of the kidnappings, the Cathedral bells would toll out the number of children missing with each newly discovered crime. The macabre practice meant that the people of the city knew on the fifth ring that the danger was over – until next time.

Despite the patrols, and the offering of a generous reward, none of the children were ever found. Rumours circulated the restless city, some blaming the Evoran slave trade, others the Lae Velsanans, or witches, and on occasion even the forbidden cults of the Horned God.

On this day, such a day of misfortune, the Cathedral bells had already rung out four times. It meant that Maria never left my sight, and that we were always accompanied.

The visit to the old Evoran's shop had been successful. The dark owner had sold me some herbs to stew and give to Maria as a watered broth. As I left the store, I asked Kurt to take us home via the waterfront only streets away. It had been a long time since I'd escaped the confines of Newbank, and I was eager for some of the city's other sights.

The coach rumbled down the cobbled street and soon rounded a bend to reach the port. On one side stood tightly packed warehouses, stevedoring businesses, and a few rough taverns, on the other the wharves busy with a maze of moored ships and labourers.

A spectacular ship lay moored alongside one of the main piers. Its three masts stood tall, sloping gently backwards, and all cut of silver timber that caught the sun. The graceful lines of the ship meant it could have come from only one place – Lae Wair-Rae.

Lae Velsanans!

My Flet blood cried out at their presence, a chill reminding me of the dark history our two peoples shared. Despite it all I was curious, curious to see a Lae Velsanan first hand, and to have a closer look at their sleek ship.

In the cab of our coach, I leaned across to slide open the port and called to Kurt, "Take us towards that great ship and draw us near. I want to have a closer look." Sef was sitting opposite Maria and myself, he shifted uncomfortably, but didn't protest.

Kurt brought us closer before coming to a stop.

The crew hurried about the deck of their great ship and also up a gangplank linking it to the wharf. The uniformed Lae Velsanans carried aboard crates and sacks of supplies. To my surprise, it seemed to be a military ship and not a merchant vessel.

Feeling relatively safe and with my curiosity only starting to stir, I said, "I'm going to get out and have a look."

Sef helped me dismount, and then lifted little Maria down to put her on the cobbles beside me. She looked about with big blue eyes, setting her long curls to bounce.

I said, "We're going to look at the ship, Maria."

"Why, Mama?"

"Because I haven't seen one so big before. Come along now."

Kurt stayed with the coach while we walked forward.

I held Maria's hand tightly as if some part of me expected the Lae Velsanans to turn from their duties and charge. Despite their apparent ignorance of our approach, I just couldn't forget that these exotic foreigners had tried to destroy my people.

We stopped half a ship-length from the gangplank.

Intricate rigging webbed over the magnificent vessel, all of it artfully reinforcing the ship's picturesque lines and curves. It may have been built for war, but I felt it could also manage a great speed out on open water. Festooned with brightly coloured flags and tattooed with intricate carvings, it was as much a ship of art as of war. It was amazing.

Behind us, I could hear the banter of a more refined tongue than that of fast-flowing Heletian or rugged and blunt Fletlander. I turned to see three uniformed Lae Velsanans walking towards their ship. They looked to be officers with bands of copper at their shoulders, it clamped over leather armour and sea-green tunics. Nervous, I watched them as they passed.

They all stood lean and tall, taller than men, or the *common* or *middlings* that they called us, and moved with powerful grace. One of them even smiled at me.

My nerves faded.

We watched them board their beautiful ship while the air sang full of their noble tongue. I wondered at my fear; they seemed so civilised. Finally, I said to Sef, "It's fantastic."

He nodded, but it was a stranger's voice that answered, "Thank you."

We both turned to see a silver-banded Lae Velsanan. His sea-green uniform, light armour, and helmet spoke of his heritage, but his strong face, blonde hair, and blue eyes, startlingly, were those of a Flet. Unlike the others, he stood thickly muscled with a broad chest, and barely reached my own height. He seemed at ease, but still radiated quite a presence.

He reached up with one of his muscular arms and removed his helmet to reveal the small pointed tips of his ears. In a moment, the resemblance to a Fletman was gone. "I didn't mean to startle you." He spoke in *Quorin*, Dormetia's common language.

"I'm sorry, I didn't hear your approach," I answered.

"I was just heading back to my ship when I heard your kind words."

I smiled, he seemed friendly enough.

He continued, "We've just resupplied and are about to leave."

And then, from across the city, we heard the Cathedral's bells toll.

Dong...

The deep ring rolled out, seeing everybody stop and wait.

Dong...

And so we counted.

Dong...

Maria looked up to me. I bent down and picked her up.

Dong...

The Lae Velsanan officer watched us intently. About us, the people of the port tensed.

And then it came.

Dong...

Sef shifted, relaxing. I could feel my own demeanour change, a great weight lifted.

Thank Schoperde, Maria would be safe!

To temper the thought, the sound of sobbing arose in the distance. Slowly, mournfully, people went back to work.

The Lae Velsanan asked, "Excuse me, but why does the bell toll?"

For a moment, with my relief making me giddy, I had to fight to maintain my composure. "There've been some kidnappings."

He nodded, looking to Maria. "We have heard as much. We were warned of this place. I can see pain in your eyes, the kidnappings have already touched you. Take comfort; those responsible are being hunted by more than your own kind."

For the first time in seasons, I heard the voices rise within me to whisper their support.

They liked him.

His words seemed simple, but they gave me hope. It was then that I realised it'd been a long time since I'd tasted such a thing.

I had to stop myself, suddenly taken by the urge to embrace this Lae Velsanan and thank him for his soothing words. Perhaps I was no longer alone in holding some of the truth and guilt.

Perhaps there was hope.

He gave a little bow and gestured to the ship. "I must go, it has been a pleasure."

I nodded, and even Sef wore a smile.

The officer had indicated another Lae Velsanan waiting for him on the ship's deck, his senior.

He stood there watching us, stark and handsome like a crisp winter day. Tall and lean, with a powerful frame, and all of it topped with cropped black hair and cold eyes of grey.

Within me the voices' whispered chorus fell from warmth to an empty silence. There was no doubt, the officer was beautiful, but it was a beauty of a chilling kind.

The strongest voice within me hissed, "Soul Eater!" And for a moment I felt overcome. I still held Maria, but pushed her towards Sef. He grabbed her, surprised but ready. I put my other hand on his shoulder to try and steady myself.

I was going to faint.

"Juvela!"

And the Lae Velsanan we'd been talking to stepped forward and reached out with strong hands.

I wanted to refuse him, to say that I was fine, but the next moment my legs buckled. I'd barely begun my fall when the officer caught me.

Maria cried out.

The Lae Velsanan said, "Careful now."

Sef tried to comfort Maria as he said, "Please Sir, I have my hands full, could you help her to our coach."

"Of course."

I protested, "I'll... I'll be alright, I just need a moment..."

Sef said, "Lady Juvela, you're unwell!"

The Lae Velsanan nodded. "Please, my lady, I'm used to much heavier burdens. You will be no trouble." And with a quick nod to Sef he moved to lift me.

Kurt had seen me faint and already had the coach coming forward. In moments, I was no longer under the sun or being held by the officer, but being fussed over by Sef while my poor daughter watched. With a barely managed goodbye to my rescuer and a thank you Sef swears he gave, we were on our way.

Strangely, as we left the docks, my colour returned along with my strength. I wondered at that, but it wasn't easy to explain. All I could say for sure was that I'd left something behind us, something at the docks - and it was hungry.

Soul Eater...

The name rang out in my mind, again whispered by the voices that seemed to be rising stronger with each visit.

Sef was staring at me. "Juvela, are you alright?"

"I..." My thoughts were confused.

"Yes?" he prompted.

"I don't know. I mean, I feel much better, but before I felt..."

"Yes?"

"I don't know how to describe it."

"Try," he said, and there was something about the way he asked that made me realise that he thought it important.

"There was something back there..."

He interrupted, "Where?"

"Back at the docks."

"Yes?"

"Something scared me, it made me feel weak."

He frowned, but it wasn't because he didn't understand - it was because he *did*. It encouraged me to go on, "Well, it was not so much that it scared me, but that I could feel it threaten me. It felt like it was somehow feeding off me, stealing, sapping my strength..."

"Go on."

I shook my head. "I don't know what to say, it sounds crazy."

"No, it's not."

"Well, anyway, now it's gone."

He nodded and leaned forward, giving a sidewards glance to Maria who'd calmed and was now lost in the view of the passing street. "And where did that feeling come from, *what* was so hungry?"

"I don't know."

"I think you do."

I shook my head. "Whatever do you mean?"

"The Lae Velsanan?" he asked.

"No, he was nice! How could it be him?"

77

"Their ship?"

All this was only adding to my confusion. A moment ago I'd thought that I knew what I was talking about, but only for an instant. Now I was lost again. With my uncertainty came defensiveness and a guess that sprang from the anxiety that nurtured it. "The Soul Eater."

"The what?"

I looked down at my hands, to where they sat in my lap fidgeting with the fabric of my dress. "I don't know." I was embarrassed.

"Juvela, who is the Soul Eater, who was feeding off *all* of us?"

Finally, after my confusion, another moment of clarity came: It hadn't been the Lae Velsanan officer, but his senior, that's what the strongest voice had hissed. I took a deep breath and said, "The ship's captain, but I can't say any more." I shook my head. "I don't know any more, I just know it was him. He was the one who drained me, though I don't know if he meant to, or even if he knew that he did. There's something hungry about him."

"For souls?"

I looked to Sef, helpless. I didn't know what I was talking about, I wasn't even sure I was communicating my jumbled thoughts clearly.

A knock sounded. It was Kurt.

Sef opened the sliding panel at the front of the cab to talk to him. At the same time the coach slowed.

Sef asked, "What's happening?"

"We're at Market Square, but there seems to be some kind of problem ahead. We'll get through, but not quickly. I just thought you should know seeing as our lady is ill."

I spoke up, "I'm much better, thank you, so you needn't hurry."

"Good to hear, my lady."

Sef said, "I'll come out and have a look. Give me a moment."

"Right you are."

Sef turned back to me, his expression serious. "Are you alright, *really?*"

"I'm well enough, *really*. Have a look at what's happening and let me know. If we're going to be stuck in the markets for a while we might as well get out and have a look around."

He nodded, smiled to Maria, who grinned back, and then opened the door and jumped down to the cobbles. I could hear him talking to Kurt and people in the crowd. Some spoke gravely of the latest kidnappings, others about the commotion ahead, but he got no straight answers.

I opened the door and called to him, "Help me, we're coming down."

He frowned.

"It's safe enough."

He grumbled, but helped me before turning for Maria. Looking up to Kurt atop the coach, I said, "Work your way through this mess and wait for us on the other side. We'll go through the crowd."

He glanced at Sef, but nodded.

I took Maria by the hand. "Let's go."

The three of us began passing through the crowd, the square abuzz with gossip and the sounds of relief. Spread amidst it were a few tightly packed mobs centred on weeping women and distraught men; the relatives of the missing. They headed for the Cathedral. The Church of Baimiopia's head in the city, Benefice Vassini, would be waiting within to bless them and then join them in prayer.

Market Square would be busy on most days, but this day the area seethed under the crush. I said to Sef, "We're not going to be getting anywhere quickly."

"Are you sure that you're well?"

"I'm fine. Let's have a look at what's causing the problem."

He grudgingly nodded.

Maria walked between Sef and I as we headed towards the heart of the crowd. I still couldn't see anything of what was happening.

Sef looked about, he seemed nervous.

I asked, "Are *you* alright?"

"I'd rather we were getting you home."

I thought he was being silly, after all I felt fine and the bells had tolled their full count.

We continued on.

To my surprise, the fuss was over nothing being sold, nor the theatrics of a street troupe, just a lone monk. He wore a sash of red tied around the waist of a faded grey robe with his ruddy face crowned by a scalp of stubble.

Through yellowed teeth and waving arms he spoke while a small metal amulet bounced about on his chest to catch the light. "Dark days require strong protection, the protection of the saints! And nothing gains a saint's attention *and* protection more than prayers. To them, prayers and the swearing of devotion earn favour, and favour *is* protection. Such sanctuary is salvation!

"In evil times all seek sanctuary, and prayers *earn* sanctuary. If a curse is upon a city, one such as we bear, surely one should seek the favour of the *Saint of Children*. Is there such a saint you ask? Of course; the most-holy Saint Santana. Offer her your prayers!"

He lifted a small wooden box, its sides lovingly carved and polished. "Behold, a relic of the mortal remains of our most holy saint! Pray to it, kiss it, or buy a blessed amulet of *Santana's Seal* for you or your child to wear. It will secure safe passage through this life *and* the next!"

A table behind him held a pile of amulets and an assortment of boxes.

While I was not overly familiar with the Church, I knew I'd never heard of Saint Santana. It looked more like a way to get wealthy. I turned to Sef, unconsciously tightening my grip on Maria's hand.

He grinned at my unspoken thoughts.

I nodded; it was time to go.

He led the way.

We left the monk behind us. He looked to be a Heletite, one of the missionaries the Church set loose upon the world. I found it hard to believe that the Church had sanctioned his actions. Yes, it was greedy, but this was just shameless.

We headed through the market's bustle towards our coach, still a good two hundred paces away. The sea of people going about their business seemed so normal, so ordinary, but above it all lay a simmering tension.

The city couldn't go on like this, not with the kidnappings, nor with charlatans profiting from such misery.

And that's when it happened.

A voice whispered, "It comes!"

I turned to look for the speaker, only to realise it was one of the voices in my mind. The rest of them then rose loud and clear as a chorus, all becoming frantic, "It comes! It comes!"

They cried out within me, repeating again and again, "It comes! It comes! It comes!"

Then the strongest hissed, "Beware, it comes!" And the others fell into wailing.

Distracted, it took me a moment to realise that everyone about me had stopped and that the square stood silent – but for the tolling of the Cathedral's bells.

Dong...

Sef tensed, placing a hand on Maria.

Dong...

I again tightened my grip on her hand.

Dong...

The very air chilled.

Dong...

People about us looked to each other with growing fear.

Dong...

Then silence.

Complete blessed silence.

Just five as it should be...

Dong...

And thousands of voices arose as women wailed and men groaned to drown out the sixth tolling of the bell.

Sef picked up Maria and put his other arm about me to shepherd us towards our coach. The square surged with people, and as we hurried, we passed a woman who'd dropped to her knees amidst the panic to clutch at her young daughter. She cried, "Only five, not six, you can't take any more!"

As if in answer, the daylight dimmed about her. Black sparks danced and snapped on the cobblestones, and then in a swirl of chill darkness, a vortex opened up beside her to leak a celestial shadow. The form took shape; it was a man robed in black.

The woman cried out.

He stepped forth on to frosted cobbles, reaching out for her daughter's hand.

No one stopped, no one even seemed to notice – just me. Then I realised that no one else could see him. They were blind to the truth.

My accursed witchery had returned to burden me with yet more guilt!

Her daughter, with eyes sparkling amidst gathering tears, reluctantly reached out. She trembled with fear. Still, as if she had no will of her own, she moved to fulfil his unspoken command.

I couldn't witness this, not again, not after the red-haired boy.

I had to do something!

I slipped out of Sef's grip and snatched the knife from his belt.

Maria looked to me with her beautiful blue eyes while a voice fierce with love hissed in my mind, "Be careful!"

Witchery!

I was stunned. It was her, who else could it be? I nearly stopped, but the mother's desperate pleas grabbed back my attention.

Sef yelled, "Where are you going?"

I ignored him.

The cultist looked down at the girl, waiting for her trembling hand.

Her mother held her tight, and though I didn't think she could see him like I could, she somehow sensed his presence.

The voices cried out for me to hurry.

My vision then regained the clarity it had only once held before. With that finer view, the black celestial sparks became storms of energy cascading off the cultist and radiating out from the magic he cast to hide himself.

I was nearly there, each step closing the gap.

But how was I going to stop him?

The sounds of the crowd, the whirlwind of movement, and the dazzling flare of magic combined to be dizzying. Amidst it all I could still hear Sef yelling. "Damn it Juvela, wait!"

The girl reached out to the cultist.

I wouldn't get there in time.

I called, "Get away from him!"

She seemed oblivious to me, and then took his hand, sliding her fingers across his own and deep into his palm.

He grabbed them tightly.

In an instant I saw her lose the colours of life.

Her mother howled.

Then, still charging, I finally arrived.

I slashed at the cultist with Sef's blade while diving between them to force them apart. The knife clumsily cut into his shoulder.

He cursed and fell back.

I pushed the girl aside and broke their hands' grip. At the same time, a shower of blue sparks flared to dance about us.

The crowd screamed and fell back.

They'd seen something!

I fell to the cobbles and rolled to a stop.

The girl lay limp in her mother's arms, but with life's colours returning.

In front of us stood the cultist, now back on his feet. For the first time the crowd could see him, I think they could even see the sparks spilling off from him as his broken spell bled away.

Sef ran towards me with Maria in his arms. He dodged around the cultist to stand between us, passing me Maria before turning back to face him. He looked to the cultist with threatening eyes, and in a slow but determined movement drew his sword. He mumbled a prayer, his words in Flet and their substance hidden under his breath, but every Flet in the square knew he'd just asked for a blessing from our battle god; Kave.

The cultist ignored him, instead turning to me. "And how will you explain this to the Church?"

A bitter stink grew, and in a swirling flash he was gone.

Beyond where he'd stood loomed the twin towers of the Cathedral. Priests crowded at the top of its steps, amidst them Benefice Vassini. They'd seen everything.

The woman beside me rose to her feet clutching her rousing daughter. Over and over she whispered, "Thank you." But she was so shaken that all she could do was stumble away.

I got up off the cobbles with Maria. "Sef, we should go."

People milled about, confused and frightened, many in a panic that only grew. They pushed past each other to knock others over, as well as stalls, and the fences of the livestock pens.

I risked a glance over the commotion, looking back to the Cathedral. Predictably, a group of priests advanced through the crowd. Benefice Vassini, robed and regal, watched over them from atop the steps, his face glowering.

Sef acted quickly, moving ahead to clear a path. With Maria in my arms, I darted after him with every pace putting more confusion between myself and the churchmen.

Finally, we reached the coach. Sef opened the cab's door, helped us up, and then threw himself in. He yelled to Kurt, "Make haste!"

The coach lurched into movement.

Sef turned to me. "You saw him before the rest of us!"

Gasping after my dash through the crowd, I could only nod.

And behind us the Heletite cried out, "Witness the power of Saint Santana! She fights through her chosen *Lady*, bestowing blessings and wonders to protect those who accept her into their hearts!"

He was besieged by frightened people.

5

The Coming of Chaos

We returned home through streets full of anxious people rushing to seek safety, amidst units of militia and city watch trying to cut through the crush. While we travelled as fast as we could, the streets remained choked, so by the time we got back to Newbank, it was to find that news of events had preceded us, carried by people who'd travelled more speedily on horseback or by foot.

Pedro ran from our small courtyard. "Juvela, is Maria alright?"

His eyes gave him the answer as she reached for him from the opened cab door.

He took her into his arms and kissed her. Finally he turned to me, reaching forward with one hand to run it softly down my arm before helping me from the coach's step. It was a surprising affection. "What happened?"

His questions irritated me, but only because I feared that they were the first of many. I could also see that he wasn't the only one struck with worry: My parents also stood in the courtyard, and with them a deputation of Flet guildsmen.

My mother asked, "Are you well, Juvela?" Her true question was of headaches and magic.

"We're alright, Sef protected us."

A guildsman snapped, "With magic. You've been careless, and now there'll be no end of trouble!"

Pedro looked up at the mention of magic as if someone had cursed.

I said, "There was no magic. We simply helped a woman in need."

My father shrugged. "No matter, *they* will be here soon. What will you tell them?"

Pedro nursed Maria, but looked to my father in bewilderment. "They?"

"The Churchmen. They'll want to know what happened, and they probably won't be interested in the truth. They'll label her a witch and a cultist, and probably try to blame the kidnappings on her."

He was right, I hadn't thought about it.

What would I tell them?

Pedro fumed at the suggestion, but deep down knew it held some truth. He'd returned from the monastery a shattered man. While he'd since rediscovered some of his old backbone, it now came wrapped in the meat of an ambiguous devotion. If hearing our talk of the Church made him uncomfortable, I feared what he made of our mention of magic.

I offered, "I just knocked the cultist down when I ran past."

My mother shook her head, she was pale and close to tears. "The Inquisition won't be happy with that. We heard you attacked the kidnapper with a knife, and that you fought him off with blinding flashes of magic!"

I said, "The Inquisition isn't here!"

My father shook his head. "No doubt they've agents, but even without them the Church isn't likely to let such a public display of the arcane go unpunished."

I looked to Maria. "There was no magic, not by me! They can't take me away, surely I'm protected by my connection to the Liberigos?"

My father nodded. "Let's hope so, but for now you'll go into hiding. The Guild's sending a carriage and, when you're safe, we'll meet with Lord Liberigo and ask him to guarantee your protection."

The unmarked carriage arrived amidst a steady flow of people coming to see the lady who'd fought off the kidnapper.

Me...

By the time Pedro, Maria, Sef and I were packed into it, we were surrounded by a crowd. Some called out, others begged for my touch. It was unnerving.

Things were getting out of control.

My mother pushed past their beseeching hands, knocking them out of the way as she lifted herself up to the window. "Be careful..."

I cut off her words, "Mother, I've far too much to live for." In Flet I whispered, "Take care, my husband is listening."

She fought the urge to glance at him, but nodded. "Remember what happened to your grandmother. Expect no mercy."

In the common tongue, I said, "I'll be alright," but my words were hollow. I couldn't hide my doubts.

She tried to smile.

Regardless of how we might want to control such things, our secrets and our lives, it's impossible. Pedro was my husband, and so was involved. He would come with us to the Guild despite there being so many truths that had to be hidden from the Heletians - and he was one of *them*.

My mother stepped down to the cobbles as my father yelled to the driver, "Go, get them out of here!"

The crowd cried out, some holding up the holy star of Krienta while others bravely clutched the symbols of other faiths. To do so put them in as much danger as me, but they were desperate and frightened - and had good reason to be.

For the first time there'd been a sixth kidnapping, and we'd already seen the seventh attempt. We could only assume that there'd be more. Would the cultists stop at seven, or would they continue until the city was bereft of children?

Our driver pulled on the reins as the Cathedral's bells began to toll.

Dong...

The mob cried out.

Dong...

The carriage lurched off.

Dong...

Someone yelled, "She's the chosen of Santana, and our only hope!"

Dong...

My father bellowed, "Sef, keep her safe!"

Dong...

And the mob around us fell back as the horses forced their way on to the road.

Dong...

I whispered, trying to drown out the sounds of chaos, "They've got their seventh in any case."

Dong...

And behind us the mob broke into mourning.

Our journey saw us head through the heart of the district, taking the widest roads so we could gain some speed and get away from the crowd. Before long, those following us were left far behind. Our driver swung us around, steering us towards the Cassaro, and then along the riverside road until we reached the Guild's compound.

Pedro sat glumly with his shoulders slumped, a lost look haunting his eyes. "Just what are we to do?" He shook his head and then glanced up to focus on me. "Please, tell me what *really* happened?"

Sef turned to look out the window, watching the passing streets through black lace curtains that worked with the day's dying light to hide our faces.

I didn't know what to say.

Could he handle the truth? Would he support me, or would he side with the Church? He'd returned from the monastery shattered, but also a believer. Just how deep was his faith? How dangerous would it be to expose the truth of the Flets; of our adherence to our ancestral beliefs?

This was getting complicated, and it was only just beginning.

I did have to tell him something, but what? Whatever it was, it had to be believable as he was already feeling alienated.

"We were in Market Square when the bell tolled six."

He nodded.

"People panicked, and in the chaos I saw a lady and her daughter being harassed by a man in robes, some kind of cultist. Sef had Maria, so I grabbed the knife off his belt and charged the man. I slashed at him hoping to ruin his spell. It worked, giving the girl and her mother a chance to flee. People didn't seem to notice him until I hit him, it sent sparks flaring when I did, but I don't know why. I didn't do anything but try and stop him."

Pedro's gaze left me, moving to Sef. Inadvertently I'd made my daughter's treasured bodyguard and my good friend look bad. I added, "Sef followed, giving Maria back after my charge. He drew his sword against the cultist to face him. By then we had quite an audience including the priests and Benefice atop the steps of the Cathedral. The cultist cast some kind of spell in front of everyone and then disappeared. We came straight home from there."

Pedro grumbled at Sef, "You would mind the baby, while my wife attacks cultists?"

"I hadn't seen him."

I placed my hand on Pedro's knee, trying to still his anger. "No one saw him. It was not Sef's failing."

"But you did?"

I shrugged.

Pedro nodded and then said, "I should have been there."

"We're all safe, let that be the end of it."

He looked to me. "But it isn't, is it."

We arrived at the Guild, our coach racing through the compound's gates to enter the courtyard beyond. A guildsman stood waiting. He hurried us into the Guildhall where we were led upstairs to a small lounge. "Please make yourself comfortable." Behind him, a staffer hurried to close the window's curtains. "As soon as we've cleared safe passage, you'll be told." Then he left, shutting the door behind him.

Pedro asked, "Safe passage to where?"

"I don't know, we'll have to wait and see."

Sef wandered to the other end of the room, looking at the paintings that hung on the wall and leaving the seats to us.

Pedro sat with an arm around Maria. She fell back and into his lap, playfully snuggling. He smiled as he stroked her long dark hair. Before long she was asleep.

It was then that he looked up, suddenly grave. "I had to do it."

I stared at him not knowing what he meant.

He continued, "They were all doing it. So many were joining that I didn't feel I had a choice. And they told me of the benefits, of the blessings of *Avida*. A lot of the young men were getting involved. To succeed you had to be a member. To talk and deal with them you had to be a member. It was plain, I had to join."

I finally understood. "When we first met?"

His voice was weak, "Yes, that was my initiation."

"The..." my throat froze.

He winced, sensing the sorcery as it choked off my words. He finished the sentence for me, "The ritual. I'm so sorry. I thought it was all a superstitious joke. I knew I had to take a virgin, and the higher her power and beauty the better the return."

He leaned forward, but took care not to disturb Maria. "I didn't know of the boy's part in it, not until it was too late. I was drunk and overcome with lust. When I... When I saw what they did to him, I just didn't care." He shook his head as tears welled in his eyes. "My only thought was that he was just a Flet." He looked down at Maria as tears rolled down his cheeks. "I'm sorry, I was such a pig."

I was stunned. He'd never spoken of the ritual. I'd almost believed that somehow the monastery had cured him of its memory.

I didn't know what to say, or what I *could* say: The magic still held me even after all these years. I could only try. "How much do you know?"

"Not enough. Nothing really. Just that there were a few chapters in the city. They recruited from everywhere, but particularly amongst the rich. I don't know who we can trust."

The door opened and a guildsman looked in, "My Lady, Guildmaster Kurgar is ready to see you – alone."

Pedro shifted uncomfortably, but nodded. "Go, I'll watch Maria."

I followed the man down a passage to another room. It was well appointed and finished in timber, sporting the colours of both the city and Newbank hanging from the walls. Those grand ensigns were accompanied by smaller pennants, those of the fortified cities of Fletland, and even a shield of the Praagerdam, the land lost to our forefathers during the horrors of Def Turtung. All of it, along with three framed maps of those territories, gave the room a deep sense of heritage.

Behind a large desk rose the man I knew my father had so often dealt with. He stood at a good height with a solid build, but wasn't overly bulky. Ironically, jet-black hair capped his head – a rarity amongst the Flets, it made our Guildmaster look almost Heletian. He carried an air of determination, but it was the intelligence in his eyes that stood out.

"Juvela, your father's asked for our help, so I'm happy to give it."

"Thank you."

He gestured to a seat as he sat back down, looking to me from across his desk. "You have power?"

At first I was uncomfortable with the question, but I knew it held truth. I also understood why Pedro hadn't been invited to join us.

He continued, "Don't be afraid, the Guild has more involvement in these matters than you might think. We don't only keep alive our people's culture and faiths, we also nurture those of us touched by the arcane."

"I can't do much."

He smiled. "Not yet, but you're young and your skills only emerging. It's all the more reason for me to make you aware of the help we can offer. Do you know much about the three magics?"

I shrugged. "The three?"

"The magics of the heart, mind, and soul. Soul magic is based on faith, it's what the best priests wield - blessings bestowed directly from the gods. Mind magic is that of the forbidden Sisterhood. It's conjured by gifted women who join collective minds, using their combined power or intuition to create effects we can only explain as magical. Then there's the magic of the heart, the stuff we attribute to the mages and witches of the Cabal. You know of the Cabal?"

"A little."

"It's a network of mages. All who work with the magic of the heart must join. To refuse is to be renegade."

I'd heard of renegades, they were known locally as the *Sanjo Drago*, or Blood Drinkers. They powered their castings not just from their own efforts, but by also spilling the blood of others. They spent their victims' very lives.

I asked, "What am I?"

He smiled, a warm and comforting thing. "I think you're a mage. We'll arrange for you to meet with members of the Cabal after the current excitement dies down, but from now on you must be more careful. Here, unlike in Fletland, all magic is illegal except the soul magic of the Church. If they catch you, you'll be burned as a witch."

"Like my grandmother?"

"Yes, like your grandmother." He sighed. "It's best that you're a cabalist considering what's happened. People who use the same kinds of magic can often sense the truth of each other. Those with stronger gifts can even read others' thoughts or send their own. If you were an emerging practitioner of soul magic, someone we might've trained as a priest, it's possible that a senior priest or inquisitor of the Church could have sensed you. He could taste *it* in you, your heresy."

"Is it that easy?"

"Only for the best. You're a mage, so to most of their priests you'll be as good as invisible. Only the most powerful in one field of magic can sense the users of another. You should be careful of the Benefice or others of high office." He began to chuckle, his smile growing wide. "Mind you, I think you'll be safe from Benefice Vassini, he's risen to his rank through family connections and politics, not ability or devotion. Just remember, potentially, they can sense you. Be wary, try and maintain your distance from them. Your very life may depend upon it."

I sat there horrified at how easily I could be discovered. What if Lord Liberigo didn't offer me protection, would I forever be running from priests who could smell my corruption?

As if reading my thoughts, Kurgar said, "Don't fret, we'll keep you safe. Within the hour, we'll have arranged protection, and while you'll need to speak to the Church, their influence isn't as strong here as in the rest of the League. They can't just take you. Ossard has been too lax in its faith for too long. The Church just doesn't command that sort of power. Besides, even the faithful in the streets are calling out your name, claiming that you've been sent by the saints to protect them. If the Church tries to imprison you the city will riot."

I took little relief from the suggestion.

A knock sounded at the door before a guildsman looked in and gave a nod. Kurgar said, "We'll take you to the Lord's Residence. Once there, we'll negotiate through him for you to be interviewed by the Church. That's something they're demanding."

I tensed at the suggestion, as the Residence sat on Market Square facing the Cathedral.

Kurgar stood, indicating it was time to go. "Don't worry, Juvela, your family is well connected. This will all be over soon."

He walked out with me. We met up with Pedro, Maria, and Sef who'd just been roused by the same guildsman, then made our way back down to the courtyard.

When we were back in a coach and on the road, Pedro asked, "Are you alright?"

"I'm fine. We're going to your father's."

Pedro didn't seem pleased. They'd never got on well.

Maria sat opposite us next to Sef, the four of us filling the cab. She looked to us with her big blue eyes.

Pedro said, "Don't worry, my little princess, everything will be alright." Then he turned to smile at me, something warm and honest. Without a word he reached for my hand and took it. A feeling of girlish excitement flared in me, yet my anxiety moved to smother it. Too much had already happened today, I didn't know if I could stand any more surprises.

6

\-

The Bells Toll

On the way to the Malnobla the bells tolled eight, their deep call rolling across the sky and through Ossard's empty streets.

Sef rode with us. The old bodyguard's presence irritated Pedro, it always had. In my husband's eyes he was only the paid help, but to me the warrior's presence made me feel safe. After the events in Market Square I was certain that he followed Kave, something I'd long suspected – even expected, considering his extraction from the battle-weary wastes of Fletland. The knowledge was its own comfort.

The Church of Baimiopia was right to fear the cults of the Horned God, but some of the faiths they included in that group held more honour than they'd ever know. If I was to live in a time of war, then it would be my choice to do it with a band of Kave's warriors at my side. It was said that the god of battle was not about slaughter, but the honour to be found in the skills of combat and defence. In truth, the survival of my people through all of our history's bloody travails came down to the labour and sacrifices of such men and women.

Our coach drove down Ossard's empty avenues unhindered and eventually into Market Square. The Lord's Residence loomed ahead, its grand three-floor facade of sandstone standing out against the drab renders or dark stone of surrounding buildings. I didn't turn to look, but knew the Cathedral rose across from it.

Would the Benefice be watching our coach race across the square, guessing who sat within?

Our driver took us to the stables at the rear, the gates opening to admit us. All about the Residence, along the walls of the courtyard and the building's roof, the liveried men of Liberigo stood on guard.

The Residence made up three sides of the large courtyard, the stables and gate the fourth. We rarely came here, and even though I was familiar with the place, it never felt comfortable like a home should. It was a seat of power, not a place for family.

Lord Liberigo came into the courtyard with concern on his brow. He patted Pedro on the shoulder and eyed Maria with worry before looking to me. I noticed that he kept his distance. "Let's get inside, it will be cold tonight."

We followed him as another coach from the Guild arrived. Lord Liberigo pointed it out to an assistant, indicating for it to be seen to.

We entered the house in silence, climbed the stairs to the second level, and followed my father-in-law into his office. Once inside the timber-finished room, not unlike that of Heinz Kurgar's, he pointed to some chairs and took his own behind his desk after drawing the curtains across the window behind him.

Maria looked across to her grandfather with big eyes, confused into silence by the day's events. I asked, "Would Lady Liberigo be available to see to her granddaughter?

He nodded, calling out, "Jericho!"

One of his assistants appeared at the door. "Yes, my Lord?"

"Take young Maria to my wife. See to it that she is never left unguarded, not for a single moment."

Without question he came forward and took my daughter by the hand, gently leading her away. She looked to both Pedro and I with fear in her eyes. We both smiled and whispered encouragement.

Sef began to rise from his chair to follow his charge, but Lord Liberigo said, "No Sef, little Maria will be safe. You have other tasks to attend to."

The big Fletman sank back into his seat, clearly uncomfortable at the parting.

At the sound of the shutting door, Lord Liberigo sighed. "The Church wants to interview you, Juvela, and they want to do it this evening. I can refuse them, but it makes you look guilty. Tell me, why shouldn't I let them have their meeting?"

I shifted in my chair, but not half as much as Pedro. His irritation at being in the background showed. I said, "I'm concerned that they'll simply brand me a witch and be done with it."

Lord Liberigo didn't even flinch at the mention of magic, he just asked, "And are you?"

I gasped at the question.

Where were Heinz Kurgar and his guildsmen to help me?

Pedro's frustration boiled over, seeing him snap, "What's all this fear of the Church? We're dealing with cultists, it's the Church who's trained to deal with them. They're here to help!"

His father frowned. "I believe Juvela is merely concerned that she'll be caught up in the middle of their battle."

I nodded.

He went on, "I've arranged a meeting. It's to be held downstairs in one of the public rooms. We'll all be present, myself representing the city, Heinz Kurgar for the Flet Guild, and Benefice Vassini for Krienta. The Church will get to ask its questions.

"Once done, we'll pool our knowledge of what's plaguing the city and *together* try and find a solution. I shan't be encouraging witch burnings or the like." He looked to me, his features softening to reveal a genuine affection. "As the Lord of this great city, I simply won't allow it."

Relief ran through me.

"But that meeting *will* happen, the messengers have already been sent."

We went downstairs and entered *the Chamber*. It was from here that the *Council of Merchant Princes* ruled Ossard.

At the moment, the grand room with its panelled timber ceiling and wonderful wall murals showcasing the city's history sat empty. The large room contained a twelve place round table at its centre, and hanging above were the colours of the city, its districts, guilds, and merchant houses.

Lord Liberigo pointed at four chairs. "Take a seat, they'll be here soon." He stopped me as I passed, looking deep into my eyes. "Juvela, consider carefully what you say. Legally I control Ossard and they can't force you away, but if Vassini raises a mob I might not be able to save you."

I nodded.

The door opened and Kurgar entered with three other guildsmen, leaving four seats for the Church. He looked across to me and smiled.

The room fell silent, something we left undisturbed.

Not long after, footsteps sounded at the main doors. We all turned in our seats and waited. The moment stretched on until they opened to reveal Benefice Vassini.

He walked in grandeur robed in white, with a wide band of golden silk about his generous waist. The silk's colour matched the rich embroidery of his garment, the rings on his fat fingers, and also a small crown he wore upon his head. The Benefice moved with a stiff back, and an even stiffer sense of self-importance.

I couldn't see this spoiled man ever working up a sweat, sobbing with sadness, or growing red with honest rage. He existed to be smug and exert control, something centred on the gold-topped staff of office he carried.

Behind him followed two senior priests and a monk of the *Calbaro*, a holy scholar. The priests came wrapped in embroidered white while the monk seemed much plainer, his grey robes only marked by a yarn belt.

The Benefice led them to their seats. Before he sat he hefted his staff, letting it drop with a sharp crack.

Led by Lord Liberigo, we all stood.

The Benefice spoke a prayer and then lowered himself into his seat.

When we were all sitting, Lord Liberigo said, "I welcome you all and ask you to respect each other and the peace of this place. No one here has special rights or is in any position to make demands. Let us solve the city's problems, not add to them."

Benefice Vassini ignored him, instead choosing to stare at me. I wondered; did he have any celestial talent? Was he sitting there searching my soul for some sign that I was the witch-wife of the Horned God and the source of all heresy?

The Calbaro monk spoke, his voice polite and almost fragile, "Please, if I may start, Lord Liberigo?"

Pedro's father nodded.

"The city has seen eight kidnappings since dawn, leaving many frightened, especially after the very public happenings of this afternoon. That event, as the only witnessed kidnapping attempt, also gives us almost all of the little we know of the problem. For now we need to confirm what happened with those who were part of it, and ask *why* they were part of it."

Lord Liberigo shrugged. "A fair question."

Kurgar interjected, "Fair? Fair for whom? We would like to remind everyone here that there is a long history of antagonism on behalf of the Church towards the Flets of this city, a hostility that is not deserved."

One of the priests shot back, "Nothing untoward has happened in years, and you'd do well to leave old wounds closed. We welcomed your people more warmly than most. You should be grateful..."

"Enough!" Lord Liberigo growled.

The monk said, "Please, let us get back to the question at hand."

I sat not knowing what to say, but they all turned to me nonetheless. Taking a deep breath, I began, "I saw a woman cradling her child in the crowd, she was in trouble and crying for help. It happened amidst the panic after the bells had tolled six. I ran to her aid. It was then that I saw a robed man..."

The Benefice bellowed, "Witch!"

My own voice died as his pronouncement rang out.

"Even now, the crowds call out your name! You have been claimed a servant of the saints, or more specifically, of a saint I've never heard of. You are a false prophet and a fool to think we'll allow you to continue such a divine association!" the Benefice damned.

"I never claimed to be of Saint Santana, and had never heard of her until this afternoon."

He scowled. "None have heard of her. We apprehended the man selling the relics and charms. He claims to be a Heletite missionary."

Lord Liberigo asked, "You doubt him?"

The Benefice said, "It's possible he's genuine, but not likely. I'm suspicious of the timing. In a wealthy city of merchant princes beset by child stealing, now seems the ideal time to discover a saint of children and have a cartload of relics to sell. It's not just that, but also the instructions given for ritual and prayer. If the monk is a fraud, he's abusing our faith and a heretic. It cannot be allowed."

Kurgar asked, "How can you not know if the saint is real?"

The Benefice narrowed his eyes, daring the Flet to find fault with his answer. "The Church of Baimiopia is a growing faith that is spread across Dormetia. It dominates the eight nations of the Heletian League and has great influence elsewhere, including in Burvoy, Evora, and *even* Fletland. Some of the missionaries working to establish the faith in those heathen lands discover locals who work selflessly for the greater good in spreading Krienta's message. Such people who endure hardship to the point of death can be rewarded with sainthood. Word of such elevations can take years to be confirmed and circulated throughout all the provinces of the Church. It is not unheard of in such a situation for a saint to be well known at one end of our growing holy empire, yet unknown at the other. That is why I cannot discount the possibility that Saint Santana is real."

Pedro asked, "Benefice, what kind of prayer ritual did the Heletite ask of his converts?"

"Witnesses have told us that he instructed them to repeat prayers to Saint Santana in the evening while burning an offering of oleander leaves. The ritual is strange and unlike any of the Church's other rituals. The monk in question is also not proving very helpful. He babbles like a fool of the wonder of Saint Santana, but seems unable to give us anything but the vaguest detail."

I asked, "Oleander, isn't that strange, as it's a poison?"

The Benefice looked to me as his eyes narrowed. "There are many odd ingredients in rituals of sanctity and power. Oleander may seem a queer choice, but so could many others upon close examination. Some owe their use more to symbolism or tradition than their true properties."

Irritated at having to dwell on a saint he'd never heard of, the Benefice's face hardened. "Enough of that, let's get back to the matter of Market Square. There are witnesses who claim you attacked the man with a knife, and there are others who said your escort," he indicated Sef, "spoke a prayer to Saint Santana that turned the cultist into shadows and wind."

With a tremor in my voice, I said, "I merely tried to help. I made no claims of saintly affiliation. I just heard a lady cry out and went to her aid."

The Benefice could see my fear. "It became clear years ago that there was a pattern to the kidnappings, but the city has been slow to act." He scowled at Lord Liberigo, offering the blame.

The Lord said, "The kidnappings have haunted us for years, it's true, but until now there's been no clue as to their cause. In the past, we'd looked into it as best we could, but in the crowded slums of Newbank..."

"For a Heletian, it's impossible to tell friend from foe," finished Kurgar, a frown marking his face. He went on, "Let's not hide the truth; because it was restricted to the poorer parts of the city, coincidentally the Flet parts, it just didn't seem that important."

Lord Liberigo's gaze dropped to the table. "That's a discussion for another time, but we all know it holds some truth. For now, can we please stick to the problem at hand?"

The Benefice stifled a laugh. "If you feel it necessary, but in the end we all know that there is only one group to blame for this mess; those representing the rule of this once great city."

Lord Liberigo rolled his eyes. "Can we please move on, Benefice?"

The fat man smiled, but with his point made he did. "The kidnappings carry the stink of the cults and forbidden magic, that can't be denied. On that basis, and as guardian of the souls of this city, I've already sent a request to the most Holy Benefice Verrochio in the Sacred City of Baimiopia for assistance."

My breath caught. The last thing I wanted to see was the Church getting more involved.

Kurgar's eyes narrowed. "What kind of assistance?"

"The Inquisition."

I felt the blood drain from my face as protests sounded from around the table.

Lord Liberigo demanded, "You did what?"

The Benefice ignored him, instead focussing on my paling face. "It was sent a while ago, well before this current sad chapter. We expect an Inquisitor to arrive any day, and when he does, we demand that the Church be given free access to all involved."

Lord Liberigo raised his hands and said, "No demands can be made. We need to work together. There's no one here who's done any wrong or holds any guilt..."

Angry voices sounded from outside to silence him.

The main doors burst open to see a priest rush in. A couple of Lord Liberigo's men gave chase while Jericho, the Lord's assistant, appeared and bowed to his master. "My Lord, my apologies..."

Lord Liberigo waved him away and called off his men.

The priest went straight for the Benefice to whisper in his ear.

The Benefice's face hardened, he then muttered a prayer before offering a hushed reply. The priest nodded and stepped back.

We all looked to Benefice Vassini, waiting for him to share his news, but he seemed to still be digesting it. Finally, he cleared his throat and said, "I have several things to share. Firstly, there have been two more kidnappings."

We winced.

"Secondly, some children have been found - dead."

Lord Liberigo sprung to his feet with questions while others cried out.

Pedro turned to me and took my hands, his own trembling. Both our minds ran with dark memories of moments of blood and power.

The Benefice raised his voice, "I am going there now. I suggest we all go, we should all see the horror of this thing."

Lord Liberigo nodded and we rose.

Being a woman, I received several looks and even a whisper from Pedro and his father; *I would be excused.*

I didn't want to go, but I had to. My feelings of guilt meant that I couldn't just walk away. I needed to see it.

We walked from the council chamber to the Malnobla's entry, Sef also with us. On the way we passed Pedro's mother who stood there with Maria. She'd also heard the news. Pedro and I both kissed our sleepy daughter, leaving her for a little while longer in her grandmother's care.

Our group was flanked by half a dozen priests and monks, and a dozen of the Lord's own men. The front doors opened to let us step out and into the cool night. The air held a strong and bitter scent, seeing me turn to Kurgar and ask, "What is it?"

With wide eyes, he said, "Oleander!"

Across the square where the Cathedral and its spires rose above the city, a small crowd prayed by candlelight. Some of them tended smouldering braziers. From those burners and others unseen in the streets about us, the city wore a shroud of swirling smoke.

Saint Santana had found her followers.

Our sombre procession of coaches passed through the city's empty streets, and everywhere we went the air hung heavy with the stink of burnt oleander, but it seemed like roses compared to what greeted us. We stopped in front of a disused port warehouse. It was huge, built of faded grey timber, and run down with its doors and windows boarded up. In front of its main doors stood four priests and two patrols of militia; they'd all tied cloths over their noses and mouths.

How could such a stench only now have been noticed? How long had the locals known something was wrong within a warehouse that reeked of a corruption so rich?

The militia captain handed out face cloths, hesitating as he reached out to me. He looked with apprehension, but I took the offered cloth before he could take it back, leaving him to shake his head as he continued on in his duties.

A masked priest came up to us. "They were found only this evening, it was the stink that gave them away. It looks like most of them have been killed elsewhere and then brought here." He began to turn away, but stopped. "There's no shame in revulsion, only proof of your decency."

Behind him I noticed that some of the militiamen wore stained shirts. The sour smell of vomit lay as an undercurrent to the sweet reek of decay.

A crowd had started to gather. They'd followed the coaches and suspected why we were here. We'd arrived with a handful in tow, but now scores waited. Some of them wept while most stood in silence. They were waiting, waiting for answers.

Lord Liberigo looked to each of us and then nodded that we were ready.

A priest opened the door.

Six priests led us in while burning incense and chanting the prayer for the dead. The militiamen stayed outside and were glad of it, but many of Lord Liberigo's men who'd accompanied us on the coaches now carried lanterns to light our way. We entered the dusty warehouse like a funeral march, and only to leave a rising tide of mourning behind us in the street.

Bare wooden floors met us, only marred by the remains of broken crates. Cobwebs stretched about, some reaching up to cover the thick beams above our heads. The high roof was barely visible beyond our lanterns' light while the distant walls were also lost to darkness.

Pedro walked beside me, and for the first time since we'd met I found his presence reassuring. In that moment I needed him. We needed each other. All of us in that group did.

The air grew chill, a light mist giving each lantern a soft glow. The sombre voices of the chanting priests left me feeling as though we were crossing from one world into another - perhaps into the realm of the dead. Maybe for those moments we did.

Something terrible had happened here.

The floorboards we walked upon sparkled with frost.

The priests not already chanting began to recite prayers. They knew, and somehow I did, that the cold mist and dusting of ice remained as an echo of the magic that had been worked here. As if to remind us, the carpet of white crunched underfoot with each of our steps.

Gently, the voices in my head rose in a mournful chorus.

We were close now. It lay just ahead.

The men who carried the lead lanterns of our macabre march were the first to reach the victims. The sounds of their gasps and moans warned us, yet nothing could see us prepared.

The light spread with our arrival to show off the entire scene. The priests continued their chant, only faltering for a moment.

The floorboards rose up as though something huge had crawled into the warehouse to unload its gory cargo. Piled about that gaping hole, arranged in three towers, stood the bloodied remains of scores of children. Most had been dead for a good while, looming as mounds of discoloured flesh and bone. The iced and splintered floorboards surrounding the hole and ghastly monoliths lay covered in forbidden symbols, all of them painted in blood.

A chorus of gasps and moans arose from us. It was too much. The sounds of sobbing and the raw cry of retching filled the air. The chanting of the priests weakened, yet somehow continued - they never stopped.

My vision swam to take on the clarity that came with touching the celestial. With that I could see everything in all its horror and taste the terror of innocent death. And all about us a million celestial sparks danced in the colours of black, violet, and crimson as they glittered along blood-painted symbols. Some of them swirled through the air to be sucked up high and through a matching hole in the roof.

This place was damned!

The Benefice stood in defiance while the rest of us fell back. He bellowed in a voice that drowned out his priests and carried to the crowd in the street, "Behold the work of the dark powers that strive to ruin our city!"

I wiped at my tears and turned to Pedro, who just stood there pale and stunned. I looked to see what had caught his eye; it was the bloody outline of a diamond painted on the frosted floorboards around the closest tower of bodies. It was the same symbol they'd painted on his back when we'd first met.

I took his hand and squeezed it. For long moments he didn't seem to notice until he turned and said, "We have to stop them, they could have taken Maria!"

Kurgar stood in silence beside us.

Lord Liberigo, normally a stern man with a quick mind, just stood staring at the pit. Finally, he said, "I don't know how to fight this, I don't even understand what *it* is."

The pit yawned open, the lantern light unable to penetrate its depths. It came up from the city's sewers. My celestial vision showed a constant stream of sparks drifting up on a nonexistent wind like the smoke of a smouldering fire's steady breath. It seemed to be a residue, a celestial residue. Whatever had happened here was finished.

Benefice Vassini said, "Lord Liberigo, this is a site of powerful magic, ritual magic – a most serious crime. I must insist that we cordon off this building and leave it for the Inquisition to examine upon their arrival."

Lord Liberigo, still stunned at the carnage, could only agree.

When one of us turned to go, the rest were quick to follow. Some of the priests stayed behind to make notes. In all we left one hundred and one bodies behind in three towers, each with a bloody monolith centred on a different symbol and ringed by more markings.

Together we stumbled out of the building to find a crowd waiting for us in the street. Their eyes and ears wanted answers, but their hearts demanded hope. Our pale faces offered neither.

At that moment, all I wanted from the cruel world was to hold Maria and to know that she was safe. I could see the same thought in Pedro's eyes. He took my hand and squeezed it. The action stirred my heart. And us? What of us? Despite all that had happened, had we begun to build something new, something crafted of love amidst all this death?

We returned home via the Malnobla to collect Maria. My part in the afternoon's dramas was not forgotten, but dwarfed by the evening's events. Once home, Sef left Pedro and I downstairs as he carried our sleeping daughter up to my room and put her to bed. I knew he'd wait with her.

Pedro leaned against the wall and watched Sef go before turning to me. "It's late and been a full day, as will tomorrow."

I nodded. "They're yet to question me..." my words trailed off.

"Are you worried?"

I looked to him hoping that he'd understand. "I've done nothing wrong. I saved a child, yet I fear the Church and what it will think of me." I shook my head.

He stepped forward and put his hands on my shoulders, his touch gentle and warm. "You've nothing to fear. Like you said, you've done nothing wrong. You're no cultist, you worked no magic, and you've never claimed to have anything to do with this new saint." He stepped closer and slid his arms around me. His embrace was reassuring.

We stood for a while savouring each other's company - like husband and wife. Finally, he stepped back and let go. Smiling, he said, "Time for bed." Then he turned and left me.

I wondered if he planned on going to my room or his own. We'd kept separate beds since our marriage and never shared, but tonight I could not only tolerate his touch, after seeing what I'd seen in the warehouse I wanted the comfort it would give.

Our maid watched from the shadows with her mouth open wide. She'd never seen the two of us show any affection for each other. In a flurry she turned and ducked away.

Pedro had already climbed the stairs. Not wanting to be alone, I followed.

I found him standing at his door. He was looking back at me as I got to the top of the landing. He offered a smile, one that was genuine if rosed by blush.

I matched it.

He looked down at his hand on the door before whispering, "Not yet, my wife." And then he opened his door and passed through to close it behind him. For a while I stood there, but eventually I moved on to my own room.

Sef greeted me. "Are you alright?"

I nodded as I walked past to sit on the bed I shared with Maria. She lay under the covers, her face placid in sleep.

"Are you sure?" Concern filled his eyes.

With a weak voice, I said, "Did you see him?"

"Pedro?"

"Yes."

He sighed. "Ah yes, Pedro."

"He embraced me downstairs. He hasn't touched me since..."

"Since you were a Mint Lady?" Sef offered.

"Yes."

He softened his voice, "And did you mind him touching you just now?"

"No, I didn't want him to stop."

"Despite what happened when you met?"

"Sef, he's changed."

"Yes, he's a different man, but one we know so little of. Take care in giving yourself to him even if it's just hopes and dreams. Remember, he doesn't know of your witchery yet."

I nodded, and as if to emphasise the point the long and deep lament of Schoperde's song of sorrow, a Flet prayer for the dead, began to rise over Newbank. Its lingering notes cut through the night while more voices sounded to join it. To Heletians the song was heresy.

Sef turned for the door, but stopped. "Please, Juvela, you're like a daughter to me, I just want you to be careful."

I nodded and offered him a smile.

He left.

The song rose strongly outside, it the only sound to disturb the cold night. It seemed my people no longer cared if the truth stood revealed. The parents, families, and friends of the missing demanded time to mourn, and if the Church of Baimiopia couldn't protect the city from such calamity, then it also couldn't harm them.

For my own part, led by the sorrow-filled voices in my head, I went to my bedroom's balcony and joined in. Its long melancholy rose and fell across Newbank, soothing the wounds of loss and asking for mercy for the souls of the dead.

7

A Clash of Faiths

Dawn saw Ossard a cold and bleak place. There was no gradual awakening, no rising sounds of bustle or rush to the markets, even the port lay still and the fishing fleet idle.

A slow wind laden with the bitter scent of burning oleander pushed through empty streets accompanied in Newbank by the last strains of Schoperde's song. Overhead grey skies glowered.

Ossard was mourning.

Pedro spent the dawn fussing over Maria. He spoke little to me and kept his distance. It reminded me of his manner upon arrival into our home years ago and had little in common with the man I'd glimpsed last night. Watching him frustrated me. For a while I'd dared hope that we could change, that our marriage might somehow bloom, but now...

Finally, I asked, "Is something wrong?"

He ignored me.

I repeated the question.

He met my gaze. "What did you sing last night?"

"It's a Flet song; the Song of Sorrow. I heard it being sung and it felt right to join in after what we'd seen."

He shook his head with exasperation. "I can't believe you sung it *after* what we'd seen!" he hissed. "It's forbidden!"

His anger surprised me, but worse made Maria back away. She might not have seen us be close and loving, but she'd also rarely seen us argue.

I kept my voice soft and level, hoping to soothe her as she watched. "It's just a song."

Pedro shook his head, "It's wrong, like the rituals and kidnappings!"

"No, it's not."

In a hard tone he hissed, "The Church calls it heresy!"

Maria began to wail.

Wondering of his time at the monastery, I whispered, "What ever did they do to you?"

A knock at the door silenced us. I turned to see to it, leaving him to hiss after me, "Witch!"

It was Jericho, Lord Liberigo's assistant. "Lady Juvela, an Inquisitor has arrived. You, your husband, and your man-at-arms are required to attend a meeting in the council chamber – urgently."

The news stunned me.

Jericho lingered and then added, "You need to come directly."

I gathered my thoughts. "Of course."

He nodded and left.

An Inquisitor?

My fear of being caught hadn't even been earned. If I was a witch, where were my spells?

I had no power.

And Pedro certainly offered no comfort.

Last night I'd glimpsed a new life opening up. In that life we could have become the loving family of my almost-forgotten lotus-fuelled dreams. Now it seemed impossible.

Anger stirred within me.

Life...

What kind of a life did I have? I was stuck in a marriage based on a terrible crime with a damaged man who resented me.

I hated it!

My anger once stirred only began to fire. The few things that gave me any solace were Maria, my parents, and Sef.

I closed the door, cutting the view of an empty street and a city enslaved by fear.

Once upon a time I'd married Pedro because it would give me power, perhaps now was the time to start using it.

I walked out of the entry hall and back to him.

He looked up, his face cold.

I said, "Get ready, we're going back to your father's."

"Why?"

"An Inquisitor has arrived. If you like, you can tell him I'm a witch."

He gasped. "You *are* a witch!"

Maria sobbed.

My eyes narrowed. "Regardless, I'm sure he can find a way around the castings *your* master put on me, and then your own shameful secret will be out. If I burn at the stake at least I'll have company."

He could only stare at me as the colour drained from his face.

I reached forward and picked up Maria, my poor daughter trying to push me away. With her in my arms, despite her resistance, I growled at Pedro, "Get ready!"

Without a word he got up and headed upstairs.

One of the voices in my head roused itself from its silence. It was the strongest and only stirred to laugh. Behind that hard bark I could hear the crack and snap of flames and the cries of a horrified crowd.

A large crowd waited outside the Malnobla. The people of the city, scared and insecure, had come to see the newly arrived Inquisitor. Some waved branches of oleander while others clutched holy symbols such as the eight-pointed star of St Baimio. Many simply prayed.

We arrived in our own coach with Maria and Sef. Our daughter was to go straight into the care of Pedro's mother while the three of us would head for the council chamber.

Each of us said an awkward goodbye to her in the entry hall; Pedro, because like all of us he loved her; Sef, because he hated having her taken out of his care; and me because I wondered if I'd be handed straight to the Inquisition and never get to see her again. At such thoughts the voices within me stirred in riled indignation.

They'd never let that happen!

I cursed them. They'd done nothing for me so far but bring me grief.

I picked up Maria and held her close. She sensed something was wrong, but I couldn't bring myself to speak of it. I just thought of my love for her. Lost in that focus and oblivious to all else another voice whispered in my head, "I love you too, Mama."

I opened my eyes to see hers locked on mine. Her gaze began to soften, and as I stood there certain we'd again touched minds, Pedro pulled her away.

He whispered, his voice apologetic, "We must be quick, they're waiting." His anger had faded.

Heinz Kurgar sat at the council table smiling in greeting. Beside him sat another guildsman, while four more stood behind him. I was shown to a seat, as was Sef, but Pedro, to his annoyance, was asked to stand.

About us also sat Lord Liberigo, the captain of the city guard, and the head of the Merchants' Guild, while other lesser officials stood. The five remaining chairs were reserved for churchmen with three of them already taken by the priests and monk who'd sat with us yesterday. The arrangement left two empty seats for the Benefice and Inquisitor.

Pale and tired faces sat around that table. I guessed, like me, no one had slept well last night. Hopefully today's proceedings would bring some reassurance, but I couldn't help but think we'd only hear more unsettling information.

After a short wait, the door opened to reveal the Benefice. He entered wearing a smug grin and leading a tall man robed in black. That other man wore a matching skullcap embroidered in golden thread set in a repeating pattern. With a stern and long face, its length exaggerated by a neatly trimmed beard, his hair, once black, now shone through white. His appearance lent him a distinguished air, but it was also severe.

The voices in my head rose to hiss in anger, and for a moment the stink of smoke and burning flesh haunted me. I had to close my eyes and concentrate to take back my senses. The feeling left me shaken and even less prepared for the meeting.

Vassini led the man to their seats. All the while the Benefice glanced about the table challenging anyone to disrespect him now.

They arrived to stand before their chairs. One of the priests called, "All stand for the righteous, Inquisitor Anton and Benefice Vassini."

Hesitantly, but led by Lord Liberigo, we did.

Benefice Vassini and the Inquisitor nodded in acknowledgement before taking their seats. That done we all followed.

Lord Liberigo cleared his throat. "Benefice Vassini, would you care to handle proceedings?"

The Benefice gave a wry smile. "To cope with this time of great crisis, something I might add foreseen by the Church, we have requested and received the services of the Holy Inquisition. I present to you Inquisitor Anton of the Expeditia Puritanica.

The man gave a curt nod, but didn't speak.

The Benefice, a little flustered, continued, "Immediately after his arrival this morning we took Inquisitor Anton to the ritual site at his own request. He has already begun his investigation and convened this meeting, and thus I give him to you to speak."

And all eyes went to the Inquisitor.

He seemed distant, as if he hadn't been listening. Instead he sat there looking at the centre of the table as though staring at something only he could see.

Was he searching the celestial?

I forced myself to relax, my vision growing clearer as it jumped to a new level. Everything fell into shades of blue and black, the only exception being the flaring soul-lights of those who sat about me.

I looked to the same spot as the Inquisitor, and there it was; some kind of beast.

It hunkered down snarling and snapping. Jagged lines, something akin to horns and barbs, showed through its bright glare. With its every move it sent showers of black sparks spraying off of its horrid brilliance. It let out a deep and rumbling growl as it focussed its bitterness on the Inquisitor.

He showed no fear.

A straining sensation made my newfound perception falter and fall out of that world and back into ours.

In the real world, all those about the table still waited for him to speak, yet he made no effort.

Just as Benefice Vassini turned to prompt him, the Inquisitor's eyes found focus and his hard voice rang out. "This city is doomed." And after a deep pause he added, "The taint of many things haunts the streets of your city, a city that needs to be reborn to be saved. It is my grave duty to tell you that much birthing blood will flow before it may yet rise again."

And silence followed.

"The agents of the Horned God walk here and do so almost freely. In their company are many who would smash the glory of Krienta. I can taste forbidden cults, cabalists, the wicked Sisterhood, and even the basest of magics, Green Witchery. This city is damned in many ways, but worst of all because it has chosen to be."

He then turned to stare at me, and I knew that my truth was revealed. "How can you hope to save the city when you're so blind to the problem and its enemies?"

Lord Liberigo and Benefice Vassini, both in their own ways responsible for the state of the city, sat stunned at the Inquisitor's easy damning. Angered by such words, Lord Liberigo replied, "If those before you are so ignorant, why don't *you* explain the problem and how to fix it? We need solutions, not theatrics!"

The Inquisitor, cold and calm, gave him his answer. "Only an army of butchers can clean this place." Then he resumed his silence.

We joined him, stunned and mute.

At first I wondered if he was mad. Then the thought arose, cold and clammy, trying to lift itself out of a chill sea of stinking brine; what if his words were true?

A deep corruption *had* taken root in the city. Pedro had even said as much, it infesting the highest levels. As hideous as it sounded, perhaps we *did* need an army of butchers.

As I considered his words others recovered. Kurgar was the first and simply laughed. "You can't be serious! The city is beset by nothing more than a gang of kidnappers, perhaps with links to some cult or other. We're probably up against twenty men, not some dark army!"

"Silence!" The Inquisitor bellowed, and his voice roared backed by angels.

Thoughts of laughter died.

He began afresh. "I fight a war, a war to keep my people and my Church safe from corruption. While you consider yourself Heletian, of Krienta, or part of the Heletian League, you will listen to me *and* do what I say.

"Some of you believe that all that is happening in this incestuous city is the usual good business against an unfortunate backdrop of a little kidnapping. In truth, some of you wouldn't care if the missing children were just being sold into slavery, and are only marginally more concerned that they're being used to feed ritual magic.

"This is wrong, and I have come to correct your thinking.

"There are more factions sitting around this table than you know, and if we work together we can all get out of this what we need. There will be hard work ahead and much of it unpleasant, but you must believe me when I tell you that the situation is desperate."

Lord Liberigo interrupted the Inquisitor. "I assure you that I take the threat seriously, but what is the threat, what is happening to our city?"

Inquisitor Anton looked at the assembled faces, his gaze lingering on me. He stood and said, "I wage a war against the servants of the Horned God. You all know this, it is after all what the Inquisition is for, but do you have any idea of what it means?"

He let a silence settle, and then continued, "It means that I right what is wrong. I don't do it for one poor soul, but for all our people. It sounds noble and I suppose is, but in its doing I am tasked with terrible deeds. I have orphaned children because their parents succumbed to heresy, but that's not the worst of my judgements, I have also razed villages and even once a whole town.

"Because of my work I am marked for damnation by a hundred different gods, all aspects of the same dark power. You see, I am the one sacrificing all, not the ones I judge, and I do it so the rest of you may live on through salvation.

"You all have a chance at an afterlife. It's your reward for the hard existence we lead here, but I will never see those heavenly fields, walk those olive groves, or see us dine together in a golden vineyard while relishing divine wine. My reward for fighting heresy in this life is damnation in the next. I shall be a plaything of the pits, the bitch-slave of dark powers, yet I would not change a thing. It is my penance."

His eyes came to rest on me as he continued, "If it means burning the high ladies of every Heletian city for witchery, I will, even if I have to build the pyres and light the fires myself. But on occasion some types of evil can be found to work towards good." His eyes shifted to Kurgar. "Then there are times when we all need to work together regardless of where we come from or who we think our real enemies are.

"Tell me of the people waving and burning oleander. They speak of Saint Santana, protector of children, an unknown to me. They also speak of her lady, one Juvela Liberigo."

The Benefice answered, "We'd not heard of Saint Santana either, not until yesterday. A lone Heletite began preaching of her in Market Square. Amidst the fear of the kidnappings he's found it easy to gather believers."

"And what was this so-called Heletite doing for his flock?"

Vassini answered, "Selling relics and amulets."

"And where is he now?"

"Dead," the Benefice said curtly.

Surprised looks passed about the table.

"I see, and how did that come to pass?"

"He killed himself last night."

"I see. How convenient. Has word spread of our Heletite's death?"

Vassini looked down to his hands where they nursed each other on the table. "We tried to suppress the news, but it still seems to have found the street. They say that I killed him, personally, that I strangled the very life out of him. They call him a martyr!" The Benefice opened his hands and flexed his plump fingers.

The monk beside Vassini added, "And already there are other Heletites preaching."

Inquisitor Anton nodded. "I see, and what of Lady Juvela? I believe she is here amongst us." His eyes turned to me.

"I am, Inquisitor."

"So, what is your connection to this false saint?"

"None, we just saw the Heletite selling relics in Market Square."

"Did you speak with him?"

"No."

"Did he talk to you as part of his preaching, perhaps pointing you out in the crowd or some such thing?"

"No, not that I know of."

"Did you buy one of his trinkets?"

"No."

"So, why are you claimed as the saint's lady?" His gaze was piercing.

"I don't know. We never spoke to the Heletite, and only listened for the briefest of time."

His eyes narrowed. "What happened after you left him?"

I took a deep breath and told my tale, "The Cathedral bells began to toll for the sixth kidnapping as we moved on. People panicked. In the chaos I noticed a lady crying out and trying to shield her child. I went to help, and it was then that I disturbed the kidnapper..."

He corrected me, "The cultist?"

"Yes. I was scared, but also so angry about the kidnappings that I just charged him."

"And stabbed him?"

"Yes."

He cocked an eyebrow. "Do you normally walk the streets armed?"

"No. I took a knife from my daughter's bodyguard, grabbing it from his belt."

"Did it never occur to you that your bodyguard might be a better person to handle such a weapon?"

"It all happened so quickly, and I was so angry..."

"And scared?" he asked.

"Yes! But I just wanted to get him away from the child he was about to take. That the blade wounded him at all was as much luck as anything."

He nodded. "Then what happened?"

"The child fell weakened and listless, but back into her mother's arms. I think the little girl had fainted. At the same time my daughter's bodyguard arrived and drew his sword. The kidnapper, startled by the challenge, worked some kind of magic and disappeared."

The Inquisitor nodded. "We will speak of this further another time." And in my mind his voice whispered, "I know your truth!"

The air prickled around me as a chill crawled over my skin. As if in answer, I heard the rising growl of the voices inside my head, they snarled like wild dogs, starved and desperate. They hated him, and the heat of that hate quickly melted away the chill.

Inquisitor Anton cleared his throat and continued, "To the matter at hand; the ritual. I have examined the scene and issued instructions for the warehouse to be piled high with wood, oiled, and burnt. The place is an open sore and will lie weeping until it is cleansed. We can live with a scar, but not a festering wound.

"Lord Liberigo, when the fire has burned down to the ground, taking those poor defiled bodies with it, you can see about sealing the sewers and rebuilding the warehouse if need be."

The Lord asked, "What if the families wish to retrieve the bodies to conduct funeral rites?"

"There can be none."

Benefice Vassini looked appalled. "But what of their souls?"

"It's too late, they're already gone."

Vassini paled as did the others about the table. "Gone?"

"Consumed by the ritual."

Lord Liberigo queried, "And the purpose of the ritual?"

The Inquisitor sobered for his answer. "To create something."

"What?" Lord Liberigo pressed.

"A beacon, and if we don't act quickly it *will* attract who it calls."

Lord Liberigo whispered, "And who is that?"

With fatigue in his eyes, Inquisitor Anton replied, "The Horned God."

During the course of the day we spoke of many things.

The Inquisitor voiced suspicions that the Santana sect might be a front for one of the forbidden faiths. He feared it was just a bridgehead, and perhaps the first of many, something that would allow the *new* and *unknown* to become accepted.

It made sense, for in our spiritually lax city the new saint had already achieved a following in just a few days.

He'd said, "And what happens when those perpetrating this myth provide something to lend it credence? What happens when the frightened see proof of this new saint's power? We will lose them. We have to discredit the sect and quickly."

No one disagreed, and in truth I think we were all impressed. Yes, he had a pit of venom to draw upon, spouting dogma and easy hate, but a good deal of what he said came considered.

By the late afternoon we'd finished our discussions, with most of the time taken up in the planning of various searches of the city by the watch. Many attendees left the chamber quickly, rushing to act on our discussions - but not the Inquisitor.

He walked across to Sef, Pedro, and myself, greeting us with a bow. All the while he never took his eyes from mine. Finally, he said, "You *see?*"

There seemed no point in denial. "A little, but it's all I can do."

"For now, until you receive training."

"I'm alone. I have no plans for training and wouldn't know where to go in any case."

"You are a Flet. Your people have a long history of magic, something that has always been of concern to the Church. The forefathers of this city were well meaning when they accepted your people as refugees, but they were also blinded by the promise of cheap labour and convertible souls. Sadly, it's not come to pass. You Flets have only maintained your old ways, spoiling what was once a god-fearing city. Such divisions cause weakness.

"The people of this city will pay a high price for their forefathers' decision, and Ossard will not come out of this as it went in. The city will be reborn, but afterwards there will be no place here for you or your kin."

His eyes narrowed. "This is your warning: If you were of no use to me, I'd drag you outside and into the square and burn your tainted hide to cinders right now. Instead I ask you to help me clean the city. When all is done I will help you gain shelter elsewhere, we could even see you and your family settled in Fletland."

I was stunned by his words.

His lips then curled into a scowl. "Fletland will be fine for you, anywhere will be as long as you leave here. You'll not be welcome in the *New Ossard*. You are Demon. Even if you begged me to let you take Krienta as your saviour, I would deny you. Your soul is filth!"

Pedro gasped.

And any hope of last night's warmth between us being rekindled died.

As if reading my mind, the Inquisitor said, "My son, mind yourself, if you give her your love she'll take your soul."

Pedro stood stunned by his words, yet accepted them.

The Inquisitor added, "If you want Krienta's salvation you must be free of demons. You live with this one and bravely deny her, yet... yet there is another..." His eyes squinted as he concentrated, slipping his perception into the celestial to skim Pedro's very being. His face tightened with the effort and then his lips drew themselves into a sneer. "My son, you have already given your love to the other. You are forsaken!"

My own mind raced; who could Pedro love?

And my husband paled. "I haven't, I love no one!"

The Inquisitor's sneer faded, but only to become grim. "You have thinned your Heletian blood by having issue with this witch, you have fathered a daughter of damnation!"

Pedro's face lost its fear, colour flushing his cheeks. He raised his arms to fold them across his chest, the movement squaring his shoulders. He would listen to me be branded a demon, but not his beloved Maria.

The Inquisitor said, "See, the little beast has already ensnared you. She no doubt uses her big blue eyes, curly black hair, and honeyed giggles as her weapons."

I turned to Pedro to see his eyes sparkling with anger.

The Inquisitor said, "Such spirit! Most melt away, some have even dropped to their knees and offered me their own kin for burning, but not you, oh no, not you our *most* pious Pedro. I've heard about you, and I know that you will offer me nothing, not even your own wife despite the crippled feelings between the two of you."

Pedro didn't flinch. "I offer you nothing, but to my god I offer everything."

Anton smiled. "And what god is that?"

"The same god as you."

"But your daughter is demon-spawn, do you not fear her?"

Pedro unfolded his arms, and reached across to grab one of my hands, "*Our* daughter is but a little girl, innocent and loved."

Anton looked down at our joined hands. "Nothing is what it seems." He then turned to me. "And what of my offer?"

I noticed Kurgar loitering behind the Inquisitor, distant but listening.

"You speak to me as though I'm nothing, but also ask my help?"

He smiled. "Strange, isn't it. I am genuine. You help me get the city through this, and I'll spare you and your family, but you will have to leave it along with your people."

I said nothing, so he added, "Please, there is so much more happening here and no one is telling you the full truth of it. If you help me, I will give you one morsel of it here and now."

"What do you want me to do?" I asked.

"I will address the crowd gathering in the square, you need do no more than stand tall and proud and deny any involvement with this new saint."

"And this truth?"

His tone softened as he took a step forward so only Sef, Pedro, and I could hear. Gently, like a father, he said, "There are countless factions at work in this city, and they all want power. Across all of them there is only one thing that they fear."

"What?" I asked.

"You."

8

The Inquisition's Answer

Anton and I took the stairs to the third level, heading for the balcony that ran the length of the Malnobla's front. We followed Lord Liberigo, the Benefice, Pedro, Sef, and Kurgar. Word had come via an attendant; the crowd was demanding to see the Inquisitor.

Maria and Lady Liberigo were waiting for us in the ballroom that opened onto the balcony, accompanied by two men at arms. Before we reached them we could hear the crowd's rumble.

The Inquisitor said, "The Lord and Lady will step out first to address the crowd and introduce me. Benefice Vassini will accompany them, but shall not speak."

Vassini looked affronted.

Anton ignored him. "I will follow with Pedro and Juvela." He then turned to face Kurgar and Sef. "You two shall stay here and well back from the doors, we don't want to confuse our message with too many faces."

Too many Flet *faces...*

Pedro said, "I'll bring our daughter."

"Yes, of course." Anton paused before continuing, "Once out there, I'll undo the damage caused by the fraudulent Heletite, and offer the people some reassurance. That will be all."

The square spread as a sea of scared faces with thousands upon thousands holding branches of oleander in the air. Clearly those preaching the word of the *Protector of Children* had been busy.

The crowd hushed at the sight of their Lord and Lady, not so much out of respect, but because they wanted answers. The silence was short-lived. When Benefice Vassini came into view many began to shake their oleander in anger and boo.

A lone voice yelled, "Remember Saint Santana's martyr!" And thousands of voices sounded in agreement.

Lord Liberigo let the crowd settle while the dusk sky grumbled in its own disquiet. A thunderstorm had come rolling across the heavens bringing with it a whipping wind.

The Inquisitor and I waited for our turn, watching from a window by the doors. Pedro stood with us and held Maria. Sef and Kurgar watched from another window where they'd been exiled to a far corner.

The air grew tense, suddenly cooling.

Anton closed his eyes for a brief prayer, before opening them to ask, "Did you feel that?"

And I did.

Outside, a growing vortex of power made the air prickle as it hung over the city. "What is it?"

"Take a *look*."

I relaxed as the room before me sprang into clarity. I looked further, my view fading into the hues of blues and blacks while the soul-lights of those around me flared. My perception shifted as I swung it about.

Market Square spread as a blinding sea of life-lights, but above it all swirled a dim blue whirlpool of gathering power. At the heart of that disturbance lay a huge circle, as wide as a warship is long, and within lay a stunning cobalt-blue iris that was split by a sharp edged pupil. It was an eye.

My soul felt brittle.

Only one thing could be so big and make me feel so small.

It was a god!

I lost my concentration and fell back into normal vision. The shock of it left me weak with my legs buckling to send me slumping against the wall.

Anton moved to my side, but not to help. "See, he's sensed the beacon and now comes for Ossard!"

Pedro paled and took a step back.

I cursed; I'd just let him see me look into another world. Turning to him, I reached out with a hand and begged, "Please, Pedro..."

Anton laughed.

Pedro flinched at my reaching hand, but stilled himself at Anton's mirth. He composed himself as he stood there. He didn't take my hand, or step closer, but neither did he step any further away.

Outside on the balcony, Lord Liberigo addressed the crowd, "People of Ossard, it is true that the kidnappings threaten to spiral out of control, that they are linked to ritual magic, and that last night the city watch discovered the bodies of many victims.

"My people, we of the city are working hard to get answers, and each new answer brings us closer to the guilty!

"Still, it is such a diabolical thing, that we've felt it wise to accept the offered aid of the Inquisition. The Black Fleet is currently moored in distant Lucera, but has heard our cry and dispatched a ship. That ship, the blessed *Ba-Mora*, has arrived this very day. I present to you Inquisitor Anton, their mission's leader."

Anton grabbed my hand and led me onto the balcony.

People generously applauded the Inquisitor, but a cheer erupted as they laid eyes on me. Some in the crowd yelled, "The Lady of the Saint!" It didn't take long for those calls to fall into a chant, "Lady of the Saint! Lady of the Saint! Lady of the Saint!"

The Inquisitor stood before them with me at his side, while Pedro followed but kept a couple of steps back with Maria.

My husband watched me with questions in his eyes. He loved his daughter, loved her more than life itself, and not so long ago a seed of love had begun to sprout between us despite the barren soil of our marriage. That poor love, a union that had waited so long to take, still seemed determined to struggle on.

Briefly our eyes met.

I offered him a smile to try and reassure him.

His tense face relaxed, but he couldn't hold my gaze.

Maria also looked to me.

I called to her, "Be good, Maria, be good for your father."

She smiled and then nuzzled into his chest.

He again met my gaze and this time held it. There was hope there, in his beautiful brown eyes – but also so much pain.

The noise of the crowd faded, but Inquisitor Anton waited for silence. Finally he addressed them, "People of Ossard, you live in grave times, the gravest, but know that I have come to put things right!

"You think the kidnappings are out of control, but they aren't. It's your faith that's run amuck!

"What kind of city allows its people to grow so lax? What kind of people accepts it becoming so? Your home might be rich in coin, but it's a pauper of devotion!

A lone voice yelled, "Saint Santana will save us!"

The Inquisitor's face grew sharp with rage. "You have been deceived, there is no such saint! She is nothing but a fraud and vile heresy!

"It is the weak-willed and feeble-minded who are prepared to adopt a new saint on a whim that have allowed the cults to gain a foothold in your city. You have been fooled by the very people who are stealing your children!"

The crowd grumbled with several voices rising above the noise.

"They said Saint Baimio was a false prophet too!"

"Our faith is strong!"

"Saint Santana has kept my child safe!"

"The Lady fights with her blessing, we saw it!"

Inquisitor Anton turned to me and beckoned me forward.

So this was what he wanted me for.

I stepped up, nervous, half expecting him to denounce me. Behind me, Pedro moved closer in support, but Anton waved him back.

Maria looked to me with sad eyes while the air of unease grew.

Pedro stood anxiously. He could also feel it.

I whispered something to him that surprised me, "I love you."

My husband, that tall, strong, and handsome man I'd always dreamed of, stood there with our daughter in his arms and tears in his eyes. He nodded, and for the first time in years no fear beshadowed him.

Something *had* grown between us, and not something to keep us apart, but something to bind us together. Regardless of what might come, right there and then I found some solace. It was as if, finally, we were a true family.

Inquisitor Anton turned to the crowd and said, "Before you stands Lady Juvela Liberigo, a symbol of this city. She is a Flet with a Heletian husband and name, and a mixed-blood daughter, little Maria. Many of you also believe that she is the servant of Saint Santana, I ask her now: Are you in the service of this so-called saint?"

The crowd fell silent for my answer.

THE FALL OF OSSARD

So the Inquisitor wanted me to denounce Saint Santana, fine, simple enough. I cleared my throat and said, "I have never been in the service of the false saint, Saint Santana."

"Had you ever heard of this fraudulent saint prior to the events of yesterday in which suspicious third parties anointed you her instrument?"

"No."

"Would you describe yourself as a particularly spiritual person?"

I hesitated, not sure what answer he wanted. I'd promised my soul to Schoperde, and while he probably expected that, I doubted it was the revelation he was after. "My faith is strong and righteous, and it isn't owed to any false saint."

He raised an eyebrow, but didn't look angry. "And you have never, in any way, felt that you have been touched by the questionable power of this supposed saint?"

The vision of the huge eye watching over the city came back to haunt me. With a slight shiver, I couldn't help but glance skywards. "No, never."

"So your actions yesterday were your own, and not guided by divine power?"

"They were my own. I saw a mother crying for help and went to her aid."

"Do you believe in Saint Santana, or that she is the protector of children?"

"No, she is a fraud."

And the faces in the crowd began to drain of the little hope that had lit them.

Inquisitor Anton turned back to the packed square, raising his arms beseechingly. "You have been lied to! Cast aside your false relics and oleander. Krienta will look kindly on those of you who renounce your heresy, but only if you do it now!"

Across the square, oleander dropped to the cobblestones amidst the clatter of discarded amulets. Satisfied, the Inquisitor didn't even bother to suppress a grin.

Then the sky winked.

In a moment everything changed.

A coldness rose in me to make my soul shiver. The voices within whispered in frightened tones, their fear making them quake.

Something terrible was coming, and then even the Inquisitor lost his grin.

I heard Pedro gasp behind me.

As I began to turn, the voices began whispering bittersweet sympathy, urging me to be brave. Then I heard Maria's mind-voice, and she only had two words to say, "Bye, Mama."

I turned to see Pedro staggering back as his arms tightened about Maria. They both stared with wide eyes at a swirling vortex of darkness that opened up in front of them.

"No!" I screamed.

The crowd cried out.

Beside me the Inquisitor turned to face the challenge.

The vortex sucked at the light, the dark within it chill and malicious. Out of it stepped the robed man I'd first seen almost five years ago, the cultist who'd taken the redheaded boy.

I hated him!

I yelled, "Get Maria away!" And then rushed forward to put my body between them.

Pedro stepped further back.

Behind me the Inquisitor chanted.

The robed man, calm and in control, looked straight at me. A hungry grin split his face to reveal bloodstained teeth. "We're well past that now, we don't *just* need children."

The thought hadn't occurred to me.

Was I his target?

Pedro called from behind, "Juvela!"

I looked over my shoulder.

Pedro stood with his arms pinned by four cultists while a fifth snatched Maria.

I turned my back on their leader to lunge for my daughter.

More blackness arose about me, not of vortexes, but swirling robes. We were outnumbered.

Sef charged through the ballroom, heading for the doors to the balcony. Despite his desperation, I knew he wouldn't make it.

In the square below, the people of the city began retrieving their discarded oleander and amulets. A voice called out from amongst them, "The Lady of the Saint is *forsaken!*"

Something then hit me from behind to send me sprawling.

I blacked out for a moment, but then came to. Ignoring the pain, I tried to get back on my feet, only to realise that it was already too late.

A dozen cultists stood at the far end of the balcony with knives held to the throats of Lord and Lady Liberigo, and Pedro and Maria. Dark vortexes swirled about them, ready for their escape.

Pedro looked to me with fear in his eyes, and with my celestial vision I saw the colours of life drain out from him. I could see his fate; a pale, stiff, and cold body lying butchered and cursed, with his soul eaten by ritual magic.

Their leader strode past to join them. "We don't just want children, now we need whole bloodlines."

I cried out.

Inquisitor Anton stood behind me still chanting his prayer.

The cultist leader laughed and then ushered his people through their vortexes. I got up and leapt after them, but only succeeded in grazing myself on the balcony's paving.

They were gone.

Sef cursed as he finally got through the doors.

The Inquisitor finished his prayer, one I now recognised as the litany for the dead. He'd never intended to stop them.

On my knees, I threw back my head and wailed. My heartfelt cry fell into the long and deep notes of Schoperde's song of sorrow.

Anton cursed my heresy before kicking me in the back of the head.

The darkness that followed was a mercy.

COLIN TABER

Part II

-

Ossard, The Pious Empire

9

Sorrow

I awoke in my parents' home, nestled amidst the linen of my childhood, and in the familiar surroundings of my old room. My mother sat beside me mopping my brow with a cloth, while whispering for me to be still.

For the briefest of moments I lay calm and blank, until the agony of my daughter's goodbye ruined me afresh.

She was gone!

That misery was then doubled by my memory of Pedro having a knife held to his throat as he too was taken. I cried out, "My family!" and struggled to rise, but my mother's hands held me down.

"Hush, you can't do anything for them now."

I gave up my failing efforts. "What happened?" And behind her I could see Sef standing at the doorway with downcast eyes.

"In the absence of Lord Liberigo, Benefice Vassini has claimed rule of the city. There'll be a proclamation tomorrow at noon."

No wonder the Inquisitor had done nothing; the kidnapping of the Liberigos had delivered control of Ossard to the Church.

"What kind of proclamation?"

"Your father says that the Benefice and Inquisitor have claimed governance, and that the Council of Princes is to be disbanded."

"What about the other council members?"

"They've all been taken."

I was stunned.

She went on, "And Pedro's brothers are too far away." His three older siblings acted as ambassadors in distant Porto Baimio, Lixus, and Vangre.

"Sweet Schoperde!" I whispered.

"Oh Juvela, there's such misery in the streets!"

I struggled to sit up, and this time she didn't stop me.

My mother took a deep breath. "There was a new round of kidnappings. So many have been taken that they've stopped ringing the

Cathedral's bells. People say that well over a hundred are missing, including all of the council, and five of their family lines." And then tears overwhelmed her composure. "The city is ungovernable."

"Pedro and Maria?" I asked.

She just shook her head.

They were gone, my husband and daughter – gone!

My own tears came and their issuing hurt, them running hard and hot.

Some witch I was, something I'd still probably die for, yet all I could do was sob.

I'd grazed my hands and knees back on the balcony. My once smooth skin now swelled black and blue, and spread with rugged scabs, but the real hurt lay underneath. My heart wasn't just bruised, it lay smashed and ruined – trampled by an army of cultists and then worked over by the Inquisition.

It seemed that the Church had got everything it wanted; control over the city, a free hand to deal with the cultists however it saw fit, and then perhaps me. Would Anton still allow me to go into exile? I doubted it. I couldn't in any case, not until I knew I'd done all I could to save my family.

My family...

That night, standing at my old bedroom window, I looked out across the rooftops and watched the distant warehouse of the ritual burn. The flames leapt high in flashes of orange, blue, and yellow, fed by oil and wood. They consumed the building and my memories of a city forever changed. The Ossard I'd grown up in, the free and easygoing place where anything could be bought or sold, the city known as *The Whore*, was gone – and I dreaded what might replace it.

Taking in that sea of countless rooftops only dragged me further into despair.

Where could they be?

Even the most thorough search would have trouble finding them, it complicated by a tradition of giving buildings hidden cellars and exits long ago used to avoid raiding pirates and tax collectors. And if the orderly districts of the city would be difficult to search, then the slums would be all but impossible. The filthy warrens of tightly packed buildings and twisting alleys dominated the city, including most of Newbank, the opposite riverbank, along the city walls, and around the port.

It seemed hopeless.

For a real chance of finding them I needed help. Quite frankly, I needed a miracle.

A knock sounded at the door. I turned to see my mother enter and Sef's shadow haunt the corridor behind her - as always he watched over me.

She said, "Your father's at the Guild, they're talking of organising searches. Don't worry, they'll find them."

I nodded, but wasn't much cheered.

She carried something behind her back, something heavy that strained her arms. "I have something for you."

I finally smiled and went to her.

She held before me an old book, something thick and dusty. It was no ledger, no family tree, nothing at all like that. Within me, for the first time since Maria and Pedro's disappearance, the voices again whispered.

Mother said, "It was your grandmother's." She shook her head trying to fight off tears before pushing on, "I don't know what it is, but she used it. I think it gave her power."

The strongest voice in my head whispered, "The Book of Truth!"

And I was sure it was her; my grandmother.

I reached for the tome amidst a rising babble of head-bound voices and could feel the power within me begin to stir. My fingers touched it and the voices gasped.

Hope was here, hope, hope to see Pedro and Maria returned!

I took it from my mother's trembling hands.

My sense of awe faltered, and then crumbled, giving way to despair. "Mother, I can't read!"

She guided me, forcing me to turn and put the book down on the bed. With a smile, she said, "Neither could your grandmother."

"What?"

She indicated the closed tome. "Just try it."

I opened its stiff leather cover, stained where so many hands had held it, to reveal brittle pages yellowed with age. They spread before me covered in lines of dense script marked by slashing and generous strokes. It was beautiful. Before I knew it, I found myself running my fingertips along them, and with that the voices in me spoke, "...their only choice, for the Goddess of Life existed in a time of only one other god, Death, and between them, together and in union, they forged a mortal world..."

Stunned, I lifted my fingers from the page. The action brought silence. I turned to my mother and said, "I think I know it!"

My mother embraced me. "You should rest. Your father will do what he can with the Guild, and perhaps tomorrow we'll see what *you* can do."

I nodded.

She broke her grip and step by step backed away. She remained scared of the magic, the Church had done that to her, but she knew there was more to it than the priests' dark dogma of fear. When she reached the door, she said, "I'll bring up a lamp in case you wish to read."

I smiled. "I'd like that. Thanks, Mother, you've given me hope."

10

The Book of Truth

In the bedroom of my childhood, by the light of a lone lamp, I let the voices read to me led by the strongest, Vilma, my haunting grandmother. She was there to help, to see me through this *awakening*, and to see me become more than I was. I felt her presence, and almost glimpsed her, as if she was woven of drifting smoke.

Never did we speak to each other, but read on she did. I listened to her whispering voice as my fingers slid along the tome's lines of slashing script. She didn't tire or miss a word, she just continued on, through the night's long darkness until the flames feasting on the warehouse faded, and up until the coming of dawn.

It was only a start, and we both knew it, but it left me forever changed.

Afterwards, it was hard to describe how I felt.

I sat by the window lost in thought as the sun rose to wash over me with its golden rays.

Strangely, I felt born anew and so alive, but also cold and numb. No, it was more than that. I felt uncomfortably *chill* and deathly *stale*.

I wondered at that, at such contrasting sensations - life and death. Perhaps in some way I'd been reborn and in the process part of me had also died. Regardless, one thing was certain; I'd begun to see the world differently.

The Book of Truth...

There was nothing in the book about how to use magic, let alone anything to help me understand what talent I might have. In that regard I felt disappointed, but it did speak of the cost of utilising such gifts.

It said that a responsibility came partnered with working magic, something that touched upon more than oneself. The passages concerning this were brief but grave and also warned of being greedy for power. It gave me a premonition, it rank with dread, and I knew that a day would come when that cost would weigh heavily on me. Still, I told myself, such worries were for another time. Fatigued and distracted, such a thing was easy to believe.

The beginning of my illumination came through the book, but it was only the start. The ancient tome wasn't what I'd expected, neither a listing of spells, lessons of the magical, or a guide to a witch's art. Instead it was a record of the world's history, its true history, it holding the divine truth.

It left me shocked, but also exhausted and confused.

Astounding as it was, I just didn't have time for it. I mean, all I really wanted was to find Maria and Pedro, but these new revelations, I wondered; could they help me in my search?

"Yes!" my grandmother whispered.

I couldn't see her, but I sensed her as the air chilled.

The feeling didn't sit well though, not after all that I'd read. From where I sat by the window, I looked back to the tome where it lay on the bed. It set me to shiver.

The divine truth...

It was unbelievable and so well hidden, yet obvious all at the same time. And it had already touched me, but until now I'd never known.

A war was raging, one that was being fought right around the world. It was a secret war, a divine war, and it pitted the goddess of life against the god of death. Sometimes it was a war of bloody battles, other times bandits and raiding pirates, or plague and famine, or even cultists stealing children from dark and dirty slums. Each of those happenings was another victory for Death and the bleak world he promised.

Unknown to most, this war had been going on for thousands of years, and only now was coming to a close. And that was the worst part, for Life, Schoperde, had all but lost.

Now was a time for the last empires to fall, sanctuaries to be overrun, and for peace to choke on gore. In the end there would be nothing left but ruin and whatever Death chose to build upon his bloodily won ground. That was why Ossard had become a place of abductions and murder with only worse to follow.

And here I was with so many burdens weighing down on me, and no idea of what to make of it. I wondered if it wasn't my problem, but with my family stolen away that simply wasn't true.

With a grim face, I turned back to gaze out the window. The sky above the city was busy with long grey clouds moving in from the west. By the light of the rising sun, something that should have painted them gold and amber, they only looked ominous.

Drifting in my thoughts, I eventually found myself lost. It was a sanctuary of sorts and led to another; daydreams, in particular, the dream that had given me respite from the lustful fevers inspired by my mother's lotus.

It returned as before, with me passing like a bird over the steep and narrow valleys of the coastal sounds. Eventually, I arrived at an area of rolling hills, green and spotted with herb-brush that climbed from behind rocky bluffs and beaches. Nearby, but back from the water, and amidst the heights of those hills, a canyon opened wide. Its sides fell away deep into the soil with small streams of water seeping out to trickle down until they found its bottom. There, half hidden by mist, they watered a wondrous fern forest.

The images of my sanctuary left me feeling settled and content, but I had to drag myself away from it. It was an indulgence, and such daydreams weren't going to save my family.

My family...

I felt confident that they were still alive. With so many people taken in the past few days the cultists had to be building to a ritual beyond anything they'd already run. Simply, I had to find Maria and Pedro before it was enacted.

A knock sounded at my door.

I got up and went to it.

Sef stood there taking in the sight of me, his eyes wide with surprise.

I smiled. I was changed, not only did I feel it, but from Sef's reaction he could see it.

He said, "I came to check on you."

"I'm good, the night has agreed with me."

"So it seems." His surprise faded, replaced with a cautious smile.

"At noon I'm going to go to Market Square."

"For the proclamation?" he asked.

"Yes."

135

"I'll accompany you."

I shook my head.

"Juvela, you'll be in danger. *They* may try and take you."

"Sef, I know I'm new to this, but I also know that I'll be safe. It would be better if you went with my father and found out what the Guild is doing about searches. I'll need to know when I return."

He nodded, reluctant, but willing to trust me.

11

Founding The Pious Empire

For the first time in my life, I walked from Newbank to Market Square. I passed under grey skies, dawn's dark clouds having moved in to smother the sun and lend the city a sombre air. The tight streets about me were again busy with traffic, but all of it subdued. It was as if everything held its breath waiting to see what would come, waiting for the Inquisitor's unveiling of the new.

Before long I was crossing the wide way of the Cassaro Bridge and leaving my home district for Ossard's Heletian heart. Here the streets ran thick with late-morning crowds, many also making their way to Market Square.

Oleander hung from many doors, twigs of its long leaves tied with bunches of the shrub's wilting pink blooms. Some homes even hosted braziers or pots that sat in windows or doorways from which the bitter stink of their smouldering offerings arose.

The crowds grew thicker, but moved aside for me. I saw their sideward glances and heard their whispers, some from their lips, and others escaping their thoughts, "The *Forsaken Lady!*"

I pitied them. Yesterday I was their hero, but today I was their villain. They'd changed so quickly, yet in that they weren't alone. Not so long ago I'd been an innocent girl, but now I was a learning witch, an angry mother, and also a lonely wife trying to avoid being widowed.

And the voices had changed with me.

Their whispered messages came clearer now. It wasn't as though they sounded out any louder as they offered their advice, instead they came on a different level. I no longer *heard* the thought to beware or to look with celestial eyes, now it instinctively happened.

In much the same way, I found myself sensing the thoughts of those that I passed. Those mixing their thoughts with strong emotions came easy to sample, yet most were lost within confusing veils, and then there were others who came across as simple voids.

Those that hid their thoughts so completely turned their knowing faces away. To read so many startled me, but to be *refused* by so many others was unsettling. The Inquisitor was right; the city *was* riddled with cultists, cabalists, and the Sisterhood.

How could we have missed it?

The thoughts I did read ranged from anger and disgust, to sorrow and fear. They combined to create a stinging bitterness in the celestial, the scent of souls turned sour.

They hated me.

The followers of Santana believed my denunciation of the new saint had endangered the whole city. In penance they'd rededicated themselves.

I shivered. The city *was* a whore willing to sell itself for yet another turn of luck.

Others pitied me. To them I'd become a mourning widow and mother, the very thing they so desperately wanted to avoid.

Mothers held their children close as I passed, fathers averted their eyes, and some recited Santana's prayers. I noticed on more than one occasion that their mumbled, whispered, or wailed verses were offered up to more than Saint Santana. The name of another saint, Saint Malsano, also came into their good graces.

Those who'd accepted the new saints didn't trust the Inquisition. They remembered the city's long history, the conflicts, the rigid dogma, and the upheaval of The Burnings. They wanted safety for their families, not the hatreds of firebrands from a distant and almost *foreign* Black Fleet. Benefice Vassini might question the legitimacy of the new saints, but none of those who offered them prayers seemed to have suffered at the hands of the kidnappers. They'd won protection. In contrast, everyone knew that the one person who'd openly denounced them, me, had lost her family.

A circle of space followed my progress down the avenue, it eight paces wide. I think it had been there through Newbank, across the Cassaro and St Marco's, but now it was unmistakable amidst the thickening crowds. Still, with more and more of the city's ugly truths revealed, I was glad to be outcast from it.

I finally reached the square to find it almost full. Well over ten thousand stood across its cobbled expanse, a sea of people extending all the way to the Lord's Residence. More joined the mass every moment, all come to hear the city's fate. A subdued murmur sounded out from the crowd to build over a tense and deepening air.

The Lord's Residence stood festooned with both the long white and yellow and gold-starred ensigns of the Church, and the dour black and navy, with gold star and sword of the Inquisition. Anton and the Benefice were making a point; now they were the lords of the city.

I went forward, wanting to be close enough to hear.

A few Flet guildsmen stood out amongst the masses, recognisable by their guild jackets and caps. They'd be here to listen to the proclamation, the Guild no doubt worried that our people were going to be blamed for the woes of our beleaguered city.

I came to a stop at the centre of the square where my circle of space remained, but even that had shrunk under the crush. I hoped it was small enough to keep me hidden: I wanted to hear the proclamation, not become a distraction from it.

Looking about, I could see many in the crowd holding on to objects of faith; holy symbols, charms, and countless sprigs of oleander. The square was a focus, a divine focus, a focus of yearning and belief.

I glimpsed skyward and let my perception drift into the celestial. The eye remained above, huge and wide, watching and waiting...

But waiting for what?

I feared I knew the answer; the next ritual, the ritual that would see Pedro and Maria slaughtered along with the rest of the Liberigo bloodline. The thought made me shiver, sending my perception back to the real world.

Just in time...

The noise of the crowd began to fade, and at noon the previously empty balcony of the Lord's Residence became full. At the centre stood the Benefice and the Inquisitor, the two flanked by priests, monks, and even some of the Inquisition's feared knights; the Sankto Glavos.

Inquisitor Anton raised his hand in greeting to the crowd, but wasted no time. "Welcome Ossard, welcome to your judgment!"

Ossard had been judged once before...

"For twenty years you have been without your shepherd, the Inquisition. Left untended, you, our most northern flock, surprisingly did quite well, even going on to recapture some of your past glory and wealth. Together you earned it, through your hard work and continued faith, but alas it could not last.

"Amongst you were some who wanted more, those who were jealous of their neighbours, yet too slothful to apply themselves. Instead of working harder, you just watched for an easier way.

"Inevitably, and without your shepherd to watch over you, the wolves that the Inquisition guard against found you, even here in the cool north. The ragged beasts slunk in during the long night that you were without us, them looking to feed and build a dark fort. Before long they met with those from amongst you who were of like minds and desperate for power, and together they struck a deal.

"Your betrayers gained favour by not only selling their own souls, but by agreeing to supply the souls of others - souls not theirs to sell. In return they gained wealth and power, and into their dark conspiracy they recruited others. Soon the city of Merchant Princes became a place of secret cults conducting child-theft and murderous rituals.

"Ossard, the wolves are amongst you! The Council of Merchant Princes has unwittingly let them in, delivering you into unclean fields - fields of heresy littered with the butchered ruins of your own children!

"Why? Because of sloth and greed, and a lust for power! They have cursed this once-great city and endangered your eternal selves!

"Ossard, you were once strong and united, but are now weak and divided as you tremble in fear. Because of the Merchant Princes' failure they have been damned, and if you do nothing to save yourselves, so to will you be!"

I could feel the crowd and its factions. Some listened with hope to the Inquisitor while others listened with deepening contempt.

Those who'd embraced Santana and Malsano seemed to grow only more hostile to the Inquisitor's words, closing their minds and whispering to their like-minded friends. They began shifting towards the back of the square, repulsed by his message.

Others who still clung to the traditional teachings of the Church and accepted the authority of the Benefice and Inquisition stepped forward, drawn towards the promise of salvation. Their minds overflowed with doubt and fear, but here they found hope and a rising sense of elation. It grew stronger with each step they took, encouraging them always on. Some of them began to call out, crying praise and glory, and even taking to singing the Church's holy songs.

My vision slipped into the celestial to witness sparks of light raining down from above. They struck and enriched the souls of the advancing faithful, a glowing rain of blessings from Krienta himself.

Looking about, I could see a similar display of power at the back of the square. Violet blessings raced about like fireflies, weaving through the crowds, striking those already taken by the new saints. That swarm of blessings came from a twisting column of swirling light, a pillar that turned quickly and reached up into the sky.

The two magics were the same, both divine, but of rival sources. Two gods battled here, and I could feel the tension as the real world strained.

What would happen if more gods were attracted to a city of so many lost souls?

And so the crowd split.

The followers of the new saints were drawn away, lured by the swarming blessings visible only in the celestial but felt by those open to them. Their pursuit took them from the square, and the Inquisitor, but they didn't care.

Behind them they left the crowding followers of Krienta, all trying to get closer to the Inquisitor because of their own god's unseen gifts. People cried out in prayer, sang hymns, or just wailed in pious ecstasy.

Ossard would never be the same again.

Inquisitor Anton called out, "The city needs to be reborn! It needs your devotion and your vigilance! It needs to leave behind all those things that have brought it to this terrible point, and be rid of them forever!"

Like parched drunkards they greedily drank of it.

"Today we divest the city of the institutions that have failed her. There is no more Lord of Ossard, no more Council of Merchant Princes," and he sniggered, "as if merchants could be princes! And all that is just the start!"

The crowd cheered.

"We will also do away with the Flet Guild and the Merchants' Guild. The old establishment is not welcome in our new and holy Ossard!"

The cheer of the crowd grew louder.

"In our new city there will be no cultists, cabalists, or witchery, and we will work together to prove our devotion. In a place of pure faith, there will be none to commit the crimes of kidnapping, and any who hold true will enjoy Krienta's protection!"

The crowd roared.

"I hereby proclaim the founding of the *Pious Empire of Ossard*, the first city-state of the Inquisition!"

The noise rose to be deafening.

Anton raised his hands and went on, his voice miraculously clear, "Will you stand with us and save yourselves and your city?"

And in their rapture they cried out that they would.

Above it all came a clarion call, but the players were nowhere to be seen. Their work rang out in notes pure and strong, making their listeners' souls sing.

"The Church will rule your city and work for this crisis to be over. When Ossard is secure, we will then seek out other places of sin that may one day threaten to return the blight!

"We will start a crusade!

"We will seek out heresy!

"And we will establish missions in Fletland and *woeful lost Evora!*"

The shimmering forms of winged angels materialised above him, scores of them, and each played a long golden horn. Robed in white, they smiled with beautiful faces marked by nothing; not age, pox, nor ill form.

The crowd grew louder, many letting tears run free. Most cried out of miracles and offered still more devotion.

The angels finished their clarion call and dove down to glide over the square. They swooped low to lay their hands on the sick, to bless the needy, and to chase away any lingering despair.

How could any doubt the Inquisitor and his declared pious empire? How could any doubt the future when it came heralded by angels?

Those devoted to Krienta poured in from across the city to replace the followers of the new saints as they left.

And amidst it all, in the centre of the crush, I remained alone and forsaken.

Having got what I came for, to know the future of the Inquisition's Ossard, I made to go.

I began to cross the square as one of the angels glided down, unknowingly heading straight for me. At the last moment, he looked up, but then averted his eyes as he set his great wings beating. He still passed above, but at a greater height, and I swear that as he did he shivered.

It reminded me of Anton's words; that the city's factions feared me.

Was I something to fear?

With my anger stewing over my missing daughter and husband, I knew the answer; and it was yes. Deep within me a power stirred, and it was only just beginning.

After leaving the square, and those loyal to the Church, I passed through those who'd given themselves to the new saints. They headed towards the port district to where the razed warehouse had stood, lured by the swirling column of blessings.

I left it all, heading back down the main avenue and towards home.

The future of the city seemed clear: It divided three ways, two powered by gods, the other by a strong sense of community not without its own divine help.

As Anton had said; the city would have to be washed in blood. Now I believed him.

I arrived at my parents' home to be greeted by one of their maids. The young woman failed to stifle a gasp when she opened the door. I could sense it, she was frightened, her mind crying out, "The Forsaken Lady!"

I was surprised to see a fellow Flet so affected. She seemed confused and unsure. I didn't sense that she'd pledged herself to the new saints, perhaps just to the street's gossip.

My mother took her place. "Where've you been, we've been worried?" The maid retreated into the shadows.

I said, "Sorry, is Father back from the Guild?"

"He's in the rose garden."

"Is Sef with him?"

Surprised at the question, she answered, "Yes?"

I nodded and stepped past her.

I found them in the courtyard sitting on the benches by the roses I'd planted almost five years ago. Strangely, as the city slipped towards chaos, the bushes seemed to have decided to bloom.

Father looked pale and his face was grim. "Oh Juvela, are you well?"

"Yes, I'm fine."

He nodded, but kept looking at me to check me over. Finally he said, "I've been talking to the Guild, to Heinz Kurgar, they can't help - not to find Pedro and Maria. They've too much else to worry about."

I nodded.

"I'm sorry Juvela, but they think they're going to be shut down by the Church, so they're preparing to go underground."

Sef watched him, but his eyes just as often darted to me. I realised that his vision focused not on this world, but the next, the celestial. He sat beside my father surveying my soul.

He also had power!

Slipping my perception into the celestial, I couldn't read his emotions or see any telltale glow or spark. If anything, it was his soul's blandness that gave him away. It was a false image, all too ordinary - something he projected to hide his true self.

Could I trust him?

It was Sef...

Of course I could.

I said, "The Inquisitor has declared Ossard the first city-state of a new and pious empire. He has also denounced and ordered the ruin of the Lordship, the Council, and both the Flet and Merchant Guilds as he blames them for the city's demise. He won't help us. He's too busy using this as an opportunity to take power."

My father asked, "That was the proclamation?"

"Yes."

"You were there?"

"Yes, along with tens of thousands of people - and angels! Father, something terrible is coming. The city is divided three ways; the old of St Baimio, those of the new saints, and the Flets. The gods are at war, but it'll be the ordinary people who suffer."

My grandmother's voice hissed, "Not all of us are ordinary!"

Sef looked to me and nodded.

Had he heard?

Father sat quietly, but after consideration asked, "And what of you?"

"What do you mean?"

"Your mother tells me that she gave you your grandmother's book. Can you use it? Will it keep you safe, or will it just see you burnt at the stake by Anton and his ilk as he did her?"

Anton had claimed my grandmother?

He looked me over, sensing something different. "Sweet Juvela, I don't want to lose you, and least of all to the Inquisition."

"I'm changed, it's true, but I'll be safe. I'm more worried about you and Mother."

Shaking his head, he whispered, "Juvela, what's happening?"

In truth I didn't know. I knew bits and pieces, but only a little more than he did. I shrugged. "What of Heinz Kurgar and the Guild?"

"Like I said, he's worried that they'll be shut down."

"It *is* going to be shut down. Does he have a plan?"

"He wants to take the Guild's workings into hiding."

"Father, our people *are* going to be used as scapegoats. We can't let that happen. Don't let Kurgar take the Guild underground, let it stand tall and proud as a symbol of hope. When the trouble starts our people will need something to rally to."

He asked, "What can we do?"

"Gather our people into Newbank, two thirds of our number are already here and most of the rest on the riverbank opposite. We should then take control of the bridge. If we can hold it, we can be safe. Once we've done that the Guild can govern us."

My father spluttered, "You talk of insurrection!"

"Father, the city's already divided. Let the Heletians work out their differences and then we can deal with the victor."

He thought about it, his eyes wandering over the rose garden. "It might work." He looked up to meet my gaze. "Where did you get such wisdom?"

I frowned. "Wise women don't lose their families."

"Don't be so hard on yourself."

Perhaps he was right. "Father, has anything been said about where Pedro and Maria might have been taken?"

"Nothing for certain, only suggestions of the port district. Some of the guildsmen also talked of the Inquisitor's linking of the cults and Santana. They think he's right, but not all agree."

"There's something else you should know."

"What?"

"There's another new saint."

"Another?"

"I heard people speak of a Saint Malsano."

My father shook his head. "How can this be?" He looked about as if even in the privacy of his own courtyard he no longer felt safe.

"We've heard that the followers of Saint Santana want to build a chapel on the ashes of the razed warehouse. They're claiming that it'll purify the ground. It leaves me to wonder; could they actually be trying to build something there to use the ritual's power?"

His words stuck in my mind. Could the cults use whole bloodlines to sanctify such a building, some kind of dark temple? And would that blood be Maria's and Pedro's, or did they need the bloodlines for something else?

I began to feel anxious. I had to get started on my search and go to see the ruined warehouse. "I'm sorry, Father, but I must go. Have the Guild stay open, our people will need it."

He nodded, but was reluctant to see me leave. "Where?"

"To look for Maria and Pedro."

"It's too dangerous. There are people out there who blame *you* for all this."

"Sorry, but I must."

He stood and took a step towards me. "I still can't believe you went to Market Square by yourself." And his gaze moved to Sef, his eyes narrowing in disapproval. "You were lucky not to be arrested!"

"Father, I appreciate your concern, but don't blame Sef. I insisted on going alone. No one touched me. In fact they went out of their way to avoid me. They're scared of me."

He reached out to put his hands on my shoulders, looking me lovingly in the eyes. "Juvela, frightened people can do terrible things. Remember our history; during Def Turtung the Lae Velsanans nearly destroyed our people, and in turn they brought down their own dominion. They didn't do it because of hate, but because of fear. Don't tempt the masses of Ossard, they're more scared of you right now than the Lae Velsanans ever were of us."

He had a point.

While I might feel born anew and could sense my soul stirring with rising power, I was still untested. "You're right, I promise to take greater care, but I do need to search for my family. I can't just sit at home and wait for news of their..." my voice broke, "...slaughter."

He nodded as his strong hands rubbed my shoulders.

I loved him; the care in his eyes and his deep passion for my mother.

He said, "Take Sef with you, we all know he can help."

"I will, and I'll be careful."

"Juvela, to lose you would be to lose half my world. Please take care, for I think the city has already lost its way."

I shook my head, refusing to accept such a thing.

"It's true, just look at it! As you said, Ossard is split three ways, and two will align against the other, and those alliances will shift. We will all suffer. There'll be mobs and riots, and lynchings and lootings. The only thing missing will be justice." He shook his head as he pictured the tragedy to come. "I can live with the city falling into chaos if I have to, but I can't live if it takes you and your mother."

I hugged him, my voice muffled by his shirt, "I'll be careful."

He opened the embrace, taking a step back to look at me. Pride filled his eyes as he smiled, and with that brightening his worries faded.

I nodded and turned to leave.

Sef thanked my father and moved to follow.

"Juvela, please wait!" It was my mother. She was standing at the door to the house from where she tried to bravely smile - but faltered.

My poor mother...

My heart ached to see her try and support me, but at the same time be so crippled by her fears. I offered, "It's alright, I'm learning so much and so quickly, and the more I know the safer I'll be."

Her eyes sparkled with gathering tears. "Your grandmother knew a lot more, but she wasn't safe. They still came for her..."

I hurried to her, throwing my arms about her. "Mother, please..."

"No, you have to hear it!" she insisted, choking back her tears. "They came for her in the middle of the night, beating her senseless in her own bed. They drugged her to stop her from casting, and then dragged her away." She looked at me with wide eyes. "Despite all her power they still got her. Do you hear me? She didn't even get a chance to scratch them!" She was digging her fingers into me.

"They tortured her for days until they finally judged her. Once damned by the Inquisitor they tied her unconscious and naked to a stake in Market Square, and she wasn't alone." My mother relaxed her grip. "Oh Juvela, forty eight others joined her, them all roused with smelling salts just in time for their burning."

I rocked her in my arms. "It's alright."

She pulled back from me as she wiped at her tears. "They made me watch! They held me at the front of the crowd and made me watch as they burnt her alive, and I still have nightmares about it!"

I couldn't help but shiver.

She went on, "I've learnt to live with them, but I couldn't live with having to watch you suffer the same fate. You have to be careful. Don't put all your faith in your power, put some in Schoperde as well!"

I nodded.

She said, "*He* sought her out, *he* can smell witches."

"Anton?"

She gave a nod, and then paused to take a deep breath as my father stepped up beside her. With a calmer voice, she said, "It was the worst day of my life, but also the best; it was where I met your father. Without him and his family I'd have been destitute," and worry and love rode in her words together.

Standing there, I realised this was a day she'd long feared would come, and now that it was here she was drawing upon all her reserves to push through.

She smiled. "Juvela, you're revealed now, yet I imagine you've much to learn. Please, just be careful."

She was right. The book had done little for me in the ways of using my power, yet I still felt confident I'd master it.

My mother's smile broadened, but it came tinged with sadness.

Thinking that she was still burdened with her worry, I said, "I'll be careful, I mean it. I won't go anywhere without Sef."

She nodded and said, "You look so much like your grandmother." I smiled, but she went on, "It's almost like she's back from the grave."

And laughter rang out from the celestial.

12

Rising Smoke

The afternoon warmed, and with it came a slow but determined breeze. It arrived carrying Ossard's usual stink, but today its blustering breath also delivered a new and bitter aroma; of burning.

Half a dozen columns of smoke rose from the heart of the city, climbing to feed a growing haze. They seemed anchored around Market Square. Not long after some of the Flets living in the wider city began crossing the river to seek the safety of Newbank.

Behind them came a chorus of distant cries and yells. The arrivals spoke of riots at the heart of the city, all saying the same thing; the Heletians were fighting amongst themselves.

Some of the followers of the new saints had forced their way into the Cathedral taking armfuls of oleander and relics with which to build a shrine. They were challenged by Vassini's priests and told to leave. They'd refused and argued, and then been forcibly expelled. Dragged from the Cathedral and hurled down its front steps, scuffles broke out as a mob gathered. Some died in the fighting that followed, failing to establish a shrine, but giving their fellow believers something as powerful; martyrs.

Worse would come, I was sure of it.

Sef and I left my parents' home, passing through streets abuzz with news and rumours from across the river. We headed to my own household barely a few hundred paces from where I'd grown up. Both homes were in the good part of Newbank, a small elevated area without the chronic overcrowding that marked the rest of the low-lying district.

I noticed, as we walked, that even here some people kept their distance or stared at me. The city might be divided three ways, but it seemed it could still breakup further. The realisation left me wary.

If they thought I was forsaken, then they were most likely followers of the new saints or somehow aligned.

Flet followers of the new saints?

My pace quickened as I waved Sef up to my side.

"Yes?"

"I need you to be honest with me."

"Of course," he said, but his tone was guarded.

"You've been to Fletland and survived its battles."

"Yes?"

"You've also seen its many faiths."

"Yes?" and his voice grew tight.

"I need you to tell me about them."

"What do you want to know?"

"It's the cults that I need to know more of."

He merely grumbled, "Hmmm?"

I whispered my question, "The cults of the Horned God; I've heard that they come in many different forms, but all follow the same power?"

Sounding relieved, he said, "Yes, but you need to understand that while they follow the same power, they're aligned to different aspects. That's what I've heard and on occasion even seen." And his eyes clouded over to be darkened by grim memories.

"So in my understanding, it's not unusual to find followers of the same form or aspect that are knowingly worshipping the same god, but *also* using different names?"

He nodded. "Yes, despite how confusing it sounds. Generally the larger cults have gained some uniformity in their rituals and terminology, but there are always splinter groups. For example, some may follow Rabisto the god of bandits, while another group may owe allegiance to Tabiro the god of thieves, and yet another to Ranndolf of the footpads. In the end they're all following the same god and similar aspects despite their differences."

I asked, "And their dark lord doesn't get angry about such a thing?"

"About them getting his name wrong?" He smiled and shrugged. "Apparently not. In the end only one thing matters; their souls *and* his true name."

"His true name?"

"His true name is the only name that holds any real power over him."

I smiled, realising my next question was unlikely to get an answer, but asked it anyway, "And that is?"

He grinned, "A well guarded secret!"

We both laughed, relieving some of the afternoon's tension.

When we'd settled down, I asked, "So, do you think it's possible that these two new saints, Santana and Malsano, might just be different names for different faces of the Horned God?"

"It's possible. You know Santana is similar to the Southern Heletian word for blood."

I stopped and met his eyes. "What, Sanjo?"

"No, the word from the southern cities, in Vangre and the like."

"What word?"

"Sanjana."

"I suppose it is." To have my theory supported sent a chill down my spine, but it wasn't solid proof. "Alright, but what of Malsano?"

"Malsano, well, I don't know..."

I shrugged. "Well, I guess that would have been too easy."

"Well, maybe it is."

"What do you mean?"

"Well, Malsano is obviously a Heletian name, it rolls and is soft, coming with long and rich sounds."

"So?"

"Well, you're never going to find a Flet word that sounds the same. Our words are short and sharp, some might even say harsh."

"It doesn't have to be a Flet word."

"I know, but there's an aspect of the Horned God in Fletland known as Malssarcht."

"Malssarcht? I've not heard of him?"

"A bringer of disease, one you might invite to visit your enemies."

Such a horrid thought had never occurred to me.

He went on, "I'd have thought that you'd know him in Ossard; Malssarcht, the night angel?"

"Why?"

"Because of Maro fever."

"You mean the dark angel, Tykarcht."

"Yes, well, there you have it."

"This is only making me feel worse about things."

151

He laughed, but his face was grim. "So, Santana might be some kind of blood power and Malsano just another name for Tykarcht - perhaps." He frowned. "You might be right, and the Inquisition must be aware of it too."

"I'm sure they'd know."

By now we stood only steps away from home.

"Juvela, do you still want to go to the warehouse?"

I nodded. "I have to. I need to look into anything that might give me an idea of where Pedro and Maria might be. I can't stay home and wait."

He turned for the door as he pulled out his key. "I'll see to Kurt and the coach. It won't be safe for us to do this, but if we must, let's do it now while we still have light. I don't want to get caught on the other side of the river after dark, not tonight."

I didn't have a good plan, I'm not even sure that you'd say I had a plan at all, but I knew I had to go and check the ruined warehouse. I reasoned, if a chapel was going to be built there, then perhaps my family was being kept nearby.

In truth, my only real hope was that I'd be able to hear Maria's mind voice. If I couldn't, I didn't know what I was going to do.

We set out in the coach. Sef was watching me, but I ignored him as I lost myself in the rolling drum of the coach's wheels. There was peace in that repetitive rumble. After a while I couldn't help but notice something else, and it was wondrous, a subtle but almost overwhelming power. It radiated like heat from a failing bonfire as if made of a million glowing embers. Individually they could barely be sensed, but together they combined to give off something incredible: It was the gathered life force of the city-state's people.

A million souls from the city and surrounding valleys!

It was a revelation.

I shook my head to stop myself as I tried to settle my thoughts. I had to focus on Maria and Pedro, if I kept losing myself to these distracting discoveries I'd never find them.

I forced my attention back to the window and the real world outside.

We'd reached the Cassaro Bridge and were crossing out of Newbank. It ran full of traffic, most of it Flets leaving the Heletian districts of the city.

Sef broke the silence. "Are you alright?"

I turned to him as my vision slipped between two worlds, both in the real and the celestial. "I'm well, but you..."

His eyebrows raised as my words trailed off.

He asked, "Yes?"

"You have your own loyalties?"

He leaned forward. "Only to our own people's gods, nothing more." Then he sighed and straightened his back. "At the moment, with the Inquisition taking over the city, the less we know about each other's business the better."

I raised an eyebrow.

"Juvela, you can trust me. I'll make any vow before all the gods, that's if all my years of service aren't enough."

I nodded, feeling bad that I'd pushed him on his loyalty, and so clumsily. "I trust you, Sef. I'm sorry."

We passed through streets filled with confusion and a growing haze of smoke. The sound of trouble rumbled in the distance, coming from the direction of Market Square at the city's heart. Behind us in Newbank, the Guild raised a red flag atop the Guildhall - the flag of assembly.

I hoped Kurgar wouldn't announce the Guild's closure. If the Guild went underground, it would only leave our people lost. Right now we needed leadership, not to be left directionless.

Outnumbered, we wouldn't stand a chance if forced to fight. And in such bloody times, it wouldn't take the Inquisition long to discover easier ways to get rid of us than shipping us back to Fletland. To survive we had to stand together, and the Guild had always provided our leadership.

Such thoughts led me back to Kurgar; I hoped he knew what he was doing. Only days ago, Lord Liberigo had thought he controlled the city, but now he was kidnapped and perhaps even dead.

I closed my eyes and whispered a prayer, "Please Schoperde, let us get through this."

As always, she didn't answer.

Our ride to the charred ruins of the warehouse took a long and winding path. The streets on the way lay almost abandoned, until we reached the southern district where they spread thick with crowds. Many were taking part in open-air services dedicated to the new saints. Oleander hung from doors, wreathed windows, and sat in braziers where it smouldered to free smoke in wisps of grey. The area, home to much of Ossard's Heletian poor, seemed to be a stronghold for the new saints.

The streets about us seemed peaceful enough, if full, but the people we passed in our unflagged coach held the energy of those who'd found new faith. None of them subscribed to Inquisitor Anton's pious empire, they looked to have another answer in mind.

Taking in the sight, I could only doubt the Church's chances of controlling the city. Without the port, south, east, and Newbank, they held only a fraction of what they needed. Eventually, one way or another, the city would again be united, but I doubted it would be under the black, navy, and gold of the Inquisition.

I hid my face as best I could in the carriage, keeping back to the shadows. I hoped we'd be able to look for Pedro and Maria, and then get out without commotion. Watching the crowd, so many with the sparkle of newly devoted eyes, I began to wonder at our chances. "Sef, look at this place, at these people, have you ever seen such a thing?"

He turned from the window, his gaze cold and hard. "Yes," he hissed, his neck corded and his fists bunched. "I've seen it before. It haunts the battle-scarred plains of Fletland where packs of those who follow the gods of thieves, murderers, and whores roam that wasted land." He took a deep breath and shivered, battling memories that threatened to overwhelm him.

"Sef, are you alright?"

He nodded, but it was a lie. "They've been given something, something divine, and they'll find euphoria in it, but before long its buzz will fade, leaving them hungering again for its high. The longer they have to wait for it, the more desperate they'll become. Eventually, they won't be able to stand that deep hunger, so they'll do anything to sate it. Once dependent on it, the blessings, the dark power that bestows them will start to make demands. In time, it will not only enslave them, but drive them mad." He shook his head, something that freed tears. "Yes Juvela, I've seen it before."

I felt for him. I'd grown up on his tales, some of them terrible indeed, but I'd never stopped to consider that he'd lived through them. Leaning forward, I put a hand over one of his fists. "I'm sorry to stir such memories, but I need to know what I must. Please, tell me?"

With an awkward move, he raised a fist to wipe clumsily at his eyes. "They've been seduced by the cults. Having seen this, I'm convinced that all this is nothing but a front for the Horned God. As they always do, they'll be working to conduct a *soul harvest*, for they're after only one thing; power."

I turned back to look at the crowds. Some offered prayers at makeshift shrines, while others paraded in packs waving oleander and banners.

I asked, "Is it that definite a path? Is it that certain an end?"

He nodded. "It always is. Look, Juvela, I've many enemies here, just as *you* do. We'll work together, and we'll stand together, because it's the only way we'll get through this."

I swallowed nervously. "How do you know?"

"I've seen it before, but never on this scale. I've seen hamlets and villages fall to the coming madness, and even once a whole town. The city can't avoid it. No one ever has." He paused, turning back to the chanting crowds. "By the time you can see the sickness it's already too late. And it is a sickness, like a plague, but not of the mind or body, but of the spirit."

I trusted Sef, I'd always trusted him. To see him grow so tense and upset sobered me. What could *I* hope to do about what grew outside? I still remained a user of magic who'd never cast a spell.

It seemed hopeless.

We reached the ruins of the warehouse to find a large crowd listening to a Heletite missionary. The robed man spoke from a small stage, talking of corruption and politics in a church rotten with greed. He spoke of the righteous power of true-faith, and how that bypassed fat benefices and their hypocritical entourages. He urged the crowd to never doubt the new saints, naming three; Santana, Malsano, and Rabisto.

Rabisto!

What was wrong with these people? Rabisto was well known amongst the Flets as a god of bandits, a forbidden *Heletian* god. The crowd seemed oblivious.

As if in answer to my thoughts, the Heletite emphasised that this new saint was not of crime or trouble, but a jolly-maker and the keeper of comfort. He explained that the politics of the Church had seen the truth hidden by vested interests directing the Calbaro's scholars.

The Heletite called, "Embrace Rabisto and he will embrace you! He offers comfort to those who need it, and who could need it more than the parents of stolen children!"

A woman cried out in answer, "I'm in need of comfort!" With greying hair and a tired frame, she stumbled forward as though life had thrown her too many challenges.

The crowd parted.

"My child's been taken by the kidnappers, and only a season after the sea left me widowed! Look at me and my years, I'm dry and barren, and nothing any man would wed. Without my husband and son I'm destitute, but still I'm in need of comfort."

The Heletite urged her forward.

She stepped up onto the makeshift stage.

He asked, "And why have you come here seeking comfort, my lady?"

"Because there's none to be found elsewhere. I've looked across the city, and even begged at the foot of the Cathedral, yet the only attention the Church has given me is to push me off their steps."

The Heletite said, "Are you coming forward to ask for the help of Saint Rabisto?"

"I've asked everywhere else, so I see no harm in it..." her voice broke with grief, "if it's not to be granted, I'll only go to *The Graves* and cast my bones into the sea."

The Heletite pulled an amulet from his pocket, it crafted as a small arrow hanging on a slender leather thong. "Kneel and put this around your neck, kiss it, and pray for his intervention in your sad and sorry life. If you open your heart to him, he will hear you."

She took the amulet, knelt, and hung it about her neck. She then lifted the golden arrow to her lips and kissed it with the resignation of one all but spent.

The crowd fell silent.

The hag let the amulet drop to rest against her worn tunic, it sitting in the valley between her sagging breasts. Her head bent forward, her eyes closed, and then she clasped her hands together in prayer. She mumbled through something of her own making, the words unclear, but the intent deep.

Silence took the moment, only disturbed when the Heletite called, "Aid this poor woman, aid her good people, aid her please!"

And many in the crowd also bowed their heads.

It was working...

I could sense the energy building, the rise in power as Rabisto stirred. She'd kissed his amulet and he'd chosen to kiss her in return.

Sef and I swapped glances – he could feel it too.

In the celestial, the eye above the city watched, and as it did a single tear formed within it to drop free. It glowed like a lit crystal, but in the real world remained unseen. It came towards us falling faster and faster.

The seed of a miracle...

It landed in the street behind the gathering.

At the same instant, the sky erupted with the chorus of a sea gull flock, they'd come from nowhere to break the silence, and then as quickly moved on.

Nervous laughter peppered the crowd.

And then, above it all, a weak voice cried, "Help!"

The crowd turned towards the sound.

The Heletite smiled.

The old woman clutched the amulet tightly as she got to her feet, her eyes sparkling with hope.

Where the divine tear had landed lay an iron grate.

None in the crowd moved.

And then the manhole cap, a grill of bars, rose up and slid free.

A dirt-stained boy struggled weakly to lift himself out of the sewer as he gasped, "Help me! Help me please!"

Some of the crowd rushed forward and grabbed for him before he could slip back down.

His mother's eyes flooded with tears as she croaked, "Stefan?"

The boy's head jerked up. "Mama!"

She called out with joy, "Stefan! Oh sweet Rabisto, thank you!" And she hurried from the stage towards him.

Stefan lurched forward on unsteady legs, until they came together in a tear-filled embrace.

The crowd cheered, while above it all the Heletite cried, "Witness the compassion of Saint Rabisto, the bringer of comfort!"

I looked to Sef.

He asked, "Was that staged?"

I shrugged. "Not by the woman."

He shook his head in disbelief, yet still managed to balance his surprise with a practical suggestion. "This'll be a good time for us to look around, while they're distracted." He reached over and passed me a plain robe. "Put this on with its hood up to hide your blonde hair. Hopefully they won't recognise you, but if they do let's be ready to get back to the coach and out of here."

"Yes."

Sef opened the door and jumped down to the cobbles, using the coach to hide us from the crowd. He helped me down and said to Kurt, "Wait for a while. When we're well on our way, I want you to go over by those buildings and keep an eye on us. Watch me for signals, and the crowd for trouble, otherwise meet us when we reach the other side."

Kurt nodded, but looked nervous. He'd only served my household for a season, and by the look of him I wondered if he'd still be in my pay by dusk.

I turned to face the warehouse's ruin, a black and grey wasted mess. Taking a deep breath, I took my first step.

Sef whispered, "We must be quick, the crowd will grow with news of the boy's return."

He was right.

Not long after, as we made our way into the charred ruin, Kurt moved the coach to where Sef had instructed. While I concentrated on the search, I could see Sef glancing back. He whispered, "Already some watch us."

I wasn't sure if I'd be recognised, but as the Forsaken Lady I seemed as well known as the Benefice or poor Lord Liberigo. Still, there was nothing for it, but to try and do what we'd come here to do.

Step after step, nothing much remained. What had once been a sprawling warehouse, and the site of powerful ritual magic, now lay as a field of charred posts, charcoal, and ash.

Up ahead, a cluster of shoulder-high lumps rose blackened and lopsided – the remains of the ritual's victims.

Approaching them chilled me even though they'd lost all their features. Now they loomed like a set of fire-scorched monoliths.

The wind picked up, the gust lifting the ash as a fine dark haze. Amidst its bluster, I could hear the moans of the dead coming from the celestial to haunt this terrible place.

My steps became slower and my breathing deeper, but I continued on as I neared the mounds. On reaching the nearest, I saw that just past it opened the great hole that sank down into the blackened ground. It lay between the three monoliths, yawning wide and now plugged with rubble and ruin.

Sef followed, but slowed. He had no wish to come any closer.

I took a few more steps, absorbing the bleak and soot-covered scene.

What a waste...

Coming to a stop, I braced myself, and then let my vision drift into the celestial.

The bright sparks of energy that had flared here two nights before as the ritual's residue were now gone. I looked closer to find that something subtler remained.

Shadows hung about me in that other world. Dark and insubstantial, they seemed lost and incomplete. They didn't react to me, or each other, instead they just moved about senselessly.

They were something left over from the victims, perhaps their last gasps or thoughts. Sadly there was so little left that these *Shades* had no sense, no knowing, and certainly no chance at rebirth.

They were chilling, so much so that I had to pull away. With relief I returned my perception to the real world.

What power had been unleashed here?

Back in the real world, most of their bodies were also gone, taken by the ravages of the fire. The macabre towers in front of me were barely distinguishable from the slumped piles of charred timber that had been packed about their ruined forms. It was sickening.

I tried to sense if anything of interest lay nearby. It seemed like a good idea, but my mind became stabbed in a thousand places by the feelings, thoughts, and other sensations emanating from the crowd. The overwhelming force of it saw me stumble.

Sef asked, "Are you alright?"

"Yes," I said as I gathered myself.

He nodded and turned back to check on the crowd.

Shaken as I was, I noticed sweat on his face and that he'd paled. "Sef, are *you* well?"

He turned to me and said, "I'll manage, but it's so uncomfortable." After a moment, he added, "Can't you feel it?"

"Yes," I said, but answered too quickly. I wasn't exactly sure what he meant – there was just so much to take in.

He realised. "Look at the ground, at the *focus!*"

My gaze fell down to the ash at our feet.

Dust rose from the charred soil, black and grey, it drifting across my boots to pass by. I followed a particular wisp of it as it climbed and tumbled, and after a moment realised that it wasn't following a straight line. It travelled slowly along the edge of a circle, a wide circle, and that circle centred on the heart of the ritual.

I asked, "What is it?"

Sef was checking on the crowd. "I was hoping you'd know."

Me?

He went on, "My guess is that it's the seed of something, the seed of the ritual, perhaps the seed of power for all their rituals to come."

I hated this, it all being such a mystery. Everybody else seemed to know so much more about what was going on.

I tried to settle down and focus myself. More than anything I'd come here looking for something that might indicate where Maria and Pedro were being held. That's what I needed to worry about, nothing else.

Again I opened up to the celestial, but this time I listened specifically for Maria. I couldn't be sure, but seeing as I hadn't heard from her since her kidnapping, I assumed that my talent for it was quite limited. If she was close, maybe I'd hear something. For long moments I stood there, my perception half in the celestial world and half in the real.

Nothing...

I kept trying, listening, and sensing.

Nothing...

Searching and seeking, desperately straining.

Nothing...

Sef's voice made me jump, "We should go."

I followed his gaze; a growing number of the crowd were watching us. I nodded. Sef signalled to Kurt, and he in turn started to take the coach around to the far side of the ruin.

Sef said, "Don't look back. Let's just get moving and keep at a steady pace. If we don't look nervous and don't rush, perhaps we can get away before any of them think to stop us."

I said, "Last time I looked, they seemed to be ignoring us."

"That was a long time ago. The birds have stirred them since then."

Birds?

I looked to the west where the sun had noticeably dropped. "What birds, what do you mean?"

Sef took hold of my arm and steered me forward. "Keep walking, I'll watch your footing, but look up."

I did.

A huge flock of gulls circled above. From their numbers, an endless stream of lone birds dove down towards us as if pointing. They'd pull up suddenly as they neared us, and then head back to rejoin the flock.

We were being marked.

Taking in the sight, I tilted my head further back, the movement freeing my robe's hood to fall away.

Behind us, voices hissed, "The Forsaken Lady!"

The call was repeated as we neared the coach, Sef forcing me forward faster and faster.

He whispered, "You get in, I'll ride with Kurt in case they try and climb aboard."

I nodded while my mind raced; could I do something, some kind of witchery that might help stop the pursuit?

Footfalls sounded only strides away.

Sef's other hand dropped to the hilt of his sword. "They'll try and stop us," he whispered.

Our coach was close, only a dozen paces ahead. I watched as Kurt slowly reached for his own weapon.

I wanted to run, but Sef hissed. He knew any sudden move would bring them onto us.

Kurt sat with his eyes on us, his look indifferent. He refused to look at the mob, but it was clear there were many of them, and the growing murmur of their voices only confirmed it.

With a few paces left, Sef whispered, "I'm going to push you forward, don't stumble, just get in the coach and out of my sword's way."

"Yes," I answered with a dry throat as I cursed my own mind's emptiness. Surely there was something I could do to help? Where was my damn witchery?

The push came and I literally flew, landing hard against the coach door. Behind me, I heard Sef's sword ring as it slid free of its scabbard.

I jumped onto the step, got inside, and then turned about to check on Sef. He stood there with his sword out, the blade held high and ready.

In front of him, a crowd spread several deep, with more crossing the charred ruin. Someone yelled, "Forsaken whore, you'll damn us all!"

I growled, "Leave or I *will* damn you!"

The noise of the mob died.

I held my face firm and tried to look dangerous.

The mob glared back, but none of them moved.

Sef reached behind him with his free hand to grab at the coach's railing. All the while he swung his sword back and forth, and then yelled, "Kurt, go man, go!"

Our driver didn't need encouragement.

Sef jumped up for the coach's step while holding onto the rail.

We lurched forward and sped up to leave the crowd behind. They yelled their curses, some of them picking up half-burnt timber from amidst the ruin to hurl after us.

Sef slid inside and then closed the door. He opened the front port and said to Kurt, "Take us back to Newbank, but keep away from crowds."

He didn't need to be told.

The ride home should have been fast and uneventful - it wasn't. Kurt planned on skirting the heart of the city by heading for the docks and using lesser streets, that way he would follow the river and get us back to Newbank.

The port's streets were strangely quiet, and the docks almost abandoned. It became clear why when we looked back over the city.

In several places towards Market Square, great columns of oily black smoke arose. As we studied the soot-dusting plumes, we noticed more of them further back, and about those twisting pillars many lesser but similar trails off to their western side.

Sef said, "The riots are getting worse."

Kurt brought the coach to a stop and then slid open the front port. "There's a second group of fires further back," he paused before adding, "I think it's Newbank."

I had a terrible feeling he was right.

Did the Guild still stand?

I'd never felt myself to be a person ruled by overly strong feelings for my people, but at that point, with my mind filling with memories of our dark past, of a history of murders, massacres, and genocide, a sense of duty stirred in my breast. Its depth surprised me. If my people were in trouble, I needed to help them. On top of that, I still had to try and find my family. Could I do both?

Damn it, I'd try!

And in that moment, the power within me began to stir. Spirits gathered around my soul, I could feel them, and amongst them was my haunting grandmother.

In my mind, I screamed at her with frustration, "Show me what to do!"

She didn't answer.

My perception slid into the next world, and for the first time I saw her: She appeared stark against that dark void, all painted in the bright hues of celestial blue. In some ways her pale face was like my mother's, but her eyes were nothing but deep pools of sorrow. Long hair blew wildly about her, it moving quickly as if caught in a rugged gale; that lively action was matched by her billowing dress, the motion, on one so dead, gave her a strange sense of the vital.

She was searching my soul, her own face plagued by frustration.

It was then that I realised her dress was woven of flame and smoke, her whole spirit defined by her fiery death.

And all the while my power stirred, growing restless, yet somehow trapped.

What was wrong?

Back in the real world, Sef's voice grabbed my attention, "Juvela, where do you want us to go?"

It dragged my perception back. "If Newbank's under siege, we have to help."

He growled at Kurt, "Go man, get us to Newbank!"

Kurt yelled at the horses, striking them as he sent us speeding home.

13

Fires at Sunset

The sun had begun to set behind us, tinting the sky a fiery orange and making the thick columns of smoke all the more ominous as they took on the tones of red. The very air seemed to glow, the sun's last rays catching the haze and ash to give it a golden edge.

Our coach charged along as if out of control, but Kurt somehow managed it. He yelled for people to clear the way as he dared people to dither, the crack of his whip offering encouragement.

While the streets surrounding the port had stood mostly empty, they became crowded closer to the river forcing us back near Market Square. Kurt slowed, having to pick his way more carefully.

We turned near the rear of the Cathedral to miss the worst of the crowds, and from there took another street that came into the bottom corner of the square. Kurt took us along its edge, its centre full of people cheering at a fire where smoke billowed to rise.

My grandmother's spectral voice howled, "No!" and around her climbed a maddening chorus. She commanded, "Go there, seek him, kill him!"

Her intensity shocked me.

She growled, her words striking like blows, "He's doing it again!" and demanded, "Stop him!"

I began reaching for the sliding panel to instruct Kurt, but Sef grabbed at my hands. His grip was firm and tight, he'd never held me like that before. Leaning forward to meet me face to face, he hissed, "No, he'll kill you!"

Had he heard her?

I whispered, my voice weak, "She wants to…"

"I know she does, but you must fight!"

"She's so strong. She wants me to, all of them do."

"Yes, but it'll cost you your life!"

I gasped, "Not if she can strike him…"

He called out, "Kurt, get us away from here!" Then he turned his attention back to me. "She *will* kill him, but in the process she'll possess you to do it. Once back in flesh, she won't relinquish it!"

Tears crept from my eyes. "I can hear the fire and feel its heat!" And I could, the searing burn of it licked hotly at my feet.

He called out to Kurt, "Faster!"

The coach turned and launched into speed. The movement threw us to the side, leaving us staring into the heart of the crowd and a distant bonfire.

Sef cursed, "Damn it, Kurt, move or I'll have your balls!"

I gasped as I stared into the hungry flames. Amidst their yellow glow stood three stakes, each with a charred form slumping from it.

The voices within me howled, my grandmother's calling, "Damn you, take me to him!"

The Inquisitor had been busy.

Sweat ran from my brow and down my trembling arms, yet Sef's grip held firm. He gave me an anchor from which to drive back her rage. Gritting my teeth, I gathered my will and closed myself to her anger. At the same time, and working to my advantage, each moment saw the coach move further away.

Sef hissed, "Fight them, Juvela! Fight them for Pedro and Maria!"

And I did, forcing them back while whispering that there'd be another time for vengeance - a better time.

Finally, they relented.

I sighed with relief, conscious of my body's tenseness and dampness after washing itself in sweat. I gave a nod that saw Sef relax his grip.

Breathing heavily, I said, "We haven't even got to the bigger fires, I dread to think what's happening there."

He shrugged. "We'll see soon enough. Are you sure you're alright?"

I nodded and leaned back into my seat.

We turned out of the square, slowing for the corner as we passed the city's old opera house. Then it happened, coming out of nowhere, a whisper cutting through my mind and straight into my heart, "Mama!"

I screamed, "Stop!" and lunged for the door. The energy that had spent a lifetime building within me surged and bucked.

Sef tried to stop me, but as I opened the door and stepped out of the slowing coach, I gasped, "Maria's here!" He froze in shock.

I hit the cobbles hard, but somehow managed to keep my feet. Around me people stared, wondering who this mad woman was who'd stepped from a moving coach. Then they knew. I heard it whispered on dozens of tongues and in a hundred minds, "The Forsaken Lady!"

Kurt stopped the coach nearby.

Sef called out to him, "Wait." He jumped down to run across and join me. "What is it?"

"Maria's here!"

A crowd began to gather.

Sef glared at them to keep them back, but it didn't hush their minds.

The Forsaken Lady!

Sef asked, "Where?"

With frustration, I said, "I don't know!"

Already part of my perception dove through the celestial calling out her name. Searching alongside my soul were others, including my grandmother - this time helping.

Into the celestial I called, "Maria!"

Only silence met me, not even a taste.

Sef, worried about the gathering crowd, asked again, "Where?"

The air swirled about us, dragging the smoke of the bonfires low and bringing with it the stench of burning meat.

I shook my head while again calling into the celestial, "Maria?"

Silence.

Tears came to me. A great flood of bloody things that trickled down my face as though my heart had broken to release its store.

The crowd gasped and fell back.

I could also see Sef's pain; his eyes wide and ready to shed his own grief. How could I have ever doubted him? Despite his own secrets, he remained, as he always had been, loyal.

I fell to my knees, landing hard on the cobbles. It hurt, but the pain was nothing compared to the celestial's quiet.

I screamed again into that strange black and blue world, "Maria!"

Silence.

"Maria, I love you!"

Nothing.

Sef looked down at me with sorrow-filled eyes, but I barely noticed. Every ounce of my being listened in the celestial, waiting and sensing for some sign of my daughter's life.

It didn't come.

With hands bloody from wiping at my tears, I reached out to lean on the cobbles in front of me. So close to finding her, yet having failed, I could feel the gorge rising within; I was going to be sick.

As my bloodstained fingers touched the cobbles, the font of power within my soul sparked. The air around me chilled and crackled, taking on a metallic stink, and then my senses in both worlds were blinded as I released a ring of power. It rushed out from me to roll away.

Sef gasped as the crowd fell back, but the best part cut through it like love into loneliness – it was her celestial voice, "Mama?"

"Maria! Where are you?"

"Mama!"

"Maria, I'm just off the square. Where are you?"

"I don't know, but it's dark and damp. I think I'm in a cellar."

"Is Father there?"

"Father's here and others, but they can't talk. They're asleep."

I looked to Sef. "I've got her. She's nearby, maybe in a cellar."

He looked around us only to turn back confused. "How close does she have to be to hear you?"

"Not too far, the link isn't that strong." But I wondered; why couldn't I see her soul?

Sef nodded. "Well, she's either in a cellar of one of the shops behind you or in the opera house."

We both looked to the imposing building. Somehow it seemed right that she'd be in there, it'd been closed for a while and was big enough to keep a large group in. I started to get to my feet, but the link with Maria broke as soon as I lifted my hands from the bloody stones.

After worrying about her for so long, to have the link cut so abruptly saw me throw myself back down. Straight away I could feel her.

Sef whispered, "Juvela, the crowds, we should come back later."

I looked about. People were again gathering close, and behind them climbed the smoke of the bonfire. Having denounced the new saints, I was of no further use to Anton. He'd have me burnt, after all, in *his* Ossard I was part of the problem.

Sef grew nervous as the crowd thickened. "If the Inquisitor hears that you're here, there'll be no hope for any of us. Let's come back tonight and I'll bring some *friends*." As he spoke he opened his shirt to expose a metal symbol hanging on a leather thong.

It rested on his broad and battle-scarred chest, shining as it caught the light. It was a sword held within a circle; the holy symbol of Kave.

If I returned with such a group we'd have a real chance. Right now, by ourselves, we didn't. I sighed but nodded, and then sent a thought of love to my daughter. "We have to go. Maria, but I love you, and will be back for you tonight. Can you be brave and wait?"

She was frightened. "Mama, do you have to go?"

"I do, but I'll be back soon."

"Mama?"

"Be brave, be brave for me and your father. You have to watch over him until I come back, alright?"

"Alright."

"I love you, Maria."

She giggled.

Reluctantly, I lifted my bloody palms from the cobbles, and walked back to the coach. Tears blurred my vision, a mix both red and clear.

Sef was quick to follow as he ordered Kurt, "On to Newbank!"

Kurt forced the horses through the crowd, getting us back on our way.

Kurt called out a warning, and a moment later the coach slid as we took a sharp turn. The air stank of burning as smoke billowed hotly past my window. We'd taken a side street to get off the avenue, and I could see why as I glimpsed a Heletian mob pelting a row of burning buildings: It was a block of homes and businesses, all Flet owned.

Kurt called, "We'll be in Newbank soon if the roads are clear!"

Sef grumbled, "The city's going to the Pits!"

I said, "We'll get through the night and see how things stand in the morning." But even I wasn't listening to my words, my mind focused on Maria and Pedro, and the feeling of desolation consuming me after leaving them.

Kurt took us around more tight bends, and dodged other crowds, before finally turning a corner to come within sight of the bridge across the Cassaro. He cursed loudly as he brought the horses to a stop.

Over the river, Newbank spread under a pall of smoke. A dozen fires dotted the district, the biggest flaring from the city-end of the bridge where flames ate hungrily at its old timbers. Between it and us spread a mob of Heletians praying for the flames to spread.

Sef said, "We have to get away from this."

I nodded.

Kurt slid open the port and suggested, "If the city gates are still open, we can get out and head up the valley to cross the river at the old Goldston bridge."

The round trip would take most of the evening, but we didn't have much of a choice. "Do it," I said, and Sef agreed.

By the last light of dusk, we passed through unmanned gates and up the valley road, heading for the ancient bridge.

For most of the trip I watched Ossard recede behind us. The city was lit in several places by the glow of fire, and above it all climbed great plumes of smoke. The terrible columns twisted as they rose, catching the garish glare of the fires' orange light.

The city was dying...

It would be hard to get back to Maria and Pedro without the Cassaro Bridge, but not impossible. Regardless, I'd have to try.

14

Newbank at Night

A cold wind blew in from the sea to blast smoke up the valley and fill our approach. It haunted the scene with an aura of fire-lit haze, the stinking exhalation rushing up and over the city's wall aglow in orange, red and yellow. Through it loomed the dark silhouettes of a handful of towers, one itself ablaze. It looked like the end of all things, and I could only guess at what horror unfolded beyond in the fire-ravaged streets of my home district.

We followed the road up to the gatehouse, but could see that the gate stood shut. Kurt slowed the coach.

Amidst the crackle and roar of the flames came little else, but we realised that while such sounds did rumble on they seemed distant. Kurt offered, "If Newbank was doomed, the gate would be open to let our people out."

Sef agreed and climbed onto the roof of the coach. "Ho Newbank, open the gate!"

A moment of silence followed, only to be broken by a thankfully Flet voice, "The gate is closed!"

Sef replied, "We've come from the city and are trying to enter Newbank. The bridge across the Cassaro is down, so this is our only way home."

The voice came again, and this time the silhouette of a head could be seen. "Home you say? Name yourselves!"

I am Sef Vaugen, in the employ of Lady Juvela Liberigo - once Van Leuwin - who awaits entry with myself and our driver, Kurt Baden."

The clink of chains sounded as more figures appeared atop the wall, this time lantern-lit. "Come through, but be quick!"

Before he finished, the gate was already opening.

We passed through only for it to groan closed behind us.

A team of guildsmen manned it, and waited for us on the other side. One of them, the man who'd questioned us from above, appeared beside our coach. "Lady Juvela, Newbank is under siege. The Guild and others, such as your father, are making plans as we speak."

"What's happened?"

He shook his head. "I can't be sure, things are very confused."

Sef asked, "But Newbank burns?"

"It looks worse than it is. The Guild moved to block the bridge, but not before the Inquisition got some men across - they tried to close the Guild. When we moved to stop them, they began torching buildings. Some have died, dozens in fact." He shook his head in disbelief. "Guildmaster Kurgar feared that they'd try again so he ordered the bridge torched. Many are glad and feel safer, but we know that won't be the end of it." He looked me in the eyes. "I fear what tomorrow may bring."

Sef asked, "And what of the fighting across the river?"

"We don't know much, only that there've been riots. Many take comfort in seeing the smoke rise from all across the city and not just here."

I nodded. "Thank you for admitting us, but we should be on our way." My thoughts were on Maria and Pedro and the time we'd already spent.

We travelled slowly through crowded streets.

Many of the people about carried burdens of bagged and wrapped belongings - they looked to have fled their homes on the far side of the river. Wherever I looked, I saw people confused and fearful with their lives forever changed, and all in the space of a single day. I realised then how vulnerable we were, not just individually, but as a people. What had stood as the most prosperous Flet population in all of Dormetia now cowered: If the Flets of Ossard were lost it would leave nothing but besieged Fletland.

One day the genocide would be complete!

We headed near to the ruin of the Cassaro Bridge. Its timbers still burned, the fire now only sparking and smouldering compared to its earlier incarnation. People also watched the spreading flames that flared along the opposite riverbank, while over there, mobs of Heletians looted and torched abandoned Flet homes.

Many of the owners of those properties stood in front of us, wrapped in the night, as their tears caught the light of the fires that consumed their worldly wealth. The looters showed as silhouettes against the glare of the flames. From the safety of the far shore, they, Heletians all, jeered and laughed at the Flets of Newbank.

Sef hissed, "They're bastards. Look at them, look at how they tear our people's lives apart!"

I agreed. "They're cowards." I could feel the hate amongst them.

"I didn't survive the battlefields of Fletland to watch such a thing. If you're not going back tonight I'll have to be excused, for my sword hungers for the blood of cowards!"

"I share your anger, Sef, but I *will* need your help. I can't leave Maria and Pedro over there. Please come with me and bring as many of your friends as you can. Once I have my family back, I'll ask nothing more of you for the evening."

A smile lit his face, and in his eyes I saw death – not his, but of a hundred fools. My perception dipped into the celestial to deliver the realisation that Sef was not only a follower of Kave, but also one of his priests.

The Guild's compound was made up of various structures from warehouses to stables, dormitories, and of course the Guildhall. It sat along the riverfront by the bridge, its water-facing windows now shuttered closed. Guildsmen hid behind a hastily prepared stockade that also lined the river's side, the defences already covered in a crop of spent arrows.

Guildsmen waved us off from approaching the main entrance by the water, obviously worried about archers. Instead they sent us around to the rear gate that led to the stables and courtyard. We left our coach there in Kurt's care and headed straight for the main building. The courtyard was crowded and chaotic, and it looked like the Guildhall would be no better.

Inside people rushed about and talked the place full of noise, their hectic energy balanced by sobering clusters of refugees. One of the groups we passed talked of taking a boat and leaving Ossard. Again it seemed my people might be forced to try their luck at sea.

173

The idea haunted me. I could picture myself weathered and sick for lack of food and water, while clutching Maria to my sunburnt breast. It wasn't an option. I didn't want to run. I wanted to survive the fall of Ossard – and my people with me.

Sef and I found an attendant who led us up some stairs and down a passage, the building like a maze. Soon enough we rounded a corner to find my father waiting in a small lounge where he studied a map of the city. He looked up. "Juvela, Sef, did you find anything?"

I said, "Not at the warehouse, but at Market Square. I think Maria and the others are being held in a cellar, perhaps in the old opera house."

His face lit up. "Are you sure?"

"I'm sure they're in the area, but not so certain where. It doesn't matter, we'll find them."

His relief faded as his eyes filled with concern. "You can't go back, it's too dangerous!" he hesitated, but then continued in a softer tone, "Juvela, there've been some burnings."

"I know, but I have to go."

He sighed, but gave in for the moment. "How did you get back?"

I told him and then asked of happenings in Newbank.

"Things are bad, but we've managed. Kurgar wants to try and negotiate with the Inquisitor, but there's so much anger outside. I think it's too late, already too much blood's been spilt. We know of sixty deaths in Newbank, and there are still thousands of Flets trapped on the river's other side. We hope they're alright, but the fires are spreading, and with them the violence."

A guildsman called to us.

My father turned and nodded. "Come, we can go in."

We entered Kurgar's office, but he wasn't alone. Several guildsmen sat and stood about his desk, and back against the wood-panelled walls. To either side of him also stood two other men. One of them wore robes of blue and a string of amulets. I could feel their power. The grey bearded Heletian looked to me with curiosity, his bald head beaded in sweat.

A mind-voice whispered, "Welcome."

The other man stood as a warrior cut from the same mould as Sef, he openly wearing the sword-in-circle of Kave. Upon seeing him, Sef bowed, suddenly full of an embarrassed reverence. The man carried a good deal of energy both in his physical presence and in the celestial. He nodded to me in greeting.

The mind voice whispered again, "That is Seig Manheim, Ossard's most senior priest of Kave. I am Mauricio Ciero, the most senior Cabalist."

Kurgar stood and gestured for us to sit in the chairs before his desk. We took them.

"Juvela, how are you?"

I supposed he meant after the kidnapping of my family. "Well enough."

He didn't believe me, but he couldn't know of the changes wrought in me. "Your father says that it was your idea to close the bridge and seal the district?"

"Yes."

"It was a good idea. It seems that the Inquisitor had ordered his men to torch this building and then as much of Newbank as they could. Many would have died. We owe you our thanks."

"I'm just glad to have helped."

He nodded. "And you've been looking for your husband and daughter?"

"Yes, and I think I've found them."

Surprised, he asked, "Really?"

"They're being kept just off Market Square."

"Market Square?"

"I believe they're in a cellar, perhaps of the old opera house."

He considered my answer. "That's possible, the building hasn't been used in seasons."

"We couldn't stay because of the crowds, but I'm going back tonight."

My father added, "We were talking about it."

Kurgar asked, "By yourself?"

Sef said, "I'll help, and take some of my brethren."

Kurgar nodded and then leaned back. He spread his hands on the desk in front of him. "The city..." He shook his head. "The city is in a terrible state. There's fighting in many places, and it's aimed at all parties. It's more like there are three cities, and we've each elected to go to war with each other. The Inquisition controls the north and centre, we have some of the east and Newbank, and the followers of the new saints have claimed the port and the south. It's lunacy."

"How much of the east do we have?" I asked.

"Only what's still to burn. Thousands of our people are stranded over there, but I doubt we'll hold it by sunrise."

Sef shifted uncomfortably as did Seig Manheim.

"Can we do anything?" I asked.

He shrugged. "What can we do without stoking the hatred that's already burning? If we send an armed force across the river, it's an escalation. So far most of the violence has been by angry mobs, but if we're seen putting militia into action, we might end up fighting whatever's left of the city guard and the Inquisition's own forces."

I shook my head in disbelief. "But if we don't our people on the other side of the Cassaro will perish!"

He sighed. "I know, but hear me out. I've been trying to work another solution: I've sent a message to whoever leads the new saints, asking for their help in establishing a truce."

I was appalled. "No!"

Kurgar took great care with his next words, them coming out oiled and smooth, "I understand your anger, but let me explain."

I sat in silence – he could have his chance.

"I've considered events, and wonder if this is an opportunity."

My father growled, "An opportunity!"

Kurgar waved him down. "Yes, an opportunity! Listen, the Inquisition has been in control for a day, and already they've tried to outlaw the institutions that have run Ossard for years. They can't do it. We still exist despite their proclamation. They're playing games, delusional and dangerous games. I'm more interested in what's real..."

My father interrupted, "Like the hundreds or thousands of our kinfolk stranded across the river?"

Kurgar clenched a fist and pounded his desk. "Hundreds or thousands, what rubbish! The true figure is closer to ten thousand, and maybe half of them are already dead!"

Gasps sounded from around the room.

He went on, "We can't deny the possibility. We've no accurate number for how many of our kin live over there, the Guild stopped counting years ago, but we *can* see the flames. If we're already taking losses in Newbank from city-side archers, as we are, I don't hold out much hope for any of our people unprotected and alone over there."

Appalled, I whispered, "You're giving them up!"

He shook his head and growled, "Let me finish! The Inquisitor and Benefice have used the kidnappings as an opportunity to take control, but we can't let them succeed. We know what'll happen if they do; at best they'll dump us destitute across the sea in ravaged Fletland, and at worst they'll try and finish the job the Lae Velsanans started two centuries ago!"

Silence greeted his words, for we all feared that they held truth.

He went on, "And you're right to worry about this other faction. It's chaotic out there, and their new saints dubious, but might they be open minded enough to accept us for who we are? If they're prepared to defy the Inquisition and turn their backs on the Church's dogma, might they also understand how those same limits restrain our own beliefs? All they want is freedom to worship, so why would it be such a leap for them to understand our own wish to follow our own faiths?

"Think of it; the temples of our gods built in the streets, no more hidden chapels, whispered hymns, and clandestine gatherings.

"This terrible moment in Ossard's history could become everything we've ever wanted. We might even win the right for the Cabal to walk openly!

"Let's see what the followers of the new saints want; at worst it might be the same as the Inquisition, but it could be so much better. If we can work together in an alliance of mutual respect and benefit, perhaps we can create a new Ossard, one that finally accepts our people."

The cabalist and priest beside him both stood lost in the promise of the idea. No doubt the thought of being able to walk openly in the streets, or of building real and visible temples sounded grand, but what of the darker side?

I asked, "Aren't you forgetting the kidnappings? You saw the bloody mess left behind from their ritual magic, how can you even contemplate this?"

He shook his head. "Juvela, I understand the kidnappings are a terrible thing, but we don't even know for certain that they're behind them. I'll grant you it's possible, but we're yet to see solid proof. However, we do know what the alternative under the whip of the Inquisition is. They'll be killing thousands; who knows how many are already dead!"

Mauricio the Cabalist said, "To openly walk the streets!"

Seig, the Kavist whispered, "To build a temple!"

But all I could think of was my daughter and husband waiting to be slaughtered.

My family!

How dare they even consider an alliance! My voice threatened to break as I stood, disturbing the growing acquiescence to the Guildmaster's idea. "I've listened, but can't agree. Right now I need to get my daughter and husband, that's what's important *and* right. You'll have to excuse me." I turned and left.

I didn't realise how sick the whole idea made me feel until I reached the corridor. Yes, some kind of alliance might seem best for our people today, but what of tomorrow? How could you trust an ally that had risen to power murdering children?

I walked down the passage listening to the dutiful footfalls of Sef behind me. His presence was reassuring.

For now I pushed the matter from my mind. I had other things to think about. We'd prepare and go and get my family and anyone else being held. Right now that was what was important.

When we reached the courtyard, Sef said, "I'll go and gather my brethren."

I turned and saw my father standing beside him. He'd also left Kurgar's office.

I asked, "How much time do you need?"

Sef smiled. "Not as long as you'd think. If you're ready to go just wait in the coach, I'll not be long."

My father begged, "Please, this is too dangerous, it's madness!"

"Not as mad as what they're contemplating back there."

Sef kept quiet.

"Juvela, you might be right, and Sef and I both agree with you, but going back into the city after dark and amidst this rioting is insane!"

"I know it'll be dangerous, but I have to try."

His voice broke, "You said you'd be more careful!"

"If it was me locked up in a cellar at the age of four with Mother, you'd try and get us too!"

He sighed. "Please, Juvela, just be careful."

Sef offered, "She'll be well protected."

Father gave a reluctant nod and then embraced me before heading back into the Guildhall.

Sef said, "I won't be long."

I nodded, and then watched him disappear through the compound's gates into the alleys beyond. His absence would give me a moment to think on Kurgar's words, so I went back to the coach, greeted Kurt, and then climbed into the cab to sit alone.

Was I being selfish?

I knew the answer to that, yet my doubts lingered.

Would I have come to the same conclusion if my family hadn't been taken?

Of course I would.

The followers of the new saints looked to have links to the Horned God, but did I really know enough about such things to judge? My own faith in Schoperde was innocent and true, yet Heletians also classed her as a power of the dark. Was I just showing the same ignorance?

> *Sweet Schoperde,*
> *goddess of life and mother of us all,*
> *losing a desperate war against Death,*
> *please bless me with guidance...*

My prayers were just words, empty wishes for wellness for myself and others, they always had been. What a whimsy. While faith in Schoperde remained common amongst the Flets, there was no longer any organised priesthood, not in Ossard at least – and that meant there were no divine blessings. Schoperde had been cut off from her believers.

If a god was weakened and unable to provide for its faithful, it only discouraged new believers and even the old.

> *Dear Schoperde,*
> *goddess of life and mother of us all,*
> *I wish for nothing but wellness for you...*

I sighed, my silent prayer drifting through my mind along with a rising feeling of hope and comfort.

I'd done well...

I laughed at the notion; as if a god needed my blessing!

As if indeed!

As my mirth faded, I became conscious of the sounds of the city. The other side of the river rang out with noise; the cries of fighting and the snap, crack, and roar of hungry flames. Crossing over to rescue Maria and Pedro amidst all this chaos would be risky, even foolhardy, but I did have to try. I wouldn't be able to live with myself if I didn't.

I'd follow Sef's instructions, after all this was about battle - something of his world. We'd go and be careful, and I'd seek to let my stirring power loose if need be. In the end, I'd brave any risk to free my family.

And, I wondered; what might happen if we also found Lord Liberigo? If he lived, could he try and reclaim control of Ossard? The Inquisitor and Benefice would have to listen to him, also Kurgar, and even the followers of the new saints.

There was still hope for the city.

I waited there in the dark of the coach, running so many things through my mind. The more my thoughts wandered, the more my frustrations deepened. My ability for witchery seemed stunted, yet the Inquisitor had said that the city's factions were scared of me.

Why?

I had no reason to believe anything Anton said, but I did about this. Too many times I'd felt my own power stir, generally when my emotions shifted. It was as though it lay trapped within me. If I was to make a difference to the fate of my family it had to be free to flow.

I shook my head in irritation. Why did everyone else seem to know so much more about what I was, or what I was going through? Kurgar had said that I'd be trained, yet nothing had happened. They were just empty words that saw me sitting around waiting on other people's favours.

The coach door opened, it was Sef. "I've found them. They're just gathering what they need."

"How will we cross the river?"

"Don't worry, it's all arranged."

I tried to smile, but it faltered amidst my doubts. I wondered; in going would I only succeed in getting myself killed?

He sensed my unease. "What's wrong?"

I shook my head, not sure where to start, but then settled for the obvious. "Why can't I do anything, I mean magically? I can see into the celestial and feel my power, but I don't seem able to release it..."

He held up a hand to quieten me, but my frustration overwhelmed both my manners and patience. "Shouldn't I be able to start fires or turn people into toads?"

"Juvela, these things take time. I'll admit that you're not following any normal path, but what's happening in Ossard isn't normal. Perhaps you need to find your own way and not listen to the advice of others..."

I snapped, "Don't say that! I've got nowhere by myself in twenty years, what makes you think I'll get anywhere now?"

"Did your grandmother's book help?"

"Not in the sense of enabling me to do anything. I think it's made me more acquainted with magic, more comfortable and sensitive to it, but it's a book of true history, not a book of spells."

He sat down and closed the door. "And what of the power you feel?"

I just shook my head in irritation.

"What are your feelings about it?"

"What do you mean?"

"Do you feel an affinity for anything, for anything of the Cabal?"

"Like?"

"Like elementalism; do you feel drawn to the elements?"

"No, I don't think so, but I'm not sure I understand."

He took my hands in his and patted them. "Where do you feel it, your power?"

"In the celestial, in my soul."

He leaned forward. "And what of your grandmother, is she helping?"

"I don't really know."

"Sometimes you hear her voice?"

"Yes, and the others with her, and sometimes even the crack and snap of angry flames."

He went on, "She can talk to you, so does she help or just look for opportunities to possess you like back at Market Square?"

"Sometimes she gives me advice. I hear her words in my mind or have sensations that tell me to be careful. I think she could do more. I wish she would."

"Maybe it's hard for her to talk with you?"

"Perhaps. Look, I'm glad of her book. I've learnt something from it, even if it wasn't what I thought it was going to be. It's helped me understand the truths of the world, but not how to use my magic..." I shook my head as my words trailed off into confusion.

181

"Juvela, do something for me tonight, and one thing besides trying to save your family?"

"What?"

"Open up to your magic – and not just with your heart, but also with your mind and spirit. What we're going to do isn't going to be easy. We'll need any kind of help you can give, and I want you to offer it without any preconceived ideas."

I nodded, but remained unsure. "What are you saying; that I'm stopping myself from using my own witchery?"

"Maybe, because perhaps you're not a witch."

I just looked at him, and then started to shake my head. "Of course I am, I can feel the power and see into the celestial."

"So can members of the Sisterhood, spirits, the gods, *and their priests.*"

I sat stunned by his words. I couldn't be any of the first things he'd listed, but a priest?

Sef watched the confusion run across my face. With tender care he stroked my hands and said, "All I'm asking is for you not to shut your mind to the possibilities. Such open mindedness could make all the difference – all the difference in saving your family."

I nodded.

"We need to go and get ready, but we'll talk more about this tomorrow."

"And what of tonight?"

"Just relax and do what comes naturally."

15

To the City

It was after midnight before our party was ready.

Fires burnt along much of the opposite riverbank, but they seemed to be dying down, and the sounds of riot too. Cloaked in darkness, our group of twenty crossed the Cassaro near the city wall by way of three small boats. It was one of the few stretches of water not illuminated by flames, instead it lay lost under thick drifts of smoke.

On arrival, we climbed the slime covered river wall to be greeted by an empty but ash-filled street. Sef took the lead and darted across the cobbles to disappear down a shadowed lane. Without a word we followed.

In our trek, we stuck to winding alleys and cover, walking, running, and even crawling as we sought Ossard's heart. The Kavists moved with surprising speed, particularly for a group weighed down by arms and armour. I just worked at keeping up.

I wasn't used to such rushing, let alone in the dark lanes of the city. Before long a rising tide of adrenalin began to energise me. I tried to keep quiet as I followed, reminding myself with each step or turn that I drew closer to my goal.

My family!

The Kavists treated me as one of their own. They advanced with me, acknowledged me, and I realised, expected me to fight. That was sobering. I was no longer in a world of maids, drivers, and bodyguards – this was a harsher and more *real* life. Only once before had I fought someone; the cultist in Market Square. Tonight I might have to draw blood again.

Sef had given me a knife and dagger, both of which I'd hidden away in my dark cloak. I knew I'd use them if I had to, by all the gods I'd do anything to get my family back, yet I hoped I wouldn't have to.

On our way through smoke-filled alleys, and past occasional burnt out ruins, we also saw other groups. Those dark silhouettes fell away from our larger band, always seeking the safety of other lanes and shadows.

Sef hissed at us to keep quiet, particularly when others were about. It wasn't the noise of our armour, boots, or swords that worried him, but our voices. Any Heletian would recognise our accent, and such a thing could be the death of us.

We moved from alley to alley, only crossing streets and never taking to them, and hoped with our quick and twisting progress to be too hard to track. After a while, it began to seem like we were trapped in an endless maze from some dark nightmare.

Over time, a change became apparent in the districts we passed through, from the ramshackle buildings next to the flood-prone river to the well-built stone of more prosperous areas. We were getting somewhere. All the while the sounds of riot and flame continued, but remained distant. Finally, like all things, our journey came to an end.

Sef stopped us and gathered us about. He pointed ahead to where the alley we were in continued after crossing a narrow street. Before long its worn cobbles finished in a dark dead end surrounded by the glum walls of a tall but tired building. He touched a finger to his lips and whispered, "The opera house."

We were there!

I didn't recognise the building, yet I'd never seen its rear, and certainly not from a back alley after midnight. With a grim smile I savoured how appalled my mother would be.

It loomed four floors high, with walls marked by missing render, the lowest level, windowless, hosted generous clumps of moss. One thing was certain; the back of the building lacked the grandeur of its front, giving off a more honest air to resemble the bankrupt theatre that it was.

The cobbled lane wasn't empty though; it held a timber platform at its very back. The loading dock stood waist high, with crates piled underneath, it backing onto two solid doors chained shut.

We stood in silence, watching for any sign that the building might be occupied. After a while, one of the Kavists whispered, "Nothing, no guards, not even a candle's light. No signs of anything."

He seemed to be right.

I slipped my perception into the celestial and searched for Maria, sensing here and sensing there.

Nothing...

Deeper and deeper I went, through seas of blue and voids of black.
Nothing...

My worries stirred. What if she was asleep, would she be able to sense me? I could only try again.
Nothing...

Sef whispered, "Can you..."

I was already shaking my head.

He turned to the others. "We'll be back."

Sef led me down the alley and onto the street, it heading to an avenue that would end at the square. It was the same avenue that I'd been on when I'd last connected with Maria. He took me to the same spot, and then checked for anyone watching. "Try again."

I did.

Nothing...

"Get down on the cobbles like this afternoon."

I dropped to the road and gripped the cold stones.

Nothing...

My tears came.

Sef asked, "Might she be asleep?"

"I don't know."

"Try again. Call out to her soul, call out with everything."

I did as I tried to use my power.

Nothing...

I stood up and shook my head.

Sef said, "We'll still go in."

"Thank you."

He nodded, but grew tense as he searched the surrounding shadows. "We must be careful, the night whispers; we're not alone."

We hurried back to our band.

The Kavists stood eager and ready. They knew tonight might deliver a fight, but they were also aware that the kidnappers of children would be less than honourable. Surviving such an adversary would require caution.

Some of them stretched their limbs, while others whispered prayers, yet all tried to hold the quiet that luck had so far allowed. With relief and weapons drawn, we began our advance.

Though they were warriors who'd shed blood and taken lives, my upbringing made me see them as more than bringers of battle and death. To the Flets of Ossard, Kavists were the defenders of Fletland, and for that we were grateful. We felt we owed Kave a great debt.

We crossed the street and tried to keep to the dim night's shadows. Leading us, Sef soon discovered a door halfway along the short alley's length. We gathered about it, while a young Fletlander dropped to his knees to check the lock and work at it.

He was about to force it when we heard something behind us; a chuckle from the dark.

The Kavists turned with raised swords, but there was nothing to see besides the alley and its shadows.

Sef hissed, "Juvela, get your back to the wall!"

His tone wiped the surprise from my face. "What is it?"

"The followers of Mortigi."

The God of Murder!

I found the wall, and planted my back against it.

And again laughter sounded, this time from the loading dock.

Sef said, "The light is poor, we must be careful *and have faith.*"

The Kavists broke into a chant.

In the silence that followed the air grew chill, my breath icing up in front of me.

The coming of magic...

The alleyway began to brighten under a weak but rising light. The smoke haze cleared to reveal the moon, the great orb's blue face marked by swirls of white.

The Kavists uttered a chorus of thanks.

In answer, a woman's voice sang a slow counter-prayer, it coming from the dark.

Sef hissed, "Lady Death."

Again laughter sounded from the shadows.

The moon's light began to fade, the haze returning to cloak it like a shroud.

Mortigists killed for pleasure, and to offer the stolen souls as morsels to their cruel lord. They were the antithesis of Kavists who fought out of necessity. They were bitter rivals.

Damn them, I just wanted my husband and daughter!

Lady Death purred from the advancing dark, "We've been hunting since dusk and claimed many, but I can see blessed Mortigi has saved the best sport for last!"

Sef spat in her direction. "Sport you can't handle!"

Laughter greeted his retort.

To be so near my goal, only to be delayed fired my anger, and with its stirring my soul's power began to churn.

Damn it, my family was so close, but Death's servants closer!

It just stoked my fury, yet it wasn't focused on anyone else, just my powerless self – and that fury began to burn.

Where was my damned witchery?

The Mortigists came forward cloaked in the dark that they'd called, the lack of light tilting the balance in their favour.

I was useless!

Yet my trapped power boiled inside of me.

I didn't need much of it, just a bit, just a taste of its searing heat and shadow-killing glow.

Please Schoperde, I just wanted my family – was it too much to ask?

My power bucked as it mingled with my anger, the two painfully merging as they tore at the very fabric of my soul.

The agony!

Hot and rampaging, it threatened to consume me.

Then it happened...

Under all that pressure something finally gave.

The barrier stopping my power was no longer whole!

It began to leak through. It came as a trickle and was only a start, showing in the real world as a flourish of sparks.

I groaned at the pain.

Was my soul going to burst?

A new round of agony shot through me.

I gasped, "Sweet Schoperde!"

And then came relief.

A wave of green light rushed out from me. For a moment, the lane flared while I slumped to the cobbles, listening to the deafening thump of my heart.

Something had broken.

Something was free.

And that something was *me*.

My mind felt like it was spinning, and my heart kept drumming out, finally the power in my soul was ready to use – if only I knew how.

My vision drifted from the celestial to the real world, fading between one and the other as it cycled round and through. In that collage of images I saw the Kavists ready themselves, movement in the shadows, and two gods face each other through their followers and their truths.

And amidst it all I heard my grandmother gasp, "Oh, I thought they were all gone?"

Back in the alley, I began to lift myself up as my hand grabbed at a loose cobble.

Sef called over his shoulder, "Juvela?"

"I'm... I'm alright."

And then the last of the sparks faded to let the Mortigists renew their advance.

Without thinking, I lifted my hand that clutched at the cobblestone, opening it so that it sat in the flat of my palm. With a sense of wonder I could taste the coming of magic – *my magic.*

I was going to cast.

It stirred as a cool sensation in my belly, and then deepened to grow wild. It spread to my chest before surging along my arm, to my hand, and then to set the cobble's dark surface to sparkle. Within a heartbeat its surface became covered in a skin of frost. My palm tingled with the flow of power, but I seemed otherwise immune to its bite.

Wisps of mist began to rise from the stone and lazily drift about. The glimmering ice crystals didn't last though, they melted to become short-lived beads of water that were then turned to steam. When the steam began to fade, the water gone, and the ice only a memory, the rock came to glow.

A soft red light bathed the flesh of my hand, but I still felt nothing of it. The stone went from red, to orange, and then to yellow, giving me light enough to see. I lifted it above my head as it brightened to illuminate the alley.

The Kavists cheered.

And in a dozen places about us, the black clad cultists stood revealed. They fell back, but not before the closest of the Kavists stepped after them to strike. Two warriors cried out as they landed hits.

One of their victims dove to safety in the dark, but the other fell. The cultist landed on his back, exposing a deep gash to his shoulder that showed bone and gushed blood. My flaring light lit his head and chest, but the rest of him was lost to the murk of shadow.

The warrior who'd struck him stepped forward to finish the job, but a whispered prayer from the dark caused him to slow.

Sef called, "Stay in the light!"

The warrior snapped, "The kill's mine!"

But Lady Death challenged, "No, the kill is mine." And two black-gloved hands slipped from the edge of the dark, one brandishing a knife. She hissed, "I take this for Mortigi!" And then slit the cultist's throat.

The Kavist was already lunging forward with body and sword, his swing ending in the doomed man's chest - but his soul had already been claimed.

Sef growled, "There's no honour in this!"

But the gloved hands stayed there, not even flinching as they sat on the cultist's chest as it was cleaved. Then, like a striking snake, they darted forward to fly up the Kavist's bloodied blade, the darkness following to keep Lady Death hidden.

The warrior's own body blocked the detail of what happened next - and for that I'm glad. I saw him stumble back, but too slowly, leaving himself open to her attack. He grunted in shock as the cobbles about him took the spray of his lifeblood, the noise tapering off into a sigh.

In an instant more gloved hands appeared to grab at him, them dragging him into the dark. A brief silence followed, only broken by the horrid sounds of stabbing, tearing, and the wet thumps of butchery.

Sef hissed, "He was a fool!"

Something landed on the cobbles in front of us - a severed hand.

A moment later, the warrior's body loomed up at the edge of my circle of light. He'd been stabbed and carved, his armour and clothes shredded, and his lifeless face marked with Mortigi's five-pointed star. The body then fell forward to land with a sickening crunch. His own sword stuck out of his back, standing straight and bloodied.

A silence followed, it broken by Lady Death, "An eye for an eye."

I reached up and split my molten cobblestone, hurling a gob of the white-hot stuff after her. It hit the cobbles to spray flaring lumps and a galaxy of sparks. Robed figures spun away, giving us a moment to gather ourselves, yet still the lane wasn't safe - it was time to move into the opera house.

Sef turned to the big warrior next to him. "Cherub, force the door."

He then looked to me with a wry smile. "Thank you, Juvela."

I grinned as I marvelled at my flaring light. Finally, I'd cast something, and been able to help by gaining us some time. But my pride was short-lived.

Lady Death hissed, "Curse you!"

And I thought they were just words...

Sef's face lost its colour as fear filled his eyes.

But my perception had already taken flight.

> *And in the celestial, Mortigi came to put his mark on me, him incomprehensible and immense.*
>
> *His attention shot through me like cold shards of ice, hurled by a gusting gale built of nothing but sleet and death.*
>
> *Pain stabbed and slashed, and at the same time his anger burned into me, all of it leaving me squirming under its volcanic heat.*
>
> *His hate torched my soul, working to extinguish my life's light, yet somehow, through some miracle, I managed to last through it and survive.*

I found myself slumped on the ground.

Someone began lifting me, holding me under the arms and pulling me into the opera house. I wanted it to stop, to get back on my feet, until I realised I couldn't move.

I watched one of my hands, the knuckles being rubbed raw as it was dragged over timber boards. Somehow it still gripped the blazing stone. All the while, lost in shock, I drooled and dumbly hummed. It took a long time for my sluggish mind to recognise what; it was Schoperde's song, a song of sorrow, but also hope.

16

-

The Opera House

Sef looked for somewhere to put me amidst the cobwebbed clutter of the opera house, it all lit by the blinding light flaring from my hand. In the end he settled on the first thing he saw that would hold me, a stage prop; an old and dusty divan.

He talked fast and looked worried as tears ran from his eyes. I couldn't understand him, my mind running slow and haltingly. Still, the confusion eventually drained away to be replaced by a rising tide of excitement.

We were inside!

Kavists rushed past us to spread throughout the darkened building. This was it, the rescue of my family – and I lay prone!

Damn myself, this would never do!

It took a good deal of effort, but I found I could use the energy boiling within me to reawaken my stymied mind. I had to force it, and it hurt to work at, but I persevered as things improved.

That done, I set to work on my stuck muscles, as I tried to recover my mobility. I found I could ease the pain by losing myself in thoughts of Maria and Pedro and their proximity. Amongst those hopes, I could have endured anything.

Recovering movement happened quickly once I understood how to manipulate the magic, but it left my muscles heavy and stiff. Unsteadily I sat up, and then tried to get to my feet.

Sef panicked at my awkward attempt to rise, until I slurred, "I'll be alright." I swallowed and then added, "Please, see to the search, or we'll be here all night."

He stared at me in awe, so much so that I had to turn away. After recovering himself, he glanced at the shattered door and said, "Watch it, they might try and come in."

I stretched my arm, the one that still held what remained of the flaring stone, and hurled it at the opening. It sprayed across the cobbles outside as it broke up to blaze with fresh fury. "No they won't."

He smiled in disbelief as his tears continued to run. "Be careful in any case, if they want to get in they'll find a way. We won't be able to stop them."

I nodded. "Please, worry about Pedro and Maria."

He turned to follow the others, but kept gazing back.

It was dim and quiet, with far too much of the space about me lost to shadow. A string of glowing orange-rimmed holes smouldered along the floorboards, they'd been born from where I'd dripped molten rock as I'd been dragged inside. None of it had caught to come aflame – and in that we'd been lucky.

One of the Kavists had lit a lantern he'd found, but here on the backstage, amidst countless rows of props and backdrops, anything could hide. Simply, we needed more light.

I took a deep breath and tried to grapple with some of the power still churning away within me. This time I had no rock, instead I grabbed a handful of coins from a prop treasure chest – they were wooden.

I closed my hands over them and prepared to make them glow, but not in the way I'd unconsciously ignited the stone. I released some of my power amidst thoughts of the moon's silver-blue light. My hands tingled and the air cooled: It was done, whatever it was.

I hesitated in revealing it, so much so that I whispered a quick prayer to Schoperde before opening my cupped hands. And there the coins were, shining, but without the heat and glare of the cobblestone.

It was good.

I grabbed more and charged them, yet after a while my head began to ache. It left me wondering at my limits.

Limits...

To my mind, I'd still done nothing worthy of being burnt at the stake for. I needed to try harder things, yet now was no time for experiments.

I scattered the coins around the backstage and passed on handfuls to the Kavists so they could better light their own way.

It wasn't long before we'd covered the backstage, the main stage, and the dressing rooms. Still, even with the light of the coins and an increasing number of lanterns, far too many shadows remained.

I followed Sef through the curtains and onto the stage. The light we had with us barely reached the first few rows of benches. I charged another handful of coins and threw them out into the dark. I sighed and said, "We'd need fifty men to search this place."

Sef answered, "Yes, and more to defend it. It's too big. We'll get straight to the cellar and then out."

We both stood there looking at row after row of seating and the shadows that waited beyond.

He said, "You could hide a hundred people out there, and that's without any kind of magic."

As if in answer, the roof beams above creaked. Was it just the movement of the building, perhaps the wind, or someone up there hiding amongst the rigging? Could Mortigi's followers have found a way in, and even now be creeping about searching for fresh kills? Aside from the faint outlines of rafters and dangling ropes, the detail of the heights remained a mystery. Sef was right; we had to concentrate on getting to the cellar, and then out.

He said, "Don't worry, if they're here we'll find them."

His presence was reassuring, as it always had been.

He called out for two Kavists to watch the theatre hall as we returned to the backstage.

Cherub came looking for us moments later. The big man said, "Found it, it's back here!" And he pointed down a coin-lit passage.

My heart raced, something only doubled when Sef smiled and patted me on the shoulder. He gathered five Kavists and set the rest on watches.

Cherub led us down the dusty and worn corridor made narrower by racks of covered costumes on one side. Half way along we came to a door that had a sign above it. I couldn't read, but guessed it said *cellar* as Sef and Cherub both swapped knowing glances.

I whispered, "Did you go in?"

His voice rumbled, "It's locked, so I thought I'd get some help."

Sef nodded. "Alright, let's get ready. Juvela, stand back and let them through."

Reluctantly I stepped back.

They bowed their heads in prayer, the whispered chant the only sound to disturb the quiet.

For the first time since leaving Newbank, I began to feel uneasy. We were so close, but it could all still go so wrong. A panicked guard might use them as hostages, or shields, or even kill them. Maybe even now the cultists rushed through their ritual.

The anxiety building within me nearly won out, almost making me cry for Sef and his fellows to stop. Before I could say a thing, though, Sef nodded, and Cherub rammed his shoulder into the door.

It didn't stand a chance.

The door exploded in a shower of snapping planks and splinters, its ruins following him as he charged down the stairs and into the dark. He carried his sword in one hand while the other flung my charmed coins about.

If the big Kavist's arrival hadn't brought enough chaos to the cellar, the others who followed him certainly did. They all cried out, and showered wooden coins about, while carrying their swords ready.

I slumped against the wall unable to watch.

Sef gave me a sympathetic look, but it faded along with his cool confidence.

Something was wrong...

He turned to the doorway as his brow furrowed and nostrils flared.

I could smell it too.

Death...

The yelling died down beneath us as disappointment soured its tones.

Sef called out, "Well?"

Cherub answered, "They've gone!"

Sef led me down. "Watch the door." Its ruin lay strewn the length of the stairs.

I descended fearing what I'd find at the bottom. Before I reached it I was trembling and covered in a cold sweat.

The kidnap victims had been there and two of them still were - dead.

It wasn't Pedro and Maria or Lord and Lady Liberigo, so I let out a selfish sigh of relief. The unfortunates were Heletian; an old woman and a young man. I didn't recognise them. They'd been left hung from chains and their throats slit.

Piles of flattened hay lined one of the damp cellar walls. It had been used as bedding. I walked its length until I reached a corner. Somehow I could sense who'd lain there; my husband and daughter. Dropping to my knees I put a hand to it.

It was still warm!

Tears flooded my eyes.

So close!

Amidst my disappointment came something cold and bitter, it whispering to me with a celestial voice, "They were still there when you were showing off in the alley." It was Lady Death.

My heart sank.

While I'd been using my meagre skills against her hunting pack, my daughter and husband had been spirited away.

In a hoarse voice, I said, "Let's get out of here. They may have planned a trap."

Sef nodded, but got some of his fellows to search the room for anything of import while he led me back up the stairs.

We withdrew and fell back through Ossard's alleyways. Sef and four others took me back to the river, and then saw me safely across to home.

Before they left me to rejoin their brothers, Sef said, "Juvela, the search hasn't ended. I'll watch for them tonight. We'll begin afresh if we have to tomorrow. Have faith."

I stepped forward and embraced him. "Thank you Sef, be careful." The move embarrassed him, but he didn't fight it. After a moment he even returned it with feeling.

"Take care, Juvela, and eat before you retire. Your castings will have drained you."

I nodded and watched them leave before turning to go inside.

My home was cold and quiet. The maid wasn't about or her belongings. Like so many others, it seemed she was frightened of me and had fled. After walking the abandoned halls with only the rhythm of my footsteps for company, I retreated upstairs.

My bedroom only seemed emptier.

I sat on the edge of my bed and tried to kick off my boots, only to end up wrestling with them. The effort made me angry - and then came the tears.

Eventually I found myself barefoot on the balcony in the cold night air. I needed no goading to join the chorus that rang out across Newbank; Schoperde's song of sorrow.

It felt good singing its long and mournful notes. Through it I burned away some of my grief and disappointment, and rediscovered my resolve. I would find my family, I had to, and I'd discover how they'd been moved moments before our arrival.

How did they know we were coming?

17

Momentous Times Indeed

Eventually, I left the balcony and sat on my bed where I cradled my grandmother's tome. I was exhausted, but still fell into a restless urge to search for my family, to at least do something. From there I dipped my perception into the next world and began to search through a city-state of a million souls. I started the hunt at the celestial equivalent of the opera house, and then spread towards the port and the south.

It was tedious work involving far too many souls – still, I persisted. I also supposed whoever held them would be using some kind of shielding magic to keep them hidden, as they had before. Nevertheless, I continued.

Sef roused me from my hopeless search midmorning, to drag me from its misery. Of them, I'd not found a hint.

"Juvela, don't fret, we'll find them," he said grave-faced.

My eyes burned from my tears. I'd also become cramped and lost to shivers, something that saw my voice shake, and my breath wheeze. All of it only made Sef fuss over me like my mother.

With a hoarse voice, I said, "Sef, I'm alright!"

"You look terrible..."

"Really Sef, I'm just a little tired."

"You haven't eaten, have you?"

"No."

"Or slept?"

"No." So lost in my misery, it hadn't occurred to me. My stomach growled. I tried to laugh at its timing, but the sound came from me as a weak rattle that sent aches shooting through my chest.

"Juvela, you have to understand that magic is a taxing thing. I know what you did last night might seem simple, but I could feel the power you gathered, and the way it surged and boiled." He knelt down in front of me with concern in his eyes. "You keep a great well of power in there," he pointed to my belly, "but crafted only the smallest portion of it. To do so, to gather such energy and not spend it, or recover by properly resting and eating, will only see you waste away."

I didn't know what to say. Wasn't casting magic all about other people suffering the consequences?

He saw my confusion. "Juvela, the power's corrosive, so much so that only a healthy body can withstand it. If you're half-starved and tired, it'll work away at your muscles and bones, it'll even boil your blood away given the chance. It becomes a cycle, one that's harder to recover from. If you're not careful, it'll kill you by burning you out."

I nodded; what he said made sense, even if I didn't appreciate the gravity of his words.

He saw that, and shook his head in anger. "Please, Juvela, you must be careful! You're no ordinary magician..."

And that comment got my attention.

He went on, "I don't know what you are, but I can feel such strong currents of power around you when you reach into your font. If you're not careful, it'll kill you; just look at your hands!"

What about my hands?

I looked down at them.

My long fingers normally lay thin and fair, and well covered with skin stretched not too tight. They weren't now. I spread them before me as they trembled, my body lost to some kind of shock. Wrinkles ran their length, and the skin hung loose with folds and creases deep in the thin flesh, yet that wasn't the end of it. I could see liver spots and other shadows, and a mix of sickening colours finished with yellowed nails.

I gasped.

Sef looked me in the eye. "Have I got your attention now?"

I nodded, horrified by the hag's hands in front of me.

"We'll get you some breakfast, and then we must go."

My hands were reaching up for the flesh of my face, but I was already cringing at the wrinkles and folds I knew I'd find there. I whispered, "Go where?"

"Juvela, you need to change and eat. Don't worry, you'll get your youth back, and sooner than you think. Please, just do as I say. I'll answer your questions downstairs."

I nodded, still stunned. "Thank you, Sef."

He got up and left me.

I went downstairs to find him stirring a pot of porridge over a freshly lit fire. He looked up and smiled. "It won't be long."

"Thank you." I sat down, grateful to rest my weary bones.

"You're tired, aren't you?"

"Exhausted." It seemed that the casting had taken a lot out of me.

My gaze left him to settle on the cooking fire, where I lost myself in the dance of its flickering flames.

"You *really* are tired, aren't you?" His smile became a grin.

I rested my head in my withered hands. "I'm glad you find it so amusing."

To my surprise, he laughed. "I'm sorry, but I'm as confused as you."

"You are not!" I snapped, and then took a deep breath. "I'm sorry, Sef, but I don't understand any of this."

"It's alright."

I smiled, grateful he'd chosen to ignore my tone. "Sef, why has it taken so much from me, to produce so little? Last night, I could feel a storm of power brewing in me, but all I magicked was a bucketful of glowing coins and handful of hot coals?"

He tended the oats before pulling up a stool. "Juvela, all power comes at a price. To be honest, I worry for you."

"Why?"

"A good question, but one I can't answer." He shook his head in frustration, though he felt only a trifle of what troubled me.

"Sef, I need your help. Tell me what you can, even guesses, for it's more than I already have."

He sighed. "I don't know where to start, so indulge me." He gathered his thoughts for a moment, and then said, "I guess your own words are a good starting point."

I nodded.

"You said that you felt your power brewing?"

"Yes."

"I could feel it too, as could anybody sensitive to such things. You need to learn more discipline in that regard, so you can hide it, just as those of us who wield the celestial learn to hide our souls."

"Why?"

"To keep them safe."

"From what?"

He checked the oats before continuing. "The celestial is another world, but not like ours. It's where magic comes from, and where spirits, souls, and the very gods dwell. It's where the spark of life is born to flare, and we in this world, our mortal selves, are merely the smoke of those eternal fires."

"I think I understand."

He nodded. "The magic you work, as do I as a priest of Kave, is just us pulling some of that fire through, not just the smoke, but the actual flame. It's a skill for only the strongest of souls. Simply said; the more power you can pull through, the stronger you must be. Learning and experience will expand your limits, but in the end we all have them."

"I understand."

He went on, "I'm surprised at the amount of power you can draw upon, even though you know so little of what to do with it. I suppose in time you'll learn, but still, what you can gather astounds me."

"Learn through the Cabal?"

He looked thoughtful for a moment, until the pop and hiss of our breakfast drew his attention. After giving it a stir, he turned back. "I first noticed your soul when I started working for your parents. It's old and powerful, and always held a complex weave."

"Am I a Cabalist?"

He shrugged, "I don't know. Perhaps you need to talk to others..."

I snorted. "Others! Sef, my parents know nothing of this, and I can't trust anyone else. I can't rely on my grandmother, as her aid is sporadic, and Kurgar promised to help me with the Cabal, but has done nothing since. If I've a powerful soul, then you'd think it might be a priority, the way the city is falling apart, to teach me how to use it!"

He grabbed two bowls and split the steaming brew. He handed one to me, the biggest, and then topped it with some syrup. "Eat up, all of it."

I took it, but only felt bad again for my tone. "Sorry, Sef."

"It's alright."

We began to eat.

After a short silence, he looked up and said, "What about your grandmother? What's going on? I saw what happened when we neared the Inquisitor and she tried to use you to confront him. Is she always struggling for control?"

"No!" I was surprised at his choice of words. "I sometimes hear her voice warn me of things, and often it comes accompanied by others. Only once has she tried to force me to do anything, back then in the coach. I think she wants to help me, to awaken my magic, but Inquisitor Anton's arrival has also awakened her thirst for revenge."

He gave a grim smile. "We'll just have to watch her. It would also help if you tried to talk to her."

"How?"

"In the celestial. You know how to get into that world, to drag your perception across?"

I nodded. "I can do it, but I'm not really conscious of *how* I do it. It seems more a reflex."

"That's good; it took me a full season to master. When you've time, you need to go into the celestial and speak with her. She's bound to you, so I'm sure she'll not be hard to find. Talk to her and discover her truth. It's the only way to work out what her part in all this is."

I sighed as I put down my half empty bowl. "And what will *that* do to me?" I asked, while spreading my wrinkled fingers, though their colour had already improved.

"All magic has its costs, but shifting your perception between worlds is one of the easiest things to do. When you finish your meal, you'll be surprised to see how much your skin will renew itself." He gave a wry smile. "The years will just fall away."

I raised an eyebrow, not sure if I should believe him, yet I picked up my bowl and got back to eating.

"Juvela, you gathered enough power last night to torch Market Square, but you didn't release it. It's a miracle that you didn't burn yourself out – and I mean that literally. That's why you look as worn as you do.

"You need coaching, guidance, and improved skills, all those things will help. Most importantly, you need to learn to gather only the power you want for whatever casting you're trying to complete."

I interrupted, feeling that I finally understood something. "The power I felt last night used my soul as a gateway into this world, didn't it?"

"Almost. It used your soul as a gateway *out* of the celestial, and your body as a gateway *into* this world."

"It felt incredible, so vital and alive."

He nodded. "And after you summoned it, drawing in such a great flood, all you did was hold onto it and melt a single cobble!" He shook his head in disbelief. "You could have turned night into day, or called a firestorm!"

I didn't know what to say.

He went on, "You stir such power, and so easily, it's why so many people are interested in you."

"Who?" I asked around another mouthful of porridge.

"I'm sure Lady Death is curious, as are some of my fellows, and also the Inquisitor. And then," he paused, "then there was when Mortigi himself came and marked you." He watched for my reaction.

I remembered the icy pain, and the feeling of being overwhelmed by an anger so hateful that it had to be divine. It had all come after Lady Death cursed me. Chilled by the memory, I swallowed and whispered, "Yes."

He nodded. "Yes!"

I just looked to him.

He said, "It's true, Mortigi himself branded you with his mark!"

With a hesitant voice, I asked, "And what does that mean?" I then took another mouthful of porridge.

Thankfully, his animation drained away, his manner becoming more sober. "It means that all his followers will know you, and that their master has a bounty on your head."

I choked on my breakfast. "The god of murder wants me dead?"

"Yes, but don't fear..."

"Don't fear!"

He shifted, becoming uncomfortable at my distress. "Trust me, you'll be well protected."

I gasped, "Sweet Schoperde, what hope is there?"

With a firm voice, he said, "There's always hope, that's why we search for Pedro and Maria."

He was right.

I took a deep breath and tried to calm down. "Why didn't he just kill me?"

"Because, to be honest, this way you suffer more; living each day while wondering if it's your last."

I just stared at him.

"Don't worry about it."

I was shaking my head. "How can I not worry? I just want my family back!"

"In all this you're not alone, others also live with divine marks."

"Who?"

"Anton is marked by many gods, and so too is Lady Death..."

Such exalted company...

"...and even me, your loyal Sef."

"What?"

"I'm also marked, but in a lesser way. Regardless, one day my time will come."

And then I had a thousand questions and fears for him, but only one found my mouth. "Who?"

"It's something we can discuss another time, and I mean it, but for now we need to talk about you."

I nodded, but sat in silence, still stunned by his news. After a while, I asked, "Why did Lady Death curse me; because of the light?"

"It was more because of the power she sensed stirring in you."

"Can I really call on that much?"

He nodded again. "Though it all comes to nothing if you can't do anything with it."

He was right.

"Juvela, the gods have never looked to me in the celestial, or moved to mark me with such a strong curse. If they did, it'd kill me."

This was all getting to be too much.

"Juvela, you're not a witch of the Cabal – I think you're something else."

We sat in an uncomfortable silence, looking to each other. Sef then checked my bowl, chuckling, pleased that I'd nearly finished. "Good eating and sleep will solve your problems in regard to the cost of magic. You're still human and need to take care of yourself."

His words reminded me of how tired I felt. "I believe you."

"Good."

"You know, last night I felt something in my soul *weaken* and *crack*. I don't know what it was, but with it breached, I seemed to be free to draw upon the power that leaked through."

"What?" Now Sef looked confused.

"It was holding my power back, blocking it, but I got so angry and frustrated that I think the barrier somehow broke."

"A barrier?"

"It allowed me to gather power in the celestial, but stopped me from bringing it through. I'm certain it remains, but now it's damaged. Do you know what it is?"

He shook his head. "Let me *look* at you."

For a moment his words puzzled me, but then his eyes lost focus; he'd slipped into the celestial. I followed.

The blue-white of his life-light shone out against the dark of the void. I could sense that he was scrying me, as he looked deep into my soul.

Without thinking, my soul shifted and threw up a layer of soul-stuff to shield me from his prying. I marvelled as I studied it, realising I could draw it back or add to it to dim the glow of my own life-light. It was a kind of armour, and the more layers I put up, the more my soul dimmed. Of course, that wasn't helping Sef as he tried to examine me, so I pulled my newly discovered defences down.

I heard his voice, "Juvela?" His perception was back in the real world, so I also returned.

He looked to me and asked, "How do you feel?"

"Alright, not so tired."

"You've learnt to shield yourself?"

"Yes, just now. The first movement came as a reflex, but I think I can control it."

He nodded.

I asked, "What did you see?"

"A couple of things, but firstly look at your hands."

I did. The skin had tightened, not yet back to its norm, but well on its way. "That was easy."

"Hmmm, don't be fooled. Recovery can sometimes take days, or even seasons. That's if the casting doesn't kill you outright."

"I'll just have to be careful."

He nodded, but was still largely lost to his thoughts.

"What's wrong?"

After a moment, he said, "Nothing."

"Did you see something?"

He looked me up and down and nodded. "I noticed... I noticed a couple of things."

"Like?"

"Well, some of what I'm going to say will just raise more questions, but maybe we need to discuss them. You should also remember that they're only my opinions. You need to talk to other people; cabalists and the like, and your grandmother too."

"Alright, but you're a priest of Kave, so you're celestially capable and know something of all this. I really want to hear what you think. You're the one I trust."

"I do know something of this, but you're more powerful than me. In truth, I haven't seen what you are before. You're different."

"How?"

"The song, let's start with the song."

"Schoperde's song of sorrow?"

"Yes, many Flet women sing the song to help them mourn. You do too, but when you sing it, I can feel the power ripple around you. It's why Anton silenced you on the balcony when Maria and Pedro were stolen away; you'd begun to sing it out of grief, but he thought you were casting."

"Casting?"

"When you sing it, it's as if Schoperde joins you in song."

I shook my head in confusion. "Why would she do that? I believe in her, you know I have my faith, but she doesn't even have the strength to offer blessings, let alone to sing with me. By all the gods, in Ossard she doesn't even have priests! Why would she offer me anything?"

"That's the real question." He left his stool to kneel in front of me. "Juvela, I think you're to be her priest."

I just stared at him, stunned by the idea.

And at the back of my mind, my grandmother hissed.

I asked, "How could that be?"

"Why not? Witchery often passes from mother to daughter, or on to granddaughter, but it doesn't have to. What's really being passed on is a bloodline's taste for the celestial, something that attracts strong souls."

I didn't know what to say.

Sef went on, "Look at Ossard and what's happening here; the gods are coming, and they're rallying their servants to their banners. I think you've heard some kind of calling and are reacting to it," he paused, swallowed, and then whispered, "perhaps you're even an avatar!"

An avatar – a mortal born god yet to awaken!

"No!" I gasped, frightened by the very idea. "How could that be? How could that happen when I know so little?"

He patted my hands. "Maybe *that's* the shackle that binds you."

"An avatar? It's too much, I can't be! I'd be more aware of it, wouldn't I?"

"I don't know, but I don't think so. Avatars are always alone and very rare." He chuckled to release some of the tension. "I'd certainly be worried if more than one was around!"

"Why, what would that mean?"

"The end of the world; the divine war at the end of all time."

His words reminded me of my grandmother's tome.

He got up and off his knees, and went back to his stool.

I said, "Perhaps you're right, perhaps my magic is aligned to faith." I went on, thinking aloud, "I suppose with the suppression of our people's religions such a calling might somehow be delayed."

"Our beliefs are here, but weak. The dogma is half-forgotten. Look at Schoperde; there are still a few priests in the wilds of Fletland, but there's none left here in Ossard. Her last priest here was forced out twenty years ago."

"Really? I didn't know that."

"Seig told me. He said Ossard's Flets don't talk about her."

"Why?"

"Because someone gave her truth to the Inquisition during their last campaign; it's what caused the Burnings."

I was horrified. "Sweet Schoperde! What happened?"

"She fled. She got out of the city and headed into the Northcountry, from where she planned to cross to Fletland. It was Iris I think, Iris Grendabanden, or something like that."

"I've never heard of her, or of what you say, but I can understand people not talking about it if a Flet willingly gave up her name. Such an act would have shamed all of Newbank."

He nodded. "From my understanding, a faith like Schoperde has dogma that's not overly deep. It's more a matter of accepting your connection to her, and then submitting to it."

"Yes, that's right. Of course, in Fletland they also have traditions of celebrations and observances tied to the seasons and the like, but that's not something we can do."

"No, not while the Church watches."

We sat in silence for a moment before I asked, "And if it's not that, if I'm not a newly discovered servant of the gods," I snorted in laughter, "or an avatar?"

"Juvela, *we've* been talking about you."

"We?"

"The Guild, and those who've sensed your emerging power. You're no trickster, and what I've said here is not unlike what's been spoken elsewhere."

My jaw dropped. "Sef!"

"Truly."

"This is nonsense! I'm a wife and a mother, not an avatar!"

"Listen to me, and listen with an open mind. You're not just gifted, or able to draw upon great power, you're also something different."

I shook my head.

He went on, "I, like most priests, can only draw upon thin streams of magic, anything greater would burn me out. As soon as I draw it into me, I have to manipulate it, and then cast it out. But you can handle it. You let it flood in so much more than anyone I've ever seen, and then you can *even* hold it!"

"Sef, this is too much!"

He shook his head. "Listen to me, look at how quickly you learned to defend yourself just now!"

I held up my hands. "Please, let's leave it!"

He took a deep breath and nodded.

"Why don't you tell me what's been said, if it's that important."

"There are many faiths in Fletland, more than you can know. Some speak in terms of prophecy, and such things often become tales to be told in taverns, or by the glow of camp fires."

"Like what you told me when I was young?"

"I suppose, but what I'm telling you now is what some people actually believe."

"I understand."

"Most of them speak of the same sort of thing: They tell of one of our own who'll rise to lead us to sanctuary, a time and place free of catastrophe."

"What! And people think that's me?"

He shook his head. "No, this saviour is suppose to be a warrior, but he's put onto his path by a priest from amongst us; a *spirit-guide*. This priest helps him awaken to his truth, which is what will trigger his rise. In the end, that saviour becomes our leader, and also the king of our foes."

206

I sat back, astounded that anyone would link such a thing to me. "You don't believe this, do you?"

"No, prophecy is the talk of fools. The world just doesn't work that way." He sighed. "Juvela, look at our people; we're dying. Our time in Ossard seems over, and our place in Fletland has never been secure. In another one hundred years, with or without the genocide, our people will be finished. Something as simple as a few bad harvests or a plague will end it."

I'd never heard such talk, but knew it held some truth.

He went on, "Banditry, disease, and the lingering hatred of the genocide; it's all taking its toll. The bitterness is killing us."

It was a glum thought. Ossard, even as a *Heletian* city-state, stood as Unae's largest Flet community. Its loss would be a terrible blow. If Ossard went, so would an important branch of our people - the branch that gave the rest hope.

I said, "There aren't tears enough for our history, let alone any prophesied calamities to come."

He grinned. "Don't worry about it, they're just stories." He laughed. "Besides, have you met anyone who'd make a good king?"

I smiled as I shook my head. It was ludicrous, all of it.

Sef asked, "How are you feeling?"

"Better."

"Good. Now, if you're up to it, we should go to the Guild."

"To check on things?"

"Kurgar has sent out a declaration to the Inquisitor and the followers of the new saints; it confirms Newbank as a self-governing district."

I laughed.

He smiled. "Yes, I think we can guess the Inquisitor's response, but who knows of the new saints?"

"But no one knows where their leaders are, or who they are?"

He nodded. "That's the thing. If an answer comes, I was hoping we might learn something from it."

"You're right."

Sef began looking about, suddenly distracted. He got up and walked towards the kitchen's high window.

"What is it?"

"Can't you smell it?

I stood and joined him. "Fresh smoke."

The window rose above us, small and barred. It was made more for ventilation than views, yet through it we could see a sky turning grey and dark.

Sef fetched a stool and stood on it. "The port burns!" He couldn't see the port itself, just thick plumes rising from its direction. They marked fires that looked to be worse than those of yesterday. "Someone's torching buildings."

I said, "Come, we'll hear more at the Guild."

18

Answers

Sef insisted on us using the coach for the short trip to the Guild, he wouldn't say it plainly, but I think he was worried about me mixing in crowds. It made for slow going on the packed streets, but I wasn't going to argue, not as I came to terms with my newest burden; being cursed by the god of murder.

As we reached the Cassaro, we could see what remained of the opposite shore after last night's fires. It spread as a blackened ruin with less than half its buildings still standing. The charred wasteland still smouldered.

Many of Newbank's residents had headed to the river to watch the port fires, and to use the last of the morning to share news. Some openly wore the symbols of their true faiths and there were even cabalists amongst them. Strangely, as the port burned in the distance, a sense of liberation reigned over Newbank.

I looked about at my home district's cramped buildings, standing shoulder to shoulder, and leaning out and above narrow streets with each new floor. Given the chance, fire would devour the place faster than a drunken sailor could jump a tavern wench.

Nearby, the river's waters flowed thick with ash. I looked past it to St Marco's Square, a mid-sized market on the opposite shore; as always my eyes were drawn to the tall belltower of the church that lent the area its name. Suddenly, the stone spire burst into flames, consumed by a blinding blue fireball. The deep growl and whump of the explosion caused screams and panic, all of it followed by the rumble of masonry as the bulk of the tower fell into the square.

"Gods!" whispered Sef.

"Would that be the Cabal?"

"I suppose, and what hope is there if even the Cabal is prepared to join the fight so openly?"

"It's not too late," I said, "not yet."

Sef just shook his head.

We were ushered into the Guildhall amidst a chaotic mess of rushing guildsmen and spiritless refugees. In the crowded compound it was obvious, despite the more relaxed air outside, that the situation across the city wasn't improving.

They took us straight to Kurgar's office. Inside he sat flanked by half a dozen guildsmen, as well as Mauricio of the Cabal, and the Kavist priest, Seig. My father was also present, rising from a chair in front of his desk.

"Welcome," Kurgar said.

I offered my father a smile of reassurance.

Kurgar continued, "Your father has also just arrived, so I'll share some news, but before that I'm sure we'd all like to know how you fared last night. I've heard that you were almost successful?"

"Almost, but they'd been moved moments before we got to them."

He frowned. "I'm so sorry."

"We'll try again."

"Do you know where they are?"

"Not yet, but we'll find them."

He nodded. "I wish you well with it, but now to other matters: Events are moving fast in the city, so I'll be brief. The messengers have returned. The Inquisitor will have no part in allowing Newbank to administer its own affairs. He has a simple demand; that we repair the bridge and prepare for the return of law and order."

Many in the room muttered.

Kurgar went on, "On the other hand, the followers of the new saints are willing to work with us."

Some offered smiles at the news, the cabalist going as far as clapping his hands together and calling out a cheer.

Kurgar nodded and resumed, "In fact, they're urging us to join them in working to expel the Inquisition."

I held my tongue. He knew, as did the others, that I wouldn't be a party to such a thing, and that made me wonder; why did they humour me? Why even allow me to be present for this discussion? My father had a right to be here as a wealthy and influential man who put much time and coin into the Guild, but me? Sef was right; they wondered about me.

I looked up to see the Cabalist gazing at me as if trying to get into my mind - he'd done it once before. The thought of it put me on guard. I slipped into the celestial and raised a shield to protect my soul. When that was done, I called up another layer, and then one more.

Kurgar continued, "Most of you will have already heard that the Inquisition sent gangs into the port this morning. It seems they went in looking for shrines dedicated to the new saints, but they've been forced back amidst much bloodletting.

"There's a very real thirst for revenge out there, and many will die today. Strictly, no one is to cross the river. Those two sides won't just be rioting by dusk, they'll be at war."

A ban on crossing the river would stop my search!

Sef half turned, waiting for me to dispute Kurgar's words.

As if in answer, the Guildmaster added, "Such a ban falls upon *all* of us. It's our duty to our people, to better place us for what comes next..."

I interrupted, but was determined to remain calm, "And what of my family?"

"Things are moving to a head, we can all see it." His tone came hard, making some in the room flinch. "You had your chance to save them, and despite a valiant attempt have failed. Do you really think another chance will present itself?"

"Yes, I'll get them."

His voice softened, "Juvela, I hate to be the one to say it, but we all know that they're probably already dead."

I glared at him.

"Juvela, we have to think of our people and not ourselves. I have more news this day, something I hope is nothing, but in truth is the real reason for the ban on crossing the river."

My father asked, "What other ill tidings could there possibly be?"

Kurgar sighed with fatigue. "We've heard that there's a rising sickness."

"Maro Fever?" A guildsman queried.

Kurgar shook his head. "No, something different."

Silence took the room.

He went on, "It's too early to say for certain how much of a danger it is, but with all the troubles in the city, Ossard could soon be ripe for plague."

Someone asked, "What is it?"

"It's a kind of pox, and it's appeared in a Heletian slum in the east of the city."

My father asked, "You're right to say the city is weakened, but this is so sudden?"

"The first case came to the attention of healers twelve or so days ago. It starts with a headache, and goes on to a mind-fever, one marked by delusions and some bleeding from the nose. At that point, the malady usually passes, but some go on to suffer small dark blisters." He looked around the room. "For those so touched, about one in six, it foretells their death."

My father whispered, "The city is doomed!"

I asked, "How far has it spread?"

"Our sources talk of it being centred in a Heletian slum, mainly in one area, but with a new outbreak nearby. The first site is the worst affected where half a dozen have died."

"Where?" I asked.

"Along the valley wall in the east, not near Newbank."

Sef voiced my own thoughts, "An Inquisition area?"

Kurgar's eyes widened with surprise. "I suppose so." He shrugged. "Until we know more, I don't want anyone crossing the river."

There was a murmur of agreement.

19

A Fourth Saint

That afternoon, I let Sef tend to his own business, while I finally got some sleep. I fell into bed exhausted, lost to slow and bitter tears.

I wept for my missing daughter, who I loved so very much, but also for my husband, a man I'd once loathed, but now longed to see. Eventually I drifted off and found some respite. I needed that, that moment to rest and gather my spirits.

When I later awoke it was midafternoon. I could have so easily just rolled over and closed my eyes, but instead I got up, planning to check on my parents.

I walked the short distance, leaving Kurt behind in his quarters above the stables to watch over the house.

I planned on a quick visit, one done to see how my mother was coping with all that was going on. It was there that I was when the news came, news that changed everything.

Everything...

I sat with my parents in their sitting room where we played at polite conversation and pretended that all was well. We talked of many things, but nothing of consequence, while we ignored the obvious topics of my stolen family, and the city, divided, burning itself slowly to the ground.

Then Sef arrived.

He burst in through the front door like a clap of thunder, earning a squeal from a maid. My mother opened her mouth to reprimand him, *the help*, but then she saw his obvious bewilderment. Instead, she asked, "Sef, whatever is it?"

He looked to me while holding up a hand as he caught his breath. Finally, he said, "The followers of the new saints have proclaimed a fourth!"

And the wail of horns sounded in the distance.

I stood, shaking my head.

He went on, "He's been named in the burning port, where his faithful are armed and dangerous, and readying to march to war!"

My heart faltered; armed and dangerous? He couldn't mean...

And a second set of horns blared in answer, sounding from somewhere much closer. The traditional instruments evoked images of the battle-scarred plains, lakelands, and deep forests of Fletland.

Sef forced it out, "It's Kave! The Heletites across the river are claiming that he's one of the new saints!"

I gasped.

"There's more; they're raising an army of Kavists, and they're on the other side of the Cassaro rallying their Flet brethren to war!"

My father gaped in horror. "If you go, Newbank will be defenceless!"

I said, "You can't, Kurgar has banned crossing the river."

Sef shook his head. "They say the Guild has retracted the ban. Regardless, fighters are already being ferried across!" His voice quaked with excitement, at once fearful, but also euphoric.

"Proclaimed amongst the new saints? Sef, is this a trick, or are they willing to allow any faith into their reformed church? Will Schoperde be next?"

And that was when I noticed the air's growing edge.

Sef shook his head, as veins stood out at his temples, and bulged about his neck. His eyes sparkled with excitement, while spittle flew from his lips. "Look into the celestial, look and see!"

My perception dipped into that other world, and there it was; the change I'd felt. Divine blessings were again about.

He called out the truth, while his hands clenched into trembling fists, "A rain of blessings! It's true! We're raising an army to reclaim the city!"

With his soul energised, I wasn't going to be able to stop him. Still, it was a chance to cross the river. "Sef, you're free to go, but you need to take me."

"No! This is a sacred duty, a pilgrimage!"

"I just need you to help me cross the river. Once done, I can search for Maria and Pedro behind your faithful line. Sef, you'll be free of me to do what you need. I won't have you mind me."

He wanted to refuse, and started to shake his head.

I glared at him, making it plain there was only one answer I'd accept.

In the end, desperate to get going, he gave in. "Alright, but I can only guarantee your crossing. On the other side, I won't be serving you, but Kave."

My parents rose to protest, but we left them.

Sef and I hurried towards the river, from where cheers rose along with the wail of horns. We spotted Cherub on the way, the big Flet greeted Sef by taking him into a great bear-hug, the two of them sharing their euphoria. I was all but ignored.

Moment by moment, they were both becoming more distant to me, and well and truly focused on the task at hand – Kave's task.

Thousands of Flets crowded Newbank's river shore, the mass thickest by the bridge. They cheered a group of Kavists at their heart, the big knot numbered in the hundreds. From there the warriors waited to cross the Cassaro by way of a dozen boats that ferried eager loads to the edge of St Marco's Square. The landing Kavists wasted no time on arrival; they climbed the river-wall, waved their battle colours, and drew their weapons.

Yet if Newbank presented a spectacle, the city-side did doubly so. On that other shore, tens of thousands of Heletians cheered a gathering of a couple of thousand devotees to Kave – they new, fearless, and raw.

The Flet Kavists arrived to be embraced by their Heletian brethren. They gathered to kill together, to shed blood and battle, yet on their faces played nothing but joy.

Watching it, I couldn't doubt that Kave sanctioned this. His warriors held his glory in their eyes and his strength in their arms. Kave *was* of the new saints, and with that acceptance came a realisation; in the end, despite how honourably combat might be conducted, it was nothing but bloody violence with death at its core.

Death...

I'd been blinded to the truth by a childhood awash in tales that celebrated the bloody defence of Fletland. Somewhere in all that, while the defence was necessary, my people's culture had become twisted so that we revered the bloodshed and tragedy, instead of the life it sought to protect.

Today, the god of battle had come to Ossard and raised an army, and now he'd go on to expel the Inquisition. Kave didn't do it because it was just, but because he wanted people dead. It was simple greed, nurtured and driven by the divine addiction of soul-feeding. He was in league with Death because of it, or more so, the great and mighty Kave was Death's bitch.

I was appalled.

Truly, the goddess of life had no allies, and now the divine war spoken of in the Book of Truth had come to rage openly on my own home's streets. And worst of all, Death would win here too.

Unless someone stood against it.

But how could you do such a thing without bringing more death – the very prize the war-gods sought?

It seemed like a riddle, something frustrating and confusing, and for an answer I only had hope.

There had to be others willing to make a stand?

In a city that found its nights haunted by the sombre notes of Schoperde's Song as surely as its days came veiled in smoke's grey, 'there had to be more than a few souls who shared allegiance to the goddess of life. If they were out there, I'd have to find them.

That realisation stirred another, one built of chilled whispers.

Grandmother hung close by.

I'd still not talked to her. Now, while being put into a boat with Sef and Cherub, didn't seem ideal, but it'd just have to do. So I passed my perception from one world to another.

I called into the celestial, "Grandmother!" And thus began my search.

Her cold blue spirit, gaunt and neglected, soon appeared. It seemed she was always close by. Long strands of spectral hair stormed about her illuminated face, rising like a halo in contrast to the dark pits that were her eyes. It gave me caution, especially after sighting her *other* halo.

Faint enough to be almost missed, scores of skulls circled her with each of them joined to her by a thin, silvered chain. They stared at me, and in an instant I knew them; it was the chorus of whispered voices I'd so often heard, the innocents who'd perished with her at The Burnings.

What had she become?

I'd been told that she'd once been a caring woman, wife, widow, and mother, but that was a lifetime ago.

She was changed.

I looked into the deep pits that should have held her eyes, but they only gaped darkly at me. "Greetings, Grandmother."

She gave a curt nod. "And to you, Granddaughter."

"You've watched over me all my life, haven't you?"

"Yes." She smiled afresh, but in the blue hues of the celestial, such a thing held no warmth.

"I'm no Cabalist."

She nodded. "I'd hoped you were, but it's not to be."

"I'm aligned to the gods, to Schoperde."

Her smile faded. "I'm surprised."

"Why?"

She sneered. "Because I thought Schoperde only took virgins, and not sluts who gave themselves away at the first sign of a gifted drink!"

The comment hurt, but I didn't reply.

She waited.

I said, "I don't have time for insults."

She studied me and then relented. "I apologise for the slight."

"It's alright, I've greater burdens."

She nodded. "I've been here a long time and it's not been easy."

"I can't imagine."

Again, she nodded. "This would've been easier if you'd been a witch, but I guess I have to *live* with that." She sniggered at her own joke. "And of Schoperde as well! A pleasant calling, but with no real power."

I waited.

She shrugged, a movement that stirred her haunting skulls. "Juvela, I'm more friend than foe. Over time I've lost my chance to be reborn, but I can wander, yet this realm isn't safe. I can't survive it by myself. I need to stay near you."

"Me?"

"Don't act surprised, you know that you're special - you've had a whole morning of your hulking bodyguard telling you that very thing. He's right. Your soul *is* old and powerful, and being near it gives me sanctuary."

"How?"

217

"Your untapped power keeps the sad predators of this place at bay. They hunger for it, but it's so strong and pure that it's poisonous to them, and that keeps them back. Me, perhaps because of our shared bloodline, I can get close and shelter in your soul's glare." Her face fell into a grim smile, something ominous. "And for that I'm grateful, it's given me a lair."

Her words chilled me.

"Juvela, only one thing overrides my concern for you, and that's my hunger for revenge. I want to kill that dog, Anton, and as many of his brethren as I can. I want to drag him from the mortal world and torment him, I want to shred his soul and twist it, I want to curse it and piss in it, and then I want to scatter its ruins to the *feeders* and see him lost to Oblivion!"

"It's true that he's a man with blood on his hands, but my priority is my family, then my people, and then my city. Do you understand?"

Reluctantly, she nodded.

I regarded her. "Will you hinder me?"

She shook her head, setting the skulls about her to shift and their empty eyes to flash. "Juvela, I'll work with you."

And that would just have to do.

My perception returned to the real world, where I found myself packed between Kavists on our cramped river crossing. The men and women about me were restless, some talked quietly while others prayed. A few glanced at me with questioning looks, but most accepted me, knowing of my respected family and having heard of my part in the opera house raid.

Our boat reached the opposite shore to grind against the river-wall, as Kave's newest followers called out greetings from above.

Sef went up first, then me. I waited beside him for Cherub, uncomfortable amidst a crowd of blessing-drunk Heletians. Watching them in this exuberant moment, I couldn't help but wonder at how many of them had spent the previous day looting Flet homes.

I slipped *part* of my perception into the celestial to see this strange moment in both worlds. The darkness of the void didn't show in that double vision, only the luminescence of souls and magic.

The glowing bolts of the first blessings that had initially energised the Kavists, Flet and Heletian, had now faded away. The battle god had finished bestowing them, but now prepared to gift a second wave.

Scores of deep blue lights began to race across smoke-dimmed skies. They only got faster as they sought out the souls of a select troop, and then, one by one, they found them.

The gifted power set the hearts of the chosen racing, crazing their minds, and flushing their eyes red. Of all the blessings I'd so far witnessed, this one came promising to be the most violent. In it Kave bestowed nothing but bloodlust, anger, and the hunger to see all life bowed. This was his blessing of ultimate glory; to be made, for a time, one of his *Berserk Guard*.

His so-blessed warriors drew their weapons, arched their backs, and growled out deep and loud battle cries.

The Kavists about me cheered their honoured fellows, while Flets continued to climb up the river-wall, and into the arms of their Heletian counterparts. They sang and cheered together, lost in their strange joy. Watching it all, I wondered if the Inquisitor had any idea of what would soon be coming for him.

Soon enough, their cheers began to fade and give way to a rising chant. It boomed rhythmic and rough, banged by fist on armour. It rolled out to dominate the river districts with its simple tones, and in it Kave's faithful prayed for success, honour, and yet more power.

Standing amongst them, I could only wonder what such a large gathering of cultists could do when so blessed. Surely they'd take the city – after all they had the numbers, skill, and the backing of the god of battle.

How could they fail!

I fell back from them to find some space amidst the gear of a nearby cart. Sef and Cherub didn't even notice; they were lost in their exuberance as they waited to work Kave's commands.

Sadly, I realised that this was where Sef and I parted ways. Today, his loyalty to Kave overcame any coin my family could offer, and even our deep bonds of friendship. If Kave was to stand amongst the new saints, then Sef as his priest would stand with him, but I could not.

Such thoughts only fed a growing sense of loneliness.

About me, the voices of the Kavists rang out heavy as they began to punch at the sky. They sang out simply, using a small cycle of words, with most of it lost in the roll of their verse, except for the last; die!

The Flet Kavists had now all reached St Marco's, seeing the force complete. At the same time the chorus climaxed with a thunderous cheer.

They formed up on the riverside road and began to cross the square. I walked behind them while scrying the nearby buildings, seeking for any sign of my family. After me came a much larger crowd, the faithful of the new saints. While none of them cursed me, I could read their many thoughts, "The Forsaken Lady!" And for most of them I remained a symbol of ill-favour.

It was a contradiction for me to be there, perhaps even dangerous, but the Kavists seemed to have accepted me, so, grudgingly, the greater crowd let me be.

Again I trod the streets of Ossard surrounded by space.

Again I was alone and outcast.

Then something brushed my arm.

It was maddeningly soft, like a down feather, but also chill. I turned and saw nothing, yet knew that was wrong. A moment later, the celestial gave me the answer.

My grandmother haunted beside me, unseen by the surrounding crowd. She smiled, a genuine thing this time, it taking away the unease of our earlier conversation. Now her eyes weren't dark pits, but there to sparkle as if full of life. "You won't walk alone, my dear, not if I can help it."

The Kavists began their march to cross St Marco's Square.

At their front surged those blessed to be berserk; one hundred of Kave's chosen. They moved about, restless, and on the verge of charging to Ossard's distant heart. Behind them came the rest of their brethren; the new Heletian converts, and the more seasoned Flets. A command of Kave's senior priests led those ranks, it almost exclusively Flet.

The command stood tall and determined, with battle banners rising from where they were strapped to their backs. All of them wore well-crafted armour, and brandished fine blades, a few of them even wielded blessed weapons licked by running flames.

St Marco's church loomed on the far side of the square in challenge, despite its ruined belltower.

Kave's command stopped in front of it, and began to climb its rubble-strewn steps. Its great double doors slammed shut at their approach, the churchmen inside sending one of their number sprinting away from the building's rear.

None of the Kavists cared.

Seig Manheim reached the top of the steps to the cheers of his warriors and the broader crowd. He raised his hands for quiet, the motion flexing his thick arms; more than any he spoiled for battle. "We march on the Cathedral, and to take back the Malnobla for the people. From there we expel the Inquisitor and his dogma of hate!" His banner rose on a fresh breeze, its navy field opening to reveal a golden fist.

The Kavists raised their weapons and cheered, something made louder by the roar of the crowd. The berserkers, trembling and drooling under the pain of divine restraint, added a series of battle cries before loping towards the avenue that would take them to the Malnobla.

Seig cried, "For Kave!" And bounded down the stairs.

I followed the Kavists, while the crowd also began to rouse. Behind me, many of them paused to pelt St Marco's with loose cobbles and rubble from the belltower. The mob outnumbered the Kavists, perhaps by as many as five to one.

If the Kavists were an army, then what was it that followed them?

The tall windows of St Marco's became obvious targets. The tinkle of rocks punching through the rare coloured glass peppered the square, all of it followed by the ugly chime of the precious shards falling to shatter. Before long, someone hurled a ball of burning rags through one of the broken windows. By the time my own boots found the avenue, the windows loomed as gaping holes that spewed thick smoke.

The Kavists marched unchallenged. In the distance, through the haze, we could see the lone figure of the churchman who'd fled to carry a warning. He was halfway there.

The Kavists kept a good pace, set by the rhythm of their chant. The crowd behind me also pushed on. I strode on between them, alone, aside from my haunting grandmother, while scrying for Pedro and Maria.

Perhaps, when we reached the Square, I'd again search the opera house...

But each step I took only fed rising doubts. My spirit, which had been so buoyed at being able to restart my search, now began to fail.

Grandmother whispered, "Don't worry, I'll help you in your search."

But I wondered; could we be too late?

"They're hidden, and that means they live."

And in front of us, Kave's march continued, all of it accompanied by prayers, horns, and cheers.

The Cathedral's bells started to toll, not long after the entrance to Market Square came into view.

And it was then that the empty avenue leading to it suddenly began to fill. A couple of hundred Heletians spilled from the streets towards its end, all of them armed with swords and makeshift shields. The Loyalists were moving to meet the Kavists.

The warriors of the cult of battle lifted their swords, checked armour, and readied themselves. The Kavists didn't mock or jeer the defenders, they simply doubled their march. They had to; the berserkers having spotted a foe finally lost the last of their control.

A great cheer rose from the mob behind us, hungry for revenge.

And the ranks of the Kavists moved faster, trying to keep up with their berserk brethren.

The berserkers gave a guttural roar, as their lope became a run.

I whispered, "Sweet Schoperde, please protect Sef, even though he follows another." And a bright golden spark sped out from me to charge into the rear of the advancing Kavists. It was magic, and woven from the stuff of love and life.

I marvelled. Somehow I'd called something, something to protect him; a blessing. I was learning.

Perhaps there was hope...

Up ahead, the Loyalists tried to link their shields.

The berserkers, frenzied and wild, now charged at full sprint.

And the main body of Kavists burst into song and took up their horns.

While the Loyalists braced themselves.

Then the berserkers were upon them.

The touched warriors crashed through the defensive line, swinging swords and roaring like animals. Blood sprayed up, along with cleaved flesh and broken shields. The berserkers didn't slow, miss a step, or even choke on their battle cries. They met the faithful of Krienta, and in a moment, cut through them.

But Kave grew bored of chants, song, and play...

The crazed Kavists emerged from the defenders' ruin. They didn't pause or even glance at their grim harvest, they just headed on.

The Kavist ranks in front of me cheered, while the mob behind roared.

I winced at their madness. How could they all give themselves so easily to hate? They disgusted me, leaving me glad to be outcast and alone...

...until I found that I wasn't.

She stood behind me wearing a worn grey dress. Surprised, I just started and stared. She was Heletian, perhaps somewhere in her late twenties, with a trace of silver prematurely teasing the temples of her hair. The colours worked well with her olive skin and hazel eyes, and when she smiled, it all joined to come alive.

"Alone no more!" my grandmother whispered.

The woman stood only a pace away, she didn't flinch or fall back, or even look frightened. With a firm voice she said, "My name is Baruna, and I'd like to walk with you?"

I gestured towards Market Square. "I was going this way."

She nodded. "Then let's go *together*."

And we turned to walk side by side, while the mob behind us fell silent.

Baruna said, "I've come to end your loneliness *and* mine. You've hope and compassion, I saw it in the square when you saved that poor woman's child. What you have is what we're poor in, and what Ossard needs in these dark days."

Her words warmed me. Already I could feel my burden lighten, as if it was now shared.

I was no longer alone!

And ahead, the berserkers leading the Kavist charge had almost reached Market Square - yet *we* barely noticed. While Death loomed up to cast his shadow over the city, we stood as a spark of life, and perhaps, as Baruna had put it, hope.

But that spark was threatened by the surrounding madness.

The Kavists followed the berserkers in their charge, their swords raised and banners flying.

Before them opened the wide space of Market Square. It stood naked of its stalls and merchants, instead its middle spread blocked by a wall of robed churchmen. Behind that priestly line of a hundred stood thousands of Loyalists fingering grim blades, many of them makeshift weapons taken from kitchens, fishmongers, and butchers.

Inquisitor Anton stood above it all in one of the Cathedral's belltowers, from where he bellowed, "Oh sweet faithful, Krienta watches and will appraise you. Be ready to work his will!"

His pious followers cried out for the chance.

From across the square, the Kavists called out in answer.

The priests waited, but did not fear.

And all the while, with each moment, Kave's berserkers drew nearer.

Krienta's holy men readied the seeds of their blessed defence. They knew that their lord wouldn't abandon them, not here and now. United, they cried, "For Saint Baimio and his father, our righteous lord, Krienta!"

And the celestial heaved as hundreds drew upon it for power.

That strange other world, normally a pool of dark calm, churned into boiling life. The air about us tingled as it tensed, filling with flaring sparks.

Behind us, the followers of the new saints surged forward. They wanted to be a part of this, the smashing of the *unreformed* Church.

The berserkers raced across the square with blood-flushed eyes, crying from drooling mouths. For these touched warriors, only kills would do, but they'd have to work for them; Krienta's priests were already casting.

The Inquisitor led that casting as he called from up on high, "Oh Krienta, heretics have dared enter the heart of your proclaimed city! We beg you to bless us so that we may show them your mercy, or if you wish it, judge them, and leave them blinded by their soul's blight!"

His priests raised their arms, "May the carriers of heresy be struck blind!"

The square filled with piercing cries.

A flock of black ravens appeared, launching themselves into the smoke-heavy air from the weatherworn ledges of the Cathedral's towers. Countless, they circled and cawed with grating voices, only to suddenly turn and dive.

Warnings were yelled.

And like a furious black hail, the ravens struck, raining down to seek the eye-flesh of the lead Kavists.

People cried out in horror.

Of all the Kavists, only a handful had helms or time to raise shields.

I looked for Sef in the chaos, finally spotting him with Cherub at the centre of the carnage. A Heletian between them had taken one of the birds in the face, the blow bringing the man to his knees, while the frenzied beast worked to puncture his eyes. Sef grabbed at the frantic bird, tearing it from the man before snapping its spine. In sober disgust, he threw the feathered lump to the cobbles and used a boot to crush the life out of it.

The stunned Heletian sported a red face with torn and bloody cheeks. He'd been lucky, he still had his sight - many others around him didn't.

The birds continued to attack, gouging and slashing, and bursting the eyes of any Kavist they could. Agonised howls filled the square as blinded warriors fell to their knees while dropping their swords.

Despite the gore of it, the Kavist charge went on - if slowed. And amidst the advance, Kave's priests desperately worked to finish their own castings to end the threat from above. Two of them in the command worked especially hard to provide such relief, chanting and praying while rubbing flints together from where they kneeled.

When the ravens ended one attack, those that escaped the swinging swords, fists, and grabbing hands of the Kavists launched themselves back into the air. They rushed to gain height, before turning about to dive back down and seek fresh eye-flesh.

After the savage fury, marked by their harsh screech and deep caw, some began to squawk in surprise. No longer did their call hold anger, now it began to ring out with fright.

Above the square, as they sought fresh victims, some of the birds began to smoulder and leave singed and flaming feathers to fall free. Before long, it wasn't just a few birds so afflicted, but most of the flock. Their pained sounds became more panicked until they started to burst aflame. The squealing birds then fell as balls of fire to land with sickening thuds amidst a haze of stinking smoke and singed feathers.

Warriors swatted other birds off their comrades before stomping them dead. In moments, Kave's priests had seen the ravens finished.

With their warriors now free, their mighty charge could resume.

Krienta's priests braced themselves. They knew that this would be a test, their biggest test, of their character and faith's truth.

The Kavists closed the gap.

And from that other realm, Kave also watched. He paid heed to his followers here, as he did to them everywhere, but only the most deserving would receive any more gifts. Ultimately, the skills of his followers would decide who won their battles, not endless favours.

In contrast, Krienta was a god worshipped by only one people, of one region, of one world. The Heletians revered him, but no one else. He didn't just *watch*, he *worked* to see his followers win, lest this be the beginning of his undoing.

The Krientan priests stood in front of the Loyalists, the ordinary townsfolk poor in weapons and skills, but rich in faith. The Loyalist force seemed outdone, until, led by Anton, their priests uttered a second curse.

The Inquisitor called out from above, "Krienta, you have seen their souls and sampled their truths, now lend us your power to cripple the heretics amongst these fools!"

His priests spread their arms, as they cried out, "May the carriers of heresy be struck lame!"

And again Krienta listened.

The lead Kavists froze with their swords in mid-swing, while their roaring voices failed. Some stood posed like statues, others just slowed as if burdened by cold-bitten joints strung with weak muscles on age-weary frames.

Many Kavists escaped this latest curse to continue the advance, but soon discovered that their way lay blocked by their crippled brethren. The Kavists' battle cry, its roar halved by sickened throats, fell into confusion.

Some of Kave's priests sought a divine solution to this latest trial, others raised their swords and called out fresh rally cries.

Emboldened by Krienta's support, his priests moved on with their plan. Half of them drew knives and stepped forward to begin their bloody tasks, seeing them slash at exposed throats and stab at undefended hearts and bellies. In moments, the white robes of the Church of Baimiopia turned red.

The square spread half full of Krienta's cursed, the Kavists too sickly to do anything but wait for the advance of his blood-drenched priests. There was hope for them though; their fellows were passing through the maze that their blighted bodies had created, and they came unaffected and free.

Krienta's priests held knives and daggers, but were poor in the skills of wielding them. Having to face the swords of enraged Kavists was an unbalanced contest, yet they didn't shy away from it.

Anton's voice rolled out again, "And with their wilting bodies and sour souls, let their minds be fouled!"

And Krienta's priests, those who'd stayed in place during the slaughter of the lame, cried, "May the heretics taste of lunacy's flower!"

Again, desperate to win the day, lest this be the first defeat in a long line that would leave his people, church, and ultimately himself vanquished, Krienta granted the request.

Kave laughed at his divine rival's desperation. He'd never so lower himself, besides the world held more than one battle this day; wars raged in far off places where the stakes were greater. He wished his followers well, but left them to prove themselves.

The advancing Kavists spilled through the tangle of their blind and lame brethren to cut into the Krientan priests, but again their charge was to be stilled. Some of their number slowed, seeming to be struck down like their fellows, but they hadn't – they suffered a different fate.

Instead of taking ill and coming to a stop, the newly cursed kept moving, but stumbled and blundered. Some left trails of drool as they wandered, others groaned and mewled, while some simply sat down and trembled. A few dropped their weapons, while others cut at themselves. One poor wretch stabbed at a lame fellow's back, as if trying to cut a way through.

Baruna and I came into the square near the opera house. We climbed the grand old building's front steps and surveyed the terrible scene. This was the bleak world promised by Death, a world of blood and war detailed with carnage and decay.

The Kavists continued their advance, passing their cursed and wounded. Some of their fellows managed to shake off their blights, only to reach for their dropped weapons and croak out renewed battle cries.

Left as it was, the Kavists would win through skill and numbers.

But it wasn't to be left.

To balance the Kavist advance, more and more of the pious Heletians pushed past their priests' breaking line. They charged with whatever weapons they had to hand, but also armed with faith and determination.

Already the cobbles lay thick with bodies and gore.

Blood and more blood...

Strangely, crowds gathered at the edges of the square to watch the macabre spectacle. Before long, some of their number also joined in.

Bloody chaos, and it only deepened...

Standing there with Baruna, I realised that it was the city that stood forsaken and not me. They just couldn't see it. Even in the confusion of battle, people kept away from me.

They were crazy!

And above it all Anton watched.

Surprisingly, I could read his feelings. Like mine, they ran strong right now, making them difficult to shield. He'd also had enough of the fighting, but for so many different reasons.

He wanted it finished; not just the battle, but the whole uprising. The disgust on his face for the Kavists and Reformers was plain. He wanted them crushed, it setting his anger to burn and flare.

He cried into the celestial, "Enough!"

And I could feel him gather power as he bound it with his rage. He asked of Krienta a mighty blessing, and his god, so desperate to hold Ossard, gave him what he wanted.

His power deepened, then doubled, and then began to surge as though Krienta himself touched the Inquisitor.

Baruna looked to me with nervous eyes, her calm shaken. "I can feel something, something coming, something woven of shadow, anger, and fear."

She wasn't alone, many in the square also began to look about with unease.

The very air began to chill and become brittle, as if haunted by Death's stale breath. The tension rose as more and more people stopped fighting to focus on a threat they felt, yet that remained unseen.

Nervous, Baruna shifted beside me, so I reached out to take her hand. Before they met, the gap between them blazed into life with a fat and flaring spark. She started, but I grabbed her hand.

I whispered, "Please Schoperde, I'll give anything to save these people from whatever doom stirs."

Power began to gather in my soul, seeping through into my body as it came into our world. I worked to control it, wrestling with it while the air around me buzzed and snapped.

Baruna turned to me. "Please, you must stop him!"

But I barely heard. I was lost in my efforts to manage the power flooding into me.

For the briefest of moments, I risked a glance at Anton to see if he was close to finishing his task. I could see his spell gathering in the celestial, some kind of fiery coil, it rank with power.

I called, "The Inquisitor brings death, get out of the square!" and my voice rang out over a sea of people looking for a threat they felt, but couldn't see.

The Inquisitor replied into my mind, "You can't save them!"

He was probably right, but I had to try!

Seig Manheim stood at the heart of the bloodstained square, his torn battle colours hanging limp from the pole strapped to his back. He could also sense the strength of Anton's casting, seeing him call, "Retreat! Get out of the square!"

The disbelief was plain on his warriors' faces: They were of Kave and had the skills and numbers to fight. They could finish this, win it, and take the city. There was no need for flight!

"Get out!" he demanded, his voice booming.

While some wondered at his wisdom, his fellow priests worked at breaking the curses still plaguing so many of their brethren.

He bellowed, "Retreat!" and something close to fear edged his voice.

His tone saw others take up the call, while the alarm on his face washed away doubts.

I realised that he knew what was coming; he could read Anton's casting.

All the while, the Reformers of the new saints kept pushing into the square at the Kavists' rear. Unaware of the coming danger, they were blocking the Kavists' best line of retreat.

My eyes began to sting, my stomach knot, and my legs cramp. There was going to be much death here, too much.

I had to do something!

Anton commanded from his belltower, "Rally to your priests, the heretics run!"

And the Loyalists charged to attack the Kavists in their confusion.

Anton grinned from above as his eyes came aglow with power.

Baruna begged, "Do something!"

I lifted my arms as the font within me boiled. "The Inquisitor brings death, get out of the square!" This time my message was powered by the energy that filled me. I didn't just think it or hear it, but felt it thrum through my heart, bones, and flesh.

COLIN TABER

In a moment, thousands of eyes locked onto me.

Someone yelled, "The Forsaken Lady cries doom!"

Seig and his priests bellowed, "Retreat!"

And Baruna called, "*She's* trying to save you!"

Finally, the Reformers pushing into the square behind the Kavists began to slow and the first of them turned and fled.

Despite all that was happening, the Church's Loyalists continued to fight on. Unknown to them, their priests fell back behind them to head for the Cathedral.

The Kavists were mostly caught between the Reformers and the Loyalists. They were never going to get away.

I called out, "This way!" repeating the message in the celestial.

And every Kavist heard me.

Those with no better choice ran for me. They forgot the jammed streets, the mobs, and their foes and fallen comrades; they just ran for the opera house.

I clicked my fingers on both hands.

A wind rose up as a sudden squall to gust across the square. It knocked people over and tore at banners, before blustering past to punch open the main doors of the opera house.

The first Kavists came sprinting up the steps followed by hundreds of others. Sef was amongst them. "Juvela, you must come inside!"

I shook my head. "Go!" And my perception was lost to him.

I searched the Inquisitor's gathering power, trying to understand its weave.

What was it?

I held my hands out, my fingers tingling. I was about to begin casting, but I still didn't know what to do to or how to protect us.

And then the Inquisitor finished brewing his magic.

His words spilled across the square like a mountain's deep rumble to make the ground shake and draw dust from buildings, "May they be cleansed by your fury!"

Silence...

The smoke-heavy sky started to flare and spark, as though the night's stars had come out early to discuss the bloody events below. The white and yellow lights only got brighter, their heat growing.

I looked closely, my perception straddling both worlds. Something was up there working to nurture it, whatever *it* was.

Angels!

230

Krienta's winged servants laboured without question, using their sacred swords to cut into the very fabric of our world. They opened a tear between it and the third; the elemental.

What I could see was elemental fire!

The anger of that primal place boiled through, and from there it spilled to begin its long fall to the ground. It let out a chorus of fiery screams as it scorched the very air.

I had to hurry!

I still didn't know what I was casting, but I could feel the beginnings of its power flow.

Someone in the square yelled, "A miracle!"

The falling fire wasn't a divine gift, it wouldn't know friend from foe. It would incinerate everybody.

The Kavists continued to flood past.

Baruna said, "We should get inside!"

"Go, Baruna, I've got to cast."

She looked to the sky. "We need shelter!"

"Go, I have to see this through."

My fingers stung as though pierced by nails. I could feel the power, it invisible, yet rushing out.

Again from the crowd, "A miracle!"

And then the rising scream of the falling fire drowned out everything else.

The Reformers were now retreating, some even running up the steps and into the opera house. Many others stood to stare skywards in bewilderment. About them lay hundreds of injured and a thousand dead.

Anton's casting howled louder, its light now blazing brighter than the sun. Those still in the open no longer spoke of miracles, instead they finally began to turn and run.

Too late!

I flicked my fingers to see the opera house doors slam shut.

It was time to ignore those caught in the open, and to concentrate on my casting: Whatever I was going to do, I had to get it right.

Baruna whispered, "Sweet Mother!"

Then all I knew was blinding heat, hot enough to redden my skin and draw sweat to dampen my clothes. It was madness! The whole square was going to burn, thousands would die, and the heart of Ossard would be scorched!

My grandmother hissed, "Any time now, dear!"

Nasty bitch!

The air filled with the stink of sweat and singeing hair, while the clothes of those still trapped in the open began to smoulder. A searing wind came up to squall about, its gusting blast seeing me go from being wet with sweat to being as dry as the brittle pages of my grandmother's tome.

Thinking of her, I whispered, "Time enough, indeed." And the power that had been running through me burst out tenfold.

What had previously seemed like a strong flow had just been leakage, now the real magic began. It left me gasping: It was ecstasy, orgasm, and childbirth, and so much more.

My spine arched back as my arms were thrown out wide, and my fingers lost to sparking jets of blinding blue.

My grandmother's voice sounded, its bitterness gone, "Control it, but don't slow it; just push it out. If it hurts, push harder!"

And I did.

The square about us became cooler as the power flooded out from me. It raced for the heights of the surrounding buildings, working as it weaved something between them. Long strands became visible that reached across the square to form a kind of arched web. The strands kept growing thicker and more numerous, until they joined to dim the light and ease the heat.

Another fool cried, "A miracle!"

I wove my casting by forcing it this way and that. I yelled, "Get out of the square!" And then the power in me began to stumble.

The elemental fire still fell from above, but was now seen through a laced roof of deep blue ice.

The crowd responded to my words. They ran and crawled, and did what they could to escape. Through a haze of exhaustion, I realised that I'd accomplished something; I'd bought them time.

The flow of power through my aching fingers slowed, and then came at last to a stop. My back straightened, but my legs just wanted to drop me. I opened my mouth to reveal a swollen tongue overcome by an unbelievable thirst, as I rasped, "Elemental water."

And the threads of the thick weave joined to turn into a roof of rippling liquid, its cool bulk haunted by great shards of ice.

The temperature in the square dropped, as did the glow and howl of the falling fire.

I grabbed Baruna, pulling her to one of the opera house's columns. "Hold on!"

A thunderous boom sounded.

The elemental fire flashed a blinding yellow, forcing us to close our eyes.

The next moment, the air was replaced by water, not a solid flood, but a thick spray that seemed more liquid than not. It blasted past us to knock us off our feet, and went from cool, to warm, and briefly to hot. Just as quickly as it had come, it was gone.

The sound of running water filled the square. It ran from roofs, facades, and steps, seeking the gutters as it made its escape.

I let go of Baruna, and together we left our shelter behind the column to take in the scene.

Above us the sky was clear, just as the square before us spread almost washed clean. It sat sparkling in the afternoon sun, flooded in places, as rivulets flowed to drain it away.

People cautiously appeared from buildings, streets, and laneways about its edge, their eyes wide with wonder.

The tops of the taller buildings - the Cathedral's two belltowers, the roof of the Malnobla, and the heights of the Turo - all stood blackened. The stark burns made it clear where my watery shield had ended.

Baruna looked to me and laughed with relief. I could only smile. She said, "What a wonder, you saved all of us!" And then she glanced over my shoulder.

I turned half expecting to see the beginnings of some new outrage, or hopefully Sef, but it was just a man.

The Heletian stood at my side and of a similar age to Baruna. His face lit up as we turned to him, it carrying the dark weathering of too much sun - or perhaps too much grief. "I'm Marco, Marco Cerraro, and I'd very much like to help you, as you alone seem to be working to save the people of the city."

Joy shone in his eyes, the same kind of honest happiness that Baruna shared, yet for him I could see that it also battled a deep sadness. There and then, I knew that the troubles of the city had already touched him.

He lifted my hand to his lips and kissed it, and the thrill of being alive raced through me. "Welcome Marco, I'm Juvela, and this is Baruna."

He smiled as though my words were a balm.

Behind us, a young woman skipped through the square. "It's a miracle! Saint Baimio's tears have washed the city clean!" She trailed a streamer of the Inquisition's black, navy, and gold behind her, as the depths of the receding waters began giving up the bodies they'd hidden.

I shook my head. "It's time to leave."

20

Words of Warning

The three of us left the square - I couldn't stay, not in a place so marked by death. I led us towards the port to leave behind emerging crowds that wandered in shock, spoke of miracles, or who simply stared after us.

To some of them I was still the Forsaken Lady, but for others I'd become something else. I didn't notice it at first, but some of them followed.

Now seemed as good a time as any to walk the streets sensing for Maria and Pedro, as I didn't think anyone would stop me. I felt tired, and doubted I could stand any more casting, but time for finding my family was running out.

Such thoughts reminded me of how I'd looked after the magic at the opera house. I lifted my hands to examine them, expecting to find them marked, stained, and wrinkled like a hag's. With relief I saw that the skin hung a little loose, but it was barely noticeable.

My grandmother whispered, "You pushed it out, the gathered energy. You pushed it *all* out and didn't let it wear you down."

I slipped my perception into the celestial to answer her, still stung by her mockery as I'd been casting.

She was there waiting for me.

Her spectral form smiled with sparkling eyes as she welcomed me to the cold and dark void. There was something comfortable about her, about the way she carried herself. She seemed different to the way I sometimes saw her; the form marked by dark and empty eye sockets, and haunted by her skull halo.

I wondered at that. Her mood often seemed to differ, swinging easily from one extreme to another. Right now she waited to be warm and helpful, but at other times she'd been stubborn and bitter. I'd have to watch her. She was complicated, as if she came with two faces.

Regardless, this was no time to linger. I thanked her and returned my attention to the real world, to my new companions, and the search for my family.

Back on the cobbled avenues of Ossard, I walked with Baruna and Marco, along with a few others who shyly followed behind. They trailed in calm silence, not like the mob that had come down from St Marco's, or the hateful crowd that had waited to meet them.

Those with me seemed to be gentle souls looking to bring Ossard back to peace. They'd been changed by recent events, shaken from their own complacent lives, to realise that *they* had a part to play in halting the city's death.

Beyond any doubt, I was no longer *forsaken*, but that being the case; what was I? Of Schoperde, certainly, but the power I handled seemed to be more than priestly – after all I'd just bested an Inquisitor.

Every day only brought more mysteries.

Quite a few of the buildings we passed had been looted and some razed by fire. The streets were thick with rubble and ash. Scavengers picked over the ruins; rodents, birds, cats and dogs, and even people. Increasingly, the townsfolk weren't after valuables, just food.

What had happened to my city?

The streets seemed deserted, but if you stopped and listened you could hear the movement of looters as they rifled through the rubble. More often, drowning out all else, came the mournful sobs of those left bereaved or homeless.

All of it dared me to consider that perhaps the city *was* too far gone, but I refused to accept it. I thought I could still have the old Ossard back *and* Pedro and Maria too. I had to believe it.

By the time we'd reached the waterfront, the numbers of those following me had tripled. Two dozen walked behind me, a mix of Heletians and Flets.

Thankfully, something distracted me from that uncomfortable realisation; the Lae Velsanan ship that had been in port only four days ago was again moored. A full score of its soldiers stood on the wharf, armed and barring access, while they eyed the smoke rising over the city.

Even at a glance, it was obvious that the sleek ship had taken damage. One of its three main masts was down, snapped near the base, other harm was also clear.

I walked towards it with Marco and Baruna, and followed by the rest. The Lae Velsanan guards in their sea-greens didn't move, but watched our approach. I slowed as we neared.

Looking across the deck, I searched for the officer I'd spoken to before, but was wary of his cold-souled senior.

Activity covered the ship. Reset rigging dangled and strained as it was adjusted, a section of the bow's railing was being mended, and new supplies delivered. The crew were busy, and amongst them laboured a bare-chested common-man.

The blonde Flet, broad-backed and muscled, toiled to move heavy crates into position on the deck. He turned about to expose his thick arms and toned chest, his torso covered in a gentle mat of golden hair. He laboured alone amongst the Lae Velsanans, but showed no sign of fear.

I looked to his face, from where sweat ran down his brow and temples, despite a cloth tied about his forehead. He straightened up and stretched, brushing back his hair to take with it the sweatband. The movement uncovered his pointed ears.

He was no middling; it was the Lae Velsanan.

If not for his ears, he could've so easily passed for a Flet. His chest spread twice as thick in width and depth compared to those surrounding him, and he stood around my height, making him very short for one of his own kind. He also carried a hard masculine air that his tall and lean fellows lacked, consequently he'd missed out on their innate sense of grace. He was an enigma.

He'd noticed that the crew about him had fallen silent, so turned towards the city and saw me. Casually, he waved, as if we were long-time friends, and then he bent down to grab his shirt as he called out orders.

After squeezing into his sea-green shirt, he made his way towards us. Behind him, three of his fellows moved to finish his hard tasks.

I felt embarrassed. I'd been ogling him, and now he interrupted his work to come and see what I wanted.

What did I want?

My mind swam with shameful images of his chest and strong arms. They were quickly chased away by guilty thoughts of my own family, and a city being lost to Death.

How could I think of such a thing, and with a Lae Velsanan!

He smiled as he closed the gap between us, but I still had no idea of what I wanted. His warm manner disarmed my growing unease. "How are you?" he asked, remembering that last time we'd met I'd fainted.

"Well, and much better than before."

He nodded, and glanced past to the rising smoke that marked the city. "It has begun?"

I turned to look behind me, to that growing forest of twisting plumes that climbed over Ossard. Fresh fires were being lit all the time, adding to the haunting pall.

I said, "The city has split into factions."

He grimaced as he wiped late sweat from his brow. "We lost a mast and some supplies at sea. You can't see it from here, but just over the horizon is an arc of diabolical storms. Our Cabalist says that they've been raised with magic. It left us little choice but to return."

"So you'll stay?" My hopeful tone surprised me.

"No." He looked to the skyline and shook his head. "None can stay, not now. We'll try to leave again, and if necessary we'll die in the trying. We have to get news of this to home."

"Home, to Lae Wair-Rae?"

"Yes, to our High King."

I began to worry. "Why? What business is it of his?"

"This is the business of everyone. It's not about mortal politics, but divine power." He then shook his head in anger at himself for his bluntness. After a pause, he forced a smile and asked, "Your child is safe?"

I could feel the blood drain from my face. "She's been taken."

He winced. "I'm so sorry."

"Her father and his parents as well; they took the whole bloodline."

And his jaw dropped in surprise. "The whole bloodline?"

"All of it, three generations."

"By Velsana!"

"What does it mean?"

He took a step back as he looked to the smoke-dressed city. His eyes then darted back, but now held a mix of sympathy and fear. "It means too much..." and his words trailed off.

"I need your help, I need to understand."

He shrugged. "I can't tell you much, I'm no priest or cabalist."

"Please, tell me what you can."

After a moment, he said, "They need sacrifices to feed *things* during their rituals. Using souls linked by a bloodline boosts the power harvested, it means they can use less people to get the strength required. If they're gathering them, then a ritual can't be far off."

"A ritual for what?"

"For control of the city. They want to create a haven, something that will become a base from where they'll build an empire of corruption."

I whispered, "They? The cultists?"

He nodded. "High King Caemarou won't let it happen. He'll go to war to stop it."

"But Ossard is part of the Heletian League, and only the smallest member – just a city-state despite its wealth." And how those words tasted sour, for the evidence about me spoke only of ruin. "If Lae Wair-Rae went to war against Ossard, King Giovanni of Greater Baimiopia would be forced to intervene. The Church of Baimiopia wouldn't allow any other action..." my voice failed as I pictured the carnage.

He spoke my thoughts, "And the remaining Heletian League states would also be drawn in. It would make Dormetia a battlefield, and the sea at its heart a foul pond littered with butchered bodies."

"It would be lunacy."

"Letting Ossard fall to the cults is a greater madness."

"Is it? Could they possibly cause as much destruction as Lae Wair-Rae and the Heletian League going to war?"

"Please, listen to me..." He shook his head as he waged some inner battle. "I want to help you, but..." he hesitated before finally speaking, "You ask if a cult-controlled Ossard could be worse than a war that took in all of Dormetia?"

"How could it?" I sighed. "It's but one city!"

"Yes, but that dark Ossard would launch its own war, one waged with ritual magic. And with that they could win!"

Sincerity rode his words, yet how could one city bring such doom?

He saw my doubts and challenged them. "Look around you at the carnage and destruction, and this has only just begun. Imagine this happening in every village, town, and city. Imagine all nations falling into chaos, all streets seeing discord and riot, and all farms and houses being looted and razed. Imagine every child abducted, and every parent willing to take up arms to get their kin back. Imagine, in that chaos, how many innocents will die."

His words reminded me of what Sef had said. I asked, "Will peace never have a chance?"

He shook his head. "If the cults ruled Ossard, peace would only come when all else has fallen. Any survivors would then have to suffer through war's closest friends; pestilence and famine. Afterwards, Dormetia would spread as a bleak and wasted land, from the misty forests of Wairanir, to the icy coves of Quor, and the sunbaked bluffs of Serhaem. All of it would lie ruined and lifeless as a shrine to madness."

He was right. I hated it, but he was right.

He went on, "Ritual magic will give them that power, and that's why they must be stopped."

Smoke rose over the city to add to the dark pall. A haze hung everywhere, and through it, I could hear occasional screams and distant fighting. Ossard had already fallen far, but had it fallen too far?

I still wasn't sure...

I asked, "What are these rituals supposed to do?"

"There are many and they come in stages, and I'd think the first have already passed. The easiest things to watch for are three major rituals. The first uses the blood and souls of ninety-nine *innocents*. It creates a celestial beacon that will attract the gods."

"Innocents?"

"Children."

I swallowed. "Do you think they've already done that?"

"Yes, not that we know the when or where of it, but the beacon *is* lit and calling into the celestial."

My mind went to the gory discovery in the warehouse of only days ago.

He went on, "Then there's a ritual that requires one thousand and one sacrifices. It sanctifies the city."

I nodded. "Is that what we're facing now?"

"I would think so."

"And the next?"

"The last ritual is the largest, and the most important to stop. It happens a year and a day after the city has been sanctified..." he paused, screwing up his mouth in revulsion, "and it takes ten thousand and one souls."

I cursed, trying to conceive of the power.

He went on, "It creates a gate, a divine focus, a place where the celestial and the real world meet. It's a place for raw energy to spill through, even the gods if they so wish. With such power behind it, a cult-ruled Ossard would be unbeatable."

My grandmother whispered, "He speaks the truth."

I asked, "Can we stop it?"

He nodded, but his face was grim. "It would be best to stop them sanctifying the city, but for a place this size, one thousand and one souls are not hard to find. We have to assume that they'll be able to do it, and if they do, then our best course of action is to deny them the ten thousand and one souls they need for the next ritual."

"How?"

He shifted his gaze to Baruna and Marco. "Who are these?"

The question surprised me, but worse still I didn't have an answer.

Marco offered something in my hesitation, but his words only startled me more, "We follow her."

I blushed. Gods had followers, not Flet housewives.

The Lae Velsanan looked back to me to share my surprise.

I glanced away in embarrassment, my gaze coming to rest on his ship's crew. Some of them were watching us. Without even trying I found myself sampling their thoughts.

"Half-breed, look at him panting after that Flet!"

"Only second in command because of his family!"

"Look at the back of his shirt, already stained with sweat. He's an animal, just like the middlings he mixes with!"

"Hairy mongrel, it's demeaning to serve under him!"

I flinched at their resentment, but the officer didn't notice, he'd dropped his eyes and was bowing.

"I am Felmaradis of House Jenn."

I offered a curtsy in turn. "Juvela Liberigo."

He said, "I know what I'm saying might sound incredible, particularly coming from a Lae Velsanan."

I gave a slight nod.

"But Ossard is tainted, and now that corruption is blooming. There's no easy way to stop it. You need to understand how much danger you're in."

I said, "Isn't it possible that these troubles will pass?"

241

COLIN TABER

"Every city sees disturbances, even majestic Yamere, but this is different. This is not about local grievance or injustice. These aren't mortal problems, but those fuelled by the divine. None of the factions involved will stop, not until they win control or are destroyed in the trying."

I was beginning to believe him. "But I worry that Ossard will free itself of the cults, only to end up in the hands of the Inquisition."

He said, "That's preferable to the cults winning control and establishing a gate. If they're collecting bloodlines, then they're already preparing for powerful magic. When the city is dedicated to the Terura Kala, the cults of the Horned God, they'll be able to conduct other rituals to secure their power. The more souls present in their sanctified city, the stronger the magic that they can call upon. Ossard will become a bridgehead, a place of dark magic, and the starting place for all things to come."

"Can we stop it?"

He grimaced as he shook his head. "Them taking the city, no, it's already lost. What we have to do is stop them keeping it, and going on to found their gate. You should leave the city and take any who'll go with you, and you should do it while you can."

"I won't leave until I find my family."

He grew intense. "Juvela, you don't understand: I'm not asking you to leave and save yourself, I'm asking you to leave and save the rest of us. If you can get enough people out of the city, you might weaken them and delay their rituals."

"Me? What if I can't?"

"Ossard becomes a city of damnation. From here they'll spread through their celestial gate to deliver their followers wherever they want. In time they'll bring down all of Dormetia; from the Holy City of Baimiopia, to the cities of Fletland and Evora, and even the pillar-cities of Lae Wair-Rae and its colonies. In the end, we'll all taste the bitterness of their corruption."

I was confused. I just wanted Maria and Pedro back. "You're telling me that my world is dying. It's too much."

He took a small step forward before whispering in perfect Flet, "I am second in command of this expedition, it led by Prince Jusbudere. We've been searching for the nest of the Terura Kala, and that search has brought us here. We've been watching for the last few seasons with suspicion, but now we know: *They* have chosen Ossard!"

"You can only stop them by taking away what it is they want; Ossard's souls. Find your daughter and husband if you can, but regardless you must get out."

I protested, "Ossard has suffered upheaval before. Only twenty years ago the Inquisition was expelled amidst rioting!"

"Look around you. This is no simple upheaval; it comes with kidnappings, ritual magic, and sacrifice. This is wrong, and not something done alone at the whim of mortals. There are greater forces at work here, and they'll tear this place apart. Get your family and get out!"

He was only making sense.

Felmaradis sighed. "We're leaving to carry word of the city's slide into chaos, and that word will be passed on to King Giovanni of Greater Baimiopia. He will send Heletians to liberate the city, most likely the Inquisition. Just get out and take as many innocents with you as you can. If you can get enough people to safety, you'll delay their rituals, and maybe even stop them."

"Where can we go?"

"Follow the next northern sound as it cuts inland, there's a set of ruins along its north eastern shore. It's far enough away, yet reachable, with fresh water, and defendable."

"And how long should we stay?"

"As long as it takes; maybe a season or two, perhaps a year. I will visit and bring news. This ship can moor right alongside the old ruins."

Who was I to lead people away from their homes and comforts, and into the wilds? It was crazy, yet he was right; something was terribly wrong in the city, and I couldn't sit back and wait for someone else to do something about it.

I asked, "How long do you think we have?"

"I don't know, but the gathering of bloodlines means it can't be far off. They're preparing to sanctify the city, and you'll know when that's close because there'll be a rush of kidnappings. Remember; they'll need over a thousand souls, and because of that they'll go for bloodlines. Each blood-related soul is double the worth of those that aren't. That's when you need to get out, even if it means turning the city over to them, or leaving your family behind."

For one last time, I asked, "Is it really that bad?"

"The city is what will power them, or more so, the souls within it. The only way to stop them is to keep Ossard in the hands of a *safe* faith, the Church of Baimiopia, otherwise the city will have to be razed." He lifted his strong arms to put his hands on my shoulders. I looked into his eyes and felt a buzz of understanding, almost of kinship. He said, "It's that bad, really. You're a Flet, and I'm a Lae Velsanan, and we both know of the bloody history between our people, but you need to trust me."

I gave a nod.

After a pause, he said, "If Ossard falls and becomes a nest of corruption, something ruled over by a demon-king, High King Caemarou will want the city taken. He'll give King Giovanni and the Heletian League their chance, but if they fail, he'll order the forces of Lae Wair-Rae's Fifth and Final Dominion in. He can assemble a great fleet and army - one that will succeed. Once the city is secured, that gathered force will be put to use in nearby areas, and we both know where the next campaign will be."

Weakly, I whispered, "Fletland!"

"I shouldn't tell you these things, but I, unlike so many of my kin, love your people and hold them dear. Please believe it. It was a Flet woman, Una, who raised me, and it's because of her that I speak."

I nodded. It was common knowledge that the Lae Velsanans used middling slaves back at the Core of their dominion, many of them Flets.

"I've seen the plans: First they take some coastal towns to cut the roads between the three port cities, then, one by one, they lay siege to them before advancing up the river valleys. The coast will fall in a season, and the valleys and lakelands in a year. If Ossard is already gone, there'll be few Flets left - and none that are free."

I grew angry to hear such a thing. If he was right, the genocide would be all but complete. I looked to him, his sincere blue eyes and warm face. There was something about him. He cared. He wasn't like the others, either his guards, or his cold-souled senior. I said, "I'll do what I can. I'll leave the city *and* find my family, and then find those ruins you spoke of. Thank you, Felmaradis, but I also have advice for you; watch your back. There are those amongst your crew who don't think you deserve your post. I think otherwise."

He grinned; he already knew. "In a season I'll arrive at the ruins and expect to meet you *and* your family."

A smile eased my doubts. I could trust him, even if he *was* Lae Velsanan.

From the centre of the city came the deep roll of thunder, its anger shaking the ground. We both turned to look; a huge ball of twisting black smoke rose into the sky, its bulk streaked red and yellow.

I turned back to Felmaradis. "What if Ossard destroys itself?"

"The worst outcome is to have the city unified under the Terura Kala. If it remains divided and feuding, they can't make use of the souls here."

"The city is divided between the Flets, the Heletians who support the Inquisitor, and finally the Reformers who follow the new saints."

"The new saints?"

"Yes; Malsano, Santana, Rabisto, and Kave."

"Malsano is of the Terura Kala, and Kave is also placed there by most scholars, though I'm not sure of the others." He shrugged. "The Inquisitor might be hard to work with, but you know who he's loyal to."

"I understand."

"I'm sorry I can only wish you luck. I'd stay and help if I could, but I have my own duties. If all seems lost, just get your people out. Don't let them stay and be slaughtered."

"I will."

"I wish you well."

"Thank you."

He smiled and turned to go back to his ship.

I watched him leave, while listening to the distant sounds of fighting from the city. It was still spreading.

What lunacy.

A crowd had gathered around me. For a moment their presence irritated me - followers! What were they thinking?

My grandmother's voice hissed, "Are you not worth following?"

Was I?

Damn it, I just wanted my family! If these people were going to insist on following me about like a pack of hungry children, they may as well work for whatever comfort I gave.

"Let's go."

They smiled, just having me address them filled their faces with life. Deep down their joy even gave *me* a lift. We were helping each other.

Felmaradis watched from the deck of his ship, and watching him was his brooding Prince.

We travelled up a street that would eventually lead us back to Market Square. It was a different route than we'd taken to get to the port, but I wanted to search a new area. I sensed the celestial as we walked down that mostly empty way, trying to concentrate on the task at hand, but my mind wandered...

Was Felmaradis right?

Could it be true?

Was it too late for Ossard?

We turned down another street, its buildings looted, some boarded up, and others gutted by fire. A haze of smoke haunted the streetscape, rising from the smouldering rubble that lay spilled about. It was an ominous path to take, but quiet, so I led us down it.

The smoke stung my eyes, while a dusting of ash powdered my dress. The silence made it painfully obvious that the street was empty, and all but abandoned and dead. Only this morning it had held shops with homes above, its own little community, but now all of that was gone. I supposed the people of the district were in hiding from the violence - or perhaps chasing it to other parts of Ossard.

It was a place of deep shadows, ruin, and sadness, but I still believed it could be made right. Surely, for this was prosperous Ossard.

Couldn't it?

I stopped when I came to the first body.

It was a Heletian who'd been stabbed in the stomach and bled to death from the wound. He was sitting up against a wall, his bloody hands holding his stomach in, with his dying face marked by a harsh grimace. A black cloth was tied about his forehead - a follower of the Inquisition.

I took a few more steps, resolving to not let his unseeing eyes haunt me, but they did. I lifted my gaze heavenward to free myself of what else lay about, but couldn't.

A thickening pall of smoke issued from the city's countless fires to hang above and transform the day's light into something ruddy and dark.

Had the city fallen too far?

My hopes insisted that I couldn't be sure.

I slowed at the sight of another body. The bloody and torn folds of a dress covered the young woman's sad remains, but the cloth was crassly hitched up at her legs. She'd been beaten to death and raped.

We kept moving only to find another corpse, then a pair, and then some more. Soon I didn't look, I just walked between the rubble and the dead. I tried to ignore them.

How callous I felt...

We went as quickly as we could, but swirling smoke and spilled ruin made progress slow. Whatever had happened here had unfolded before the battle in the square. This was part of some other fight, terrible and senseless. It was simply a waste of life.

After trying to avoid the bodies and their glazed stares, I couldn't when I walked through the thick smoke and into one hanging from a balcony above. It was a lady, a Flet lady, and she hung there cold and stiff.

I gasped. To my horror I recognised her; it was Heifer, the girl I'd shared my Mint Lady outing with.

Others had also been hung with her, she just the first in a long line. They looked similar, perhaps related, and with a chill I realised it was a bloodline.

Had the city fallen too far?

Perhaps...

...and I cursed myself for denying it.

With the rubble, smoke, and bodies making passage slow and difficult, I began to wonder if we'd ever escape. Then things worsened as the tight street we were in delivered us into a small square.

And there I saw Ossard's truth.

The local square, not much wider than the street we'd walked down, had been converted into an open-air chapel to one of the new saints. I guessed that it'd been dedicated to Santana from the amount of oleander blossom and leaves used as decoration. The greenery now lay withered and blackened, and a small stage charred and ruined. Also there, with their hands and feet bound, were the blackened corpses of a score of Santana's followers. They'd been tortured and killed.

Had the city fallen too far?

Yes it had, and I had to accept it.

It was time to return to Newbank.

COLIN TABER

Part III

Ossard, The Nest

COLIN TABER

21

Newbank Celebrates

I shepherded Baruna, Marco, and the others across the meandering waters of the river. It was surprisingly easy. I offered to vouch for the Heletians amongst them, but the Flet ferrymen were happy enough to take them – for a fee. To get them across took a while as their numbers had again grown. By the time we'd finished it was dark, but at least we were home.

We returned to find the district celebrating. The streets about the river were busy with people, many dancing, laughing, and drinking by the flaring and ruddy light of the city-side fires. People cheered the blazes as they did each departing boatload of warriors crossing to join the fight.

It was sickening.

These weren't my people, not those who could revel in such misery and death. I turned my back on them in shame only to find myself facing Baruna, Marco, and the others.

I realised that these were my people. They were the ones seeking peace, not the blood-lusting fanatics and opportunists fighting over the ruins of Market Square, or the cruel people behind me who claimed loyalty through a coincidence of common heritage. My people stood before me; those loyal to life for its own miraculous sake.

Baruna asked, "What of your family?"

While I'd not found any trace of Maria and Pedro, the day's events had left me exhausted. I needed to rest.

I looked to those gathered, and for the first time I saw them in both this world and the next. They shone before me, their pure souls flaring, all good people caught in a tainted and dying place. About us raged flames, hate, and madness, yet between us nested hope.

An unusual green light sparkled within them, almost hidden away in the depths of their souls. I noticed it also shone out from my own, pulsing like a heartbeat. Seeing it in the dark void of the celestial, a place normally disturbed only by blues, violets, and life-lights of white, made me realise how unique we were.

We did have a link, a common purpose...

I smiled. "We have to get you settled, all of you."

Their faces lit up, and to my surprise I realised that many of them were also confused as to why they followed me.

I continued, "We'll go to my home where there'll be room for all, though it will be cramped. Once there we can prepare for what comes next."

Relief flooded their faces. They were glad to have direction amidst Ossard's chaos. Beside me, Baruna and Marco grinned.

A young man called out, "Please my Lady, what does come next?"

It was a good question, and left me only too aware of their eyes upon me. I began unsure of what to say, but with an intention of only sharing the truth. "I won't give you false comfort, for the upheaval about us is only the first flicker of the flames to come. Doom is approaching; the very fall of Ossard. You can either join the madness or turn from it. The fall's hunger for power and death surrounds us, but what of peace and life? That's what I seek. If Ossard can't host them then the city is twice damned and I'll leave."

He asked, "Where will we go?"

"There *is* a place where we'll find sanctuary, and from there we'll look for an opportunity to stop our home's final fall."

Hope sparkled in their eyes and smiles settled on their faces. They were reassured, and with that reassurance came a strengthening of their feelings towards me: They had *faith*.

Two thirds of those following me were Heletian, seeing me wonder if they'd be safe in Newbank when it spread so aroused. I hoped so. "Please follow close, we'll talk more when we reach home."

They nodded and left me to lead the way.

⁃

We got to my home to find it secure and quiet. I unlocked the door and led them in, directing them through to the courtyard; it was the only place I'd be able to talk to all of them when gathered. I hadn't counted, but I guessed that they now numbered about two score or more.

A voice exclaimed from the kitchen, "What's all this?" It was Sef.

I laughed as I got Baruna to lead on the others, telling her, "Kurt's in the stables, tell him you're my guests." I rushed into the kitchen to find Sef standing over the cooking fire where he tended a stew.

He smiled, but gestured to the parade of silhouettes passing behind me. "What's going on?"

"They followed me."

"What do you mean?"

"It started at the square."

"One of them was with you at the opera house?"

"Yes, Baruna. I've asked nothing of them, and they just want to follow me - ever since my casting."

"Yes, the casting..." he sounded troubled.

"What's wrong?"

"Didn't you sense it?"

"Sense what?"

"The strangeness of the casting, of the blessing Schoperde gave you?"

"I don't know what you mean?" But my doubts began to stir.

"Well..." he began, but his voice faded as he looked over my shoulder.

I turned to find Marco.

He said, "They're gathered."

"I'll be out soon."

He left, so I turned back to Sef. "What?"

The Kavist stepped forward and placed his hands on my shoulders as he met my gaze. "Juvela, for a while you thought you were to be a witch like your grandmother, today you thought you were a daughter of Schoperde, but now I suggest that you *are* in fact something else."

I began shaking my head from side to side as I stepped back and pushed his hands away. "Sef, I *am* of Schoperde. I handled her blessings. I know that I've never known a lot of her or been particularly devout, but today I felt her grace!"

"Juvela, I don't doubt you felt something. She's a god, the god of life, and the one who also oversees the birth of *new* deities."

I tensed as my apprehension grew. "What are you saying?"

His eyes sparkled as the big Flet struggled to hold back tears. "Juvela, someone has to shepherd in the *new*."

"But I feel a link to her!"

"Juvela, I'm just a mortal priest, but you're an avatar; the seed of a god yet to be born. You know that and so do I. Your soul is too old, textured, and layered for it to be anything else. It's strong, so strong that none in this city who'd have reason to harm you prior to your *awakening* have been able to."

"But Schoperde gave me the means to save all those people?"

"Your blessing did save many, and it was good and pure, but it wasn't of Schoperde."

I shook my head in anger at these new questions and the confusion they brought. "If not of Schoperde, then who?"

"You."

I was a god?

He went on, "Sweet Juvela, your soul's awakening. Now and in this life-time you're going from an avatar to the divine!"

I snapped, "Stop it! I'm sick of this! And in the end what does it matter?"

He dropped to his knees in front of me. "Juvela, think of it: The city is dying, just like cities have died before amidst upheaval and bloody chaos – and from the greatest of those ruins always have arisen new gods."

I shook my head in disbelief at the connection he was making. "Are you saying that people are dying because of me?"

"No! I'm saying that when cities the size of Ossard, cities rich in souls, fall, that it can uplift avatars to see them awakened into godhood. Who knows how many avatars walk the world, but right now you're the strongest in Ossard. During the coming soul harvest, when all that gathered power begins overflowing, it's going to find you."

I was horrified at the very notion.

He went on, "Look at the Heletians' second god, Saint Baimio..."

I laughed, a harsh sound in my upset. "The Heletians only have *one* god, Krienta!"

"Yes, they don't call Baimio a god because of their dogma, they call him a saint, but they raise him above all others by naming him the son of Krienta, their creator. Well, once he was mortal. We've heard their Church's tales, and not all of them are lies. He came into his power during the fall of Bar-Mor, the mountain city of the giants."

Was he comparing me to Saint Baimio? "Sef, this is crazy..."

"And the gargoyle god of Dorloth, she arose from the fall of Quersic Quor of the Lae Velsanan's Second Dominion of Kalraith."

"Sef, this is too much! Some of what you say makes sense, but linking it to me? I don't want to be a part of it. You're saying that I'm going to profit from the death of the city."

"I'm not saying you're responsible. I'm just saying that as an avatar all that's going on in the city might see you awakened."

"No, it can't be true!"

"Look at the people who've followed you here. Look at *me*!"

"What do you mean?"

"Juvela, I'm a priest of Kave with my soul and service vowed to him, yet here I am serving you! I want to. No, I *need* to! To be here to help, to see you through this."

"I don't need your help," my voice broke as I spoke, disturbed by my surging emotions. Was I having such an effect on people? What a sickening thought, yet the courtyard stood full of proof.

He shook his head, "Juvela, you must understand; myself and those in the courtyard follow you because our souls demand it. Your mere presence has broken our old allegiances and replaced them with something new."

I was frightened by his words - and that they stank of an uncomfortable truth.

Damn it, what did it matter?

What mattered was that the good people in Ossard survived the coming turmoil - and we had more chance of doing it together. I took a deep breath and cleared my throat. "I'm changed, it's true, but all I can say is that I'll try to do the right thing. I've heard you, but I don't want to talk about it."

He nodded and got back to his feet as he gave me a grin.

I hugged him, sensing his love and devotion. Those feelings had been a part of my life for so long. They gave me courage as they flooded me with reassurance. I giggled, for a moment again that little girl who loved his stories of adventure and his bawdy songs.

He chuckled and said, "You should go to them now."

I nodded and turned for the courtyard. Despite the moment of warmth, it seeped away as quickly as it had come, dragged under by thoughts of a city dying so that I might be a god.

They waited in silence, some standing around the edge of the courtyard while others sat on the cobbles. Kurt was amongst them. He gave me a knowing smile and a quick nod.

I walked to the centre of the yard, it ruddily lit by the flaring amber glow reflected from the pall hanging above. Again I hadn't planned what to say, but this wasn't a time for flowery speeches.

I looked about at their faces, taking confidence in their souls' pure taste. Whatever I might be, at least I knew that these people were good and true. Finally my gaze came to rest on Sef where he stood in a doorway. I said, "I want to welcome you to my home, though it seems we've already outgrown it."

Some of them laughed.

"I want to speak to you of many things, but one foremost: Of working to keep each other safe in a city falling apart..."

I talked to them for a good while, including some of what Felmaradis had told me in hushed Flet. As I spoke others joined us, shown in by Sef. Where they came from I didn't know, yet their purity also shone through.

It was the beginning of something; it was undeniable.

There was good left in the city, maybe not enough to save it, but certainly enough worth saving.

I spent the next part of the evening organising the household to cope with so many guests. The arrangements were temporary and we all knew it. One way or another we wouldn't be here in a few more nights, for in time Newbank would also be consumed by the fighting.

Before long bedrooms became dormitories, along with storerooms, and much of the living space. The kitchen bustled with the making of bread and the stewing of broth to serve close to a hundred. The cellar was emptied and aired, and then prepared as a serving space for meals. Only the stables remained free on the far side of the courtyard. If I had to, I'd give them over for more sleeping space, but for now I planned to use them as a store for what we gathered for our escape.

Amongst all this activity I watched two Heletians struggle to lift a heavy chest; one stumbled as they carried it, seeing them drop it after only a few steps. It fell to the wooden floor with a great crash to leave a gouge across the boards. Mortified, the men cried out.

I forced a smile and told them not to worry. Inwardly I shuddered as I thought of what Pedro would've said. Still, my husband's biggest stir wouldn't come of scratches on the floor or from scores of strange guests; it would be because of the changes wrought in me, and my unexpected fate.

People settled in as best they could as I retreated to the only sanctuary that remained, my bedroom. I asked for Baruna, Marco, and Sef to join me. There was still much to discuss.

As we gathered, I said, "Please sit." And gestured to the bed.

Sef and Marco hesitated with embarrassment.

I laughed. "I think we're beyond polite niceties, please, there's nowhere else for us to speak." The two men looked to each other before finally sitting down. In the meantime I pulled across a stool for Baruna. She gestured for me to take it, but I waved her offer away. I felt the need to pace.

Sef said, "So where do we begin?"

I looked from him to Baruna and Marco. "Well, we've all met this day, but neither Sef nor I know much about yourselves. Why don't you share with us how you came to be here?"

Shyly, Baruna looked to each of us, her nerves showing.

Marco offered, "I'll go first if you'd like?"

Baruna shook her head. "Please, I need to tell my story, and now that I'm given the chance I feel I have to grab it."

Marco nodded.

She took a deep breath. "My life started simply enough. I was raised by my family, large and loving, deep in the valleys where we lived in a poor farming hamlet." And her eyes softened along with her nerves. "You know the sort, it struggling on amidst the ruins of an old and abandoned mining town. There wasn't a lot of good land up that way, just slivers alongside the river, but it was enough. Besides, those abandoned towns might have run out of silver and been poor in farmland, but they're still rich in one thing; well-crafted buildings. Mining towns grow quickly and die faster, but while they live their hearts know how to beat. Those old stone halls, taverns, and merchant houses just sit there waiting for families to come and warm them.

"When my family arrived there a few generations back they managed to settle into one of the larger buildings that needed some work. It was a great home, solid against the valley winters, and one envied by many of our neighbours after we'd re-roofed and mended it.

257

"It's much the same across the Northcountry; hundreds of poor farming villages, some born-again mining settlements, and a few small towns – all there to serve this city's hungry markets."

She smiled with her memories. "Growing up in such a place, in our big stone hall, surrounded by terraced fields while tending our goats was a blessing."

She paused to look at each of us, her eyes now sharp; she was going to share her pain. "But, it ended.

"One summer, my grandmother took sick with a fever, it wasted her body and filled her lungs. She died after a long season of agony, one where the sickness seemed to peak and then fade, only to come back stronger before finally dragging her away. Yet the fever hadn't finished with us. My twin brothers and mother also fell ill. They tried to fight it off, but also failed. It left my father, a brother, and myself to bury them.

"We couldn't handle our land, not when we were down four sets of hands. It became a struggle, one that drained us. All the while our neighbours, who might have otherwise helped, had begun to shy away; the local priest had spread rumours about us."

I asked, "What did he say?"

"He said my grandmother dabbled in the old ways, in green witchery. He even suggested that she'd ruled over our household and conducted rituals to win our family favour."

Sef cursed; as Flets in Ossard we'd all seen the hard face of the Church.

Baruna said, "Some of our friends told us of his words – and others."

"What others?" I asked.

"Our home had an unused wing that we'd walled off inside its wide and high roofed frame. It was huge, almost like a small noble's house, and the most impressive building in the village. Some said the priest wanted it to use as a new home, and the vacant wing as a church."

Marco said, "There was a time when I'd thought the men of Krienta were noble and just..."

Baruna snapped, but not at Marco, "Noble and just? Our priest stood as a dishonourable man. He managed to have three sons despite his vow of celibacy, all to a Flet woman who lived not as his wife, but as his slave. He offered us no help or comfort, just threats of damnation!" She stopped to calm herself.

"We relinquished some of our fields and sold some of our goats, yet we still struggled from chill dawn to cold mountain dusk." She shook her head, her eyes glinting. Tears built there, getting ready to run.

Taking a deep breath, she continued, "A season later, when we'd settled into a new routine, my younger brother also came down sick."

Marco sighed, but he wasn't alone.

I asked, "The same fever?"

"Yes."

Sef shook his head.

"It got worse. My brother died not long after, leaving my father and myself behind. The morning after we buried him, my father awoke with a chill, and by sunset was burdened by the same fever.

"The priest offered no comfort, only more whispered words of dark curses and that he'd long suspected my grandmother of heresy.

"My father's sickness progressed quickly. He was dying, taxed by trying to manage our farm and broken by grief. A few days before the end, the priest came into our home saying it was important for my father's salvation that he be close.

"While he waited for my father to die, he counted our goats and checked over our fields. He made me cook for him, only to berate what I served and anything else I did. Finally, as my father lost his mind to the fever over one long, last night, the priest dared sit between him and me and slide his hand into my blouse. He told me he'd need to check me for corruption." She looked to me, fierce in her anger. "I hated him!

"Father died to leave me in a home I couldn't hope to hold. The priest never left, and his sons settled themselves in before my father was even buried. I awoke the next night to find his eldest on top of me, trying to get me with child. Through my struggles I landed a knee to his manhood, giving me a chance to flee, so I fetched my family's hidden savings and took to the road.

"I had enough coin to get to the city and try and make my way, but it wasn't easy. Once here, people saw me as young, unmarried, and without family, thinking me a thief, whore, or runaway. They never understood or believed what had happened, and never showed any interest in wanting to. So many years have passed since then that I've now spent as much time in Ossard as in the valleys, yet I'm still mostly alone.

"That's the way things have gone, with me doing odd jobs to earn coin and get by. Until I saw you." She looked to me. "Straight away I felt some kind of kinship, like you were alone too." She fell into an embarrassed silence.

I stepped across to be beside her, putting a hand to her shoulder to offer what comfort I could. As my hand touched her, power began to flow. It passed from my soul, through my body, and into her own. The feeling made me giddy.

She smiled. A look of contentment came across her face, as if she'd slid into a warm and perfumed bath on the coldest of winter days.

I patted her shoulder again in wonder at what had just happened.

From Baruna came a feeling of thanks and trust. She had faith in me, in my care and compassion.

Marco and Sef both whispered their own thanks for sharing her tale.

She smiled anew, it something shy at first, but blooming with her natural beauty. I could also feel her spirit lighten, it euphoric with relief. Most of all she revelled in the knowledge that such lonely days were over.

I said, "Thanks, Baruna, the more we understand each other the better we can work together." I turned to Marco. "And you, Marco, tell us how you came to be here?"

He looked about the room, his shoulders tensing as he gathered his thoughts. He began quietly, "I've lived all my life in Ossard, but also travelled much of the Northcountry as a child. My father was a merchant dealing in silks, cloth, and leathers, which he sold from the back of his cart. While he had some coin it was never enough to stop the valley rounds. He worked hard, but was always too ready to help a friend or do a special deal on a bolt for a needy widow or new bride. In the end, he was a generous man, but no Merchant Prince." Marco looked to Baruna. "We went everywhere, so I imagine we passed through your valley and perhaps your village."

Her eyes showed shadow as she remembered her home. "Minehead it is. A place that births such memories is never known by a good name."

Sef laughed, a hard and rough sound. "You're so right! Have you ever heard of ill tidings from Paradise? It's always the gloom of fever in

Minehead, the failing of the Second Dominion of Kalraith centred in Quersic Quor, or the fall of the city-state of Ossard - also known as the Whore."

I gave a grim smile. "It's true, isn't it, there's strength in names."

Baruna added, "And power."

I nodded. "Yes, but let's get back to Marco, for we can't let Baruna's woe hang idle."

He smiled, but it was weak.

"I'm sorry, I'm not jesting at your expense, but so all of us can share our burdens." I leaned forward to put a hand to his shoulder, and something passed from me to him. It was like when I'd touched Baruna.

What was happening here?

His smile filled out; he'd also felt it.

He looked up and nodded, yet waiting tears made his eyes sparkle. "Let me finish, for my story also holds something of use."

We all nodded.

"We often travelled the length of the deep valleys, and as a young boy I used to love playing in the abandoned mining towns. I've seen many such places, most of them far inland and closer to the heart of the mountains. Those are of no help to us..."

I wondered at what he was saying, but then remembered Felmaradis' suggestion.

"...they're all too cold in winter and far away. Without good preparation such a trek would be the death of us, still not all of the ruins are found in the interior's high valleys. I can remember the roads we took and that some abandoned towns lay in the lowlands. There are four such ruins in the valleys to the north; three nestled amongst rolling hills, and the last a strange place half drowned on the coast."

Sef asked, "Strange in what way?"

"The buildings, or what's left of them; they're solid and huge, and have room to shelter hundreds upon hundreds. The local shepherds keep clear of them because they believe that they're haunted. My father wasn't so cowed, instead he was fascinated - as were my brother and I.

"We'd camp there whenever our rounds took us near. Father thought that the ruin was old and crafted well before the silver rush and even the birth of this city. He was certain that it wasn't worked by Heletian hands."

Sef raised an eyebrow. "Then who?"

261

"My father thought that they were Lae Velsanan ruins, perhaps a fort from one of their fallen dominions. You see, the steps, windows, and doorways were all usable, but oversized for people like you and me."

The story was intriguing. I was also certain that he was talking about the same site Felmaradis had suggested.

Marco continued, "Only a few shepherds live on those wind-blasted hills with little protection from the squalls that blow in from the sea. Anyway, we can talk more of it later."

And we would; it sounded interesting.

Marco went on, "I had a good childhood. I helped my father on his rounds and was happy. Eventually I left his business to him and my older brother, knowing that my sibling planned to fill it with his own children.

"I went on to work as a tailor, and sometimes even as a merchant myself. I made some coin, never much, but enough, and then I met someone and fell in love." And a tear slipped from his eye.

"That was Atalia, a lovely woman, and one who tried so hard to keep me happy." He shook his head. "Well, we married and built our lives together, and then waited for the coming of children to complete our family.

"That wait went on, stretching through the seasons and into the years. It left us with nothing to show for it despite all our love and efforts. Our local priest offered to pray with us and happily took our coin in return for blessings, but in the end, after spending a small fortune, we still had nothing but our unfulfilled dreams.

"We resigned ourselves to our fate, but then she..." and his voice broke, only to return hoarse a moment later, "...but then she told me that she was expecting." His hands trembled in his lap.

"She seemed so well as she carried through that first season. She'd had some sickness, but she took herbs for it and used balms on her spreading skin..." he stopped again as his words trailed off. After a deep breath he said, "I'd never known such happiness, yet my feelings were eclipsed the day she took my hand and put it to her belly so I could feel our babe kick." He shook his head in wonder.

"Our neighbours, a young couple, also came to be expecting. So, as is the way of things, her husband and I talked of raising sons while the women talked of daughters. Amidst the chat of babies and such my wife shared some of her balms and a brew for morning sickness, something she'd bought in the port from an Evoran herbalist.

"Alas, for their household, it wasn't to be. After only a season the babe slipped from our neighbour's womb. It made things awkward between us.

"For Atalia and I, all seemed well until five days ago. My wife had begun to have dreams, strange dreams, dreams that showed her a sanctuary that was unknown to her. She told me of it even though we both thought it just some sort of fancy. She described it as a gorge with its sides greened by ledges that stepped down into the soil's depths. More greenery could be found about a beautiful pool at the bottom, something bubbling with mist and heat." He looked at us as he shook his head. "I'm not doing it justice, she made it sound wonderful."

I stared at him, all the while trying to soften my gaze.

How'd his wife shared my dream, for I needed to hear no more to know that she'd seen the same fern-forested place?

Sef asked, "And then the city began to give into chaos?"

He nodded. "Our home and our lives seemed peaceful enough despite the changes swirling about. Whispers of the new saints came, of course, then the extra kidnappings, and then the arrival of the Inquisition. Through it all our home remained a place of calm." He looked to me and said, "We were in the square when your husband and daughter were taken. We saw it, all of it, and cried out and mourned with the crowd."

I nodded, but kept quiet, not wanting my own misfortune to distract from his recount.

"That night we went home as the criers declared the Inquisitor our saviour, yet sleep came hard, but not just because of the chaos: It was Atalia, she was restless and close to birthing. Still, eventually, we both drifted off.

"I awoke not long before dawn to find the city quiet and Atalia dozing, but later she began to stir. She seemed upset, telling me of another dream she'd just had, insisting we needed to leave Ossard and that the only safe road would be through Newbank. She said that it had something to do with *that* poor lady, the Flet on the balcony who'd lost her family.

"I began to wonder if she was unwell as she just wasn't making any sense. And that's when it happened..." Tears began to run down his cheeks.

We waited.

"The front door smashed open, it startling us against the silence of the night. I jumped out of bed to find the front room filling with men, too many to stop. Three of them grabbed me and pinned me against the wall. I called out a warning to Atalia, but I was too late; they'd already found her.

"The men who had me stared with blank faces, but I could see hate in their eyes. I asked what they wanted, but they wouldn't answer me.

"A man yelled at my beloved, so I began to struggle, causing them to beat me until I blacked out. I roused on the floor to the sounds of the same man, his voice hard as he spat his venomous charge; *witch!*"

Marco took a deep breath as he wiped at his tears. "I could hear Atalia cry out for me, and I answered that I was there, yet the man's charge kept ringing in my ears."

Witch!

"With the Inquisition in the city, we both knew what that would mean.

"I began to beg, calling out that she was innocent and heavy with child. Finally, one of the men watching over me hissed of witnesses. I turned to see our childless neighbours standing outside in the street, lit like shades in the dim grey before dawn.

"Atalia screamed afresh, making me struggle anew. I watched a man stride out of our room, past me, and into the street. He opened a leather pouch and showed it to our neighbours; on seeing it they nodded. He turned back to the house and called; we have it! It was Atalia's balms and herbs.

"Atalia was led out and past me, towards the door. Grazes marked her body and tears her face, but they were nothing compared to the fear in her eyes. They had a gag about her mouth, and behind it a clove of garlic."

Garlic; many believed it could break a witch's spells.

"I cried out that she was innocent and had done nothing wrong, yet all they did was beat me again until I blacked out."

He sat there and looked to each of us. "That was the last time I saw her alive."

Sef said, "Maybe she's alright. She could be locked up somewhere, perhaps in the Turo?"

Marco shook his head. "No, I found her later that morning. She was tied to a stake in Market Square, burning along with half a dozen others. She was already dead."

The three of us sat in appalled silence.

His seemed accepting, but he'd barely had time to come to terms with Atalia's death. He added, "It's a sad story, and only finished by me telling you that I returned home to find it looted and burning. My neighbours chased me away, cursing me and the bad luck I'd brought them."

"Bad luck?" I asked.

He nodded. "At first I thought they spoke of their own lost babe, but there was more to their taunts."

"What?"

"Something about a sickness."

I looked to Sef. "Kurgar spoke of a rising sickness?"

Sef nodded.

Marco added, "They claimed it was from the new saints, and that only the Loyalists were falling ill with it."

Poor Marco, I felt for him. I'd suffered and still went on suffering, but Marco's wife and dreams of family were well and truly dead.

I stepped close to him and put my hand on his shoulder. Again something flowed between us, a kind of transfer of power. I could feel it, it running from me to him, yet it also left me sated.

He smiled as his tears stopped, and then he whispered, "Thank you for your *blessing*."

I stood back trying to ignore the reverence in his eyes, but it was a look shared by Baruna and Sef.

This was too much...

Looking for a distraction, I grabbed at the first thing to come to mind. "Thanks for sharing your story, Marco."

He gave a grateful nod.

"We've all suffered, it's true, and we need to protect ourselves and any who join us from the coming chaos and perhaps even the rise of plague. I also need to find Maria and Pedro - I'll not leave the city without them."

They agreed.

I went on, "It seems that to be safe from both plague and madness we have to leave Ossard. While that's unpalatable, it makes the question; where should we go?"

Marco nodded. "The ruins I spoke of."

And I agreed, "Call it fate or coincidence, but Marco's ruins have suggested themselves..."

Sef stopped me. "Hang on, we've only just heard about them. There are countless abandoned villages and towns across the Northcountry, how can we be certain that this is the best place to go?"

I had no trouble answering him, "Sef, while you were with your Kavist brethren this afternoon, I saw the Lae Velsanan officer again in port. His name is Felmaradis Jenn, and he spoke of what sounds to be the same ruin. It's too much of a coincidence. If Marco thinks it's a good place to shelter then I'd be prepared to go and have a look, but having also agreed to meet Felmaradis there a season from now seals it."

"Can you trust him?" Sef asked.

What he meant was; have you forgotten that he's Lae Velsanan?

"I trust him. He's good-souled if complicated, and in truth a mystery."

"How so?"

"He's comfortable with me and Flets in general. At one point he even spoke in fluent Flet."

Sef raised an eyebrow. "He is a mystery then, unless he learnt it on some sprawling estate from a downtrodden slave."

"Sef, he was fluent and without accent. He's a natural. That's not the hallmark of someone who's learnt a language just to order about slaves. If you want *me* to accept one thing, then I ask *you* to accept another. There's something about him, something honest and powerful, and he says he'll return to the ruins in a season to help."

Sef nodded, and while he was intrigued, an air of reluctance haunted him.

Marco said, "It's been years since I travelled those roads, but they were good enough back then. In fair weather it was a day's walk up the Cassaro, then a day's zigzagging climb up the valley-slopes and over into the neighbouring sound, and from there a day east along the sound's shore, and then you follow it round for half a day."

Sef asked, "Three and a half days?"

Marco nodded. "By foot."

"And food?" I asked, "How do we feed a *couple of dozen* when we're fleeing a doomed city?"

Sef said, "Juvela, it's not that we shouldn't plan and work towards it, but we *will* be able to feed them. We take what we can, mainly grains and root vegetables, foods that will keep. We'll also take some seed and livestock and buy more from the farming hamlets along the way." And then he smiled.

And gave me comfort.

He was right. It would work out, and not because we left it to fate, but because we'd look for opportunities along the way. We'd settle ourselves down and wait for Felmaradis, and in the meantime we'd make the most of whatever presented itself.

The city was doomed and we all knew it, if not by strife, then by cult ritual, or rising plague. We needed to get out.

"Well, let's get organised. Let's talk to some of the Flets downstairs who know Newbank well enough to round up some carts and food. We'll also need water, blankets, and so much more. We have to be able to move, and quickly."

They agreed and left me.

From the celestial, I could hear my grandmother stir, a mournful sound. I slipped between worlds. "What's wrong?"

She stood there, her eyes lit by the flames that had claimed her, and thankfully naked of her halo of skulls. "Such sad stories."

I nodded, almost overcome by a rising sense of grief.

Why did the world have to be such a hard place?

I said, "It's terrible what they've gone through, and poor Marco so recently bereaved."

She answered, "Yes, poor Atalia. At least she knew that he loved her and never harboured any doubts. Even their daughter, unborn and unnamed, knew of their love for each other."

A daughter...

Hot tears marked my cheeks.

My grandmother shared my grief, yet something menacing stirred in the void nearby.

She said, "Juvela, I have Atalia here, and she wishes to see you."

And another form stepped forward.

She was spectral like my grandmother and painted in wisps of blue. She had a thin face and long hair, and in her arms she cradled a plump babe, her unnamed daughter.

"Atalia?"

She curtsied, her eyes shining with pleasure – or was it the spark of her own murderous fire? I also sensed the stink of smoke and noticed her daughter's shawl was woven from it.

I asked, "Should I tell Marco? I could bring him here."

Grandmother said, "I think it's best he doesn't know, at least not for now."

Atalia, all aglow in spectral blue, reluctantly nodded.

Grandmother said, "Don't worry, Juvela, you'll find your own family. I haven't seen them pass this way."

Her words strengthened me.

She went on, "Your hope and compassion are strong things, they're *your* things. Use them."

"Thank you. I should go now, I have so much to do."

They nodded.

I began to shift my perception back as I moved between worlds.

And at the same time, that lingering sense that something watched us grew, as if it circled and was about to pounce.

Grandmother gasped.

I paused in my leaving.

And the sparkling fires in her eyes dimmed to become the dark pits that had marred her the first time we'd met. When they finished deepening, as if on cue, the halo of skulls sprang out from behind her.

Atalia and her babe faded away, yet I noticed that their skulls remained. I could see them as I left that world, anchored to my grandmother and also enslaved to her fate.

I left the celestial.

22

An Unpleasant Surprise

I found myself on my balcony taking in a terrible view. The night sky spread in amber, highlighted in yellow and red over the districts where the fighting flared at its worst. Twisting pillars of smoke rose to feed the bloated pall above, and about it all rained ash and sparks adding to the hellish glow.

I couldn't see any stars or even the broad and swirl-marked face of the moon. It was as though the world centred on the unstoppable fall of Ossard and nothing but that lone doom. Aside from the granite-flanked valley snaking away eastwards, there was only the dark sea to the west. Nothing else could be seen. We were all alone now at the city's death.

Newbank held bustle and noise, some of it angry, yet no wild fires flared. Our district's only part in the current chaos seemed to be in the endless stream of warriors we sent across the river, but such actions only added to the certainty of the coming end.

Regardless of plan or policy, the Flets of Ossard were already aligned to the new saints. The revelation of the fourth, Kave, had seen to that.

I might not have had all the answers, and been somewhat confused, and no doubt deceived by others, but my soul could sense the truth: The stink of the Horned God clung to the city.

Ossard was doomed.

There was nothing left to do, but to try one last time to find my family and then leave.

Rumours were already running of a new wave of kidnappings. It could only be the spike Felmaradis had warned of: The cultists were getting ready to sanctify the city.

Many of Newbank's Flets laughed at such stories coming from across the river, but I couldn't. I knew what it was to have my loved ones stolen away.

Word had also come of the Inquisitor sending a ship south. It had cast off to seek aid from Greater Baimiopia and summon the rest of the Black Fleet. It wouldn't get through. The unnatural storms Felmaradis had spoken of would be waiting for it. The simple truth was that whoever had worked to ruin Ossard had done a masterful job - and all the while remained hidden.

A knock sounded at my door.

I turned. "Yes?"

It was Sef. "We've just heard news from our returning people."

He meant the packs of Kavists who'd crossed the river.

"What news?"

He strode in wanting to be close.

I grew worried. "Pedro and Maria?"

"No."

I sighed with relief. "What then?"

"Juvela, it's you! The Inquisitor has declared you responsible along with Kurgar for the woe that has taken the city. He's demanded your head and body to be salted and burnt separately."

I laughed. What a fool Anton was. He was as lost at finding the real power behind the city's troubles as I was, so now he looked for excuses.

Well, that did it. Even with my emerging power, it'd now be a needless risk to walk Loyalist streets - unless I had a definite location for my family. He'd confined me to Newbank, as the districts of the new saints were already unsafe for me. I thought about it for a moment; in truth, with the growing number of people moving between Newbank and the city, I wasn't even safe here.

I sighed.

Sef asked, "Are you alright?"

"Compared to Ossard, I'm fine."

He gave me a weak smile.

I said, "I want to see Kurgar."

"We should wait until morning."

He was right, but how many more mornings did the city have? "I suppose it can wait. Sorry Sef, I'm exhausted and not thinking clearly. I must get something to eat and some sleep."

He nodded. "What do you want to see him for?"

"I should share what Felmaradis has told me."

"He'll laugh at you, as any Flet would - taking advice from a Lae Velsanan."

"Would you?"

Instead of answering, he said, "You'd be better off asking Kurgar for protection, for a secure place to stay. This house is too open and well known."

"I'd not thought about it." And I hadn't.

"You know, Kurgar has authority over the Guild's buildings and also owns several himself. He even has an unused tower, its five levels high and defendable."

"A tower?"

"It's in the middle of Newbank's slums, it was part of the old city wall."

I still felt safe with Sef, like a child in the arms of its father. "I think I'm alright here, there are scores of people downstairs."

"Juvela, it's not just the Inquisitor's declaration you need worry about, remember you carry a divine mark."

As if I could forget.

"I'll think about it. Perhaps it is a good idea."

He turned for the door. "I'll have some supper sent up and then you should rest."

"Yes, thanks, Sef."

He left, closing the door behind him.

I turned back to look out upon a city dotted with fires and haunted by the rising tones of Schoperde's long and sad song. While it wasn't being sung as strongly as it had been in earlier days, it still rose to be heard.

Food came quickly. I was so tired that I barely remembered eating it before lying down. In my bed I embraced a pillow while thinking of Pedro and then all but passed out.

I rose early to use the celestial to search the opposite shore for the souls of my family. I stayed there standing on the balcony in the crisp grey before dawn. My perception wandered every street, every alley, and even drifted through the sewers.

I didn't find them.

When Sef came I'd been crying for a good while, so long in fact that my eyes glared red-rimmed and sore. He didn't have to ask why.

I said, "Could they've been taken out of Ossard?"

"No, they're here. They need to be for the ritual."

I wiped at my tears. "Of course."

He nodded. "We'll find them, it's not too late. They'll be shielded by magic, something strong that they can't be seen through."

"You're right."

He offered a smile. "I know this hurts and that you suffer, but remember there are always others who've endured more."

"Like poor Marco."

"Yes, and Baruna, they've both had to walk hard roads."

He was right. In comparison I was lucky, at least for my loved ones there was still hope. And that thought sparked another. "And you, Sef, what of you? I know you've suffered in the past, but you've never spoken of it."

He paled, seeing me regret my prying.

"I'm sorry, you needn't speak of it."

He shook his head. "No, I know I needn't, but I will." And he paused as he gathered himself, "I was a priest of Kave tending to the needs of his warriors where the lakelands, forests, and plains meet. It was a calling I'd not looked for, but earned after the siege of my home village.

"I grew up there, a small place called Kaumhurst. I'd been a farmer and carpenter, and even married…"

"Married!"

He smiled at my surprise. "With a daughter as well."

And in an instant, the hardness of the man I knew melted.

"In Fletland it's everyone's duty to defend their village from raiders and bandits through service to their local militia. It was the only time I handled weapons, something I'd never felt comfortable with.

"One day Kaumhurst was besieged. They'd been seen coming through the dark before dawn, a gang of brigands crossing our fields. They were brazen, carrying torches and their battle colours high, some of them were even singing and blowing on field horns. By the time they arrived our village was roused and ready behind our stockade, and then began the strangest siege I've ever heard of.

"It started as a standoff, with them making little in the way of demands. On occasion they'd call out insults and fire off arrows. We had enough food and water so we were content to wait. To be honest, we were bemused about the way they'd gone about it: They drank as they sat about a bonfire, singing through each night, they seemed more intent on enjoying themselves. It was the strangest thing we'd seen, and not the kind of raid any of us had ever heard of.

"Others came to join them – and that was the only thing that worried us. Their numbers grew from two dozen to four score before..." and then his words trailed away.

I said, "You don't have to go on, Sef, I can see your pain." And I could imagine the outcome; of a final battle and the death of his family.

He shook his head. "I'm alright, and I'll finish what I've begun.

"As you can imagine, we were getting more anxious as their numbers grew – and them more foolhardy. They taunted us by firing arrows, building greater bonfires, and holding nightlong feasts that served up our own livestock.

"Then came a long day of argument that divided the village as our patience ran out. We couldn't agree on action, yet it would only take one more incident to make blood flow. Sure enough, the fools gave it to us: That dusk the bandits took flaming brands from their bonfires and began torching our fields.

"We let two bands of archers out to catch our foes by surprise. Still, they'd come for a fight, so after some success we were forced back to our stockade and back inside.

"It was a tense night, one that dragged on only to be broken by taunts. It also seemed that their numbers still grew, for we saw two more groups marked by torchlight crossing our smouldering fields. Lost in the dark of night and drifts of eye-watering smoke it was hard to follow all that went on, but one thing I couldn't miss was my wife, Anja, hit by an arrow.

"It was just a soft thud and then her ragged gasp. She fell to her knees, and so did I as I took her into my arms. She was in a bad way with too much blood running from her chest. I was scared. I just knew that she was going to die.

"My mother came forward, cradling our infant daughter, and all the while Anja knelt there, held by me, trying to take her last breath.

"Horns sounded and the cries of bandits. Someone yelled a warning from the top of the stockade as flaming arrows began to rain down to land in dirt, thatched roofs, and flesh. Fires sprang up to throw everything into a ruddy light, including my beloved's ruin.

"There and then I knew my family and home were doomed, but I wouldn't have it. I stood and roared my grief, vowing to give my soul and service to Kave if he'd bless me with the strength to save all that I held dear.

"Like a falling star, something hit me, aglow and full of power. It landed with so much force that it blasted the nearest part of the stockade apart. I emerged enraged and by Kave's blessing berserk." Sef shook his head in disgust.

"I awoke surrounded by countless bandits dead and covered in blood and gore. The scene was lit in amber, tinted by smoke and the rising sun of the new day. As I'd offered, I'd saved the village and my loved ones, and all for the cost of my soul.

"I was hailed a hero, a true man of Kave, and held in such esteem that I became his priest to serve the local Kavist patrols. And in all this I served the interests of everybody but myself."

His words made me wonder; how could such a thing happen? The giving of yourself to one you didn't hold faith in?

He nodded at my unspoken question, something I suspected he'd asked himself time and time again. "It didn't matter because it all came to nought. That strange gathering of brigands happened once more a year and a day later. They again taunted the village, but this time when they began their attack they made sure that they laid waste to everything." He looked me in the eye, his gaze cold and hard. "My village, mother, wife and our daughter are all gone and dead. I survived because they wanted to leave me to suffer. That was their revenge, not just the deaths of those I loved, but for me to survive them.

"I was so angry with Kave for allowing such a thing that I walked away from my duties and sought the peace of Ossard. I've barely served him since, and in truth there's still a reckoning to come between us."

I didn't know what to say.

He laughed at my silence. "Not your average tale, it's true. And that's the short version. Maybe I'll tell you more of it when we're sitting about a fire in Marco's ruins."

I remained silent.

He joked, "Come now, so I'm not on speaking terms with my god, worse things can happen."

Finally, I said, "I had no idea you harboured such pain."

He stilled his laughter, giving me a quick nod of thanks. "That's all for now, that's what happened, but now we need to worry about today."

It was my turn to nod.

He asked, "Do you still want to go and tell Kurgar about your chat with the Lae Velsanan, this Felmaradis?"

"Yes, perhaps he'll laugh at me, but he should know in any case."

"And what about your people downstairs? They can't all go, and I doubt they'd even let the Heletians amongst them in."

"Marco and Baruna can come with us, the others will have to stay." I paused, considering. "Perhaps we should take a few more just for appearances."

"Appearances?"

"If we take two more, Flets, it might put any fears about Marco and Baruna to rest."

Sef offered, "Perhaps, but we could just leave them all behind and be done with it."

"True, but maybe it's not a bad idea to give the Guild a sense of what's happening here. It might help add weight to my opinion."

"Alright, but who?"

"I don't know. Marco and Baruna will be familiar with some, they can pick two."

"I'll go down and get them organised. That'll give you a moment to get ready."

After changing and soothing my red eyes with cool water, I made my way downstairs. It was crowded, more so than the night before, the kitchen bustling as it served up a porridge breakfast. Sef greeted me at the bottom of the steps and grinned at my surprise. Simply, I asked, "How many?"

"Enough, the courtyard is full so they now gather in the street."

My smile dropped, replaced by an embarrassed blush. "The street?"

He nodded. "You should look, but compose yourself."

"Tell me, how many?"

"I think we've a hundred in the house and maybe that again in the courtyard and stable..."

"Stop it, Sef, how many?"

275

"And well over a hundred in the street, perhaps closer to two. They just keep coming, but ask for nothing."

"Nothing?"

"Well, nothing but to see you."

"What?"

"They're looking for the lady who saved so many in the square. They're calling you their Lady of Hope, and the rose that blooms from Ossard's despair." He paused, "They gain comfort in just being here." His voice softened, "We all do."

I turned from him to see the people in my home continue their bustle, yet slow and look my way. Standing in the shadows at the base of the stairs my blush only deepened. It was hard to believe.

So much was changing...

Despite my awkwardness I smiled, a small thing that grew. Those around me took it as my acceptance of them, and from it their own smiles were sown. The air tingled with their relief. Strangely, their feelings gave me succour, it coming to me as a rising high.

After a long moment of basking in that feeling it began to fade. It took me a while, but I soon realised that it wasn't because they tired of me; I'd just grown used to it. I needed something stronger to attain the same feeling.

I needed more of them!

One taste of their gifted power - their faith - and I *was* hooked. I could now understand why the gods thirsted for being followed: It wasn't about ego, morals, or even perhaps power for power's sake, it was for the high built of the elation it generated.

It also explained why they hungered for Ossard's chaos and the soul harvest it promised. If something as simple as faith gave the gods a rush, what would the consumption of a soul feel like? What about a dozen, or a hundred, or even a thousand? I shuddered.

Were the gods addicted to it?

Of course they were!

In a hoarse voice I said, "Take me, I need to see them."

Sef nodded, but my hungry tone aroused his concern.

He led me through the crowded room to the entry hall, all the way clearing people from my path. They looked to me offering their devotion with their souls and their hope with their hearts.

They trusted me.

Adrenalin coursed through my body while my mind burnt through thoughts and emotions as my soul lifted itself to a higher state. I sucked in their offered faith like a whirlpool guzzling at water. I forced my steps on, but celebrated every stride, and each revealed yet another soul that wanted to nourish me.

I was elated, but also struggling to come to terms with the feeling.

When we reached the door, Sef asked, "Are you alright?"

My voice rumbled, "Yes."

He looked to me with anxious eyes.

I reached out and touched his shoulder to let some of my gathering power flow.

He gasped as his eyes opened wide in wonder.

"Sef, the door."

"Of course." And he opened it.

The street spread before us packed full of people sitting on the cobbles even at this early hour. They stilled their hushed conversations, hundreds of them, a mix of Flets and Heletians, men and women, and from across the ages, as they turned at the door's sound. The morning air hung cool about them as the smoke-stained sky spread gold above, and there, like magically sprouting from Spring's garden, they all rose together as one.

I stepped out to be amongst them, seeing their faces light up, and with each smile my soul fed and grew. Some of them called out or reached for me, but all of them unknowingly touched me. And now I knew what I had to do.

Hope was here!

Aligned to me they'd sought me out.

Hope was here!

And my soul buzzed as I drank in their offered power.

Hope was here!

And something strained in the celestial; the last of the bindings that held me. They stretched as I grew stronger, my rising power making my soul flex, until, in one amazing moment, they finally gave way.

Hope was here!

And in that other world, a ring of power rushed out to swamp the souls gathered nearby. It surged so strongly that it also manifested itself in the real world as a green mist laced with sparks of gold.

It was a blessing...

My blessing.

And as it touched them I could see their faces light up.

Hope was here!

Hope had arrived in Ossard!

I couldn't deny it:

I was a god!

Sef whispered, "You must speak to them."

I stepped forward and gestured for those near me to sit so those behind could see. "I am Juvela Liberigo and I welcome you to my home."

Some of them cheered while others clapped, but most just sighed with relief. Someone called out, "Thank you, *Lady of Hope!*"

I went on, "There's little room left inside, yet you are welcome to it all the same - and to join us when we move."

A man called out, "Where are we going, Sweet Lady?"

Sef shook his head a fraction to indicate the need for discretion.

"Our destination is one that welcomes peace."

A woman asked, "How can we help?"

"Spend the day gathering what you can, for we'll have to leave the city and travel on open roads. You'll need food, blankets, good shoes, and clothes to protect against the coming of winter." I smiled. "And deep reserves of cheer."

A young woman queried, "I've a young babe, and you wish to lead us from the safety of the city?"

"The city is no longer safe with only worse to come. We seek a place of hope and compassion where there's a chance for survival."

A voice called, "Does such a place exist?"

"Yes, a sanctuary, a place of warmth and comfort. It's free from the new saints and cultists, and even the Inquisition."

"Won't we just be running?" another asked.

"To stay will see us feed these diabolical flames. We must survive them, and watch for a chance to return and help heal the city."

They accepted my words, just glad to have seen me. Above all else they wanted hope, so I'd given it to them.

Sef whispered, "Well done. Time for the Guild?"

I nodded as I waved to the crowd, turning from their cheers.

We rode out with six of us crowded into the coach. I sat next to Baruna and Sef, while Marco sat between two Flets that he'd chosen.

Marco said, "I wonder how many will be here when we return?"

I said, "Not too many more."

Sef smiled. "I'm not so sure."

I said, "We'll only get the people who are certain, and from what I've seen so far, they're the ones with wounded hearts who feel they've nothing left to lose. There are still others out there innocent of the city's madness, but yet to be convinced."

Baruna offered, "You convinced a lot of people in Market Square."

"Yesterday?"

"Yes, and when you stopped that cultist from stealing the lady's child, and also when you fought to stop them taking your family."

It'd never occurred to me that at such desperate moments I'd been on display. I opened my mouth to say something, but found myself speechless.

Baruna smiled. "It showed us something of you, of your strength and willingness to risk yourself for others."

Finally my open mouth found my voice, but it wasn't much of a pairing, "Oh."

Marco laughed, the sound soft and rich. The others were swift in joining him.

Travel through the streets of Newbank was quick at this early hour. We passed a crowd still working at last night's dark celebration, a good portion of their number Heletian - followers of the new saints. The sight of them unnerved me. While the majority were probably innocent to the truth of their allegiances, not all would be.

We arrived at the Guildhall to find the grand old building abuzz despite the quiet on the streets. Eyebrows were raised at my entourage, but we pushed past their stares, outstretched hands, and curses, their anger directed solely at the Heletians amongst us. Marco and Baruna bravely walked on, not acknowledging the slights or stares. Through it all they retained their cool and dignity to win yet more of my respect.

On reaching Kurgar's office we were asked to wait. Eventually, a guildsman returned, his eyes laying too long on Marco and Baruna. "You can go in." It seemed that all my company would be admitted.

We entered his office to find it hosting a tense air. Instead of it being crowded with guildsmen and others who'd watched our previous meetings, this time it held only three; Kurgar, Ciero of the Cabal, and Seig of Kave. The latter's presence made me uncomfortable, making me wonder again at Sef's mixed loyalties.

Kurgar began, "Juvela, you've been creating quite a stir."

"If you're referring to what happened at Market Square, I only did what I could to stop the Inquisitor."

He nodded.

Ciero stood to his right, the cabalist staring grimly. "Who'd have thought a novice could best an inquisitor? This stinks of renegade magic!"

I was surprised by the accusation. "I'm no renegade."

Seig said, "My concern is not the magic or where you learnt to cast, but your followers. I believe that's what they're calling themselves?"

Baruna said, "We follow her because of her actions."

Kurgar frowned at the interruption. "And who are you?"

"Baruna, Baruna Discotti."

"You're in Newbank as a guest, and you'll not use the Guild as a forum." He shook his head. "Juvela, I was told that you wished to speak to me, please, I'm here to listen?"

"Thank you, I have some information."

"About your family?"

"No, about what's happening in the city."

"Go on?"

"The source will be mistrusted by most..."

He interrupted, "But not by you?"

"I trust it, but it was from a Lae Velsanan."

His eyes went wide. "Really?"

"From an officer in Lae Wair-Rae's military."

"And what is this information?"

"He believes Ossard is to fall, only to rise again as a city of the Horned God – a power they call Terura. He said it will become a nest of corruption, so they've left to carry word to King Giovanni of Greater Baimiopia."

"Really, and what do they care of what happens in Ossard?"

"They worry it's the beginning of something bad, a place from which dark armies will come."

"And their work is sanctioned by their High King?"

"Yes, the expedition is commanded by one of his sons."

"And this officer told you all this?"

"Yes, a senior officer. He said that if the Heletian League couldn't recover a fallen Ossard that High King Caemarou would send a Dominion fleet." I licked my lips. "He also said that such a force, once assembled and with its task complete, would then be put to work in nearby Fletland."

Kurgar raised his eyebrows. "A very *helpful* Lae Velsanan, isn't he! I suppose he also gave you their battle plan?"

Seig burst out laughing.

I kept quiet.

Kurgar joined the laughter, as did the cabalist.

I felt a fool.

Well, Sef had warned me...

Kurgar began afresh, "Perhaps this Lae Velsanan was trying to misinform you. If that's the case, it would be safe to say that we should be doing the opposite of what he said." His brow furrowed. "Did he suggest, for example, that you should work against the Reformers and instead support the Inquisition?"

"Yes," I whispered.

"Predictable, isn't it? He wants us to side with the one force in the city that wants us dead!"

I didn't believe it, but realised I wasn't going to change Kurgar's mind. "But the kidnappings?"

"Are probably a trick of the Inquisition. After all, Inquisitor Anton didn't lift a finger to help you when your family was taken from right in front of him."

It seemed hopeless and the world too confused. "Felmaradis spoke of coming rituals, of magic that would eat up countless souls and..."

"Countless?"

"He said they'd want to open a gate, a celestial gate, and that eventually they'd need ten thousand and one souls to fuel it."

Seig again burst out laughing while Kurgar and Mauricio joined in. Finally, the Guildmaster said, "Juvela, that's an awful lot of power!"

I sat there in silence.

He added, "You know the Inquisitor has issued an order for your head?"

I nodded.

His voice softened, "Please, Juvela, I'm sorry for my harsh tone, but I've so many people depending on me that I just don't have time to consider such a thing. The people of Newbank would never support it in any case."

And that was true. "I understand."

"Please, tell me how your hunt for your family is going?"

"I've had no more success."

"Please, if you need anything, just ask."

I whispered my thanks.

There was nothing left to discuss. The Guild had made its choices, just as the people of Newbank had. In the end, I said, "I have one last question."

"Yes?"

"Did you discover who's leading them; the new saints?"

He shook his head. "While it's been difficult to identify their leadership, everything they've promised through their messengers has been honoured."

I nodded, rose, and left.

On the way home, I stopped by to check on my parents.

We passed through streets growing busy, though thankfully our passage remained quick. From a distance their house seemed calm and orderly enough, standing silent with its windows shuttered. I had Kurt stop the coach and the others - except Sef - remain behind. This, I hoped, would be a short visit.

I entered the house expecting to be greeted by a maid, but none came. The hall spread about me dark and quiet, the room lost to shadow.

Everything seemed to be in order. The only thing unusual was the lack of light and the absence of anybody to greet me. I moved in deeper. That's when I noticed that the door leading to the courtyard was open - the only source of light and also a faint breeze.

Soft murmurs sounded from outside. My steps quickened, and that's where I found them.

My father sat on a bench with slumped shoulders and shadowed eyes, his gaze locked onto the rose garden, but I doubted he saw a single petal of its ash-dusted blooms. He was lost to us. Mother sat on another bench across from him also adrift in some trance of gloom. One maid sat with her, stroking Mother's hair with one hand while the other held a cloth to her brow. The other maid knelt on the cobbles between them whispering hopeful nothings.

They hadn't noticed my arrival.

"What's happened?" I asked as I stepped into the courtyard with Sef.

The maids turned to show their pale and drawn faces, but neither of my parents responded.

The maid sitting with my mother said, "Lady Juvela, such tragedy! Your mother grew distant yesterday not long after you left, and then news came of a mob looting your father's business. He went out there with a group of guildsmen, but they were too late. When he returned, he was so shattered, he could only join your mother in grief."

She turned back to my mother to stroke her hair. I noticed she wasn't just doing it to comfort her, she was also brushing ash away from where it landed to settle on her head.

I stepped closer. "Mother, Father, it's me, Juvela. Are you well?"

The kneeling maid, her eyes red from tears, said, "They won't talk, they haven't since sunset yesterday."

Father sat there turning something over and over in his hands. I knelt in front of him to see that it was the key to the business.

And then my mother whispered, "The child?"

Maria...

I turned. "I haven't found her, I'm still looking."

She whispered again, her voice unbearably tense, "The child, the poor child!" She sat stiffly, her fingers trembling as her tears began.

In the celestial, my grandmother walked about her trying to soothe her soul while she also wept. I could feel her guilt. She'd done this to her, to my mother, to her very own daughter, all those years ago as she'd been burnt to death.

"Don't worry, I'll find her. I'll get both her and Pedro, I swear."

And she mumbled on, "The child, the child!"

I went to her and took her into my arms.

She whispered again, "The child!"

Grandmother stroked her soul, massaging it, trying to get her to relax.

Mother calmed, yet still went on to repeat her mantra.

I smoothed her hair and wiped tears from her cheeks. Something was broken in there. Whether it was the chaos of the city, the kidnappings, or the loss of Maria - it had all been too much.

My mother pulled out of my embrace to settle back on the bench. She began to relax and go quiet, now composed again. Then, when I thought she'd found some kind of peace, she hissed, "The children, we must protect the children!" And her words saw us all grow tense.

My father looked to me and said, "It's all gone, the shop and warehouse. It's all gone. There's nothing left."

"Father, I'm so sorry to hear it."

He shook his head. "And what other ill news could there be?"

"Father, the Inquisitor has put out an order for my arrest."

"Why?"

"I don't know, but he's also named Heinz Kurgar."

"Why can't they just work together towards peace?"

"Father, I don't think they want it." And it was the first time I'd given voice to the truth.

He fell silent, making me regret speaking such news.

I asked the maids to pack for them, and to have them ready for travel. I said we'd be back to collect them when we left the city, and that they were also welcome to join us.

The ride home began in silence. Marco, Baruna, and the others read enough in my face to not ask any too many questions, but Sef had other ideas. "Juvela, we could send some people around to watch over them, perhaps to make sure that they're ready to leave?"

I considered it and decided the suggestion had merit. "Do it, it'll be the only way we can make sure that they're ready to go. We can have a few people stay there, but not in the house, just the stores and stables."

Sef nodded.

On the short ride home I worked at trying to forget what I'd seen. That was when something new grabbed my attention; a familiar face on the street. The man was only in view for a moment, but it was long enough.

I knew him...

He wore a hooded robe, yet I knew that strong jaw and those cold eyes. It was the cultist who'd stolen the red-headed boy prior to my coming of age, and then later sacrificed him while I lay under Pedro being deflowered.

He'd know where my family was!

"Stop!" I yelled, as I went for the door.

The cultist stood at a street stall, but must have sensed me, for his head snapped about.

I dropped to the cobbles.

"Wait!" Sef called out.

The cultist watched my charge, my power surging.

He just stood there.

My spirit soared as I closed. I reached out with my hands in the mortal world, and with spectral limbs that rippled with power in the celestial.

But my eager hands passed right through him.

What?

I stopped hard against the stall, its merchant staring at me in fright. I stood there in confusion, the cultist's image fading as my celestial limbs also failed to entrap anything.

An illusion!

I looked around.

There, down an alleyway, he again stood grinning at me. His voice hissed for only me to hear, "You've so much to learn." And it dragged through my mind like bog-dirty fingers.

I charged after him again, my heart thumping like a drum.

He turned and ran down a dirt alley that doubled as an open sewer, heading for the heart of Newbank's slums.

I ran on, not caring for anything else. Every time he tried to lose me in those twisting ways, I'd just keep on.

He darted ahead and around a bend, past stalls, bleak refugees, and a pair of men betting on knuckles. I just kept going. Finally, the alleyway opened into a small square hosting a crowded local market.

I came to a stop, but couldn't see him.

I moved through the crowd towards an alley that seemed to be in the direction he'd been heading, but to no avail. I turned about to search the broader crowd.

Where was he?

With a sinking heart, I realised he'd chosen this place to make his escape. I searched the celestial, but already his scent was stale.

"Juvela!" It was Sef, with the others not far behind.

I fell to the ground to pound the dirt as my frustration overwhelmed me.

Sef rushed to my side

I spread the flats of my hands on the ground and cried out long and low in grief.

He looked down, not knowing what had happened, but knew it had something to do with Pedro and Maria. He also knew that whatever the clue had been, that I'd lost it. He pleaded, "What can I do?"

I hissed, "Damn them!"

"Cultists?" Sef asked as the others gathered about.

And then it cut through the celestial, "Mama, is that you?"

It was Maria!

I cried out as tears flooded my eyes.

It was her!

Sef asked, "Can you sense her?"

And again it came, stronger this time as she sang out in desperation, "Mama!"

Sef and the others started; even they'd felt it.

I spoke the words and sent the thoughts, "Maria, I'm here! Tell me, are you alright?"

"Mama, where've you been?"

And the guilt her thoughts aroused was almost enough to overwhelm me. "I'm so sorry, my darling! Please, tell me where you are!"

"Mama, they moved us. Please come and get us!"

"Do you know where you are?"

"It's windy, there are windows, but they're too high for me to see out of. All I can see is the smoky sky. Mama, Papa's sick!"

And my joy faltered. "Oh Maria, what's wrong?"

"They've been cutting him."

And my soul went numb. "Can you see him, is he there now?"

"Mama, they steal his blood. They do it every day. They've taken him away to bleed him some more."

"Maria, I have to work out where you are. Do you know? Is there anything more that you can tell me?"

I don't know, Mama. It's windy and cold."

I begged her, "Maria, please, my love, tell me more. Are you sure you can't see or hear anything else besides the wind and smoke?"

"Sometimes I can hear the city, but the sounds are always faint."

I lifted my head and looked about. "It's Maria and she's close."

Sef also started looking around. "Where?"

"She doesn't know. She says she can only see the sky out of the windows and nothing else. She must be high up."

And at one end of the square, rising up and over it, with a few ramshackle buildings crowded about its base, climbed a tower. It didn't look mighty like the Turo, but amidst a slum its strong stonewalls made the five level building loom like a fortress. Its three top levels were each marked by small square windows, one set in the midst of each of its four walls.

Sef was looking the same way.

"That must be it!" I cried.

"I guess so," Sef answered, his words drowning in gloom.

I looked to him in surprise.

He was shaking his head. "We need to be sure. Ask her about the windows, ask her where they are in the wall, how many, and if they're long, round, or square."

"Maria, we need to be sure of which building you're in. Describe the windows; where are they in the wall, and what are their shapes?"

"They're small squares above even Father's head. There's one in each wall, in the middle."

"Good girl Maria, I think we know where you are!"

"Come soon!"

"As soon as we can."

I turned my attention back to Sef. "That's it!"

He sighed in disbelief. "That's Kurgar's, the old tower I was telling you about."

"What?" I howled.

The others just stood there, but I could read their thoughts:

All else in Ossard is corrupt, that's why we follow Juvela.

Kurgar couldn't be involved in the kidnappings, could he? It had to be a mistake. If he was involved, then he was linked to the new saints, which meant the Reformers already held two-thirds of the city.

All was lost!

Felmaradis was right; the Inquisitor, the man who'd ordered my death, was the city's only hope.

As the shock of it all faded, my anger only grew.

All along Kurgar had wanted an alliance with the Reformers and been annoyed by my objections. I'd also been searching all of Ossard for Maria and Pedro except Newbank, where I thought they could never be.

Damn, I was getting angry!

And that fury stirred my power. I could feel the air about me cool and hear it crackle with energy that leaked between worlds. Amidst my rising rage a wave of black sparks rippled out from me to glitter in the dirt.

Sef and the others jumped back, startled.

Baruna said, "Juvela, you've great power, but you must control it!"

I just wanted my family back - and to destroy their looming prison brick by brick...

...yet Baruna spoke sense.

I had to stay in control. If I left it to my anger, I'd level the tower in one terrible moment, bringing its bulk crashing down upon the slums. I could wrap my family in a protective bubble and save them, but only after trading their lives for hundreds of others.

I looked to Sef. "I want to get them now. If we leave to come back later they'll just get moved. They already know we're here because of the cultist I followed."

He nodded. "Juvela, I agree, but we must be careful. When we do this we'll be turning the Guild against us and perhaps all of Newbank – and so much more."

He was right, and the *more* he spoke of was his fellow Kavists. If we moved, we'd have no friends left in Newbank and the wider city. We'd no longer have a choice; we'd have to leave.

Baruna said, "Don't worry, we'll get your family, but let's also ready our flight from Ossard."

I nodded. "Sef, do you know much about the tower? Can we get into it or do we need help? I feel like I can unleash enough power to bring it down, but not handle it carefully enough to do much else."

He shrugged. "I've passed it a hundred times, but never been inside. They left it standing when they dismantled the old wall. I'd expect its layout to be unremarkable, much like the new wall's towers. Getting in will be the hard part, and then having the strength to overcome whatever force awaits. It can't be big in numbers, or I'd have heard about such a thing, but if they're cultists they might also have priests."

I was still on my knees with my fingers digging into the hard packed dirt. Throughout the conversation I'd sent feelings of warmth and comfort to Maria, feelings she returned.

Sef said, "We can't stay here like this, it's drawing attention."

"We can't just leave!"

"Do you still have Maria?"

"Yes."

"And Pedro's with her?"

"No, they're... they're bleeding him."

Sef winced, but he wasn't alone. "Can you contact him, I mean, how can we know where he is?"

Some of my determination faded. "No, I can't, only Maria." And I could guess what Sef's next words would be.

"If we go in and get Maria, you'll lose your only link to Pedro. We need to get them when they're together."

He was right; we'd have to wait.

Distant screams and the clash of fighting drifted to us, coming with a growing haze of smoke. It sounded close; the battle for the city had again crossed the river.

"Ossard *is* chaos," I whispered.

Sef said, "If the building was owned by any other, I'd just fetch some of my fellows."

Marco asked, "If the Kavists knew of Kurgar's part in all this, would they not switch sides?"

"Seig is our senior priest and close to Kurgar. He must know what's going on. It sickens me to say it, but I think this has his blessing." He paused before adding, "Perhaps that's how they knew we were coming when we went to the opera house."

"Perhaps."

Sef looked defeated.

I reached up to him with a hand, putting it softly into his.

Poor Sef, my poor Sef, not only did he feel guilty for the stealing away of Maria, his charge, but also for the failure of our rescue attempt.

Something of a smile came to his face at my touch, and I could feel a tingle as power flowed between us. I'd not meant to do anything but comfort him, and I did, but it came as a blessing. "It'll be alright, Sef."

The sound of fighting rumbled on, coming from the river and also to the east. All the while the drifting smoke grew thicker.

Marco offered, "Our own people can help; while most can work on readying to leaving the city, someone unknown to the cultists can stay here to watch over the tower before we return in force."

Someone unknown? Obviously, he didn't mean Sef or I.

"A good idea," said Sef.

Marco went on, "In the meantime, as we move against the tower, we can arrange for our people to leave the city and regroup beyond its walls."

The rising sounds of trouble saw the square begin to empty about us.

Baruna said, "This could be our last day in the city."

Sef nodded. "We have to think of that; our last chance to pack supplies, seek out carts and drivers, and food and herbals."

I hated the idea of leaving Maria again, particularly if Pedro was hurt, but they were right. Besides, I couldn't go in there when they were handling him, they might kill him. Finally, I said, "Alright, but we move tonight."

They agreed.

I added, "We also know that the Reformers are getting ready for a big ritual, so let's get as many people out of Ossard as we can. Tell people you trust, but no Reformers." I looked to Sef. "I'm sorry, but that has to include other Kavists."

He nodded as his face flushed with shame.

I sent a message of parting to Maria, a sweet and loving goodbye. I promised to return soon, for her and her father, and for her to be brave. Reluctantly, I then lifted my hands from the dirt to break our link.

And straight away I knew it was the wrong thing to do. "Sef, I can't leave them again! We were so close at the opera house, and now we're only closer, yet still it can all go so wrong. Perhaps we should just wait for Maria to tell us when Pedro's back and then go get them?"

Sef held great worry in his eyes. "Juvela, listen to the riots, they worsen and near and so does their flames. We need to go, prepare, and then come back. We can't wait here. For all we know, Pedro may never return to Maria."

Sef's words were hard to accept.

My grandmother whispered, it passing through my mind like a cool winter breeze, "Leave them, Juvela, they'll keep for another time."

"Sorry, this is so hard for me."

Marco said, "I'll stay and watch the tower. I'll get a cloak from a stall, and then hunker down amidst the refugees."

I could trust him. I stepped forward and embraced him, it seeing my magic flare - a blessing. He drew himself back from me to look with wide eyes as his voice sounded, but only in my head, "Juvela, sweet Juvela, I can taste your love for them, for your family. I'll not fail you. Can you feel me, my heart, mind and spirit?"

"Yes," I whispered.

Aloud he said, "Go and know I'll tell you of anything that happens here, otherwise I'll see you when you return."

"I'm so grateful. I don't know how to thank you."

He smiled, a warm and gentle thing. "For you I'd do anything."

"Oh Marco, this is no time for reckless sacrifices."

"But it is; in a dying city, that's what will make all the difference."

"Marco, I ask nothing of you."

"But for Ossard's Rose, our Lady of Hope, I'm prepared to give everything. Atalia told me that you were true, and now I've seen you, yet you're still to fully awaken."

We stepped back from each other as I whispered, "I've seen your daughter and wife in the next world; they send their love."

He drew me back into his arms. "A daughter; you bring such hope!" Then he let go.

＊

We got Marco a hooded cloak from a closing stall and left. He came with us before wrapping himself in it, and then turned back. He planned to settle into position in an alleyway opposite the tower's entrance, huddled amidst a group of refugees.

The rest of us headed back towards our coach. From there we'd go home and prepare for our return to the slums, but also organise for our people's flight from the city.

The smoke thickened about us. Soon enough we passed a burning building, and not much after, our first body.

The curse of the riots had well and truly returned.

Those left in the open were hurrying through the haze, appearing as nothing but rushing shadows. I hoped Marco would be safe.

Walking in a group, our number became lost in the billowing smoke. Our world was one of dim light, haze, and the flaring flash of flames. I called out, "If we get separated, just head for home." I kept on while watching the silhouettes about me, all the while hoping that they were my people, but only Sef answered.

Lost in the murk, a huge figure loomed ahead.

Sef cried out, "Cherub!"

The big Flet answered, "Ho Sef, Juvela, the Loyalists are about!"

Sef asked, "In Newbank?"

"Yes, a reprisal for Market Square. They've got scores across, all hidden amidst the ferry traffic. They've been creating trouble ever since."

Sounds of fresh fighting came from the river, seeing Cherub's eyes light up. "I must get on, but be careful!"

We moved on in deepening dread; we both knew we'd lost our fellows.

Sef said, "Kurt should've had the sense to take the coach and go."

I'd have answered him, but I couldn't. A strong hand had clamped over my mouth, holding a wet and stinking cloth. I tried to scream, to make some kind of sound, but Sef was already stepping away while a figure darted after him.

My mouth filled with a bitter taste, it coming from some kind of herbal brew plastered over the cloth. Given a moment more – a chance for my surprise to fade – and I'd have unleashed some of my pent-up power.

Instead I passed out.

23

Alone Again

I awoke in a cell, a place seemingly built of the cold and the dark. Before long I came to my senses enough to discover there wasn't much more to it; just three stonewalls, a matching floor, and a run of rough iron bars. A passage beyond held the only light that dared illuminate the dim world I'd entered. Out there the glow of a candle flickered in a silence so complete that I could hear its wick choking on the cheap tallow that fuelled it.

I lay on my stomach as I tried to rally the strength to rise. My head hurt, it heavy and hazed, and my vision spun every time I blinked.

This wasn't going to be easy.

With a deep breath, I began to move to sit up.

It didn't happen. Just tensing my muscles earned me a feeling of nausea strong and almost complete. It convinced me that the chilling stones of the floor were comfortable enough for now, or so I thought – my movement had been noticed.

A Heletian man said, "She's awake, send word."

The sound of footsteps drifted away.

The nausea also waned, for my senses had found something else to distract them.

Something small hit my back, and again, and then another. Each impact, not uncomfortable or hard, came with the sound of a dry pitter patter. Whatever was hitting me was bouncing off to roll along the floor. A scent filled the air. I knew it. Even through my haze I made the connection.

Garlic?

A tense voice asked, "Are you sure this stuff will work?"

"Aren't you?"

Nervous laughter.

The first voice said, "Don't worry, he'll be here soon. He's been after her for a while, and you know how particular he is. He wouldn't leave her in our care if he thought she'd get away."

The Inquisitor?

"Yeah, but she's a witch..."

So, it was the Inquisitor.

"...how'd we know she won't just break the bars and walk out of here?"

"We'll stop her with this."

And another clove of garlic hit me on the shoulder before landing by my ear.

Pitter patter...

"You've heard how they talk about her. They're frightened. They think she's dangerous. I heard one of them call her a soul-eater!"

Pitter patter...

More garlic rained down. They were really beginning to irritate me.

Pitter patter...

"He'll be here soon. If this stuff can't stop her, at least he can."

Silence...

...almost.

Pitter patter...

And my mind began to rise above its fog and find focus.

I really didn't have time for this.

Again, so close to my family, only to have the opportunity stolen away – and this time by idiots.

Pitter patter...

With a clearing but aching mind, I passed into the celestial to spy on their souls.

Pitter patter...

Nearby, a heavy door groaned open, the sound followed by the stomp of several sets of booted feet.

I stilled my celestial work, but left my perception there, for at the same time that other world began to fill with a rising sense of menace.

In that cold void my grandmother roused. Her dark eyes dominated her sneering face, all of it surrounded by her skull halo. She hissed, "The bastard!"

Finally, I came to understand why her help had been so sporadic: She was a split person, a person of two halves, and such anger in her could only be caused by the arrival of one man.

His stern voice rang out in the real world, so I let my perception return. "Juvela Liberigo, I want to talk to you." It was Inquisitor Anton.

The barred door to the cell squealed as it swung open. Rough hands then picked me up to stand me in front of him. The sudden movement made me gag, but none of the five men present seemed to care.

He stood there and held a wooden cup to my lips. "Drink, it'll settle your stomach after the Moonroot." And he tipped it to pour its liquid into my mouth. It was light and tasted of cinnamon.

"Can you walk?"

I nodded.

"Come then." And he looked to the garlic scattered about the floor, and then with disdain at the guards. "Help her."

By the time we rose out of the dark cellar my head had begun to clear and my stomach eased. Soon, after three staircases, we stood in a wood-panelled room with a curtained window; it was Lord Liberigo's office.

The guards helped me into a chair while two goblets appeared on the desk in front.

Anton said, "The wooden goblet has more of the elixir, the other holds watered wine."

He leaned back against the desk as he looked over my shoulder to the guards behind me. "Leave us." A moment later I heard the door close.

"The elixir will free you up to cast again. Moonroot has many properties, and one is to stifle the flow of power from the celestial into this world. It will let you look into that other realm, but can confuse what you see. Even now, after you've had the elixir, it can for a good while afterwards befuddle your attempts to manipulate power."

I nodded.

"Speaking of which, you've become quite strong."

I slurred a little, my voice hoarse, "Not strong enough." I reached for the watered wine.

His stern face broke into a smile. "What you did in Market Square was impressive."

"I tried to stop a slaughter."

"Yes, and you did."

"I did what I had to."

"And they say that you have followers." And then he shook his head. "I'd hoped we'd got rid of the last of your kind twenty years ago."

I raised an eyebrow.

He went to the chair behind the desk and sat. "We knew you were coming, that's why we acted."

"What are you talking about?"

His lips drew into a grim line. "I'm talking about you and your role in things."

"What role?"

"Your role in the end of *everything.*"

Was everyone mad?

"Oh yes, *everything.* If only those fools downstairs knew, they'd have done more than pelt you with garlic."

I shrugged.

His eyes flashed with Krienta's power. "Everything. Don't be shy, think about it: It starts with Ossard and then moves on; first the Heletian League and the Church of Baimiopia, and then the Ansilsae Prophecy of the Lae Velsanans, and all the others until the Divine Covenant fails. You are the start of it, and your actions would ruin it all – bringing every last faith of the established order crashing down." He took a sip from his own wine and then looked back to me. "That's why I have to kill you."

"What?"

"I thought I'd done enough twenty years ago with your grandmother and the like, but obviously not."

"The city's falling apart, and you're worried about me? I'm not the threat, the Reformers are!"

"Yes, they're a threat, but one that'll be taken care of when the fresh forces I've requested arrive. You on the other hand..."

I cut him off, "Your messenger won't get through."

He stilled and looked at me, taking my measure. "Why?"

"The Lae Velsanans told me, the ones recently in port. They said that out to sea, just over the horizon, the city is surrounded by an arc of diabolical storms. They've cut off Ossard!"

"A lie!" he snapped.

"Look into the celestial, you can see."

He considered my words, but went on, "You won't escape your fate, not this time. I'm sorry, but you must die so that the divine order can go on..." he stopped, his eyes opening wide. "By the Holy Saints, you're right!" He looked to me. "There *is* a storm barrier, I can see it!" He paused, and then his voice softened, "My messenger's bloating body is already surfing the squall's damned swells."

I slipped into the celestial to see for myself. There his messenger's soul laid before us, the poor man's life-light fading as it burnt out its final embers.

I whispered with a breaking voice, "The city is doomed."

"What else did these Lae Velsanans say?"

"He said that it would be preferable to have the Inquisition rule Ossard than the Reformers, but if it wasn't to be, that I should get out."

"To abandon Ossard to the cults?"

"It would weaken them if I could lead enough away."

He thought about it. "I see the truth of it."

Silence.

He shifted in his chair. "It took until Market Square for me to be certain of you."

"Why, the power I drew?"

"Yes, though I'd held suspicions since the kidnapping of your family. Then, at the end of that episode, you fell to your knees on the balcony and bleated out that heretical song. That's when I first sensed your power."

I nodded.

"Still, you're not quite awakened, but it'd not be long now," he grimaced, "and that would be the end of the world we know."

"Help me, let's work together. We can save Ossard!"

"Perhaps, but only for it to fall again because of you."

"I'm not working to do anything but save my family."

"Juvela, you've already started this thing, this assault on the divine order. It can't be stopped short of killing you."

"But what of Ossard?"

"It's just one city."

I was appalled.

He went on, "I'm sorry, but I have no choice: I must serve, and you must be stopped."

And a breeze came to stir the curtains behind him, as the lamp-lit room began to feel chill and lonely.

I wondered; what kind of gods would let a whole city fall just to maintain their power?

Gods addicted to death.

He asked, "Do you lead many among the Flets?"

"Their numbers grow. When I left them this morning, there were about four hundred. They're not all Flets, there are also Heletians."

"Heletians?"

"Yes, they're good people looking for hope."

"Heretics!" And then he shrugged. "Oh, what does it matter! May they find what happiness they can before the end."

I sat in silence, still confused by my apparent role in things.

He saw it on my face. "You don't know your truth, do you?"

With reluctance I shook my head. "Not all of it."

"Have it then, for in the end it's all we have. You know you're powerful, and that your power is divine?"

"Yes."

"You know you're an awakening entity; an avatar?"

"Yes."

He studied my face, and I could feel him watching both my soul and filtering through the surface thoughts of my mind. I could shield myself from him, but not completely, a haze of feelings still escaped me.

"But you're not to operate alone, and you didn't know that?"

"What do you mean?"

"You're an awakening god, an avatar, one of a whole raft of new gods that Schoperde birthed across the world to replace the old order."

"Why?"

"Because she thought the previous generation had grown greedy like spoilt children."

His words reminded me of what I'd read in my grandmother's tome. "And I'm here to end them, the old gods?"

"Yes, to end their divine rule. You along with the others."

"Others?"

"The other avatars. Juvela, this was not something you were going to have to fight alone with a sword, nor a thing of wars in the heavens. It was merely a case of Schoperde birthing a new generation; of trying one last time."

"One *last* time?"

"Yes, she hadn't the strength to repeat her actions."

"And it will all fail if you kill me?"

"Like it did before."

My brow furrowed.

He said, "Two thousand years ago she tried the same thing and nearly succeeded. The established order did finally suppress it, but at great cost; the Lae Velsanans' Second Dominion collapsed and many died in the calamities that followed, yet our victory wasn't complete. One of the new gods survived."

"And still does?"

He smiled. "She can't help you."

"She?"

"Dorloth of the gargoyles. She's too strong for any of us to do anything about, but she's also isolated in her troith amidst the ruins of fallen Kalraith."

Could she help me?

Anton went on, "As long as my counterparts in the other established faiths do their parts in removing emerging avatars from amongst their own kind, the divine order will be maintained." A grim smile settled on his face. "It's one of the few things we agree upon."

"So you won't work with me because it'd threaten the dark regime you're trying to keep, even though that puts you in league with cultists?"

"Yes, I suppose so. Funny, isn't it?"

"Even though Ossard will fall and become the province of the Horned God?"

"Yes."

"That's insane!"

"The Horned God is part of the old regime – not the new."

I shook my head in disbelief. "You've enslaved the world!"

"Yes, and work to keep it that way."

"It's a crime!"

"Maybe, but not one punished by my god." He shuffled, growing restless with the conversation.

I was running out of time.

"Is it true that we could have weakened them by getting out of Ossard?"

"Yes, but a hollow victory, the city would still have fallen."

"The Lae Velsanans are carrying word to King Giovanni; Greater Baimiopia will know, and so will the Heletian League, Church, and Inquisition. They wanted us to leave if we couldn't control the city, so as to weaken it for those who come to retake it."

Anton nodded. "It makes some sense, but alas you'll not have the life to see it, and I've sworn to my god that I'll not flee." He shook his head. "I can feel him turning from me already, he knows of my failure. Hopefully, when I hand him your soul in apology, he may yet offer me some kind of salvation."

"You should leave the city and take your Loyalists with you. You could work to win it back when help arrives. We could work together."

He shook his head. "They'll sanctify the city, and they'll do it soon. The kidnappings have climaxed. I've had word that the ritual is planned for as soon as tomorrow night."

My family!

"Tomorrow night? Please, you must leave!"

"No, I've vows to guide me. I've planned to die tomorrow, but not until I've taken as many of them with me as I can. It'll be a bloodbath, and if Krienta sends me his blessings to do it, there may very well be nothing left..."

And then another voice cut in, cold and female, purring from the shadows behind his chair, "This life I take for Mortigi!" Metal flashed from a silver blade suddenly at Anton's neck.

He jumped out of his chair and spun about, but was trapped between it and his desk. His hands flew to his throat.

Too late!

Lady Death stepped out from the shadowed curtains and came into the light. She held her knife out with the blade's edge bloodied.

Anton stood with his back to me, his hands still at his throat. Blood dribbled down one of them to run into the sleeve of his robe.

Lady Death chuckled, the sound deep and rich. "You've got your facts wrong, dear Inquisitor, but it won't matter, not for you, you won't be around to see it."

Angered by such a brazen attack, but perhaps more infuriated that Krienta hadn't intervened, he growled, "Get out of my rooms, bitch!"

She lunged forward to slap him on the cheek with the flat of her blade.

He tried to dodge her teasing strike, but couldn't.

She mocked, "Soon enough they won't be your rooms, the leadership of the Reformers are already coming for them!"

Anton put his bloodied hands behind him on the desk and launched himself backwards, kicking off of his chair. He pushed its heavy oak frame back into her, giving him the moment he needed to get away.

She pushed the chair aside as he jumped to the floor beside me.

I could see an ugly wound across his throat, the cut well placed, but not deep enough to kill.

Perhaps Krienta had intervened...

He yelled, "Men, to arms!"

The door burst open behind us, but neither of us turned. From it we could hear the Inquisitor's call repeated.

A guard came up to stand alongside me with his sword drawn, another took up a position beside Anton. And all the while footfalls of reinforcements thundered from the corridor.

Anton sneered as he wiped blood from his neck. The arrival of another set of guards restored his confidence, seeing him growl, "Kill the bitch!"

Lady Death laughed, and with a snap of her fingers the room's lone lamp died, plunging us into the dark. A weak light filtered in through the door behind us, but it was as good as nothing: We were in her world now.

Sound erupted all around me; from one side, a charge forward; to the other, scrabbling back; the thump of wood, screams, blows, swords ringing as they were drawn, and then the horrid gurgle of someone drowning in their own death. Something struck me across the stomach to send me stumbling to the side and deeper into the shadows. I looked about the room, it nothing but a foul mystery of dark potential.

Metal flashed as it caught the corridor's light. It was followed by a meaty crunch and a gasp of agonised surprise.

I had to get out of here!

A circle of light appeared in front of me, and into it leered Lady Death. "Hello, Juvela, I'll be coming for you; Mortigi has demanded it!" Then she was gone, her passing marked by the sounds of renewed fighting.

This was a place of carnage, a charnel house, a den of the cursed and damned. I sprung from the wall, and ran for the door, knowing this would be my only chance.

She yelled, "Run like the dog you are, I'll give you a head start!" And I could feel the celestial surge as Mortigi gifted her with blessings.

I flew out the door, and into the corridor, passing a pair of stunned guards as I went for the stairs.

Their voices rang out in challenge, but they were quickly choked off.

"Don't worry, Juvela, I'm coming!"

On unsteady legs, with a spinning head, I rushed and drew blindly on the celestial. Despite the Moonroot, I had to try and craft something. I was desperate; without such aid she'd catch me.

A crisp breeze rose to gust about and grow stronger, slamming doors, tearing at curtains, and killing the light of the building's lamps. It took me into its wild weave, becoming more frenzied, until my world seemed to be built of only its roar, my blustering hair, and a blizzard of dust, leaves and stray papers. This strange gale, one I'd called of the very air elemental, only became harder and faster so that more and more my feet didn't even find the ground.

I was riding the wind!

And so I reached the Malnobla's entrance wrapped in the wind's embrace. From there the squall blasted aside the doors and raced me to my freedom into Market Square.

Lady Death cursed from behind, but wasn't defeated - she simply called on more power from her dark lord.

My heels found the cobbles more and more as the strength of my summoning began to fade, yet with each moment I moved further, passing the barracks, the rising silhouette of the Turo, and the university. The howl of the wind accompanied me on that empty avenue, one lit by the glow of distant fires. It was then that I heard the cry, "They've tried to kill the Inquisitor!"

Another voice yelled, "The Flets have cut the Inquisitor's throat!"

And others took up the calls or created their own, "They've killed the Inquisitor!"

"The Inquisitor is dead!"

"The Inquisitor was murdered by the Flets!"

And then joined the bells of the Cathedral.

The wind that had travelled with me, helping me to such a good start, now faltered and fell away. I'd have to finish my trek on foot. I ran on, tired and short of breath, but desperate to get back to Newbank and the rescue of my family.

People began emerging from their homes or sticking their heads out of windows to listen to the cried news. Nearby, a voice growled, "There's the witch, burn her!"

And behind it all rose the cold laugh of Lady Death.

I was only half way to Newbank!

As I ran I felt something rush past, a moment later a set of darts thudded into a nearby wall's wood.

She was making her move.

Still weak from the Moonroot, I knew I'd struggle to outrun her. I needed a fresh advantage.

I grabbed a handful of gravel from the road, splitting it between my hands. In moments, with just a thought, each closed fist was lost to a blinding glow.

She mocked, "She's scared of the dark!"

I turned towards the sound of her voice, and although I couldn't see her, launched some of my fiery pebbles.

My effort was rewarded. The alleyway flared, and in the glare from the spray of sparks, I glimpsed her retreating form. Encouraged, I hurled some more. This time their blazing light revealed her climbing up a wall. I followed her progress by throwing yet more of my flaring weapons.

It seemed like the way to handle my escape, until I realised that I'd left a thatched roof smouldering. A moment later it burst into flames.

Being immune to their heat - and still dizzy after the Moonroot - I'd been thinking of them just as balls of light. Behind me, I'd just set a very short fuse for something at the heart of the Loyalist district, and that something would become a firestorm.

There was no time to think of clever plans, or how to deal with anything other than getting away. At least with the alarm being raised people could seek safety, and that gave me the seed of an idea; was this the way to get the Loyalists out of the city?

I was closing on St Marco's.

Behind me the avenue crowded with Loyalists calling out abuse and launching a hail of uprooted cobbles, and somewhere between hunted Lady Death. Despite it all, my spirits rose.

I was getting closer to Newbank!

I saved a few of my flaring stones, throwing the rest into alleys and onto roofs. I didn't want to create hardship for people, far from it, but I needed to sow confusion.

Finally, I reached the square to stumble past St Marco's Church, the sad building standing blackened and ruined. I could feel the spectral gaze of the priests who'd perished within it upon me; they'd been marooned there. They offered no particular blessing or curse, now being of the celestial, they knew the truth of the city.

For them I whispered a warning of the darkness to come. I also shared my hopes, that in their own way, they might intervene to influence the Loyalists behind me.

I crossed the square, making for the bridge. Behind me the avenue flared and flashed as the new fires grew in their rage. The streets about filled with people, not just because of the rising flames, but also roused by the news of Anton's apparent death.

The bridge ahead, despite the numbers of Reformers and Flets coming and going across the Cassaro, had yet to be repaired – even in a temporary way. I walked along what was left of it until I came to stand at its charred end. It left me looking across a wide gap to Newbank.

It was then that I heard her, "I claim this soul for Mortigi!"

And as I spun about, I felt a burning sting above my hip.

So close to home and now this!

Her intended stab became a cut, winding around my body with my turn. She lost her grip on the knife with my movement, its handle now slick with blood.

Somehow I ignored the pain, instead growling, "Why can't you just let me be?"

She froze, surprised at my lack of response to the wound and taken aback by my rage.

Blood trickled down my side in fat lines. The wound hurt with all the venom of the Pits, but right now, under the waning influence of the Moonroot, my anger took precedence.

She taunted, "You'll never see your family again!"

I didn't need any more reasons to get wild with her, but she seemed determined to give them.

She went on, "The ritual's at dawn, and the night's already well past its mid. Before the sun clears the horizon they'll be dead!"

I'd had enough, so I gave in to my fury.

Unarmed, I reached into the celestial to try and weave a casting to stop her, something that would leave me free to go. She was powerful – a favoured high priest – so I knew I'd need to draw a lot of magic through to overcome her. I began that task, that manipulation, but straight away I realised that something restricted my power.

The Moonroot!

What I'd done before – of igniting gravel and summoning wind of the elemental – hadn't required much effort, but what I needed now demanded a whole lot more. Simply, the Moonroot blocked it.

Back in the real world, she drew a fresh blade.

I had to do something, anything, but I'd only have this one chance.

And so my power bucked!

I might not have been able to drag power through to stop her mortal form, but I could still work things in the celestial. Great tentacle-like limbs unrolled from my soul's core lashing out to ensnare her own. With a violent jerk they sought to overcome her.

Back in the real world she started and gasped.

I raised my flaring fists to rest them on her shoulders, the light of the near molten stones held within them made my fingers glow red and showed the shadow of bones. Apprehensive, she tried to wriggle away from the heat, so I hissed, "She's scared of the light!"

She whispered, "What are you?"

And for an answer, I unleashed myself upon her.

My celestial limbs tightened again, flexing and constricting to open tears along her soul's core. I upped the pressure to send her soul-stuff to bursting out, spraying off into the chill depths of the void.

Some of it hit my own soul. It felt good; the taking of power. It reminded me of the high I'd gotten from my followers, but this came more intense and pure.

Lost in that rising rush, I found myself working to take in more of her soul-stuff as it escaped. Finally, overwhelmed by the euphoric sensation, I found myself tearing open her soul to sup at her – her very existence.

In the real world I sighed, it rising into a wail, and then into Schoperde's Song. I sang it like it'd never been sung before, setting waves rushing out along the river, celestial sparks to flash and flare, and great coiling bolts of power to roll around me.

The Loyalist crowd coming into St Marco's kept back, many screaming in fright. At the same time, Lady Death's voice hissed out of her ruin as a long and mournful sigh. She'd be dead in moments, and not because of the lightning coursing through her and me, but because her soul was nearly gone.

Oblivion waited.

And then it was done.

Sated, I returned my perception to the real world.

It was hard to focus, to concentrate, to even breathe after experiencing such a thing.

So, I confessed to myself, that was soul feeding...

The taking of someone's soul until they died...

Every sense in me sung, my body tingled, the knife wound had healed, and my head spun.

By all the gods, I wished I'd never done it!

Having tasted it, I knew I'd have the urge to feed again, and its lure would forever be hard to resist. What I faced was nothing short of the temptation of Death's addiction. If I gave into it, I'd be failing not only myself, but also the cause of Life.

In front of me, Lady Death's body fell crumpled and wasted to the scorched boards of the bridge.

I still sang the Song of Sorrow, but it certainly wasn't to mourn her. I wondered at that; maybe it was because of my own loss of innocence.

What had I done?

That was when I noticed the crowds gathered in Newbank. Most of them were Flets seething with anger, riled by the accusations of murder called out by Loyalists.

In so many eyes – on both sides – burned a mindless lust for revenge. Their anger was fuelled by their bloody-minded gods, and for no good reason but to service their own divine addictions.

If I was to have a part in unseating them from their heavenly thrones, I'd be glad of it. I'd do it even at my own cost if it would bring their whole order crashing down so Schoperde could start afresh.

Above the roar of flames, yelled abuse, and my own singing, I heard others join my song. It reminded me that there was – as there always should be – still hope.

Hope.

I still had to save my family, find the innocent, and then lead them to safety. Despite all the hatred, some love remained.

The crowd of Loyalists in St Marco's glared in anger, blaming me for Ossard's ills, but I didn't care. Further along the river towards the port, mobs of Reformers spilled into the streets, armed, and coming to meet them. I then turned to look upon Newbank where tens of thousands lined the riverbank. Over there were all sorts; some who hated me, others who feared me, and my own people led by Baruna.

She had them gathering at the other end of the bridge where she stood at its charred end. It was they who sang, joining with me to call me home.

I could see others standing amongst my enemies on all sides looking on in wonder. They were *almost* convinced.

To the roar of my people, I stepped out from the charred planks of the bridge to walk across the void to Newbank.

I knew without question where my power was coming from now; my people. I couldn't deny it.

Today the world would change.

I whispered to Schoperde, "Your daughter is born." And I prayed to her; may my family be waiting while Marco watches over them, and may Sef, my most loyal friend, also be safe.

Oddly, using my celestial senses, Marco didn't seem to be there. In checking the bond I'd established between us, I realised that something was amiss.

I let the glowing stones drop from my hands to fall into the river below. With my crossing all but complete, I then took my first step onto the Newbank side of the bridge's scorched boards to be greeted by fresh cheers.

Baruna took my hands. "It's so good to have you back." And my people parted so we could pass through.

Their happiness was uplifting, giving me another high. But the sensation reminded me of a new and aching hunger I harboured – for soul-feeding.

24

-

Liberation

The crowd parted so I could move ahead, many held torches, others lanterns, and even a few clutched at candles that dribbled hot wax. My people; they'd waited for me, knowing that I'd return.

They had faith.

But with my return came the city's fall, and our exodus could no longer wait. By sunrise Newbank would be swarming with Loyalists and be at the heart of the city's woes. The city of Merchant Princes was gone, as was the Inquisition's short-lived pious empire, for now came the dark days of Death's Ossard; a bleak and ruined boneyard of violence and decay.

Beyond my people stood so many more. Most of them cheered at the sight of fresh fires across the river, some with wicked grins, but there were others who prepared to face the Loyalists with all the dignity that our ancestors had mustered to meet the fury of the genocide.

So this was Ossard's end ...

I said, "Let those who want peace and to survive the fall of the city follow, for soon we'll be ready to leave - after I've attended to my family."

Baruna nodded.

Sections of the crowd whispered about us; word had spread of the link between the kidnappings and Kurgar. I could see groups arguing, some not quietly. The news seemed to have split Newbank. Some didn't believe it, but others did, remembering a slow stifling of the peaceful faiths by a Guild always blaming the need for secrecy.

My own followers crowded deeply around, perhaps as many as a thousand. About them thronged many more who'd come to see me for themselves. It was these souls, I realised, that I had to win over to make a difference, to salvage something from the coming fall of the city.

With every step, using my footfalls as a rhythm, I burnt a little of my power; that which I'd gained in consuming Lady Death. Pulses of it rolled out through the celestial to break upon the crowd's souls like the surf on a beach. For my followers it came as a blessing, for those unsure of their allegiance, a whisper of truth. To the remainder, who'd already given themselves to Death's gods, it washed over them as if they lay under the waterline, buried beneath slime and weed.

I walked along to feel a returning flow. Most stood strong in faith, others like Baruna thrummed with extra illumination. This was the beginning of something; not just hope, but a new age.

I said, "The Loyalists are claiming the Inquisitor dead and blaming the Flets for it. They'll try for vengeance by coming into Newbank, but it'll leave their backs unprotected."

"And you think the Reformers will take advantage?" Baruna asked.

I nodded. "They already are, and then they'll move onto their ritual. We must be quick."

She said, "We have a lot to take."

"I still need to get to my family, and what of Sef; I saw him attacked?"

"Sef lives, but is wounded. He's waiting at the crowd's rear." She smiled. "Almost everything is arranged, for now the only thing we need to do is fetch Marco and your family."

"Thank you."

My followers formed a path, and at its end waited Sef with one of his arms bandaged.

I smiled. "Are you alright?"

"I'll be fine; they got some steel into me, but it was the club to the head that dropped me." His own smile softened, "I'm glad you're back."

I nodded.

He looked to the other shore as the warmth drained from his face. "And now comes the fall?"

I followed his gaze. "Yes."

Our coach waited with Kurt atop it; I got in, Sef beside me, and finally Baruna. She said, "Marco hasn't sent any word, and people are talking openly of Kurgar's involvement. If the Guildmaster has heard, he may've tried to move them."

He would've heard. The master of the Flet Guild could hear any of Ossard's gossip, and this was certainly a matter close to his heart. I said, "We'll go straight there."

Sef gave the panel a knock, seeing Kurt get us started.

Baruna said, "Others will follow to help, while yet more will see to getting our people out of the city. I've told them to get beyond the gates by dawn and to take any who are willing with them. I've also sent some to collect your parents and their maids."

"Thank you, Baruna."

Sef looked to me. "Your power has grown; what happened over there?"

"I'm awakening. They've all spoken of me as though I'm something to fear - and for the first time I believe them." And, I sensed, the effects of the Moonroot had finally waned away.

Baruna smiled.

"Anton told me some things of note."

Sef asked, "And you trust him?"

"Whether he meant to help or not, he told me some truths thinking I'd soon be dead. I'll tell you the details of it later, but the core of what he said was why they want me destroyed and the consequences if they failed. He also told me of the only other to survive their hunt."

Sef asked, "Another avatar?"

"No longer an avatar, but awakened."

"Who?"

"Dorloth of the Gargoyles."

Both of them stared.

"I don't know how, but maybe she can help."

They looked to me, too stunned to answer.

"Anton also told me that I'm not a power like those above, I'm something new. Schoperde birthed me, and others like me, to replace the old generation who've been overcome by their greed for souls. I'm part of a second chance."

Baruna asked, "What second chance?"

"Life's second chance - and its last."

Sef's eyebrows arched.

I explained, "Schoperde birthed the old gods to look after the races of man, but they've become addicted to feeding on the souls of those they're supposed to protect. Together they've grown so strong that they've blocked her attempts to raise new gods, gods that won't succumb to that same addiction. It's a battle that's gone on for thousands of years and left her drained."

THE FALL OF OSSARD

The coach slowed as we moved deeper into the slums. The afternoon and much of the night had passed since the Inquisitor's men had mounted their raids. Some of their fires burnt on, but the smoke wasn't as thick. The bulk of what now drifted about was being blown from the growing inferno raging across the river in the Loyalist district.

The streets of the slums held a scattering of traffic and also some crowds. True, it was late, but there were relatives to check on and also news wanted of the chaos unfolding across the river. An undercurrent of fear, bitter and sharp, also haunted the night; it came from the rumours concerning Kurgar.

The road only grew narrower the deeper into the slums we went. Soon enough we had to leave the comfort of the coach and take to the dirt lanes on foot. All about us people hurried, many openly wearing the symbols of their true faiths; those first subverted by the Church, and then by our own guild.

Taking in the atmosphere, I imagined that the Flets living in Old Wair-Rae had once also gathered in such a nervous air on the eve of Def Turtung. Then, the Lae Velsanans had turned against their former slaves after a generation of granted freedom, scared by my people's growing wealth and success.

For all of us, either living two centuries ago in the Fourth Dominion or today in Ossard, we stood at the cusp of our judgment. It was time to stand for our truths.

We hurried on through the slum's alleyways heading through the maze. After passing a few more turns we'd be at the tower, and I could feel my power rising with my expectations.

We were so close!

My concerns also rose. I couldn't communicate with Marco; his soul felt *wrong*.

I led, then came Sef and Baruna, and behind us walked a dozen of my followers. Unlike the streets we'd just passed through, the deeper we went into the heart of the slums the more deserted they'd become. The dark ways narrowed more and more to stand tall and ominous.

I whispered, "Let's be careful."

The alleyways lay quiet, even the open sewers dared not sound a trickle or gas a bubble.

I slid my perception into the celestial to search for Marco.

His soul was there, yet something was wrong. It glowed alive and beaming, but from it stretched a luminous trail that raged like

311

billowing smoke in a gale-caught fire. Sparks also leapt after it to add to his shed soul-stuff, all of it burning off into Oblivion.

I hissed, "Wait!" And we stopped only one turn from the tower.

Nothing seemed to be lurking about his soul, and it didn't seem to be ensnared by any kind of casting. I also looked to the tower where its celestial presence loomed dull and lifeless. I reminded myself that it'd looked that way before, no doubt masked by some kind of magic.

Sef asked, "What's wrong?"

"I can't see them.

"They may be hidden."

I shrugged as I resumed our march. "Perhaps."

"Is Marco there?" asked Baruna.

"Yes, but something's wrong."

After another turn we entered the small square, it now occupied only by shadows and the echoes of distant riots. We passed through it to ignore the tower, and turned down the alleyway opposite.

"Where's Marco?" Sef asked.

In the dim light it was hard to see anything in the alley except that it lay thick with rubbish and filth. The refugees who'd huddled in it were gone.

I slipped into the celestial to look again. There his soul was glowing with life right in front of us, but still shedding energy. It didn't make any sense.

"Sef, look into the celestial, he's right there."

He looked and cursed, "By the gods, what's happening to him?"

I took a hesitant step forward, to where - in my perception's view of two worlds - his soul lay. That glowing sphere of life, the seed of his being, seemed to be right before me, yet all I could see was a pile of dirty rags. I stopped in the dim light, finally recognising the robe we'd bought. It lay there tattered, twisted, and heavily stained. I reached down and drew it back to unveil his bloodied remains.

Sef hissed, "The bastards!"

Poor Marco, he lay there twisted and torn with meat spilling through his shredded clothes. He was dead.

Baruna gasped, "Oh, Marco!"

Sef said, "But his soul, it's as if he lives?"

Baruna began to cry.

I slid into the celestial to try and connect with him. "Marco?"

He was waiting for me. "Oh, Juvela!" he sounded desperate.

"Marco! What have they done to you?"

"Juvela, I'm trying to hold on, but I can't for much longer!"

"What happened?"

"They came, cultists, I didn't see them approach, but they attacked..." his voice broke, trailing off in a mix of anguish and disbelief.

"Marco?"

"...they killed me!"

"Oh, Marco..."

"Wait Juvela, I don't have long."

And I could see what he meant: It was taking an immense effort for him to hold out against his soul's urge to rush back to his god.

...to rush back to me.

The realisation distracted me, stirring my deep hunger.

I could feed again!

He said, "They taunted me, saying that they were going to take them away."

"Both Pedro and Maria?"

"Yes, and others, including the Lord and Lady." His soul began to shiver.

"Was there any clue as to where they were going?"

"Nothing for certain. I tried to connect with Maria, but I couldn't, – and then... then the cultists started to... to..."

"Marco?"

"...to cut at me."

I shivered. "It's alright Marco, you've done well to hold on."

My hunger was growing...

Soon!

"I wish I could've done more. I wish I could've stopped them or got word to you. I tried, but I mustn't have been strong enough."

"Marco, it's alright. When did it happen?"

"Not long after sunset. They teased me, saying the ritual was set for daybreak."

I would've been unconscious when he'd tried to send his message.

He moaned with pain.

And the thought of him dying made me shudder. I could let his soul return to me on its natural path, coming home to roost, from where one day it would be reborn, or I could snatch it up to feed upon, absorb the power, and deny him his future.

313

I tried to calm myself: He trusted me. He'd have his time of peace, and when ready, his rebirth. "Marco, it's alright. You've done well and I'm grateful. You can rest now."

"Wait; the cultists became frenzied when they attacked, and I could see things as if they were thoughts spilling from their minds. There were visions of them rallying at Market Square. I think they needed to take it, that they'd been ordered to."

That made some sense, for where else should the sanctity ritual be completed but at Ossard's heart and seat of power?

After all, Lady Death had been there...

And with that thought my hunger grew, beginning to give me deep quaking cramps. So pained, I became impatient. "Thank you Marco, but you can rest now, please."

I sensed him relax.

He said, "It's been a joy."

I almost snapped at him, wanting him to let go and end my agony. I restrained myself. "Rest, Marco, please."

And then he let go.

I knew that I should let his soul rest, it was my intention, but my hunger roused so painfully that I worried I'd not be able to resist.

His soul began to break into a glowing trail of soul-stuff, finally free to begin its race home.

Its race home to me...

I braced myself. This would be a different sensation, part of a natural cycle, as he was one of my own. I doubted it'd feel as intense as soul-feeding, but nonetheless my hunger for it and the power it would give me saw me oblivious to all else.

And then, just as I thought I had myself under control, my dark hunger bucked. It cut through me strong and vicious, each extra moment drawing me further into its agony.

I yearned to feed, to end the pain – and to take the high it would give.

And what was left of his soul flared and rushed for me.

I tensed and waited, bracing myself.

I should let him rest, but I needed to feed...

I needed the power...

I needed...

Then, just before he reached me, something blue and spectral passed between us in the void. It flared with new power, crying out in triumph before circling away.

It had taken Marco!

I cried out in anguish.

I needed that soul!

I turned my perception to search for the thief.

And there she was; my grandmother.

The dark pits of her eyes lay cold, but somehow smug upon her pallid face, and about her floated hundreds of skulls in her macabre halo.

Back in the real world, I slumped into the filth of the alley while crying out. Sef and Baruna both reached for me, thinking I'd been overcome by my mourning for Marco's passing.

I realised then how much I'd already come under Death's sway. I had to stop it, to resist the addiction - while I still could.

If I could...

I also had to break the bond between my grandmother and me.

Steadying myself, and aided by Sef and Baruna, I rose out of the alley's dirt, muck, and Marco's blood.

A cool chuckle then sounded from the shadows.

Sef's hand tensed on my shoulder, for we both knew who stalked us. "Easy, Juvela."

Tears ran down my face to fall into Marco's ruin. I was disgusted with myself: Marco had died serving me and suffered afterwards, and all I'd been able to think of was gorging on his soul as if I was at a banquet. He deserved more than that; at the very least respect, love, and my own service. I vowed to save him, not just from my failure, but also from my grandmother.

If being a god meant I received people's faith, surely I had to give something in return. My disgust at myself saw my need to feed fade, yet the hunger remained, but was no longer so urgent.

A voice again drifted from the darkness, cool and smooth, "The hunt isn't over. You may have beaten Mortigi's lady, but we're many and still coming to claim you!"

Damn them and this plague of madness!

Angered, I growled, "Don't bother, I'll come to you." And I stepped over Marco's body and deeper into the lane. "I'm coming, and I hope you, your fellows, and your filth-eating god are ready!"

And all about me the darkness opened with surprised eyes. Some of them gasped, others hissed, the lead calling, "How dare you!"

"You won't believe how much I dare!" And I offered my hands as power surged through them to flare as though a dozen suns had risen in the alleyway.

The cultists screamed as they ran, half-blinded and dazed. One of them stood frozen in terror, his eyes melting to leak from their sockets while the skin on his face reddened to peel as his clothes smouldered.

I hurled the light from my palms, it flaring as it flew. It split as it chased them, each blazing ball finding dark robes to burn through and flesh to quench them.

And then I was done.

"Juvela?" It was Sef.

I lowered my hands and what remained of the hot light died away.

"Juvela, such power, where has it come from?"

I nearly laughed, but this was no time for mirth. Still, I wasn't going to admit that my newfound strength came from feeding on the soul of Lady Death. Instead, I said, "I must get to my family."

Baruna stared, until finally she said, "We'll come too."

"No, please, you must lead the people out of Ossard before sunrise."

"She will," Sef said, "but I'm coming, and there'll be no argument."

I smiled. "You know what you're going up against?"

"I know," and his voice wavered. If he intruded on the rituals of the Reformers, he'd be working directly against the wishes of Kave.

In the celestial, I could feel the perception of a god looking our way, noticing something of what happened here. Quickly, I set layers of soul-stuff about my life-light to hide its glow. My soul, as powerful as it threatened to become, was still no match for the likes of Mortigi.

Sef asked, "Can we stop the ritual?"

"Too many stand against us, and they've too many souls to feed it. The city is lost, and nothing can stop that – but we *can* weaken it."

Hope lit his eyes. "Let's go then!" He began to turn.

"There are quicker ways." I spread my arms, my hands beginning to glow, but this time with a softer light. "Come to me, Sef. Baruna, please, see to the innocents and get them out by sunrise."

She nodded, smiling at my blooming power.

With just a thought, Sef and I rose from the blood-soaked dirt of the alley and up into the night. Sef laughed, a sound that became louder as we climbed to pass above the slum's uneven rooftops. The blue light from my hands mixed with the amber and gold of the city's fires to expose Mortigi's cultists as they fled across roofs of shingle, slate, and tile.

Sef lashed out at one with a sword as we passed. "And that's for Marco!" It seemed only a flesh wound, but the cultist slipped from his perch on the roof's ridgeline to fall to his death on the streets below.

And from our vantage point, as we rose higher, we beheld the doom of the city - the very fall of Ossard.

The rooftops about us ran alive with the followers of Mortigi. The black clad murderers swept across the heights of Newbank like a plague of rats centred on the slums, but not exclusively; they were everywhere. They numbered close to a thousand, the only things more common the roofs themselves and the fires eating the city.

Below, someone called, "Get Mortigi's marked!"

Darts, throwing knives, even arrows and crossbow bolts flew at us, but nothing struck. I refused them all.

The missiles slowed as they neared, only to stop and then be returned with greater force. Cultists screamed and cursed as their fingers were sliced and their bodies pierced by their own weapons. Some died instantly, while others slid from rooftops unable to grab onto handholds with now fingerless hands. And in the celestial, I reached out and burst each of their souls, remembering Marco as I let their essence dissipate and sent them on to Oblivion.

Such action denied them an afterlife, and their foul god a feeding.

I refused to take them despite my aching hunger. I had to be strong; for that was the path to Death's addiction.

We rose above Newbank, all of it illuminated by spreading flames. Along the roofs moved packs of thieves and cultists, and in the streets below Flets, Reformers, and Kavists. They banded together under many banners, fighting for their newfound or - in some cases - long-hidden faiths.

Loyalists also attacked on several fronts, both in the city and now in a freshly established beachhead in Newbank. They marched, charged, and died under the Inquisition's black and gold, pushing on despite their losses as they surged into Newbank to claim revenge. Behind them, down the main avenues of the city, I could see Heletians fighting each other; Loyalist against Reformer.

Slipping my perception between worlds, I could see the reptilian eye above the city. Power grew there; a dark dream of what was to come.

I shivered.

We were high enough now that we'd cleared the tallest rooftops and towers, and passed over the heart of Newbank to head towards the river. To the east, at the Newbank Gate, I could see a gathering of coaches, carts, and people.

Our people!

The sight lifted my spirits.

There were so many, thousands and thousands, and they hadn't gathered for me, but for hope and life.

I sent a thought, it not something they'd understand in a word-for-word way, just a sense of what they needed to do to survive.

Get beyond the wall to safety!

Beneath us, the Loyalists continued flooding across the river. They'd advanced from their landing to reach the steps of the Guildhall and work their way into the district's streets. With flaming brands, they pushed into Newbank's main square, the area of my own home and that of my parents. Two forces fought in that open space, Flets and Loyalists, and behind them I could see my own people still heading for the gate.

In the celestial I warned, "The Loyalists are in the square!"

And fires sprang up in the surrounding buildings.

My parents weren't at home - I could sense it - yet I still felt sickened to watch the first signs of flames. By their flaring light, I watched looters spill through their house and courtyard, trampling the rose garden I'd planted during my season of shame. I knew I could stop it, but as soon as I moved on it would only start again. It was pointless. Like the city it had grown from, its fate was to be razed.

A flash of light from below marked the beginning of the Guild's magical defence. Great waves of red power rolled out of the building to strike the bands of storming Loyalists. The attack only incited the mob, drawing more of them. Half a dozen died in a moment, while a score fell wounded.

Sickened by the sights about me, and already fatigued by a catastrophe that was far from peaking, I wondered; perhaps they deserved each other, these people in love with their barbarous city.

My own home lay behind us already aflame. I hoped everyone had got out and that someone had taken my grandmother's tome; regardless, I couldn't worry about it now. It was just too late.

I turned from the fighting in Newbank. For my people I could do no more. It was time to focus on my family, perhaps - with all that was going on - an indulgence, but to me it was a symbol of hope.

Finally, I was strong enough to get them.

Damn it, I was an awakening avatar!

We rose higher, having passed the worst of Newbank's fighting to now be above the Cassaro. Hundreds still rushed across to join the battle, but increasingly the Loyalists were turning about: Their vengeful charge had left a flank exposed.

The Reformers had been ready, heading straight for Ossard's undefended heart. They surged down the alleys of the poorer districts, to the avenues that had for so long marked the boundaries of wealth and class.

The city heaved with the desperation of thousands of separate life and death struggles. Fires flared and chaos swept its streets. Crowds fought, looted, or in some places celebrated victories. In many places buildings burnt, not just homes or businesses, but also whole blocks.

Sef gasped, "The Turo!"

The mid-level windows of the high tower flared with blinding flashes of light. After a moment, more came from the next level up as an unknown spell caster advanced.

I said, "The fighting's spread so quickly. The Reformers were ready."

As they had been all along.

The casting continued in the Turo, making its way up floor by floor. Whoever led that charge stalled on the second highest level, before unleashing another series of spells, each followed by rumbling booms.

A final flare lit up the night. The brilliant light shone from the tower's top level to roar angrily and blow off part of its roof. For a moment it drowned out the rest of the city's fury, before sending a rain of burning timber and rock to shower down on the streets below.

"Sef, keep an eye on it, they can see everything from up there - including us."

A pulse of power flew from the top of the Turo, screaming as it zoomed across to hit one of the Cathedral's towers at its base. It was lost in a ball of blue flames, the writhing fire dying quickly, but not before its stonework fractured to bring the tower down. The rumble of its collapse snuffed out the screams of those it killed, the sight of it quickly smothered by a great cloud of billowing dust. A shocked silence came to settle over the square.

More pulses of power shot out to eat into anything the Reformers considered a threat. The flurry of attacks targeted the dust-shrouded Cathedral and other church-owned buildings, most of them near or edging on to Market Square.

I slid my perception into the celestial where I could watch the amazing pull and tug caused by so many users of magic dragging power from that other world. It moved with huge tides and eddies, the energy passing from and through it, leaving me to wonder; could the boundary somehow tear?

How strong was the barrier between worlds?

In the celestial, lost spirits, shades, and feeders all gathered, eating at the fragments of soul-stuff left over from so many deaths. They also waited for another kind of opportunity; for the chance to slip back into the realm of the living.

Elsewhere, other practitioners of magic took up the fight. For the Loyalists, that meant the senior priests of the Church, and for the Reformers, both the Cabal and priests of the cults. From a dozen different locations jets of energy and crackling bolts of lightning flew. Fires sprang up, bursting into sudden life, explosions blossomed, and buildings collapsed amidst a hail of red-hot stone and rubble.

Amidst the chaos, a pulse of power burst out from the Turo to scream towards us.

Sef cursed in surprise.

As quickly as it was cast, my celestial reflexes worked to diffuse it, stripping its energy away. So empowered, I could defend easily – but not forever. We all had limits.

I gathered myself for something final.

A bolt of lightning crackled out from my hand to flash across the sky. It set the pall hanging over the city aglow, before blasting the top of the Turo off to send stones flying. When the smoke cleared, it revealed the tower still standing, but crowned in ruin.

Beside me, I could sense Sef as he wondered: From where has all this power so suddenly come?

With guilt on my mind, I ignored him.

To the west lay the Port district, in many places it also burned. The air over there swirled about to gather the countless smoke plumes and weave them together. At its heart glowed a pillar of sparks of a deep violet hue. I didn't have to check to know that it rose over the previous ritual's site.

Sef yelled above the noise of the wind, fighting, and roar of Ossard's countless fires, "Look at the River Gate; others flee the city!"

Crowds gathered there, many marked by the white and yellow or black and gold of the Loyalists. They were leaving, ushered on their way by the ghostly priests of St Marco's.

Passing over the Loyalist district, my excitement soared. For the first time I could sense that I was closing in on Pedro and Maria.

My family!

Sef's thoughts again fluttered through my mind: She's so powerful, could she somehow stop all this?

With a cold voice, I said, "To save them, I'd have to kill them – and I don't want their blood on my hands. Let them kill each other if they must." Yet, deep down, I knew I could only play with such power because of my feeding on Lady Death. The admission stirred my hunger, it rising from a nagging ache to mature into a throbbing pain.

We passed plumes of smoke as the fires about the city continued to grow and spread, and then, finally, we began to descend towards Ossard's main battleground; the bloodied and rubble-strewn ruin of Market Square.

I slipped into the celestial to search for the souls of Pedro and Maria. I could taste them; they were close.

There!

"Sef, I've found them," I said as I laboured to weave the view of two worlds together.

"Where?"

"The Malnobla!"

Sef drew his sword. "Let's get them!"

And my thoughts were also of Kurgar.

The cultists had secured the building, and now used it as it always had been – as Ossard's seat of power. The Loyalist banners hanging from the balcony were cast down as we watched.

I offered a prayer to Schoperde, begging her to lend me the strength to end Kurgar's life.

Surely such a thing would leave the new Ossard weakened?

And all the while, I guided us down into the slaughter-ground of Market Square.

It surged beneath us under the tide of battle as the two sides clashed. The dead lay scattered about, but also strangely piled in places like islands amidst a furious sea's swell. Both sides fought hard, but clearly the Loyalists had been caught out and were now being pushed back. Their only line that held, albeit as a thinning ring, was around their crippled Cathedral.

So close now to the end of all things, my anger at having had my family stolen away to start with only bucked and grew. I wanted them back, and to make the perpetrators pay, but that fury only helped work free my dark hunger. The pain of it throbbed inside me to grow more desperate and hard. At the same time its demands took strength from the deaths around me, as if it could taste them.

We came down amidst the fighting a hundred paces from the front of the Lord's Residence. There was little space, but an impatient wave of my hand called a force that pushed aside the combatants regardless of loyalties.

Some of their contests finished abruptly as one lost balance and fell on another's sword; in others, those that struggled to keep on their feet or move back into my cleared space, I dealt with by reaching into the celestial and brazenly draining their souls.

Part of me screamed in disbelief!

The beginning of that feeding hadn't been a conscious decision, more a loss of my battle to stay in control. Now, blinded by its high, I grabbed another, and another, and then only more.

Sef could feel something of what was happening, becoming restless beside me and afraid. I tried to twist his silence into an endorsement.

Surely I needed souls for power, otherwise how was I to best Kurgar and get my family back? There was also my grandmother to deal with before I could free Marco and his wife and daughter.

In that feeding I claimed six more. Of them, five had been promised to others, and I could feel the celestial shift in anger as larger entities turned to see who dared steal their own.

The fear of being caught by such powers saw me finally calm. I could feel myself stepping back from a crazed binge, one that would see me drink of all the souls in the square. Lost to such madness, I'd even sup on Sef.

The thought both sobered and disgusted me.

322

I said, "Let's go, Kurgar's already claimed the Lord's Residence. They'll be there with him."

Sef nodded, his eyes wide as we landed in the square.

Few combatants noticed us, most too busy in their own struggles. A smattering raised weapons against us, but I just snarled to see them drop.

I'd fed some more!

But I hadn't meant to...

This wasn't how it was supposed to be. I came here for Life, not as Death's servant!

I grabbed Sef to drag him forward, trying to remain focused on my purpose and get out of the square.

He flinched at my touch.

The crowded battlefield parted before us to reveal a path of blood-slick cobbles, it all lit in amber by the flaring light cast from the city's countless flames. About us rang the clash of metal amidst the crunch of breaking bones, the tearing of flesh, and the screams and moans of the dying. This was the bleak world the old gods wanted; one where souls were quickly claimed.

Sef pleaded, "Juvela, you've got to control yourself. I can see what you're doing, and if you're not careful you'll become just like our foes!"

He was right, but was it already too late?

The further we moved, the more we escaped the battle's heart and came into a strange kind of peace. It was dotted with exhausted Reformers who smiled and quietly celebrated, despite their wounds and fatigue.

We passed through them to stop at the base of the Residence's steps. Ahead of us, at the centre of the rising stairs, spread a pool of blood being fed drip by drip from a plump and robed body hanging from the balcony. Bloodied and burnt, with arrows sticking out of it, it slowly twisted and turned in the smoke-heavy breeze.

It was Benefice Vassini!

The body twitched – life remained in the poor man!

I looked into the celestial to see bonds of power humming about him. The casting was a curse, it blocking his soul from breaking its last links to his mortal form. The cultists had done it to torment him.

Unbelievably, a child played at the edge of pooled blood. Next to her, a slim but tall man dragged his own fingers through the congealed mess as it dribbled down step by step. Horrified, I moved to stop him, but at the same moment he stood and turned while rubbing his bloodied fingertips together.

The air chilled.

By the flaring light of Ossard's fires, I could see that he was neither Flet nor Heletian, but Lae Velsanan.

He looked up to the Benefice, his spell breaking the bonds entrapping Vassini's soul. The dangling form shuddered, and then gave out a final but relieved moan.

I turned back to the Lae Velsanan, but he was already disappearing into the crowd. His magic tasted familiar - it something of Life. He was an ally, if a mystery, perhaps something for another time.

Holding Sef's arm, I stepped forward to skirt the pooled blood and climb the stairs. It was time to get my family and deliver justice to Kurgar.

25

The Residence

The great timber doors stood open at the top of the steps, yet I had to stop and steady myself against one of them as I tried to deal with my roiling power.

I looked back across the square. It had seemed so chaotic only moments ago, but now I could see that most of it was already in the Reformers' grip. The Loyalists still fought on in isolated pockets, outnumbered, and being cut down. Their only organised resistance stood to ring the Cathedral, but even that force was being overrun and wasted.

The Loyalist defeat was so certain a thing that many Reformers turned from the fight. Their leaders directed them to clear the cobbles of bodies and prepare for the building of a great pyre, while behind them, from the direction of the port, a convoy of timber-loaded carts began to come into the square.

The ritual?

They were quick with their work, their hurry nagging me to also move. Beyond them, I noted, the eastern sky was brightening.

I lent hard against the door, trying to deal with the power boiling within me. It was caustic and difficult to handle, particularly now that it mixed with my excitement as I closed in on my family.

Sef put a hand to my shoulder. "Are you alright?"

I could only give him a nod, as speaking would have revealed the truth.

"Are you sure?"

I closed my eyes and nodded again, but this time concentrated on calming myself. After a deep breath, I pushed off from the door to open my eyes and said, "Let's go."

Sef's worry lifted into surprise, him staring at the woodwork I'd been leaning against. I turned to look.

Spreading from where my body had touched its polished finish ran the swirling images of white roses. Green leaves and shoots also ran through the decoration, all of it tinged with the red health of new growth.

Sef whispered, "The Lady of the Rose, that's what they call you!"

So many things were happening to me, and there was still so much more to learn. All I could say was, "Better that than the hag of oleander."

Sef smiled and gave a soft laugh. "It's a measure of your power. You're ready."

I blushed, knowing the truth of where so much of my power had come from – the souls I'd stolen.

What was I doing?

Ashamed, I promised myself; I'd not steal another, never again. I took a deep breath and tried to hold on to my calm. "Sef, with you by my side, I can do anything."

The entry hall spread before us with a layer of ash and litter covering its marble floor. Likewise, the walls' rich wood panelling had already been defaced with obscene carvings and angry scrawls.

I whispered to myself of courage and promised to be true to Life...

But the hunger was still there despite my gluttony. It ached deep down in an empty place, sending up giddy shivers of longing...

No, I'd be strong. I had to be. Feeding on stolen souls was the path to addiction and submission to Death.

Yet that hunger now lurked within me, and was always going to be there. The damage was already done...

No, control and strength would see me through. If I took one more, it'd only lead to another, and then another two.

But it had felt so good, and the power harvested could ensure my family's escape. Surely, just one more soul wouldn't lead to addiction? I could control it, and besides if it were Kurgar's, it would merely be a kind of justice...

No, I couldn't!

But what if I needed that extra power to rescue my family?

No!

But to come all this way, only to fail because I didn't have the power needed...

Well...

Just one, just to seal the rescue...

Well, just one, but then never again.

And, as we advanced across the entry hall, I noticed that I was drooling.

No one came to stop us, not at the entry, nor in our passage through the hall. When we reached the stairs we both paused before beginning our climb, knowing that Kurgar would be in the Lord's office, at the traditional hub of Ossard's power.

Noise came to us from above as we ascended. Footfalls and slamming doors, people rushing from room to room; meetings, discussions, and of course some looting.

How quickly they'd taken this place.

We came to the first landing, Sef with his sword drawn, and me with my determination. I shivered as I wiped saliva from my chin.

A voice came to us from down the corridor, a hard thing followed by heavy footfalls. "Stop! What'd you do here?"

Sef and I turned to face the speaker.

A man stepped forward with his sword out, moving to block our path. He looked to be a Kavist from his arms and armour, with another stepping up behind him to back him up.

Sef said, "Let us pass my friend, our business is not with you."

The first man frowned as the rhythm of more footfalls sounded from further back. "Your business *is* with us if you're here."

I said, "We've come to see Kurgar, and that's something we've done easily enough before."

"Before you turned half of Newbank against him!" the lead Kavist growled, and then he addressed Sef, "Brother, you've turned your back on Kave!"

Sef shuffled uncomfortably.

The Kavist's fellow snapped, "It's to be expected! If I'm not wrong, this isn't any brother of mine, he's Sef, the *lone man* of Kaumhurst."

Sef grew tense, but I had no time for taunts and bravado. I said, "I'll not be refused."

The footfalls behind them grew louder, before the silhouette of another hulking warrior showed in the dim light.

The lead Kavist, ignoring the latest arrival, sneered. "You can't pass." And he raised his blade to let it hang in the air between us.

The third Kavist stepped into the light; tall and broad, yet fresh-faced. It was Cherub.

Sef smiled with relief. "Cherub, please, your friends are holding us back from an important meeting with Heinz Kurgar?"

Cherub looked to Sef and then to me. Finally, as he blushed, he dropped his gaze to the floor, not willing to act.

I growled, "Kurgar took my family, and I will have them back!"

But the lead Kavist had his own anger brewing to make his voice raw, "Normally I'd not hit a woman, but today I'll make an exception."

Sef took a step forward. "You'll be dead before you do!"

The Kavist put on a grim smile. "Says you?"

I stepped between them and raised my hands between their drawn swords. "Damn you, I'll not be delayed. I've no fear of you – or *ending* you either."

His eyes flickered between Sef and me. "Such big words for the witch of woe."

"I'm no witch."

"Then what are you?"

"Let me show you, and if I'm greater you may withdraw?"

He laughed. "I'm no fool! Get out of here, or I'll skewer you!"

But I stood my ground between him and Sef and their steel. I let my hand slip to the breast of his armour.

He started at my touch, but stilled as if to dare me.

Sef hissed, "Juvela!" He thought I was going to feed again.

I whispered to the Kavist, "Can you feel the cold?"

A smirk came to his face as he shook his head, but then it faded.

In that other world, I'd begun to put pressure on his soul. Small tears opened in its defensive shell, and into those fissures seeped the void's chill.

His gaze dropped to my hand, to where it rested on his armour, then it rose to again meet mine.

"I'm no witch, nor charlatan, or even a cult priest, I'm much more than any of these. I'm a direct child of Schoperde, the goddess of life..."

And then I began to draw his soul's energy into mine.

He broke into a sweat as his skin paled and his lips began to tremble and go blue.

"...and because of that lineage..."

His eyes watered, and in them his life-light began to flicker.

"...I can take life away..."

He began swaying on his feet as his eyes rolled back to show their whites.

"...but also return it."

I gritted my teeth as I stilled the flow, then reversed it.

It hurt. Oh by the gods it hurt! My hunger, which had bucked at the taste of his soul-stuff, now raged at being deprived.

I hissed, "I'm no witch; I'm something so much more than that. If I wanted to kill you, you'd already be dead, but I just want to pass you by."

The colour came back to his face, his eyes righting themselves as the tremors died on his lips. He wasn't a priest, but he knew he'd just come close to death. With a quick swipe of his arm, he knocked my hand from his armour, yet with the contact broken his show of life faded. Silent, he just stared at me as he fell back into the shadows to hit the wall, and then slumped to the floor.

Sef and I went forward, passing the others as we headed for the Lord's office.

The door was closed, but the low drone of voices could be heard. I looked to Sef to see him nod, so I threw open the door and walked in.

The office sat as it always had, a large room heavy with ornamentation and wood – and now packed with Reformers. Kurgar sat back in Lord Liberigo's chair, comfortable at my father-in-law's desk. His voice stilled at my entrance, after having been busy issuing orders for a ritual that with the passing of so much of the night was now quite near.

He looked to me and said, "Juvela..."

I strode past startled faces, too many of them familiar; including the Kavist high priest, Seig, and the Cabal's Mauricio.

Had they all been a party to the city's fall? How long had they toiled to claim their positions and make their plans reality?

Did it matter now?

I just wanted my family, and to leave this bloody mess behind. "Kurgar, you know what I want."

Sef followed with his sword out.

Mauricio said, "His title is Lord Kurgar, the Lord of Ossard."

"Lord of the damned!"

Kurgar raised a hand. "Now, Juvela, really, you're in no position to be making demands."

"I hold *every* position!"

"Juvela, I need your family, and I'll not be giving them up."

"I don't think you understand what you're up against."

He smiled, a cold light sparkling in his eyes. "No, Juvela, it's you who doesn't understand."

329

My perception drifted between worlds as I unrolled tendrils of power to entrap his soul and bend it to my will. Before me his soul lay; simple and innocuous, young and newborn.

And then the image shifted – its truth revealed.

Sef tensed beside me.

And Kurgar's true soul spread before us, bloated with power and the countless souls he'd devoured.

"Yes, Juvela, you're not Ossard's only avatar. I've eaten much these past days, but also over the seasons and years."

I just stared at him as my anger boiled.

Was I to be robbed of the chance to free my family, again?

I said, "But you're serving the old gods, what of the new and our duty to Schoperde?"

He laughed. "While I'm an avatar, I'm not what you think."

"Who's your master?" I demanded.

"You really are ignorant. It's true I'm an avatar, newly born and maturing into my own godhood, yet this life came to me not through Schoperde, but from the very gods she wished vanquished."

Could the old gods bring forth life of their own?

"Yes Juvela, they can raise their own. In our world we have no need of maternal Schoperde, not any more."

"But look at the death you bring!"

"And I'm not alone; there are more, and now we gather to celebrate the rise of a *new* Ossard." He laughed. "And it's us against you," he paused as he dipped into the celestial before returning his perception to me, "you, with barely a dozen souls added to your own."

I glared at him, my anger unrelieved and my doubts growing. I'd expected to just walk in, grab my family, and then leave, being all but unstoppable. I'd certainly not expected to be challenged by another avatar, let alone one stronger. Damn it, this was where fate had brought me, and that being the case, I could only assume that if silent Schoperde was going to aid me then it would be here.

I swallowed and said, "Schoperde will help me."

Kurgar grinned while the cultists and cabalists about him laughed.

Sef shifted, uncomfortable.

Kurgar finally joined them to chuckle. "Really, Juvela, do I have to tell you everything?"

I stared at him, my apprehension stirring.

He went on, his eyes sparkling as he savoured his words, "Schoperde won't be coming to your aid."

"Of course she will."

"What makes you so certain?"

As calmly as I could, I said, "It's the only way for Life to win the divine war against Death."

Fresh laughter met my answer.

Kurgar said, "Yes, it would be, wouldn't it."

And then I realised that he knew something very important.

He shook his head, but his smile didn't fade. "Juvela, haven't you realised yet?"

"Realised what?"

"The war's over, and Schoperde lost. She's dead."

Dead?

I could only stare at him.

He went on, "The war ended two decades ago."

"No!"

"The last great battles were fought much further back. They left her so weakened that all she could do was linger on while slowly wasting away. It all came to an end only recently. That's why there's none of her priests left here and precious few anywhere else. It's why she doesn't bestow blessings, and why her faith fails."

"This is a trick!"

He gave a dark laugh. "Look at the Cassaro Valley and the Northcountry; the land's dying, it treeless and bleak. Life has abandoned this place and the whole of the world, every last bit of it."

I hated to admit it, but his words stank of an uncomfortable truth. I wondered though; what of me, how could I have been born of her if she was no longer present?

Kurgar must have read my mind. "You and the others were her last desperate attempt to win back this world. The very effort of it, of seeding you, is what finally ended her sad and crippled form. We haven't seen a sign of her since. It seems that she spent the last of her power – her very essence – giving your soul passage here."

I didn't know what to say.

But then I realised, for now and the task at hand, his revelation didn't matter. I hadn't come here to debate the fate of Schoperde; that was something for another time. I was here for Pedro and Maria. With Schoperde's aid or not, I wouldn't be leaving without them.

And amidst my fading confusion I became aware of something else; a thrumming in my soul. It was abuzz with offered power.

It was Sef's faith, given freely, and rich and strong because of it. For him and so many others, I was a symbol of hope - and that was something very much alive and worth believing in.

Kurgar may have *stolen* hundreds of souls, perhaps even a thousand, yet I stood knowing that more had already *offered* me theirs. I didn't have to steal and feed on them like a starving dog tearing meat off a rotting carcass. My people wanted me to have the power they offered, not dozens, or scores, not even hundreds, but thousands. That was something Kurgar didn't have - so I stepped forward and called upon them.

I sent out a ring of power that expanded across this world and the next. I could see their faint life-lights, now distant, yet they blazed as it reached them. With it I gave them the strength to flee the city and withstand the trials that would come. I also planted in them the knowledge that I needed them to confirm their hope and faith in me and our future.

The first new prayer of strength and wellness returned from Baruna and others also flared, at first a few, then scores, then hundreds, and finally thousands. They sent me their thoughts, love, and best wishes. After a moment the flow became a raging flood.

I looked to Kurgar. "You've no power compared to me."

The muscles in his neck corded as his face flushed red. He could see what I'd done, and he knew that through it I could at the very least equal him. He also now understood that there were other ways to gain strength, and with his realisation came mine; I didn't have to feed on souls, what was coming to me was freely given - and would be there again when needed.

Kurgar growled, "This is nothing! When the ritual is complete - and you can't stop it - the dribbles of power your misguided followers allow you will flounder. I require nothing more than what's already here!"

"I don't want the city." I gestured to the window and its view of fire and smoke. "It's already ruined, and the ground soured. I just want my family."

Behind his bravado he worried, his voice carrying a quaver. He'd never conceived that such power could be freely given, and now he wondered at which of us was stronger. I could sense his considerations.

If all she wanted was her family, and then she'd go...

He asked, "And what of your family? What if they're not all *to* hand?"

My mood cooled. "Not all?"

What had he done?

He looked to Sef, then back to me. "Your husband and daughter are alive, but not the others. They're already beyond your reach."

"The Lord and Lady are dead?"

He nodded. "As are the others who were taken."

Sef shifted, his own anger growing.

"When?" I asked.

"Some at dawn and noon, more this evening. We used them to prepare the ritual's foundations and frame. It's a gradual thing, of layers and building."

What a waste.

He asked, "If I free Pedro and Maria, will you leave the city?"

And without them the ritual would continue, but I couldn't stop that – or could I?

The cultists had already all but won Ossard. I had to reconcile myself to that. What was going to happen was unstoppable, but perhaps – in the future – not undoable. As I'd seen before, for some magic there was such a thing as a counter-casting. Maybe the ritual could be undone.

"Alright," I said, and I had an idea, a plan that would take more than a day to work. "Bring Pedro and Maria to me, but I also want the bodies of Lord and Lady Liberigo so Pedro can attend to them."

Kurgar raised an eyebrow.

"My husband is a pious man and has been ever since his time in a monastery. Such things are important to him."

"They are marred, ritual magic is not clean."

"Bring them."

He nodded to an attendant. "Fetch her family and the corpses. Bring them all here."

The attendant bowed and left, leaving us to stand in silence.

Eventually Kurgar spoke, "Where will you take them?"

"You know where, I'm sure you've heard."

He nodded. "The ruins then, and in league with Lae Velsanans." His distaste showed.

"Indeed, what bad company we *both* keep."

He chuckled. "You are powerful, but not strong enough. You can't stop what happens here. In the end, with a city this size, the departure of you and your followers means nothing."

"So you'll let us seek our sanctuary and not harry us?"

He raised an eyebrow. "More demands? In the end, it won't matter. You'll find that you can't sleep, knowing that your actions saved your family, but in turn doomed the strangers that I'll have to use to replace them. That knowledge will drive you mad."

I pressed him, "You'll not harry us?"

He sneered. "You have my promise, for I needn't bother with the likes of you."

I nodded.

The door opened behind us.

Sef and I turned to find Pedro standing dirty and bruised with his hands and feet in chains. He swayed unsteadily, his eyes lost and unfocused. I went to him, slipping an arm about his thinned waist.

Brimming with the power of my people, I let some of it flow through to give him strength. Colour came back to his cheeks, his eyes locking onto mine, while his slack jaw settled into a tired smile. In a moment, life was restored to his grim face.

He whispered, "Oh, Juvela." And one of his hands found one of my own to give it a squeeze.

An attendant came in behind him carrying Maria. She was also dirty, but in a better state.

"Mama!" she cried, reaching out for me.

Kurgar nodded to the attendant, and the man stepped around Pedro and put her down by my feet. She cuddled in close.

The attendant took a pendant from around her throat; instantly I could sense her mind again.

She was free!

I looked about for the promised bodies, but they were yet to arrive. Turning to Kurgar, I asked, "And the Lord and Lady?"

The attendant nodded at his glance.

Kurgar said, "They're coming; I imagine they're wrapping them."

I nodded.

Noise beyond the door marked their delivery. They were each carried and wrapped in cloth, the fabric already stained.

I asked, "And what will you do with the Loyalists?"

He smiled. "You know there are bigger sacrifices to come. I could probably muster a thousand willing to offer themselves up for ritual magic, but ten thousand? I'll keep them for that."

The attendants brought the wrapped bodies to me and then pulled back their shrouds. Their faces lay there, bloodied and beaten, but also pale and waxen. It was indeed the Lord and Lady.

Pedro cried out.

I nodded. "So our deal is done?"

"Yes, and how will you get them from here?"

I'll have your men take them to the roof.

"So you like to fly? That was always a part of Schoperde's way; a penchant for the birds and wind." He stood. "Let's go, then, I've much else to do - and dawn nears."

They removed Pedro's chains, seeing me hug him now unbound and free. I whispered, "My husband, be at peace until we're safely away. You'll see more strange things before then, but you'll just have to trust me."

He nodded, "You have my trust."

Before long we stood on the roof, the bodies of the Lord and Lady between our two groups with their shrouds being tugged by the predawn wind. The sky to the east had grown brighter, its grey daring to take on some colour; fresh golds, ambers, and reds, all bravely peaking through the smoke-haze that blanketed so much of the city.

Kurgar asked, "So, you'll just go?"

I looked to him, and then turned back to the tragic view.

Much of the city lay hidden behind countless plumes of smoke. The fires feeding them set every district to flare, while about it all thrummed the roar of flames and the last rage of dying battles.

What a waste.

I stepped forward to the bodies. "We'll leave in a moment." And then knelt between them to draw back their shrouds.

Kurgar's brow furrowed, his gaze intense.

I placed a hand on the breast of each body, it sitting over their hearts amidst congealed blood and opened flesh. The feel of it, chill and wet, was broken by the stiff texture of ruined clothes, and the arc and edge of smashed ribs.

335

Then I slipped into the celestial.

I searched for any sign of life; of fading embers or the sparks of souls.

Searching...

Normally, death would see a soul return to its god, but as they'd both been used to fuel ritual magic - something handled by mortal hands - the spending followed no natural or perfect path. I sought for something left over.

Seeking...

Like when stoking a fire with timber, often bits of bark and splinter would be left behind in a wood box or by a fire's grate. It was for such a piece of soul-stuff that I now hunted.

And found!

Kurgar hissed.

I found a spark from each of them, the fading lights weak and wavering, and chased by a smothering dark. Without hesitation, I took them into my care, fed them, shielded them, and then washed them in a generous share of my own stolen power.

They blazed into life.

Forged!

Kurgar growled.

Having secured them, I crafted a shell for each and filled them with strength. Back in the real world, I pressed heavily on their clammy chests to feel jellied blood squirt and cracked bones shift.

Beginning at my palms, warmth came to their bodies. It was there that I focussed my power as I worked to drag the Lord and Lady back. Colour returned to their faces, them gasping as their backs arched, while their eyes opened wide to bulge with shock and pain.

Beside me, Pedro fell to his knees.

"Sleep," I whispered.

Their breathing calmed as their eyes closed.

Kurgar snapped, "Get out of here! Get out of my city!"

I stood and looked to him, pulling Pedro up with me. I then waved Sef across, getting him to stand with us as my dear old friend held Maria.

Kurgar snarled, "Go! Get out! Take your damned family and be gone!"

Exhausted, I said, "As agreed."

Surprisingly, Kurgar's anger was quick to fade, his scowl melting into a grim smile. "Not Sef, though. Our deal was only for your family."

Sef paled.

I said, "He comes with us!"

Kurgar shook his head. "No he doesn't, he's not family - and there's more to it than that." He looked to Seig Manheim. "Go on, make your demands."

Seig stepped forward. "Sef Vaugen of Kaumhurst, formerly a priest of Kave, and *marked* in that service, you cannot leave."

Sef's shoulders slumped.

"He must be free to go!" I insisted.

Seig said, "No, this is a matter between Sef and Kave. He must remain as his divine mark demands, for that is part of his punishment."

"Punishment?" I asked, wondering if it had anything to do with me.

Sef turned, his face bleak. "My soul and service are promised to Kave."

"You can go back on that - I'll protect you."

Seig called out, "Tell her your truth!"

And Sef cursed under his breath. "I can't go, I'm sorry." His tears began to flow as he handed Maria to my husband; she was sobbing too.

I begged, "Please Sef, come with us. If you stay here you'll die!"

And Seig growled again, "Tell her!"

Sef swallowed as he wiped away tears. "I can't leave because I'm marked, and must follow that mark's conditions."

"Who marked you?"

Seig bellowed, "Tell her, Sef, the coward of Kaumhurst!"

"What's he talking about?"

My old friend shook his head in frustration. "My mark's not from a rival god, but Kave himself. I've been damned for turning from battle, for choosing not to fight to the death..." And then his jaw froze, despite him staring at me as though he had more to tell.

Watching him, I could see the muscles of his jaw and neck spasm, while his eyes seemed to plead with me to be heard.

I could feel it, there was more to his tale. Sorcery hung about him to hold him back - the same kind of casting that ensnared me at my first meeting with Pedro.

He took a step towards Kurgar, but turned to look at me. "Go Juvela, I'll deal with my penance and find a way to join you."

"No, Sef!"

Seig called out, "Yield to your mark!"

Sef winced. "Go, while you have your family!"

"Sef!"

"Go, Juvela, find your place in things. I'll see you again."

Seig growled, "Get here!"

And with one last whispered goodbye he did.

Kurgar laughed. "Not all goes to plan, does it? Now get out of my city!"

I stretched out my hands, taking the opportunity to bless Sef's soul and build a bond from it to me.

We would see each other again.

And then we rose into the smoke-heavy air, it giving way to the colours of sunrise. Pedro held Maria, as I used my power to lift his parents and us from the rooftop, and head towards the Newbank Gate.

Kurgar yelled, "You've stolen from the bloodline. I'll have to kill eight others to make up for it. You've the blood of innocents on your hands!"

His words sickened me, but I couldn't change what I'd done. In the end, I'd just have to make sure that bringing back Lord and Lady Liberigo was worth it.

Please, Schoperde...

Soon we'd be out of the city and safe beyond its walls. The following days would see us out of the valley and seeking shelter at Marco's ruins. In that time I'd have much to consider: Could I somehow contact Dorloth and enlist her aid? I also had to be ready for Felmaradis, face my grandmother, and find a way to help both Marco and Sef.

And what of Schoperde; could she really be dead?

THE FALL OF OSSARD

COLIN TABER

The Fall
of Ossard

Appendix

Appendix

-

The Goddess of Life
& the God of Death

The Mother Goddess, Life, *is*, and always has been. It needs to be understood that she *was* long before anything else could be. Trying to fathom where she came from or how she came to be is beyond our mortal minds, as is such an understanding of her partner, Death.

She is the mother of all life, of this world and others, and even the gods who reign over them. Nonetheless, she needed a partner in bringing such bounty into being, and she found it in her opposite, Death.

He agreed to work with her, to labour with her, and love her. A union that saw the universe born. It took that union, his seed and her bloom, to fill it with the magic of their offspring.

But, for all his toil, Death demanded a price: That all of her creations would eventually come home to him.

One day Life will run short of the seed her partner gave. In the meantime, she brings more life to the worlds she has woven, and Death reaps the harvest it returns.

The departed souls of our loved ones' journey to his dark and cold realm, but only to stay for a while. For again, in time, they are reborn into mortal forms.

Life and Death, though, have since become estranged.

Now Death seeks advantage. He works to win influence amongst their divine children, the gods, and their mortal children, the races of man. He wants to control the flow of souls, not just in his dark and chill realm of the dead, but also in the worlds of the living.

For souls are power.

COLIN TABER

The Fall of Ossard

Glossary

Glossary

Aespen Ocean – The wide ocean to the west of Dormetia.

Anja Vaugen – See Vaugen, Anja.

Ansilsae, The Plain of – A barren plain on the east coast of Velsana. The site where the prophecy of the same name was issued, ending *the Battle of Ansilsae*. That prophecy – or divine promise – ended a civil war that would have otherwise seen the destruction of the Lae Velsanan race. The prophecy promises that plain as the site of the Eternal Capital of the Lae Velsanans' Fifth and Final Dominion.

Ansilsae Prophecy, The – Issued by the five gods of the Kinreda. It promises their followers, the Lae Velsanans, total and final rule over the world if they can discover and overcome the four failings of their race.

Atalia Cerraro – See Cerraro, Atalia

Avida – Another face of the Horned God or Terura. A god of greed, decadence, gluttony, and more. This is the Heletian name for that aspect.

Baden, Kurt – Juvela and Pedro's Flet coach driver.

Baimiopia – The Holy City, capital of Greater Baimiopia, and the centre of the Church of Baimiopia.

Ba-Mora – Inquisitor Anton's Ship, the lone vessel dispatched with his small force from the Black Fleet to Ossard. It is named after the lost capital of the Ogres, a mountain city said to be a wonder, but sacked by Saint Baimio during the Heletian-Ogre wars. The Ogres were the fourth race of man and called the city Bar Mor.

Baruna Discotti – See Discotti, Baruna.

THE FALL OF OSSARD

Benefice Gian Vassini - The most senior churchman of the Church of Baimiopia in Ossard. He is comfortable and somewhat corrupt, and now heading towards his more mature years.

Black Fleet, The - The fleet of ships maintained by the Inquisition and used as their main means of travel for their various missions and regular rounds of the Heletian League states, as they hunt out heresy and the enemies of the Church of Baimiopia.

Burnings, The - The uprising that saw the Inquisition and its Black Fleet forced out of Ossard following excessive purging and spiritual policing by the Inquisition over two decades ago.

Burvois - The middling people of Burvoy, also the name of their language.

Burvoy - A kingdom of sun, fields, orchards, and the dark Caspas Forest, found at the south-eastern borders of the Heletian League.

Cabal, The - An organisation that spans the world and touches all races. It governs the use of heart magic by its practitioners. Much of its workings are subject to secrecy. It's also engaged in the hunt for *renegades* - those users of heart magic who refuse to join its ranks.

Cabalists - Members of the Cabal (see above).

Calbaro, The - The main order of holy scholars found within the Church of Baimiopia.

Cassaro River, The - The river that passes through the city of Ossard.

Celestial, The - The realm of gods, spirits, souls, and raw magic. This astral place is invisible to most, but able to be slipped between (from the *real* world) by those who handle one of the three branches of magic.

Cerraro, Atalia - The dead and much loved wife of Marco Cerraro.

Cerraro, Marco - A Heletian follower of Juvela, and recently widowed.

Church of Baimiopia - The only legal faith in the lands of the Heletian League. The faith of Krienta (the creator) and his chosen son, Saint Baimio. The faith is centred in the most powerful Heletian state, Greater Baimiopia, in the holy city of Baimiopia.

Chronicle, The - A position held by a Lae Velsanan who records the history of his or her age. Currently held by Forwao, who resides in Yamere at the Core of Lae Wair-Rae. The record is a detailed account of the rise and fall of the first four promised dominions of the Ansilsae Prophecy. In the Chronicle's library (the *Library of Truth*) an *almost* continuous record of Lae Velsanan history exists. Only one volume is missing - that which deals with the final days of the second dominion. The Chronicle is divinely inspired in sourcing his or her information. He or she is mortal, but receives whispered truths from the celestial.

Ciero, Mauricio - The most senior member of the Cabal in Ossard. He's a reclusive Heletian, and lives in the city's elevated and wealthy northern district.

Colonies, The - The eleven official colonies of the Lae Velsanans' Fifth and Final Dominion, Lae Wair-Rae, which are scattered about Dormetia and to its east.

Communed, Celestially - To communicate soul-to-soul through celestial means. Requires powerful magic, or a god, or cell-mind to facilitate.

Core, The - The heartland of Lae Wair-Rae, the region found on the south-eastern part of the island of Wairanir. This is a land well developed and overcrowded, thus the need for colonies to both feed the Core, but also export its excess people to.

Counter Prayer - Magic that works to counter that previously cast, usually of equal power and the opposite effect.

Covenant, The - The divine agreement that sees the elevated gods of the celestial not meddle directly in mortal affairs. They may send blessings to their followers, or via their priests, but may not directly intervene in the mortal world. The Covenant hasn't been breached for centuries. Such breaches are punished by massed actions agreed to by the remaining elevated gods.

Council of Merchant Princes - The grouping that governs Ossard through discussion and vote, and is drawn from the wealthiest families of the city-state. It is headed by the Lord of Ossard, Lord Liberigo.

Cycle of Life - The cycle the soul follows through birth and death, and on to rebirth (see appendix).

Death - An immortal figure, and original adversary to the goddess, Life, also her estranged lover.

Def Turtung - Also know as *the Killing* (to the Flets), or *New Moons Night* - Lae Lunis Pors - (to the Lae Velsanans).
    The night that marked the beginning of the Fall of the Fourth Dominion of *(Old)* Wair-Rae. The Flets had spent centuries as an enslaved race in the Fourth Dominion, and eventually began to win (and buy) their freedom. Nonetheless, the dominion was still very much dependent on Flet labour (particularly in the fields of agriculture).
    Def Turtung began in Yamere, a series of riots by the common people of the dominion against the Flets who'd gained their freedom through hard work and success. The disturbances spread and were openly encouraged by the forces of law. Eventually, what began as a spontaneous and popular expression of anger (and more than anything, jealousy and bigotry) became a sanctioned war against the Flets, forcing them to flee by sea.

Discotti, Baruna - The Heletian woman who comes to befriend Juvela, attracted by her sense of justice, compassion and hope.

Divine Focus - A place where the real world and the next world (the celestial) almost join, drawn together by bridges hosted by celestially aware individuals, or those anchored to artifacts or rituals.

Divine Mark - A brand that marks a soul, denoting the marking god's interest in it. It is a sign to their followers to take some kind of action: Some marks are a sign for followers to challenge or kill the bearer, or for more complex marks, to offer aid. Marks can also be bestowed by gods upon their own followers to mark them for penance and shame.

Dominions, The - Of the Ansilsae Prophecy. There will be five. They are as follows: Quo Ungria, Kalraith, Jhae Dalin Cor, Old Wair-Rae, and Lae Wair-Rae.

Dorloth - The awakened god of the gargoyle nation. She is now mature and ready for elevation to the celestial, at which point she will leave her physical form behind.

Dormetia - The region controlled in a large part by the rising Fifth and Final Dominion. The only other major power, though not of equal strength, is the Heletian League.

EK - See *Encarnigo Krienta*.

Elemental World, The - The third world. The *real* world is the first, the second is the *celestial* (home of gods, spirits, souls and magic), and the third is the *elemental*. It is a place of raw power filled with the primal energy of fire, water, air, and soil.

Encarnigo Krienta - Part of the Heletian calendar, the zero year, the year of Saint Baimio's (the mortal son of Krienta) elevation to the celestial after his defeat of the Ogres and the sacking of their mountain capital of Bar Mor, known to the Heletians as Ba-Mora.

Evora - A former runt Heletian kingdom (and member of the Heletian League) that was all but sold off to the middling Prabesk traders from far off Prabeq (found far to the east). The deal was done as the last Evoran king succumbed to his debts. Evora is no longer a Heletian League member, and is now used as a trading base by the Prabesk, and largely populated by their own kind. Militant factions in the League and the Church of Baimiopia (and Inquisition) refer to it as *woeful lost Evora* and dream of retaking the territory.

Expeditia Puritanica, The - The arm of the Church of Baimiopia's Inquisition that actively undertakes the organisation's many cleansing missions. All field Inquisitors and the Black Fleet come under its governance.

Feeders, The - The lost spirits, shades, and carrion of the celestial. The ruins of souls.

Felmaradis Jenn - See Jenn, Felmaradis.

Fifth and Final Dominion, The - Lae Wair-Rae was declared the Fifth and Final Dominion by High King Caemarou after the riots of New Moon's Night. He claimed that the freeing of the Fourth Dominion from its dependence on slavery spelt the end of that realm and the beginning of the next, it being cured of the fourth failing; sloth.

Some historians have suggested that Lae Wair-Rae is merely a continuation of Old Wair-Rae, but such discussions are not popular at the royal court. Such voices claim their position due to the lack of calamity at the end of the Fourth Dominion. Advocates of Lae Wair-Rae being the Fifth and Final Dominion (including High King Caemarou) point to the famines and upheavals suffered by the Lae Velsanans after the bloody events of New Moon's Night, and the subsequent war against the Flets (their former enslaved workforce). Despite the stifled debate, something limited largely to a handful of academic circles, it is widely believed that Lae Wair-Rae is indeed the Fifth and Final Dominion.

First Faith, The - The faith of the *Goddess of Life*. She is also known by the divine names of *Schoperde*, *Pordanamae*, *Bru Moar*, *Tergaia*, and *the Green Way* amongst others. This is the most basic of faiths, the worship of our natural world and the life that it gives. It is about balance and the ways of nature.

Five Faiths of the Kinreda, The - See The Kinreda.

Flet/Fletlander - Of Fletland. The Flets are of the middle race of men and have been a wandering people for over a thousand years. They most recently suffered at the hands of the Lae Velsanans in a genocidal campaign waged by High King Caemarou to chase them out of the borders of his newly decreed Fifth and Final Dominion. They can be found in the harsh and wild lands of Fletland and in Ossard.

Fletland – The current Flet homeland, found on the south-eastern corner of the island of Kalraith (to the west of Ossard). It is a place of plains, bogs, deep forests, and inland lakes and rivers.

Florin – The currency of the Heletian League states, and minted by each member.

Forbidden, The – The name given by the Lae Velsanans to their cultist kin found in the icy northern wastes of Wairanir, well north of the Core.

Forwao – The current *Chronicle* (see The Chronicle).

Gods – There are many gods, but originally there were only two: the god of life, and the god of death. Life birthed many more, and after such labour left them to govern the worlds and races she created before entering a deep sleep to recover from her efforts. After an age, Life reawakened to find that many of this second generation of gods had been seduced by the promise of easy power from their father, Death. They have since become addicted to feeding on souls and the surge of elation that such a thing delivers, instead of the constant succour delivered by living souls that offer devotion through faith.

There are three stages of godhood:

The *Avatar* – the seed of a god within a mortal shell.

The *Awakened* – the sprouting seed of a god within a mortal form. If they gather enough strength they will eventually become elevated. Such a process can take as little as years or as long as millenia.

The *Elevated* – a mature god who has come into its final form in the celestial, and abandoned its mortal or physical representation in our world. Elevated gods have to abide by the rules of *the Covenant*.

Goldston Bridge – The bridge across the Cassaro well outside of Ossard's walls, and a good ride up the valley to the small trading town of the same name.

THE FALL OF OSSARD

Grenbanden, Iris - The last priest of Schoperde to serve Ossard. She fled during the Inquisition campaign that led to *the Burnings*. She was forced to flee after her identity became known to the Church of Baimiopia, and thus the Inquisition. It is rumoured that someone in the tight-knit Flet community divulged her name and true calling.

Heinz Kurgar - See Kurgar, Heinz.

Heletian - The middling race of man who populate the Heletian League, and after the Lae Velsanans, the most widespread of peoples in Dormetia.

Heletian League, The - The grouping of eight Heletian nations, with all sharing a common language, culture, ancestry, and faith (the Church of Baimiopia).

Heletite - A monk of the order of missionaries from within the Church of Baimiopia.

High King Caemarou Quor Budasa - Ruler of the Fifth and Final Dominion of Lae Wair-Rae. He is married to High Queen Caree and has eleven sons - including the youngest, Prince Jusbudere.

High Queen Caree Quor Budasa (nee Jenn) - Wife to the ruler of the Fifth and Final Dominion. She is mother to eleven princes, and also the aunt of Felmaradis Jenn (through her brother, Rajis Jenn, current head of House Jenn).

Horned God, The - The term the middle race of men use for the many faces of the dark powers that try and corrupt man. The Lae Velsanans know the same power as *Terura* of the *Terura Kala*.

Inger Van Leuwin (nee Van Blomstein) - See Van Leuwin, Inger.

Iris Grenbanden - See Grenbanden, Iris

Isabella Van Leuwin - See Van Leuwin, Isabella.

Jenn, Felmaradis - First General of Prince Jusbudere. He is a nephew of the High Queen, and son of Rajis Jenn. His mother is unknown.

Jenn, Rajis - Father of Felmaradis, elder brother to the High Queen, and a powerful cabalist. He is reclusive, long ago widowed, and lives in Milcama. He has seventeen children, sixteen to his deceased wife, and the youngest, Felmaradis, to a mystery lover rumoured to live on his estates. All his children now govern their own estates in the colonies (many on the west coast of Kalraith), adding to their House's wealth. His heir, Jae Banadis, is governor of the Kalraith colonies.

Jenn, Una - The Flet woman who raised Felmaradis on the family estates in Milcama.

Jericho - The trusted personal attendant of the Lord and Lady Liberigo.

Jusbudere, Prince - See Prince Jusbudere Quor Budasa.

Juvela Van Leuwin - See Van Leuwin, Juvela.

Kalraith Island - The large island between the island of Wairanir and the mainland of Dormetia. It is the site of the *old core* of the Second Dominion, and now split between Lae Velsanan colonies, the Flets of Fletland, and the gargoyle nation at its wild heart. For more information regarding the gargoyles, see also; Dorloth, Kalraith Ruins, Quersic Quor, and Troiths.

Kalraith Ruins, The - The ruined cities at the heart of the fallen Second Dominion. The area is now overgrown, lost to thick forests, and home to the mysterious gargoyle nation of Dorloth.

Kaumhurst - Sef Vaugen's home village in Fletland, now destroyed.

Kave, The God of Battle - An ambiguous thing. Seen by some as a cult of honour in combat, while others see it as merely another face of the dark power of *Terura* or *the Horned God*.

Kinreda, The Five Faiths of - Five separate gods make up the Kinreda. They have a long history of fighting each other and have only been brought together through *the Divine Promise of the Ansilsae*. It is not unknown for them to still have disputes. Indeed, their own infighting has been instrumental in the first three dominions' downfalls. All faiths are now head-quartered at Lae Bareth, the holy island (see Lae Bareth).

Krienta - The god and *Creator* of the middling or common Heletian people. This god of the Covenant is what the Church of Baimiopia is built around.

Kurgar, Heinz - The head of the Flet Guild.

Kurt Baden - See Baden, Kurt.

Lady Death - The head of the cult of Mortigi, the god of murder, in Ossard.

Lae - Velsanan word for *new*.

Lae Bareth - The holy city of the Five Faiths of the Kinreda. It's found on a small island at the centre of a long gulf that runs along the south eastern coast of Wairanir. It's named after *Old* Bareth, an ancient holy city that disappeared beneath the waves during the calamities that changed the face of the world during the fall of Jhae Dalin Cor, the Third Dominion.

Lae Corster - The head of the Lae Wair-Rae branch of the Cabal, and a close ally to the High King.

Lae Velsanan - The *higher* race of man. They are on average taller, leaner, and more fine in bone and features. Aside from a crown of rich hair on their heads, they are hairless, and often alluringly *perfect*. They are also long lived with intense minds and a slight point to their ears and noses. Amongst the other races, they are known for their arrogance, melodrama, and self-absorption.

Lae Wair-Rae - The Fifth and Final Dominion. Young and now rising, destined according to the *Ansilsae Prophecy* to be eternal. A sprawling nation of Lae Velsanans who follow the *Five Faiths of the Kinreda* and are now embarking upon a wide campaign of colonisation.

Library of Truth, The - The library of the Chronicle, currently based in Yamere.

Liberigo, Lady Angela - The First Lady of Ossard, wife of Lord Liberigo, and a middle-aged Heletian woman.

Liberigo, Lord Silva - The Lord of Ossard, and head of its most prosperous merchant house. Middle-aged, he is an astute Heletian man.

Liberigo, Pedro - The youngest son of three to the Lord and Lady of Ossard, and a troublesome playboy. Married to Juvela, and father to Maria.

Liberigo, Juvela (nee Van Leuwin) - See Van Leuwin, Juvela.

Loyalists - The name taken by the traditionalist followers of the Church of Baimiopia in Ossard, adversaries to the Reformers.

Lucera - A small island kingdom, and member of the Heletian League well to the south. It is plagued by pirates, and during the course of *The Fall of Ossard* is uneasily hosting the bulk of the Black Fleet of the Inquisition.

Magic - The power drawn from the next world or celestial into our own. There are three main branches of magic; heart, mind and soul.

Magic, Blood - This kind of magic takes its energy from the life force of blood, and any practitioner of magic can utilise it. In its most common form, it means that a caster offers their own blood by cutting themselves to augment their power in an effort to increase the chances of a casting's success or its potency. This process delivers strong and raw power (drawn from the blood-linked soul) but can be fatal. It is not stable magic.

Its most reviled form is that practised by many renegades of the Cabal, the *Sanjo Drajo*. They gain their power by using the blood of others to cast. Such a practice is illegal in the Cabal, as it is immoral, and gives individuals access to great power.

Magic, Soul - The magic delivered through the soul and faith, given in the form of blessings or graces from the gods to their priests or followers.

Magic, Heart - The magic of the Cabal, derived through those naturally attuned to the celestial and strong enough to not need the patronage of a god (soul magic) or others (mind magic). They work very hard through learning, experimentation, and practise to expand their powers.

Magic, Mind - The magic of the Sisterhood. Some women are gifted with a sixth sense that enables them to network with others of similar talent to create a power well akin to that of a single cabalist. These *cells* can be connected so that they can further pool their power.

Malnobla, The - The seat of government in Ossard, and the lord of the city's residence. It's a grand building set on one side of the city's main square (Market Square).

Malsano - The dark face of the Horned God that watches over poverty and pestilence. Often invoked to curse others. Also known by the names of Malssarcht and Tykarcht.

Man, The Three Branches of - High, middle (or common), and low. The distinction has been classed by the Lae Velsanans who consider themselves alone to be *high* (see Lae Velsanan). They are taller, leaner, and more long-lived.

There are many different nations of middling men (the Pagar, Flets, Heletians, Evorans, etc.) who are shorter, stouter, shorter-lived, and in Lae Velsanans eyes', thought to be crude. The race of lower men is made up solely of the Saldaens, a short people who are the last of their kind. The three branches of man cannot successfully inter-breed; while conception can occur, the babes born are always stillborn as they are soulless.

Manheim, Seig - The most senior priest of Kave in Ossard. The Flet warrior who has seen many campaigns in Fletland against raiders and other cultists.

Maran Sea - The sea spreading to the south west of the Maroklaran.

Marco Cerraro - See Cerraro, Marco.

Market Square - The main square of Ossard, large and able to hold well over fifteen thousand people. It is used as a market, and also for civil ceremonies.

Maro Fever - A seasonal malady that is common in Ossard. It weakens its victims, is viral, leaving them open to other illnesses through the summer. Most of its victims die from pneumonia.

Maroklaran Sea - The sea that winds through the heart of the Dormetian region.

Matriarch, The - The head of the forbidden organisation, the Sisterhood.

Mauricio Ciero - see Ciero, Mauricio.

Mind Voice - Heard only in the mind between people using celestial talents to commune.

Moonroot - A herbal that interferes with the use of celestial talents.

Mortigi - The dark face of the Horned God who celebrates murder. The followers of Mortigi revel in the hunt for victims and are both skilled assassins *and* fiends.

Naskae - The soul pearl is a physical embodiment of a Lae Velsanan's soul. It is where two worlds - the real and the celestial - meet. It sits in the abdomen of every Lae Velsanan. About as big as a coin, these small blue glowing spheres are literally a chunk of magic that can be *mined* to power spell castings. Removing a naskae from a living Lae Velsanan will kill the owner. If the naskae is not harvested from a corpse, it will eventually deteriorate. When it has finally dissipated, the soul (now completely free, and no longer anchored to a physical form) is able to be reborn into our world.

Using a naskae to power magic castings draws on the energy of the linked soul in the celestial. To use all that power, to drain the soul completely, destroys it. That individual, in every sense of the word, is no more and will never be reborn. Oblivion.

New Moon's Night - The night of rioting against the Flet slaves in the Core that marked the fall of the Fourth Dominion over two hundred years ago (see Def Turtung). Known to the Lae Velsanans as *Lae Lunis Pors*.

Newbank - The main Flet district of Ossard, and found on the south east side of the Cassaro River. It is very poor, mostly unsewered, crime-ridden, and crowded.

Northern Sea - The chill and grey sea between Ossard and Fletland.

Northcountry - The rugged and steep valleys about Ossard that are farmed to feed the city, and through the rich city-state's history have been mined for valuable metals to pay for its rise to power and influence.

Oblivion - The *fourth* world, a place of nothingness, and a place where souls that are *drained* or *used* send their shadows. There is no chance for rebirth or regeneration for any soul lost to oblivion.

Old Wair-Rae - The Fourth Dominion, which fell during the upheavals caused by the revolt of the Flet slaves triggered by the bloody riots in Yamere on New Moon's Night (known to the Flets as Def Turtung - *the Killing*).

Oleander - A wild bush that grows to twice the height of a middling man, has toxic sap and leaves, and is extremely hardy. It grows out from its core, is roughly round, generally not thick in its greenery, with long and thin leaves. It has flowers of pink or white that appear in bunches, but wilt when cut. Its canes are now Ossard's most commonly used timber.

Ossard – A city-state of just under a million people, and member of the Heletian League. A large minority of the population of Ossard (a wealthy city of *merchant princes*) are Flets, although they have largely missed out on their share of the city's wealth. The wealth of the city is controlled by the Heletian majority. A third of the city-state's population reside within the walls of the city, the rest across farming settlements in the Northcountry.

Pedro Liberigo – See Liberigo, Pedro.

Pillar-cities – The cities of the Lae Velsanans, named as such for their builders' penchant for summoning pillar-towers to crown their cities. Notable pillar cities of Lae Wair-Rae are; Yamere, Lae Bareth, Akermanis, Rumaza, Milcama, Markae, Jor Jamilla, and Andrin Lae.

Pits, The – The name given to the hellish underworld that doomed spirits are sent to by unforgiving gods according to most middling folklore and theology.

Praagerdam, The – The lost land of the Flets, an autonomous district of Old Wair-Rae, the Fourth Dominion of the Lae Velsanans. It was overrun and razed during Def Turtung.

Prince Jusbudere – The eleventh son of High King Caemarou. Despite his youth, already famed as an exceptional warrior, commander and leader.

Quersic Quor – Centre of the gargoyle nation, and nesting place of Dorloth. Formerly the capital of the fallen Second Dominion, Kalraith.

Quorin – The common language used across Dormetia, particularly as a trading tongue. It has Lae Velsanan roots.

Quor – A colony of the Lae Velsanans' Fifth and Final Dominion of Lae Wair-Rae. It is also the closest Dominion territory to Ossard

THE FALL OF OSSARD

Rabisto - One of the many faces of the Horned God. He is the patron of the lucky, of the risk takers, and thieves and bandits. He is also known by the names of Tabiro and Ranndolf.

Rajis Jenn - See Jenn, Rajis.

Reformers - The followers of the new saints.

Renegade - A mage who uses heart magic and refuses to join the Cabal and follow its rules. Many renegades are necromancers or sanjo drajos (blood drinkers).

Rosa Sorrenta's - The establishment visited for Juvela's *Mint Lady* outing.

Rose Tree - The now extinct symbol of Ossard. This small tree used to cover much of the Northcounty, but was wiped out by blight and the need for timber by the booming mines and the growing city. It grew to three times the height of man, and each spring and autumn would come to flower with generous white rose-like blooms.

Saint Baimio - Son of Krienta, and leader of the Heletians in the Heletian-Ogre wars of five centuries ago. He was elevated into godhood and the celestial after defeating the Ogres at Ba-Mora and razing the mountain city.

Saint Marco - The patron saint of travellers in the Church of Baimiopia. He lived four hundred years ago in the Kramer Confederation to the south. St Marco's church and square were built opposite Newbank to appeal to the recently arrived Flet refugees two hundred years ago.

Saldaens - The low race of man. These short and squat people live a longer life than that of the middling races, and one denoted by contentment. They have a close affinity for nature. They can only be found in numbers in New Saldae and Heletian Saldae.

Sanjana - Southern Heletian word for blood.

Sanjo - Northern and standard Heletian word for blood.

Sanjo Drajo - Renegade sorcerers who almost exclusively base their power on blood magic, by harvesting it from others.

Sankto Glavos - The holy knights of the Inquisition.

Santana - One of the new saints, proclaimed by the Heletites as the saint of children. Also the Burvois word for blood.

Schoperde - The Flet name for the goddess, Life.

Sef Vaugen - See Vaugen, Sef.

Seig Manheim - See Manheim, Seig.

Serhaem - The most south-eastern colony of the Lae Velsanans' Fifth and Final Dominion. It is a city-state positioned strategically between the two Heletian League states of the Kramer Confederation and Greater Baimiopia.

Sisterhood, The - A secretive and forbidden organisation that governs the exclusively female wielders of mind magic. Local cells or covens communicate through the celestial mind-to-mind, and are able to link their cell-minds with others to create networks that augment their power. They owe their allegiance to no body, nation, or god.

Because of their secretive and single-minded nature they are outlawed and distrusted.

Soul-Eater - A slang term for a powerful being (soul) that uses others for strength by feeding. This feeding can be done unconsciously in the way of receiving loyalty or faith, or by the outright consumption of the souls of the dying.

Soul Harvest - A time of soul gathering, when gods come to claim their followers back. Usually marked by catastrophe and calamity.

Spirit Guide - The prophesied mentor for the coming saviour of the Flet people.

THE FALL OF OSSARD

Tampanna Sea - The sea to the east of the Ossard's Northcountry.

Terura Kala - The term the highest race of man, the Lae Velsanans, uses for the cults of the dark powers that try and corrupt. The middling races of man know the same groups as the followers of the Horned God.

Troiths - The climbing towers that rise from the ruins of the Second Dominion's cities in Kalraith. They're said to be built from stone and bone, and stand as parodies of the Lae Velsanans' pillar-towers. They are the homes of the emerging gargoyle race.

True Name - The key to a soul.

Una Jenn - See Jenn, Una.

Unae - The name given to the mortal world.

Van Blomstein, Vilma - The sorceress burnt at the stake by the Inquisition, and who helped trigger the riots that saw the Black Fleet forced from Ossard (The Burnings). Mother to Inger Van Leuwin, and grandmother to Juvela Van Leuwin.

Van Leuwin, Inger - Daughter of the witch, Vilma Van Blomstein, and mother of Juvela Van Leuwin. Also wife to Josef Van Leuwin.

Van Leuwin, Isabella - Wife to Juvela's second cousin, her chaperone for her Mint Lady Outing.

Van Leuwin, Juvela - Daughter of Inger and Josef Van Leuwin, wife to Pedro Liberigo, and mother to Maria Liberigo.

Vangre - The wealthiest city-state of the Heletian League member, the Kramer Confederation, far to the south.

Vaugen, Anja - Sef's wife, now deceased.

Vaugen, Sef - Bodyguard to Juvela through her childhood, and widower to Anja Vaugen.

Vassini, Benefice Gian - The head of the Church of Baimiopia in Ossard, see Benefice Gian Vassini.

Velsana - The isolated ancestral homeland of the Lae Velsanans, and the site of Ansilsae, the barren coastal plain that hosted the apocalyptic battle that gave birth to the Ansilsae Prophecy.

The Lae Velsanans were forced from their home as part of that prophecy, and now the Kinreda priesthood preach that it remains hidden by the gods, waiting for the Fifth and Final Dominion to rise and rediscover it. Once reclaimed, it will host the eternal capital.

The island continent is thought to be situated to the west of Dormetia, abandoned and laying fallow. The most ancient texts of the Lae Velsanans show it to be an island continent divided into five regions.

Vilma Van Blomstein - See, Van Blomstein, Vilma .

Wairanir - The large island that holds *the Core* of Lae Wair-Rae, the Fifth and Final Dominion, in its south-eastern corner.

White Sea - The sea to the north of Ossard and the Northcountry, often laden with drifting ice and haunted by savage winter storms.

Witches' Kiss - The casual term used by the Inquisition to denote someone who is succumbing to some kind of magical awakening.

Yamere - A great pillar-city of outstanding beauty, and *current* capital of the Fifth and Final Dominion.

THE FALL OF OSSARD

About the Author

Colin Taber lives in Australia, currently haunting the west coast city of Perth.

He's done many things over the years, from working in banking, retail, dish-pigging, publishing, landscape design, and even running a tree farm. All he really wants to do, though, is to get back to his oak grove and be left to write.

Hopefully, that day is coming.

COLIN TABER

Ossard's Hope

Book 2 of the Ossard Trilogy

Available early 2010

For information on this and other
coming titles, go to the website at:

www.fallofossard.com

Made in the USA
Lexington, KY
03 April 2010